NOT AGAIN
A novel by Maria T. Henriksen
Book 1 of the series Not Again

Copyright © 2019 by Maria T. Henriksen
Print 978-1-7333904-1-5

All scripture is King James Version (KJV).

Printed in the USA.

Cover Design and Interior Format

Not Again

a Novel

MARIA T. HENRIKSEN

Lisa,

Thank you for the joy you
have given me as an author as
I greatly appreciate your
support.

Here's to healing hearts one
page at a time!

Maria S. Henriksen :)

Dedications

To my beloved family for supporting me throughout this journey—Dave, my forever love; Brandon, my spirited son; and Kathryn, my fun-loving daughter.

To the students of Pottsgrove school district, my first love as a substitute teacher. In particular, a very special thanks to Taylor Nace, Aaron Hollinger, Morgan Muir, Amanda Tammaro and my daughter, Kathryn for bringing my novel to life in my book trailer. You were all fantastic and a pleasure to direct.

To the super talented Sandy Jorgensen for singing and producing the song for the book trailer by transforming my raw creation into a real work of art.

Last, but not least, to my students—past, present, and future. Thank you for your encouragement! You inspire me beyond words!

I can do all things through Christ which strengtheneth me.
Philippians 4:13

Prelude

"**N**O! NOOO! NO! STOP! PLEASE, STOP!"

For two whole glorious years, I cherished a little, yappy dog, named Mugsy, from the moment I laid eyes on him in 1977, at the age of nine. Our neighbors, the Martins, gave us the puppy from their dog's litter. This occurred shortly after my parents, brother, and I moved to our newly constructed house in the sleepy town of Pennsford, a suburb of Philadelphia, Pennsylvania.

The Martins kept one of the puppies—a skinny honey-colored, short-haired, homely-looking runt with short pointed ears, a bushy tail, and a short temper. He was named Elvis, as an ode to the recently departed.

I found the contrast between my Mugsy and Elvis humorous. Mugsy was the cutest mutt. He was a Shih Apso, a combination of a Lhasa Apso and Shih Tzu. His fur was sandy brown and soft. His ears were floppy and bounced when he walked. They came from the same litter, yet one looked scrappy like he needed bathing, and the other dog, my canine buddy, was lovable, soft, clean, and ready to be hugged.

Mugsy and I shared a special relationship in the fleeting time she graced us with her presence. Sometimes I pretended it was Mugsy and I against the world. She was always there for me, ready with licks and cuddles, unconditionally.

I dared not imagine life without Mugsy, until one day when we witnessed an awful and unusual event with her. She was flailing, yelping, shaking, and moaning uncontrollably. It was excruciating to watch. After consulting with a veterinarian, we discovered that our sweet addition to the family suffered from epilepsy. An epileptic episode could kill her or give her permanent brain damage—that left us with only one choice: to put her out of her misery. It was the humane thing to do.

My home endured a very different climate with no Mugsy to greet me upon arriving home from school. She did not jump up on me when I entered the family room, nor did she greet me with her wet, welcoming kisses I so cherished. It was like *Cheers* without Norm. Or, *Happy Days* without "Fonzie." There was an emptiness, a loss, and in a manner of speaking, an empty chair.

Oh, the tears I cried when she was put down. You could have floated a pontoon boat on them. I tried to bargain with God to spare her life in exchange for me being the perfect girl. I swore I wouldn't do anything bad ever again. Not that I was *bad*. And not that I really considered the meaning of the word "perfect." It was, however, my only bargaining chip. I rarely got in trouble, but I felt compelled to offer God something in return for my puppy's health. He was, in fact, the maker of the universe, after all.

When my request was not granted—when sadness overwhelmed me—I convinced myself that God did not exist. He simply could not exist. He saw my Mugsy, and He saw how great we were together. Even my self-absorbed, pain-in-the-neck little brother loved our canine sibling.

How could a merciful God take my best bud from me? *God could have* cured my furry friend, *if* He truly existed.

The conclusion that God did not exist seemed to bear no effects in my day to day life as my family didn't even go to church, much less talk about God. Therefore, I continued with my life, as if not believing in God was of no consequence. After all, at the ripe old age of eleven I must have acquired some wisdom. *Right?*

Chapter 1

FROM THE MOMENT MY MOM awoke, to retiring for bed, she smoked those dreaded cigarettes. My mom smoked for as long as I could remember. The smoking irritated me, and I told her, yet she puffed away. Nicotine-filled smoke swirled around her incessantly, like dust swirled around Pig-Pen, Charles Schulz's character from Peanuts. She sat at her favorite spot at the kitchen table and lit up one cigarette after another, all day long, day after day, while drinking a cup of tea. As surely as she lived, my mom smoked. So much so, a ring of smoke stained the ceiling above that favorite chair of hers. *Gross!*

The relentless smoker, for the most part, played the role of a stay-at-home mom. Friends and family called her Bea, short for Beatrice. I never cared for her given name. It sounded old. Beatrice. Hardly music to my ears. Bea, her preferred nickname, sounded more modern and hipper.

My mom reached vertical heights of five feet nine inches—only one inch shy of her namesake, Bea Arthur, the actress who achieved fame as the main character Maude Findlay from the '70s sitcoms *All in the Family* and *Maude*. Although I was not quite as tall as my mom, I was nonetheless satisfied with being a few inches shorter.

Once upon a time, my mom was drop-dead gorgeous. However, time took its toll on her appearance. Not only did she gain substantial weight through the years, but she stopped wearing makeup, except for special occasions, and she predominately wore her thick, dark brown hair in a simple braid hung to the left side. Fortunately, I inherited my mom's thick hair, although mine was a richer brunette. I chose to keep it long in its natural ringlet state, and never did I, nor would I ever, copy my mom's hairstyle.

Many moons ago, Miss Pennsylvania pageant promoters implored my mom to be a contestant. Her stunning face, featuring high cheek bones and big hazel eyes, framed by thick dark eye lashes — just like mine — and thin, yet shapely figure, stopped traffic. However, the promoters barked up the wrong tree because my mom generally shrank away from drawing attention to herself in that manner. She wasn't shy. She never regarded herself as beautiful, nor did she ever compliment me on my looks, as I resembled her.

I, on the other hand, did enter a so-called beauty pageant. While it was not my cup of tea at all, I, thirteen at the time, couldn't resist the pressure from dear Mrs. Martin. She did, after all, give me the gift of Mugsy. I wanted to help her. I felt like I owed her. The pageant ended up being humiliating and led to awful events in my life, but no one could have guessed that. Here is the story . . .

The Miss Blue Lagoon contest was an annual event. I was invited to participate in it one overcast summer day while I was riding my purple three-speed Schwinn around the neighborhood. When Mrs. Martin spotted me and waved me over, I complied.

She stood there barely reaching five foot one in her strappy gold high heels, cut-off Daisy Duke jean short shorts and bleached blond bob haircut, wearing pink lipstick and black mascara. She pleaded with me, "You know I am organizing it, the pageant that is. I could really use your help by participating," she said, distracted pulling Elvis on his leash.

"It's not really my thing," I replied, barely able to get the words out because I hated to disappoint. All the while, I attempted to understand why she would walk a dog while wearing high heels. Some things will never make sense, and this was one of them.

Much to my chagrin, Mrs. Martin entreated, "Please, Christina, we will have to cancel it this year if we don't get at least one more girl."

"I talked to Katie and Amy yesterday, and they said that they were going to sign up," I returned aiming to encourage her and free myself from the unwanted task.

The wannabe Daisy Duke rolled her eyes, "Yes, I already know about them. The fact is that there aren't as many girls in the qualified age group—ages twelve to fifteen. The swim club board won't extend it to sixteen. I already asked, and eleven is just too young." She pursed her lips as she tugged on Elvis's leash, "You are my only hope, Christina." She knew how old I was because her son and I were in the same grade.

"But . . . ," I winced as my voice trailed, only to be interrupted.

"Christina, you are an extremely beautiful girl. You will do fine," she stated emphatically as she bore a hole through my heart. "We are having a party at my house afterward, too," she added to sweeten the pot.

"I have never even been to one of these, let alone in one," I replied flatly. "I know nothing about it," I continued. Nothing, except that a girl who won years ago subsequently launched her modeling career. At least that was the story my friend Katie told me, and I had absolutely no interest in modeling.

"Oh, it's simple. You just walk around the pool area, one girl after the other, first in a swimsuit, and then in a dress. We have rehearsals, so you'll know exactly what to do." *A swimsuit! Are you crazy?!*

I stared blankly for a bit and then uttered, "I don't know," while avoiding eye contact as I steadied my bike. Eye contact was always the kiss of death in these exchanges.

"Please, Christina," she urged, gently raising my head with her index finger, "you would be *saving* the pageant. I already put hours of work into it. And it is a rather grand event." *Did she just bat her eyelashes at me?*

"Okay," I blurted begrudgingly. *How much begging, guilt, and pressure could one girl endure?*

"Ooh, you're a lifesaver!" she said with a quick, but firm hug. "Thank you very much! I will never forget this."

From that point on, life as I knew it completely changed.

Chapter 2

MY THIRTEEN-YEAR-OLD LIFE PLUMMETED DOWN-HILL. I despised every single minute of the pageant. The first thing to despise was "the buying of the pageant suit." The one I owned was tired and worn out from many months of use, so I had to shop with my mom and her dad's cousin—who vowed to live as a Catholic nun, of all things! What a joy that was!

Sister Mary Margaret, a gray-haired, wrinkle-faced, not-so-pleasant nun, wore a traditional black and white penguin style habit wherever her Lord sent her. I saw my first cousin twice-removed maybe once every five years, and of all days for her to visit! Her sainthood accompanied us on this embarrassing quest to secure the perfect pageant bathing suit. I worried that the cringe-worthy experience would become habit forming.

My mom in her perpetual cheapskate mindset thought that the stores in the mall would be too expensive. Therefore, her only resolve was to drive all over kingdom come from one random store to the next, hopping in and out of the car.

Her frugality greatly annoyed me, especially during this time of crisis. God forbid my mom would spend any extra money on me. Oh, right! I repudiated my belief in God and decided it was best not to broadcast my controversial lack of faith. Had I told the penguin that her boss didn't exist, my one crisis would have become two. And one crisis was all I could handle.

While trying on one suit in the dressing room of the fifth store fraught with limited options, I heard Sister Mary Margaret, an apparent expert on swimwear and teenage girls under duress, say to my mother, "What is the big deal? It's just a bathing suit for heaven's sake." Her words of disdain echoed louder than the piped-in music playing the *Chariots of Fire* theme song.

"Let's go," I semi-barked with exasperation as I half-sprinted out of the dressing room. Though moving more like Speedy Gonzales, I felt like the way Eeyore looks—defeated and downtrodden. The tune in the background didn't help matters.

"Didn't any of them fit?" my mom asked arms crossed, clearly frustrated.

"Nope," I replied curtly, head down.

Sister Mary Margaret exclaimed, "You answer, 'no,' not 'nope.' Nope is *not* proper English."

I rolled my eyes. *Could this get any worse? I guess you're a grammar expert, too,* I thought, but my mouth surely didn't say. Not only could I not find a decent bathing suit to parade around in, but I was getting English lessons from a nun when I received mostly A's in school. *Definitely not okay.*

Our final destination was Strawbridge and Clothier. There, we found a so-so bathing suit among the grimmest of selections. It was slim pickings, as they say, and unfortunately, model slim escaped my physique. Normally, I didn't mind not being skinny, but one of my preconceived notions of a pageant contestant consisted of a super thin frame.

My physical shortcomings created anxiety over finding a flattering bathing suit. Average build at best, I stood at a five feet six inches in my fourteenth year. Above my waist, my body did not scream Dolly Parton, though I recently filled out more than many. I was a tad short-waisted, but otherwise, the rest of me appeared adequate. Don't even ask me what I weighed because I couldn't have cared less.

The suit adorned diagonal stripes in blue, yellow and green with thin white stripes bordering each color, and a matching white belt that hung in a knot. The knotted-belt bathing suit was the style in 1982. It revealed nothing inappropriate, which eased my worries as I hated anything slinky and would have been overly self-conscious grabbing barely-there swimsuits with Sister Proper English present.

Chapter 3

THE SECOND THING TO DESPISE was "pageant picture day." We were required to get our pictures taken early Friday morning before the pool opened at eleven o'clock. I couldn't believe I was required to pose solo in my new swimsuit while standing on the diving board. Secretly, I feared falling into the pool, which I was certain didn't pass as glamorous. At least I would have made a splash! How graceful would it have been to fall while someone was trying to snap my picture? Maybe it would have disqualified me. Although that would have been embarrassing, it would have been a million times better than what actually transpired.

The pageant girls also posed for a group photo. I quickly surveyed the aspiring bathing beauties. It became evident that most of these girls lacked the figures and facial beauty traditionally deemed pleasing to the eye—myself included. What inspired these girls to enter the public foray? *I know why I am here—guilt. But, why are they?*

Take Cheryl Wilson, for example. She and I had been friends since fifth grade. She stood at a respectable height of five feet seven inches creating an unsightly bone-thin frame. Plagued with acne, this dorky-looking contestant with frizzy dark hair, wore big plastic glasses and metal braces. Still going through that early-teen gawky stage, Cheryl Wilson was no Cheryl Tiegs, who graced the cover of the *Sports Illustrated* Swimsuit Issue multiple times.

Now, she and Carla Carlucci were attached at the hip all summer. Carla was super friendly, but despite boasting a killer tan, her facial features were considerably lacking, featuring a big nose and a hairy mole on her chin reminiscent of the Wicked Witch of the West in *The Wizard of Oz*. As a result, I didn't see her winning this contest either. We all fell short of being pageant material. What were we doing? Were we all coerced? And what was with the pageant people acting so desperately? What possessed them to host an event when the interest and quality was clearly lacking?

Chapter 4

THE THIRD THING TO DESPISE was "pageant practice."
We spent a huge chunk of our Saturday morning practicing walking and posing and doing all such things that I considered flaky. *Are they for real?* I asked myself that question over and over throughout the morning.

The instructors called the turns "pivots." I imagined playing basketball and pivoting while dribbling, but these pivots were nothing like that. Awkwardly, like I was new at the walking game, I finally maneuvered these pivots. I asked if it was possible for me to simply turn around, rather than pivot, but I was denied that request.

The initial promenade was quite steep, and it begged one of us to trip. My dread was assuaged when I learned that we would be escorted down the concrete hill. *Thank God! Oh right, I no longer believed in God.*

Wait! I interrupted my own private rant. *Who is escorting me?* Before I experienced a full-on panic attack regarding my personal escort, I was told mine would be Stan, with whom I was already familiar.

Allow me to define "familiar." I was the makeup artist assigned to make every inch of scantily clad Stan look tan for his role in *South Pacific.* Now, let me be clear—his ratty shorts were short. Putting body makeup on the upper part of the inner thigh of a classmate was, like this pageant, not my thing, nor my comfort zone. Let's just say Tan Stan had to finish the makeup himself every time.

All the girls waited in the "screen room"—a screened-in porch— for our cue to practice. *Glide. Sashay. Pivot. Repeat. Glide. Sashay. Pivot. Speech. Oh my!*

The fourth thing to despise was "the pageant speech." It would need to be honest. What exactly does a self-proclaimed anti-beauty pageant enthusiast share in her beauty pageant speech? That she attended computer programming class and art class earlier this summer? Yes. That she babysits to earn spending money? Check. And that she volunteered at the local old folks' home? Hmm, that will work. That when she is not bettering herself, earning a dollar and volunteering her services, she heads to the pool, usually in the afternoons? Yes, that should do it.

The fifth thing to despise was "the pageant dress." We found ourselves back in the screen room later that day only to be told to hurry up and get changed into our dresses. The pageant volunteers warned us that wearing pantyhose was frowned upon for some reason beyond my comprehension, but one girl, Maureen Bainbridge, insisted on wearing them. She stood no taller than five feet two inches, with short blond feathered hair—styled like Kristy McNichol—freckles, average build and a snippy mouth. Her semi-cuteness compensated for her lower-than-average acumen.

Most of the pageant girls avoided the problem of not following the rules, aside from me, this time. I desired to wear lightweight, colored stockings to go with my rainbow colored, horizontally striped dress, and this time, I was resolute. What was up with the stripes?

"Oh, no, Christine, you can't wear those stockings!" exclaimed one of the woman volunteers with an intensity I associated with a violent death. *What?! Did I kill this outfit? Come on. They're only stockings!*

"It's Christina," I corrected her, surprising myself with my candor. I disliked it when people called me Christine. That was not my name. The "a" on the end of my name sounded prettier, more feminine, not so common, and I certainly never considered Christine a nickname. Although easygoing about most things, I was a stickler for the accuracy of my birth name.

"Oh, Christina," she said somewhat exasperated, but with much less fervor, "we prefer you to go without stockings."

"But I like wearing them with this dress," I replied. "It completes it." In my opinion, the combination created a lovely ensemble. I must have had the grimace of a stubborn teenager because she bypassed the stocking predicament and looked at my feet. Perhaps she was looking for a fight she could win.

"Are you wearing those white flats on pageant day?" she asked pointing to them with a disapproving look on her face. *Here we go again!*

I looked down at my cute white flats. "Yeah," I answered trying to show respect through my gritted teeth.

"You would look better in heels," she retorted quickly. "Pageant girls always wear heels. They are more flattering," she explained. "The extra lift gives the legs a slimmer appearance." When she said it, I could see that she believed it and I could even see a glimmer of joy in her eyes. *She really likes this pageant crap.*

"I need to wear what's comfortable," I stated decidedly, but with less frustration. *I did need to make those pivots. You should have let me simply turn around, then maybe I'd wear heels.* She dropped it. The pageant Nazi had a few larger fires to put out, sparing me further scrutiny.

One girl wanted to wear what looked like a dog collar around her wrist. It was a black band with silver spikes. She also wanted to wear black lipstick and stiletto heels.

Another girl painted hot pink stripes in her own hair but swore she would rinse it out for the show. I thought the pink stripes were fun, but what did I know?

Later, the same volunteer tried to make peace with me by calling me a "sweet, Italian girl." *Yes, that's who I am in part, but we can't forget my Irish side. That wouldn't be fair to my mother now, would it?*

The sixth thing to despise was "the vote." Before heading home that day, we were asked to anonymously vote for Miss Congeniality. Secretly, I hoped it would be me, because my chances of winning Miss Blue Lagoon seemed nil, and I wanted to walk away with something for my time and effort.

I quickly scanned the room filled with my fellow contestants:

Cheryl Wilson and I were acquaintances, but she had a flat personality.

Maureen Bainbridge wasn't even nice, *ever.*

Katie O'Leary and I established a friendship. She adorned straight long blond hair that she wore up a lot. Katie's blue eyes, hourglass physique, terrific sense of humor, and intelligence kept her in the running. Katie busted out of her shyness when she portrayed the blond bombshell in the middle school musical, *Guys and Dolls,* last year, and did a fabulous job. We hung out at the pool together the entire summer, even after her stardom.

Strangely enough, the art teacher/co-casting director pleaded with me to try out for that same part because she thought I would be perfect for it, emphasizing the actress needed to be very appealing. Although flattered, I failed to envision myself parading in front of everyone. *Yet, here I am.*

Jennie Pitman. Her face was stunningly beautiful. Jennie adorned the same fabulous hair color and style as Princess Diana and big, brown expressive eyes. This helped compensate for her being flat chested. Jennie was so flat that she looked like a boy. *Oh, stop, Christina. Be nice.*

Amy Gardner, the short, big boobed, blue eyed, bobbed brunette, with a shapely, yet slightly oversized figure, appeared overly friendly, like she was trying too hard to be popular. She and Katie seemed to be hitting it off. While Amy proved intelligent enough, I found her to be annoying at times.

There were a bunch of other girls, but I was not acquainted with them. I did not even know their names; voting for them fared impossible. *I just joined this pool for goodness sake.*

Yes, it was a local pool and many of the girls attended my school, but there were girls in different grades that I didn't know and girls like Carla Carlucci who attended unfamiliar private schools. *Now there was a possibility.*

Carla.

She was rather chatty and comical with the girls. I think she was fifteen, close to sixteen. Most of my friends were fourteen by now, but I was only thirteen, due to a late birthday in November. Okay already. I had to write *someone's* name down. I wrote Carla on the given scrap paper, folded it up and tossed it in the basket.

Chapter 5

THE NEXT DAY WAS THE *big* day, the Miss Blue Lagoon pageant. I was nervous but trying to appear casual. Quite a few people were present by the time I arrived. They were seated on the grass, on benches, and in their lawn chairs all along the path we had to walk. They'd be close enough to touch as I walked by them. *Shivers.*

My younger cousin, Jessie, short for Jessica, was almost nine years old and part of a group called Junior Miss Blue Lagoon, or Junior Miss for short. Jessie and I looked a lot alike as we shared a very strong family resemblance. She was as cute as button with freckles sprinkled all over her face. Jessie flashed big brown eyes and super long, thick eyelashes—a family trait.

As I was in the dressing room getting ready, I heard a lot of commotion. I peered out to look beyond the screen room. My eyes focused on the judges' table down the hill. *Is that ditzy Jennie's dad shaking the hands of the judges? She looks exactly like him! Except for his hairy legs. The resemblance is scary!*

I scanned the audience and found my parents. Then, it hit me; there were people in attendance who didn't even belong to Blue Lagoon. *I'm gonna be sick. Oh—My—God! Oh,* yeah, I forgot. God was nonexistent.

"Okay, ladies, take your places in the proper order and wait for your cue like we rehearsed," Mrs. Neumann directed. *I wonder if she'll have a cow again when she sees me in my forbidden flats.*

One girl after the other paraded down the steep concrete incline with their escort by their side. I was no exception. Upon my descent down the hill, I saw Avery Evans, who I considered to be the cutest boy in my grade. My mind floated to memories of the eighth-grade dance and his then-girlfriend, Amanda . . .

She sported curled under bangs and her jet-black hair was pulled back in barrettes. These were no ordinary barrettes. Nope, these were matching barrettes that coordinated perfectly with her outfit. Amanda literally had barrettes to match every single outfit she owned—a very preppy style.

She also had a very distinct feature: a turned-up nose. She seemed nice enough, but we never exchanged pleasantries. She was either shy or a snob. I gave her the benefit of the doubt; I avoided the cliché that having a turned-up nose automatically meant that you were stuck-up.

As expected, Amanda and Avery went to the eighth-grade dance together. As usual, I declined many offers to go with someone. I preferred to fly solo. Dating terrified me. My theory was that if you date someone it should be when you are older and ready to get married. My philosophy on dating screamed old-fashioned and completely different from anyone else's. It had nothing to do with religion, nor did I judge others for dating. I was somehow—don't know how or why—more conservative than any of my peers and most parents I knew.

The proof of that was in my response to Avery asking me to dance that night. "What? You're here with Amanda. I . . . umm . . ." then I bolted.

What I did seemed rude, I know, but I was so insecure. *How did I ever turn down his breathtaking blue eyes?* Remarkably, I distinctly remember the song that was playing the time when he asked me to dance was "I've Been Waiting for a Girl Like You." *I need to stop kicking myself for the way I handled that.*

This tacky pageant was much worse than that dance. *Here? Now? In a swimsuit? With him? Ugh!* Our eyes locked. I cringed. He smiled. *Breathe. Breathe. Look forward. Not at your feet. And not at him. Look forward. Be poised. Be graceful. You can do this.*

My escort felt the weight of my nerves on his arm and held me steady. I grinned a small smile of thanks in his direction.

The moment I stepped back into the screen room after our first turn, I blurted out, "Where did all these people come from? I didn't know it was open to the public!"

Amy replied, obviously suppressing a giggle for my sake, "Oh, yeah, if you don't belong to Blue Lagoon, you have to pay admission to get in."

Admission?! This pageant is like a freak show!

"Whaaat?! Are you serious? How much?"

"Five dollars, I think," Amy answered, giving in to her laughter. She was completely humored by my antics and emotional state.

I guessed that the pageant was sort of a fundraiser based on the number of outsiders, but I had no idea how huge it was. And it was only the beginning.

After I changed into my cutesy, innocent little Italian number, complete with flats and stockings, I made my way arm-in-arm with my escort, Stan, down the hill yet again. I pivoted (*yay!*) as instructed before the judges and proceeded to climb the step to reach the microphone. As planned, I proudly told the crowd about my intellectual, artistic, and entrepreneurial endeavors, along with my selfless acts to contribute to society that I experienced that summer. I eased myself off the step and headed back to the screen room. *It's almost over. Whew. Almost!*

While the judges deliberated, the Junior Miss girls each stepped up to the microphone in turn to share a little about themselves to their detainees. I missed this, but I bet it was charming. No doubt Jessie did a wonderful job despite her shyness.

One last time I had to manage a graceful saunter— this time to the judges' station. *This walk to the pool will never be the same. I'm emotionally scarred for life.*

We stood in silence together and patiently, or rather impatiently, waited for the results of this fabulous pageant.

Vomit.

Mrs. Martin took the microphone and masterfully worked the audience and volunteers with many a sweet 'Thank you' and flattering 'Couldn't have done it without you.' *Wonder how much pressure she put on them? 'Sally, really, your vacation can wait. Your kids can go to Disney next year. Help me make this pageant successful.' My gosh, without her pressure, I'd be somewhere pleasant right now!*

Mrs. Martin proceeded, "Yesterday the girls voted for Miss Congeniality . . ." Secretly, I hoped to win this award because I didn't stand a chance to win the big one, but I wanted to win something to make up for the humiliation.

" . . . and the winner is . . . Carla Carlucci." I heard clapping and a little cheering from the audience, so I decided it was polite to join in. I had to admit I was disappointed; I thought I had a decent personality. *Why didn't I win? Should I have voted for myself? Desperate times call for desperate measures.*

Carla stepped down to receive her flowers from one of the Junior Miss girls. "Congratulations, Carla," Mrs. Martin commended with an expansive smile, wide enough to span North America. She continued, " . . . and now for the results for the Miss Blue Lagoon Beauty Pageant . . . the second runner-up is . . . Maureen Bainbridge." Maureen smiled broadly looking both surprised and happy and received her flowers graciously.

"Congratulations, Maureen," Mrs. Martin stated in the same manner as she did when she congratulated Carla.

"And for the first runner-up the judges have selected . . . Katie O'Leary." She, too, smiled and covered her face with her hand. Katie carefully stepped down and received flowers from my cousin, Jessie. *You're so cute, Jessie.*

"Congratulations, Katie," Mrs. Martin said enthusiastically.

She continued, "And now, for the moment we have all been waiting for, the crowning of Miss Blue Lagoon. The winner is . . ."

I felt my heart pounding. *Did I have a chance to win?* At that moment, I wasn't quite sure if I wanted to win or not. I honestly did not care to be in the spotlight, but winning, at that moment, felt like it would be fantastic. I waited for Mrs. Martin as she announced with vigor and zest, "Jennie Pitman!"

At first, Jennie gasped placing her hand over her mouth. Then, she shook. This was followed by her screeching, and her jumping. She was thrilled. The moment was hers. She stammered down the steps to receive her crown. Mrs. Martin handed her an exquisite bouquet of red roses. Jennie beamed!

Reporters popped up out of nowhere and pounced onto the scene.

The flashes of their cameras were blinding.

"Were you surprised to win, Ms. Pitman?" one reporter questioned.

"Ms. Pitman, do you have any plans in continuing the pageantry circuit?" another inquired.

There was a pageantry circuit? This was much larger than I thought.

I quickly dashed through the crowd wanting desperately to wallow in self-pity alone. I passed Paul Martin, Mrs. Martin's son, who seemed to be scowling at me. I ignored him and continued my quest to hide from the rest of the world until my path was blocked. My dad stood in my way.

"Hey, pooch!" he exclaimed. "You were wonderful! You look beautiful!"

"But I lost," I replied, eyes wet and choking back tears.

He patted my head, "What do those judges know anyway? You were by far the prettiest girl."

I mustered up a meek, "Thanks, Dad," and met his gaze.

"I love you, Pooch!"

"Love you too, Dad." He squeezed me tight. I soaked it in. We parted. I only made it a few steps before I ran into Avery Evans.

Bump.

Oh, my gosh! "Oh, sorry," I said hiding my wet eyes and red face. I quickly dabbed them with my hands while aimlessly looking at my shoes.

"Hey, don't be. And by the way, you were fabulous!"

"I was?" I said sheepishly surprised and met his eyes quickly before hiding them again.

"Yeah, you were definitely the best looking," he commented nonchalantly as if the judges were completely clueless.

"Whaa . . ." I studied his face to see if he was teasing. He wasn't. "Oh, thanks . . ."

Undeterred by my red face, he mentioned, "Mrs. Martin invited everyone over to her house. Are you going?"

I noticed people scurrying out, carrying their lawn chairs.

"Oh, ah, I forgot about that, but it should be okay. I live up the street from her."

"Cool, I'll see you there. Later," he remarked as he started down the hill to see a friend. "I'll look for you there."

"Okay. Bye." *Wow. What just happened?* Things went from awful to . . . a big, fat WOW within seconds and before I even climbed the hill.

Things are really looking up. Nothing could be worse than the pageant.

Chapter 6

TRACKED DOWN MY PARENTS AND told them that I was going to Mrs. Martin's, but first I needed a ride home to change. I doubted that my parents would go to the party since they weren't social like that, and they were usually gracious about giving me my space. When we arrived home, I ran upstairs and donned my favorite pair of designer jeans, the Chic ones of course. I threw on my favorite purple short sleeved shirt, checked my makeup and was out the door.

By the time I reached the Martins', the party was in full swing. Kids and a handful of adults filled every inch of the floor plan. The catchy and fun "Rosanna" by Toto, enhanced the merrymaking atmosphere.

What possessed Mrs. Martin to have a bash of this magnitude in her house? She lived in a decent size house, not a mansion or a castle.

I noticed her son, Paul, sitting on his couch in the family room. He looked up and glared at me. Once again, I dismissed his peculiar stares.

As I weaved through the crowd bumping people at each turn, I heard a little girl say, "When I grow up, I am going to be Miss Blue Lagoon." *Wow, this thing is big.*

I spotted Katie and Amy. "Hey, guys, how did everyone get here so fast?" I asked.

"Everyone knows about the after-party. It's a tradition," Amy explained cheerfully.

I nodded. "Oh, Katie, congrats!" My acknowledgement was truly heartfelt.

Amy blurted, "Christina, we were just discussing how you got robbed." She looked at Katie who nodded and continued, "You should have been with Katie in the top three. Everyone thinks so. It's the talk of the night."

That was awkward. Amy didn't think she deserved top three. I honestly didn't know what to say.

"Thanks, guys." Though perplexed, I made sure to hide it with a smile.

"Yeah, it was like rigged or something. I got runner-up, but even that doesn't seem right," Katie confessed with confidence.

"Wait. Do you guys really think it was fixed or are you just kidding?" I asked cautiously.

"Oh, come on . . . everyone knows who the prettiest girl was," Katie guided.

"Yeah, Jennie," I stated the obvious.

"Naw, she's got 'the look,' and the beauty queen attitude, but you have the classic stunning looks: that great bone structure with high cheek bones, those big, brown eyes." *Technically my eyes are hazel, but I'll let that slide.* "Those crazy long, thick, dark lashes . . . and that hair! Anyone would kill to have thick, curly hair like yours!"

"Doesn't everybody prefer blonds to brunettes?" I asked realizing I should have thanked Katie for her kindness first.

"Naw, not when it compliments your olive skin so nicely! Girl, you don't even seem to know what God gave you."

Oh, my goodness, He gave me this? Not going there. Instead, *thanks, Dad, for your darker skin. Sure beats getting sunburned like Mom.*

"The problem was you totally weren't into it," Amy added, sounding a bit disappointed.

"Oh, you noticed that I wasn't all that into it, huh?" *How obvious was I?*

"Is *she* kidding?" Amy looked at Katie and then back at me.

"Oh, it's not Christina's thing," Katie informed Amy. "In fact, I am kind of surprised to see you here," Katie turned to me in a playful manner.

"Well, I . . . uh . . ." Again, I was at a loss for words. I found it distracting talking to them as people were banging into us as they walked by.

"Hey, it's cool. We're just messing with ya. We saw you talking to Avery after the pageant. He's looking for you," Amy informed me with a bit of a razz in her tone. Just then The Little River Band's "Man on Your Mind" filled the room.

Katie fished, "So, what's up with you and Avery?"

"Nothing," I responded, keeping it close.

Katie, Avery, and I were in the same class for three years in middle school. Everyone called it the Top Section. There were two top sections for each grade—one for each hall. Each hall consisted of four classes. The top sections contained the classes with the highest achieving, brainy students. Katie, of all people, understood how insecure I felt being in that class as an intellectual inferior. However, at the same time, it was socially acceptable to be smart in our school, even highly regarded, so I kept up the pretenses. At least I tried.

"Oh, come on, dish it. What did you two talk about?" Katie persisted.

"Inquiring minds want to know," Amy urged.

"You guys better not be messing with me about all that stuff about people saying I should have been in the top three 'cause that's just not cool. It's not that I agree with it . . . I'm just saying," my voice faded. Naturally, I feared being the brunt of a cruel joke.

"Seriously. That *is* the buzz," Amy stated convincingly. "We wouldn't tease you like that. That's awful."

"Christina, I would never lie to you about something like that," Katie added convincingly.

Amy inquired in a softer tone, "Why so paranoid? You really don't think of yourself like that, do you?"

"Because it was exactly what Avery said," I revealed quietly.

"Oh, man! Gotcha! Did he? That's so great; I bet he likes you," Katie speculated.

"Yeah, it takes guts to say something like that," Amy expressed.

"Like what?" Avery asked catching us all off guard.

"Oooh, nothing," said Amy tauntingly.

Avery breezed past her tease, not biting on that hook, "Well, you girls were something tonight. I don't think I would have had the guts to do what you all did. That takes a lot of courage."

"Oh, you have *no* idea!" I smiled.

"I still can't believe you didn't win, Christina," he said dumbfoundedly, shaking his head, as he looked right at me. Then he turned to Katie and Amy, "Ah, no offense girls. You both were great, too."

"Open mouth, insert foot," Amy smirked.

"Sorry," Avery sincerely apologized. He did look truly sorry.

"Let's leave these two alone," Katie suggested, smiling as she scanned Avery first then me. "Amy, come with me. I want to get some soda. Yeah, that's it, soda," Katie teased.

"Do you want a drink or something, Christina?" Avery offered.

"No, thanks. I'm fine." *Now that I'm with you, my long-time secret crush.*

"Let's say we get out of here," Avery proposed. "We can go for a walk." *Yes! Anything to get out of these squished quarters.*

I followed Avery out the side door. It was a little chilly for my tee. The temperature dropped drastically after we left the swim club. I left my sweater at home since I assumed we would be inside.

"You look cold," he observed. "You think you'll be okay?"

"Yes . . . yes, I will," I shivered.

"You sure? We can go back inside if you want," he said. "I'd lend you my jacket if I had one."

I needed space, but not cool air to the point of shaking. "I'm okay," I fudged. We walked further up the street toward my house.

"Isn't your house up here?" he said pointing to the left. I nodded wondering how he knew which house was mine as I had no idea where he even lived. "Do you want to get a jacket?"

"Nah, I'll be okay," I insisted. *Leave you now? What if the momentum of this entrancing moment passes?*

Avery stopped. He put his hands on my shoulders and rubbed them up and down to warm me up. I melted. Avery easily slipped his hands into mine and stared straight into my eyes.

He broke the silence, "You *are* cold. You're shaking." I attempted to be cool, but not like that.

I stood there breathless staring back at him. I faintly heard kids running around the Martins' yard.

Avery pulled me even closer. "You're *so* pretty!" he told me softly. "I always thought you were pretty."

He leaned in to kiss me. Our lips met. He kissed me softly. I pulled away. Stunned.

On second thought, I leaned forward, closed my eyes and kissed him back. It was nice. It was more than nice. It was FABULOUS! My heart was racing. I thought it was going to leap out of my rib cage. I never kissed anyone before, yet I found myself in a lip lock with Dreamy Eyes. *I just kissed Avery Evans! Are you kidding me? Is this real?*

"You're a good kisser," he complimented in a whisper.

"Yeah?"

"Don't be so surprised." *Okay, I won't.* I relished the compliment. After all, he should know. I had no basis for comparison, but I assumed it couldn't get much better than that.

He turned slightly, held on to one of my hands and we floated up the street. I drifted on cloud nine. I attempted to contain my delight, but I couldn't help but blush. By then it was dark, so my hot, red cheeks went unnoticed. It was at that instant when I fully relaxed and truly took in the moment. I was happy. I swung his arm playfully, stopped and gazed into his eyes.

"This is nice," I assured him. *An awesome ending to a humiliating day.*

He brushed the hair away from my face and leaned in to kiss me again. The soothing, warm kiss turned into a passionate interlude. We parted for air. I giggled.

"What's so funny?" he asked.

"Not funny as in 'ha, ha,' but funny as in *'a-ma-zing!'* " I clarified. *Did I say that out loud?*

"You're not kidding," he agreed. "It's getting late. My ride might be looking for me. I wish I could spend more time with you."

I smiled. "Me too."

We walked back hand in hand, chatting and laughing. I wondered if he wanted to go public with our private escapades. After all, I knew not what to expect. I never experienced this situation before. I broke my general rule about dating by kissing him. Oh, well, rules were meant to be broken.

"Do you want me to walk you home or back to the party?" Avery asked.

I desired to spend every minute I could with him. "Let's go back to the party."

"Great, I was hoping you would say that. We can spend more time together then," he returned a smile.

Avery opened the door for me, and we walked in together. He casually slipped his hand back into mine. I relished that. It was so sweet, and it most certainly made a statement. It said, "We are together." By the looks from others, the hand holding definitely conveyed its point.

Guys eyed us up and gave Avery their nodded approval. Girls whispered to each other. Paul Martin glared at me again. He looked like he wanted to bite my head off. *What is that about? Why does he keep looking at me like that?*

"Hey, has anyone seen Sam Glosser?" Avery asked. "Yeah, he's in the living room at the other end of the house," someone answered.

"Hey, thanks," Avery replied with appreciation. Avery pulled me gently through the crowd. Air Supply's "Sweet Dreams" became fainter as we walked away from the family room. We stopped when Avery spotted Sam sitting on the floor next to an upperclassman.

"Hey, Sam, let me know when you want to leave, okay?" Avery requested.

"Sure, sure," Sam replied with his head down. Then Sam glanced up at Avery. When Sam noticed Avery holding my hand, he said, "Hey, where have *you* been?"

"Around," Avery responded nonchalantly.

I casually scanned the room. Nothing unusual. Nothing interesting stood out.

Avery turned to me and politely asked if he could get me something to eat or drink. I gracefully declined. I was a tad hungry but chose not to spend the time eating. That was the time when Katie and Amy discovered us.

They bounded over. "Hey, where have you guys been?" Amy asked inquisitively.

"We went for a walk," I offered. Girls *always* elaborated. They would have insisted on a more specific answer if I said, "around" like Avery.

Amy boldly inquired, "Oh, so are you two, like, together?"

"Amy," Katie chastised in a hushed tone then reprimanded Amy by elbowing her.

"Give me a break. I'm just asking." That she was.

Avery and I looked at each other. We hadn't discussed it—our status, that is. I was speechless for the third or fourth time that day, but who's counting?

"I would love it if Christina would go out with me," he answered sincerely. Looking at me, he respectfully asked, "Christina, is that okay with you?" Then he quickly assured me, "You can think about it if you need to. No pressure."

This guy. I gushed.

I peered into his gorgeous mesmerizing ocean blues. My heart hammered crazily. "Yeah, I'd like that. Go out with you, I mean," I replied softly. Our pledge to each other was undisputedly official because an audience witnessed the act. *Why do I keep on having these public displays? What a crazy day! At least this time isn't humiliating and no one is twisting my arm to participate. I'm in heaven.*

We stood there for what seemed like an eternity. Everything stopped. Every sound. Every movement. Everything, except how we felt about each other.

Then he leaned in and kissed me right there in front of *everyone*. I lost myself in it. It was tender and magical as if we were transported to another place and time. The kiss was also long and passionate. But that was okay. It was more than okay. It was *wonderful*. It was my *dream* come true! I *kissed* my *crush*! *I kissed Avery Evans!*

"Yay!" Amy clapped jumping up and down, interrupting and ending the moment. "Finally, something interesting happened tonight." *Guess we didn't miss anything while we were out walking.*

"I'm happy for you guys," Katie said spiritedly.

"Wait until Joey gets a load of this!" Sam exclaimed. "Avery got himself a girlfriend! A cute one at that!"

"What? Who's Joey?" I asked.

"Joey Glosser. Sam is Joey's older brother. He should be around here somewhere."

I should have put one and one together. Joey was in our grade too, but I never had any classes with him. I only knew of him and his bad boy reputation.

We went off to a corner in the hallway. We sat on the steps that led upstairs and spent the rest of the evening holding hands, making small talk and laughing. We shared comical moments we once witnessed separately in class at school but relived together in the Martins' house.

At one point during our wonderful conversation, I felt someone far off staring at me, and again it was Paul. *What is his deal? Why does he keep looking at me like that? He is so creepy.*

When the night was over, Avery kissed me good-bye and he said he would call. We waved to each other as he drove off. *Until tomorrow,* I thought. *Wow. What a night!*

I couldn't contain my happiness. My joy. I glided up the stairs to my room. My parents were already in bed; my alarm clock taunted one o'clock in the morning. *Man, the night flew by.*

I fell asleep recounting my marvelous evening with Avery. I was actually going out with Avery Evans. AVERY EVANS! *So much for waiting to date. What a silly rule that was! It is a woman's prerogative to change her mind after all.* Besides, high school loomed this fall and I will turn fourteen. I was no longer a little kid. I was the luckiest girl in the world. Life just couldn't get any better.

Chapter 7

THE NEXT MORNING, I SLEPT in until ten o'clock as I was exhausted from the previous day's events. It was still too early to go to the pool.

I was looking forward to spending time with Avery now that we were going out. I had no idea where we would go since we belonged to different pools and it cost money to be a guest. My baby-sitting money would be depleted in no time if we did that.

While still in my pajamas, I sauntered downstairs to grab some cereal for breakfast. As usual, my mom was sitting at the table smoking her cigarette and drinking her hot tea.

"Good morning," she greeted me with a smile.

"Good morning," I smiled back as I poured myself a bowl of Cheerios.

"Any plans today?" she asked.

"I might go to the pool later."

"Sounds like a plan."

I finished up my cereal and ambled back upstairs to get dressed when the phone rang. "Hello," I answered.

"Is Christina there?" the voice on the other end asked.

"This is she," my heart pounded as I recognized the voice. I performed a little happy dance.

"Oh, hi, Christina. It's Avery."

"Hi!" I exclaimed, thrilled that he called. Still doing the happy dance.

"Do you have any plans for today?"

I wanted to sound cool and casual. "Nothing etched in stone. What's up?"

"Cool. I thought maybe we could hang out." *I like the sound of that.*

"Sure, what do you have in mind?"

"I thought we could hang out at my place. We have a finished basement. My mom lets me hang out down there with my friends, but it would be just you and me. Is that okay?"

That would be awesome!! "Yeah, I guess so," not letting on to my sheer delight, yet added new movements to the happy dance.

"Do you play video games at all?" Once in a while, I played video games. I played in spurts. All day some days and then it could be weeks before I played again.

"Yeah, where do you live?" I asked.

"How 'bout I pick you up. I could ride my bike over. Do you have a bike?"

"Yes, I ride my bike almost every day to the pool."

"Would you rather we go to the pool?"

"No, no, we can play video games or whatever."

I didn't want to disappoint him. It seemed like he figured out what he wanted to do, and I really didn't mind. I would certainly change things up for Avery. *No problemo!*

"Cool, I'll pick you up around noon."

"Wait. You never told me where you live."

"Walnut Street near Pennsford Swim Club."

"Okay, so why don't we meet part way? It will be easier and faster." *Plus, then I don't have to introduce you to my mom. Not ready for that.*

"Alright, how about the corner of Berkshire and Maple at noon?"

"Sounds like a plan. I'll see you then."

"Christina, I can't wait to see you."

"Me too." *Is that the best I can come up with? I must get better at being a girlfriend.*

"Bye, Christina."

"See ya, Avery."

Happy dance resumed in full swing! *He can't wait to see me?! He can't wait to see me! He literally said that. I wish I could say things like that.*

He's so expressive yet collected. Oh, right, he had a lot of practice with Amanda. Did she talk? I don't remember her talking much.

Maybe Avery doesn't like chatty girls. I probably shouldn't say too much. Who am I kidding? Half the time I get tongue-tied when I am with him.

Then again, our conversation flowed easily at the Martins'. We had so much fun talking.

But the kissing. Ah, the kissing was to die for. Words could not do justice as to how awesome it was.

S-W-E-E-T! Would I feel like that if I kissed anyone or is it just him? I never had any interest in anyone else. I can't wait to see him!!

It was another hot day in Pennsford with cloudless blue skies. A perfect day for a bike ride. *I love summer!*

I figured I would arrive on time rather than early; I didn't want to appear too anxious.

My plan worked as I rode up to our designated meeting spot and saw Avery straddling his bike with a huge grin on his face. He sported white tube socks, Nikes and a white Izod shirt paired with red and white sport shorts. The shorts showed off his muscular legs. My heart leaped and my face beamed. Nobody pulled off shorts like Avery.

"Hey, Christina!" He gestured with a wave.

"Hi, Avery!"

"How are you doing today?"

"Good. How are you?"

"Great! Thanks for meeting me."

"Sure, no problem!" *Any time!*

"You ready then?"

"Yeah, let's go!"

We casually rode side by side and the conversation flowed easily, even on bikes.

When we arrived at his home, we parked our bikes in his driveway and stepped inside through the side entrance and landed in the kitchen. As I walked in, a delicious smell engulfed me. The aroma was making me salivate.

"Do you want something to drink?" *A drink? I want whatever is in the oven.*

I did, however, work up a thirst riding over in the heat. "A glass of water would be great. Thanks."

"I'll grab some snacks too. What kind of snacks do you like?"

"Pretty much anything chocolate."

"My mom made chocolate chip cookies." *Ah, that's what I smelled! Sweet!*

"Perfect!" *Could this day get any better?*

"I'll grab some chips too." *Salty and sweet. Jackpot!*

His basement was warm and inviting. It showcased a functional recreational room fully furnished in deep orange, yellow, green and brown florals with a TV and a traditional green felt pool table in an adjacent part of the basement.

Right away I noticed the Atari console to the side of the TV. "So, what do you want to play: Pac-Man, Space Invaders, or Asteroids? You pick." *He's a gentleman. Very cool.*

"Okay, Pac-Man." I liked gobbling up those dots. We played for a while taking turns. It was uninterrupted gaming. His mom only yelled down once to see if we needed anything, but I did not lay eyes on her the entire day. I knew what she looked like from way back in fourth grade when she was the homeroom mom. Maybe I wouldn't recognize her after all these years. After all, it had been almost five years since I last saw her.

The day flew by; it was terrifically easy to hang with him. No fuss. No muss. Just fun and good conversation. By the time I even thought to look at my Swatch watch, it was closing in on dinnertime for me. "It's 4:30. I better be going soon," I said regretfully.

"Jeez, I didn't realize how late it was," Avery acknowledged. He abruptly stopped playing Asteroids. Avery turned his head in my direction and looked straight into my eyes. "What time do you have to be home for dinner?" he asked.

"Six o'clock."

"You can make it home in seven minutes on bike, so that gives us some more time together," he figured.

"Maybe, *you* can, but it will take me at least ten minutes." I chuckled and gave him a little shove. He gently shoved back and started tickling me. I fell back on the floor and laughed uncontrollably. I begged him to stop. He did and looked down at me. I grinned back at him while catching my breath. We gazed for a moment into each other's eyes and then he kissed me.

"You okay?" he quietly asked after he pulled away. I drifted back on cloud nine.

"Couldn't be better," I said and assured him by pulling him back toward me. We kissed until we needed to come up for air. "You are an amazing kisser!" I blurted.

"Back at ya." He sounded sincere. We continued to make out.

His hands never wandered from my waist for which I was grateful. The kissing, while somewhat passionate, remained innocent.

A while later, I glanced at my watch. It was 5:30. "I gotta go," I announced, inching my way up.

"Oh, okay," he said disappointed. "Thanks for coming over. It was fun." *What part? The kissing or the video games?*

"Yeah, it was fun," I laughed and pecked him on the lips.

He walked me upstairs. We both carried glasses and empty snack containers. He laid them on the island in the kitchen and I followed his lead. His mom stood across the counter preparing dinner. "Mom, when are we having dinner?"

"Around six o'clock," she smiled glancing over at me.

"Oh, I forgot. Mom, this is Christina." Then he turned to me. "Christina, this is my mom." We both agreed that it was nice to meet each other. "Mom, I'm going to see that Christina gets home okay." *A true gentleman. You raised him right, Mrs. Evans.*

"As long as you're home in time for dinner," she said smiling as she continued to cut up vegetables.

"Great! Let's go, Christina!" he beckoned.

I called out to his mom as we departed, "Nice seeing you again."

"Yes, it was a pleasure seeing you too," his mom smiled warmly. As I was getting on my bike, I said to Avery, "Your mom's nice." He smiled, "Yeah, she's the best."

"She gives you lots of space," I observed, reminding me of my parents.

"Cool, huh?"

"Very cool!" I agreed wholeheartedly.

———•◦•———

We rode our bikes as if we were on a mission. I could tell that he didn't want to be late for dinner, respecting his mom's wishes, and that sat very well with me.

"You don't have to take me all the way home. I'll be okay. Plus, I don't want to make you late for dinner." I was used to riding my bike all over town by myself.

"I don't mind," he said convincingly.

As we approached my house, we saw Paul Martin in the middle of the street. "Hey, Paul, what's up?" Avery asked.

"Yo, what's up?" Paul replied. "What are you guys doing?" He appeared annoyed. AGAIN!

"Not much. Just hangin'. Sorry, I gotta go," Avery said apologetically. I sensed Paul's gaze as we rode away. *What is his deal?*

We pulled into my driveway. My dad was home. His car was parked in front of the garage. "So, do you want to hang out tomorrow?" he asked.

"Sure," I smiled. Inside, I screamed, *"Yeeees!"*

"I'll call you," he stated, and then he leaned over and gave me a quick peck on the cheek.

"Thanks for everything, Avery. You better go." I didn't want his mom to blame me for not arriving for dinner on time.

"Yeah, I had fun. See ya tomorrow!"

A few seconds later I faintly heard him say good-bye to Paul as they were both out of sight. I opened the garage door to put my bike away and checked my purple Swatch watch. It was 5:54. *Avery better hustle if he wants to be home by six o'clock.* I closed the garage door and I walked into the house.

"DINNER!" I heard my mom screech. *What timing! Whew.*

"How are you doing, Pooch?" my dad asked as we all sat down to eat.

"Good," I answered, revealing nothing of my superb day.

He volleyed, "Did you go to the pool today?"

"No, I went for a bike ride instead." *I can't tell him everything! He's my dad.*

"Nice day for a bike ride," he responded.

"Yeah, it was," I agreed.

From that point forward, dinner was the same as usual: small talk, my mom nagging us to eat our vegetables, and me washing the dishes while my brother sat on his butt. He *never* helped with the dishes.

I wondered if Avery helped with the dishes at his house. I missed him already. I couldn't stop thinking about him all through dinner.

Rather aimlessly, I headed to the family room where my dad was reading only to be interrupted by the phone. I leaped up to answer it. Nobody moved. Even if I didn't get up to answer it, no one would move. They expected me to answer the phone. It was not as if I was the only one who received calls. Somewhere along the way, this became my job. *So cliché.*

"Hello," I answered.

"Christina?" Avery asked.

"Yes, hi. Can you hang on a minute?"

"Sure."

I placed my hand over the receiver. "Mom, can you hang this up when I get upstairs?" She nodded.

"Thanks." I ran upstairs to my bedroom for privacy.

I didn't want anyone to hear my conversation. Like *that* wasn't obvious. "Avery, are you there?" I asked.

"Yeah, I'm here," he answered.

"Okay!" I yelled covering the receiver. "Sorry about that," I apologized.

"No problem," Avery replied.

"Did you get home in time for dinner?"

"Just barely. My mom didn't seem to mind," he assured me.

"Oh, good. I'm so relieved. I don't want you to get in trouble on my account," I told him.

"No problem. My mom likes you," he stated.

"She does?" I fished for more, "How do you know? How could she? We just met."

"She told me that she remembers you from Mrs. Miller's class. She was the homeroom mom, remember?"

"Oh, yeah. I can't believe she remembers me!" I said surprised.

"Yup, my mom said she always thought you were adorable."

"Adorable? Really?" *Ahhh! That's sweet. For some reason coming from his mom it meant something.*

"That's what she said. I couldn't argue . . . 'cause, well, you are. Don't you know that?" he asked as if it was common knowledge.

"Ooooh, not really," I shyly responded. I knew I was somewhat attractive, but not necessarily *adorable,* especially to people who hardly knew me. Parents do not count, but in my case, dads don't count since my mom never complimented me on my looks.

"Well, you are. You really got robbed on the Miss Blue Lagoon thing. My mom thinks so, too," he stated empathetically. *Oh, not the pageant again.* That seemed like ages ago and it was only yesterday. So much has happened since then. "But that's not why I called," he got back on track. My heart sank. This didn't sound good. "My mom told me that I have a doctor's appointment tomorrow, and then I have to run errands with her." He briefly paused. Then he continued, "So we won't be able to hang out. I'm really sorry," he apologized in earnest.

"Oh, that's okay," I tried not to sound too disappointed or too upbeat.

"She just told me. I had no idea until now. Maybe we can hang out Wednesday?" he suggested.

"Sure, I'd like that." *But I will miss you in the meantime.*

"I really did have fun today. You're a great gamer!" he complimented. I thought he was going to say *kisser.* Maybe his mom was sitting nearby. I failed to get his kissing out of my mind.

"Thanks. So are you."

"You're so easy to talk to, too," Avery said. *So are you.*

"Avery, you're the one that gets the conversation going. Half the time I am too tongue-tied to say anything." *I can't believe I said that.*

"Really?" he asked. "You get tongue-tied? You always sound so cool and collected."

I burst out into laughter. "That's what I think about you. You're always so open and honest. You can say anything to anybody."

"I don't sound like a dork?" he asked humbly, wanting to know the truth.

"Are you kidding me? My heart melts just talking to you." *Did I just say that?* "I can't believe I just said that," I blurted. "I'm so embarrassed."

"No, don't be; it's cool. I feel the same way," he gently encouraged.

"You do?" MY HEART WAS POUNDING!

"TOTALLY!" he said with enthusiasm. I was falling for Avery hard and fast. *Is this normal?* He continued, "When I am with you, I have the most awesome time. When I am not with you, I think of you all the time." *He did not just say that. Oh, my goodness! Maybe there is a God after all.* I about cried. *How incredibly sweet!*

"Me too," I eked out. "I wish we lived closer or something," I said trying to make up for my weak attempt to reassure my feelings for him.

"Yeah, that would be nice." There was a pause. "Christina?" Another pause.

"Yes?" The anticipation about killed me.

"I *really* like you," he announced.

Whoah! The way he said that wasn't like casual admiration. It was almost like he wanted to say, 'I love you.' I couldn't go there; it was too soon. I felt nervously excited like a school girl experiencing her first real relationship. *Oh, right! I am a school girl experiencing her first real relationship.*

"I like you too, Avery," I said amiably. *That was pathetic.* "I mean I *really* like you!" There, I finally said it. It was officially on the table. We pledged our mutual intense "like" for one another. It didn't get much better than this.

"Will you do me a favor, Christina?" Avery asked. "Sure." *Anything for you.*

"Will you miss me tomorrow as much as I will miss you?" *Wow, that took courage! He is mushy. Step away from the mushiness.*

"Consider it done," I assured him.

"Hey, I gotta go. I'll call you sometime tomorrow?"

"Great! Bye, Avery," I said fondly.

"Bye, Christina," Avery responded tenderly. I hung up the phone, then gasped for air. My heart was aflutter.

He really does like me. Yes! I stifled a scream as I danced around my bedroom. He actually likes me. I can't believe it. My luck has finally changed. I am going out with Avery. Happy dance ensued. I AM GOING OUT WITH AVERY . . . AVERY EVANS! I can't believe I am really going out with him. He is so cute. He thinks I'm adorable. Is he kidding? He is incredibly cute. Like the epitome of cute. I wasn't so sure he liked me, at least not that much, but now I know, and the feeling is mutual. I wish I could see him tomorrow. I totally miss him already.

I guess I'll go to the pool tomorrow. Not much else to do in this boring town. I am going to have an awesome time with Avery the rest of the summer. I can't wait! End happy dance.

I dreamed of Avery and me on that enchanting night—riding bikes, playing video games, laughing, kissing, and sharing our most intimate thoughts. And yet, it wasn't just a dream; it was reality. And I relished every minute of it. The next morning, I woke up refreshed and with a smile on my face because I, Christina De Rosa, had the world's greatest boyfriend.

Chapter 8

I WOKE UP HUNGRY AND SLUMBERED downstairs for breakfast. My body was tired but filled with joy from hanging out with Avery the day before. *So, this is what it feels like to have a boyfriend.*

My mom greeted me per usual as she sat on her designated chair at the kitchen table drinking her morning tea with sugar and milk. "Good morning," she greeted me with the slightest of glances.

Although I was smiling within, all I could manage was, "Good morning," with a half yawn as I sat down to eat the cereal that was placed before me along with the milk, bowl and spoon. Having everything ready for me each day for breakfast made my mornings run smoother.

"Where are you off to today?" she asked while she watched the news on the TV.

"The pool I guess," I replied with a shrug as I poured the milk over my Rice Krispies and listened to the snap, crackle, pop. *I love that sound!*

"Sounds good," a typical response from my mother.

After I finished eating my lively cereal, I quickly showered, dressed, and tied my hair in a ponytail. I hoisted my bike out of the garage and pedaled away.

Not before long, I heard, "Christina," my neighbor yelled to me over the sound of a car driving by, "you looked so lovely in that dress Sunday. I can't believe you didn't win!"

I glanced over and waved, "Oh, thanks!" I felt like barfing up my breakfast after being reminded of the stupid pageant. The compliment was kind, but I wanted the pageant behind me. Time to move on. Literally. I wasn't about to let that spoil my day.

The fresh warm air was welcoming. I loved how the wind swept against my face as I rode my bike.

My grandmother lived on the way to the pool, which was convenient. I frequently stopped by unannounced. She seemed to like the company and I felt that it was the least I could do as I lived close by. I rapped on her bronze door knocker. *Knock. Knock.*

"Coming," she yelled, probably figuring it was me. My grandmother was no dummy. "Hello, Christina, I thought it might be you. Won't you come in?" She stepped aside to let me in.

"Thanks, Mom-Mom," I said as I walked in the living room. She, too, had the TV on. It was boisterous as usual since she was hard of hearing. She motioned for me to sit on the couch, "Have a seat."

She waited for both of us to be seated. "So how are you doing today?" she asked, looking me square in the eyes. That's the thing about grandmothers: they give you their undivided attention ninety percent of the time. I liked it.

"Great. Thanks. How are you?" I exclaimed cheerfully trying my best to speak loud enough for her to hear me over the TV.

"Can't complain," she stated, but believe me, Mom-Mom could complain. "You seem chipper today."

I loved the old fashion expressions. That kind of terminology popped into my head all the time. Must have been Mom-Mom's influence, but rarely did I have the guts to talk like that. I thought people might think I was weird.

"I am, Mom-Mom," I confirmed boldly with a smile and a likely glow.

"Oh, what brings that on?" she inquired with a raised eyebrow, leaning forward.

"Just enjoying my summer. Hanging out with friends. That's all." I responded in a nonchalant manner.

"So, you have a boyfriend?" she guessed, looking at me very intently. My Mom-Mom was nobody's fool, but of course, it was written on my face in flashing neon lights—"IN LOVE!"

"You could say that." I squirmed a little in my seat.

"So, what's his name?" she asked in a friendly and curious tone.

"Avery." *I love saying that and I love that my Mom-Mom asked.*

"Does this Avery have a last name?" she teased and showed me so with a sweet smile as she tilted her head toward me.

"Evans."

"Come again?"

"His last name is Evans." *Where is this going?*

"So how old is Avery?" she continued keeping the focus on me and not the blaring TV. *I wish she would turn off the TV. It's so loud!*

"My age. He's in my grade," I replied. "I have known him since fourth grade," I elaborated, relieved that I could say he was my age. I can't imagine her words if I said that he was younger. She was well aware that boys mature more slowly than girls.

"And you're in what grade now?" She finally clicked off the television. *Thank goodness for some peace and quiet!*

"Ninth."

With her lips pursed and hands clenched, Mom-Mom exclaimed, "Oh, that's young—too young for your generation to have boyfriends."

"Why do you say that?" I was supremely intrigued and not offended at all. These conversations usually led to me hearing tales of her youth, which was always a treat.

"Because, my dear," she began sincerely while leaning back in her chair with an air of authority, "back in the day when I was growing up, we *had* to grow up fast. We didn't have a choice. It was a matter of economics. Today, you should take your time being courted by someone. You have the option of going to college, having a career. I never had those options. Plus, you should be dated by many young suitors. You have choices now, and you should use them."

"Huh." *Maybe I got my original philosophy from my Mom-Mom, although I do not recall such a conversation.* "Well, I don't plan on getting married until after college," I stated with conviction knowing that I would appease her.

"I am glad to hear that. Best news I have heard all day. It's better to take your time and 'play the field' as they say." I was glad to be able to brighten her day.

"So, Mom-Mom, what's new with you?"

"Me? Well, people at my age don't live exciting lives. That's left for the youth like yourself." *I guess that's why she didn't do much except watch TV.*

"No new aches and pains?" I teased.

She tittered, "You're quite the character, Christina, aren't you?" She paused. "All right, come to think of it, if you really must know, my knee has been bothering me."

"Oh, sorry. Which knee?"

She pointed to her right knee, rubbing it. "The right one."

"Do you remember hurting yourself?" I wondered if she hurt something else in the process.

Mom-Mom shook her head, sounding exasperated, "No, honestly I don't. That's what's so troubling. The pain came out of nowhere."

"Did you take anything for it?"

She laughed, "Now, who are you, my doctor?"

"Just asking," I shrugged.

"I know. I know. For your information, I did. I took Advil this morning. It's feeling much better now. Guess that's why I forgot about it." She gave me a dismissive wave.

We talked for a few minutes more about irrelevant topics ranging from the weather to soap operas. She watched all the daytime dramas on channel six ABC: *All My Children, One Life to Live,* and *General Hospital.* I was careful not to get hooked on those shows as they seemed like a waste of time.

"I better get going. I think I'll stop over at Katie's house to see if she wants to go to the pool. I hope your knee gets better."

"Thank you. It already is. By the way, what does your mother think about you having a boyfriend?"

"She doesn't know," I readily admitted.

She raised an octave and sounded very certain, "Oh, don't be so sure. Your mother is extremely observant."

"Are you going to tell her?"

She waved me off. "No, that's for you to do. Why don't you want her to know?"

"She doesn't seem to care about that kind of stuff," I shrugged. It wasn't as if I was trying to actively hide it from her.

With an indignant tone, she declared, "She cares about you very much. That much I know."

"I guess so." I didn't feel like my mom cared that much about my life. I came and went as I pleased. Sometimes she even invalidated how I felt.

One time in middle school, I told her how it bothered me that this girl called me a space cadet. My mom told me I was silly and not to be so sensitive. She literally argued with me, insisting my feelings were wrong. You feel what you feel. It's not right or wrong, good or bad. It just is. Needless to say, I didn't share anything personal with my mom from that point on.

Upon walking me to the front door, Mom-Mom said, "Just be careful. You know me, sweet sixteen and never been kissed." I never understood why she always said that. She bore eight children. What a strange sense of humor.

"Now who's the character?" I couldn't resist! I enjoyed the playful banter with Mom-Mom as I couldn't talk like that with my mom.

"Touché!" Mom-Mom exclaimed. She must have had fun talking like that. "Now, don't do anything I wouldn't do," she advised with a wink and a smirk.

"No problem." I failed to think of anything clever to say that would not come across as disrespectful.

"Have a good day, Christina!" She waved good-bye.

"You too, Mom-Mom. I'll see you soon." I planted a kiss on her cheek brushing against her prickly facial hair and I breezed out the door.

I cruised down the street to Katie's house. Sometimes I stopped by her house unannounced, too. I rode up her driveway, hopped off my bike and rapped on the side door. A few seconds later, she appeared.

"Hey, Christina."

"Hi, Katie. You wanna go to the pool?"

"Yes, I was about to leave. I'll grab my stuff. Be right back." She returned in a flash and without hesitation asked about Avery, "Are you and Avery still an item?" *Why wouldn't we be?*

"Yeah."

"So, what's he doing today?" she asked in a breezy tone.

"He had a doctor's appointment or something. Then he had to run errands with his mom."

"Oh, so I'm his replacement?" she jested. Katie straddled her bike. We rode slowly side by side on the street. The street on the way to the pool was nice and wide.

"No," I said defensively. "You know we've been hanging out at the pool all summer."

Katie chortled, "I'm just messing with ya, girl. But I do want all the details."

"Details, huh? Well, I don't kiss-and-tell," I said cheekily.

With a higher inflection of her voice she baited, "Well, *hello!* I saw you kiss him already."

"Oh, right." *I almost forgot about that. Well, not really. How could I ever forget that pivotal moment?*

"So, is he a good kisser?" Nothing like getting straight to the point.

"Why, do you want to kiss him?" I tittered and lost my balance after hitting a pothole. *That was close. I don't think she noticed that I almost fell off my bike.*

Katie continued as if nothing happened, "No, not really. No offense, but he's not my type. Not that he's not cute or anything. He's more like a brother to me."

"Oh, I didn't realize you knew him that well."

"I don't actually. I guess I don't see him as boyfriend material. He's more like a friend. You should be grateful that I'm not into your boyfriend."

"I'm not the jealous type. At least I don't think I am. I figure if he liked someone else, then it would be over between us. I can't see myself groveling for . . . well, anyone. I wouldn't be able to trust him after that anyhow."

"Okay, okay, but is he a good kisser? Inquiring minds want to know," Katie persisted.

The lightbulb went off in my brain as my head bobbed wide-eyed, "You mean Amy wants to know! Now I get it!" *Amy likes Avery. Who wouldn't, besides Katie?* "So, where is she?"

"She's meeting me at the pool."

"Is three a crowd?"

"No, I didn't mean it like that. She's a planner. She called to see what I was doing today," Katie explained. "I'm sure Amy wouldn't mind if you hung out with us. We figured you would be with Avery, especially after witnessing that kiss Sunday night." *Reasonable conclusion.*

"Enough with the kissing already," I insisted.

Again, with the intonation, "Are you kidding? Your public display of affection is the talk of the town."

"I thought my not winning Miss Blue Lagoon was the talk of the town."

"That's old news." *Good golly,* this town is boring!

Chapter 9

WE ARRIVED AT THE POOL and parked our bikes. Mrs. Jenski nodded approval as we flashed our pool badges. Before I turned the corner, she called my name and waved me over. I had known her since fourth grade as the cafeteria lady and Cheryl Wilson's next-door neighbor. For some reason, she always spoke in a raspy, low voice and was always kind to me. I strained myself to hear her. She whispered, "You looked beautiful in the pageant. You should have won."

I graciously replied, "Thank you very much," and walked away with a smile. Guess Mrs. Jenski didn't know about the famous kiss.

"What was *that* all about?" Katie asked.

"Just one of my fans," I chortled shaking my head in disbelief.

"I told you it was rigged." I felt uncomfortable every time she said that. We walked over to a familiar grassy spot and spread our towels out to sit on. It was going to be a hot one today.

"But how? Why? That just doesn't make any sense, not that I don't appreciate your compliment. It's a small-time, small-town pageant."

"You say that now, but I heard that Jennie is entering other pageants and the rewards are more than just flowers and a gift certificate."

"She got a gift certificate?" I questioned, stunned.

"Yes, and so did I. Did you not pay attention to anything?"

"Guess not," I shrugged.

"You really hated the whole thing, didn't you?" she asked, in an attempt to understand.

My repulsed look could have said it all, but I also responded verbally, "Well, yeah, it wasn't my kind of thing at all."

"I realize that, but you could have faked it," she propounded.

"Was it *that* obvious? Seriously?" I still couldn't believe how transparent I had been.

"To me it was. Why did you do it if you hated it so much?"

"Because Mrs. Martin begged me to. I just couldn't disappoint her." *Pathetic!*

Katie's eyes widened with her sudden insight, "Oh, okay, now *that* makes sense. I heard that no one can say no to her. She seems to cast a spell over everyone."

"Yes, she must have secret fairy dust she sprinkles everywhere to get what she wants out of people. Just a theory."

"Wow, she actually got to *you.*" We discussed how I was asked to play the part she got in *Guys and Dolls* but refused, even though I thoroughly respected and liked the teacher who tried to persuade me to audition.

"Hey, do you regret not trying out for the part?" she asked.

"No, not at all. I thought the part suited you better to be honest." Truthfully, I feared making a mistake on stage. The thought of me tripping in high heels paralyzed me from trying out for any part in the musical. That, and the fact that I couldn't bear the scrutiny of being in the spotlight portraying a gorgeous girl.

Katie shrugged. "I didn't think so, but I had to ask." More honesty. She waved her hand in the air causing me to look up. "Here comes Amy."

Amy walked straight over to us. "Hey, guys, mind if I join you?" That was a silly question considering she already made plans with Katie, but it was considerate.

"Pull up a towel," Katie gestured with a hand motion alongside her.

"What did I miss?" asked Amy as she smoothed out her towel next to Katie.

Katie quipped, "Oh, let's see . . . Christina won't kiss-and-tell, she didn't know about the gift certificates and oh, yeah, Mrs. Martin is the devil that made her do it. That about sums it up."

"Mrs. Martin made who do what?" Amy squealed.

"Mrs. Martin begged Christina to be a contestant."

"Now I get it!" Amy exclaimed.

Am I invisible? "Yoo-hoo," I said waving my hand, "I'm still here." The three of us giggled.

"I wanna hear about the kiss-and-tell part!" Amy said both

humorously and earnestly.

"Nothing to tell," I responded shrugging my shoulders.

"I asked Christina if Avery is a good kisser," Katie recapped.

"Soooo, *is* he?" Amy asked. I contemplated what to say or if I should say anything at all. "Well?" Amy persisted. I thought some more. "Oh, come on! You're killing me!" she pleaded as she kicked her legs up and down.

I leaned over in Amy's direction. "Okay, Amy, be honest. You like Avery, right?" I pried. I had a right to know. After all, he was my boyfriend.

"Yeah, kinda," she admitted, "but I would never . . . I mean I couldn't steal him away from you. I'm not devious like that," Amy assured me.

"She's not," Katie quickly added in Amy's defense.

"I believe you, Amy. But you have to understand my perspective. What good does it do if I said that Avery was a good kisser? I mean, I don't want to rub it in. On the other hand, what if I said that Avery wasn't a good kisser? Then I would be bashing his reputation and that wouldn't be nice." *It truly is better unsaid, isn't it?*

"Hmm, I see your point," Amy admitted as she placed her index finger on her lips.

Katie rationalized, "Yes, but *I* am not interested in Avery, so if he was a good kisser, you could tell me." She was rather sharp, but there had to be a way around not telling them.

"You would tell Amy," I stated the obvious.

"Yes, but I wouldn't be rubbing it in," Katie declared. "Oh, come on. Give me a break," I implored in frustration.

"I'm just saying . . ." Katie sang.

"Okay . . . okay, couldn't you tell anything from our . . . ahem," I cleared my throat, "kiss Sunday night?" I teased. I decided to have fun with this after all.

"It looked awesome!" Amy exclaimed enviously.

"Awesome to you because you like him or awesome for some other reason?" I questioned.

"Both, for sure," Amy admitted nodding her head.

I went for it, since I wanted to know how we looked to others during our public embrace.

"Okay, Katie, how did it look to you?" I asked.

"It did look pretty great," Katie agreed by nodding as well.

"See? I told you," Amy taunted. I felt like I was a detective on a fact-finding mission, but I could end up the victim.

"Based on what you saw that night at that moment, what conclusions could you draw?" I probed.

"That Avery is a good kisser," they both replied in unison. They must have forged a closer friendship than I thought.

"And what makes you think that?" I teased.

"Because you looked like you were really enjoying it," Katie surmised. Amy nodded in agreement.

"Maybe I enjoyed the simple fact that I was kissing *Avery*," I suggested coyly.

"No way, that kiss was over the top," Katie retorted.

Now we're getting somewhere.

"Have you ever considered that the kiss was so over the top because I am a good kisser?" I planted a possibility.

I watched the wheels turning in Amy's head. "Hmm, that's possible. I mean I hadn't thought about it like that," Amy admitted.

"No, you're just saying that to sidetrack us," Katie retorted. *Bonus points for you Katie.*

I stuck my bottom lip out and wined like a crying baby, "Now you're hurting my feelings."

"You should have seen the look on your face afterwards," Katie pressed. I nodded indicating for her to continue. "Your face was all smile!" she recounted, as her face lit up. Katie was a good actress.

"Yes, but couldn't my beaming be attributed to the fact that we just declared our status as boyfriend and girlfriend?" I toyed with them, impressed with myself.

"Possibly, but I think there was way more to it than that. I'm telling you, you were like 'WOW,' as in 'That kiss was fabulous!' You should have seen your face!" Katie was able to freeze frame that moment in time after I kissed Avery with absurd accuracy. It truly was some kiss! I couldn't help but blush.

Amy pointed at me. "She's blushing!" She kicked her feet again against towel. "We were right after all!" She concluded with the look of pure satisfaction.

Katie screeched as she flicked her right index finger, "I knew it!"

I caved. "Okay, okay!" "I will give you the scoop, since you earned it," I said earnestly. "Avery is not a good kisser." I paused for effect. Both Katie and Amy leaned back and gaped in disbelief.

"He's not?" They answered again in unison. *Are they sharing a brain?*

"No, he's a fantastic kisser!" I barely contained myself. The flood gates opened wide, "I mean, he is a knock your socks off, make the hair on the back of your neck stand to attention and your toes curl great kisser," I exhaled. "It was like I was transported to a TV studio and was kissing Rob Lowe."

At the same time Katie and Amy gasped. "Wow!" They turned toward each other, then back at me and we all cracked up.

Amy's eyes grew wider as she inquired, "Seriously, he is *that* good?" Nodding my head, I looked at them assuredly.

Keeping my eyes planted on them I continued, "You have to understand that I have no basis for comparison, but," I paused for effect, "Avery . . . is . . . without question . . . a phenomenal kisser!"

"Oh my God!" Katie roared as she kicked her feet. "How many times did you kiss him?" *Too many to count in only one night and one day.*

"Let's just say I enjoyed every single moment our lips collided." I enjoyed the scintillating conversation.

"So, how come you aren't with him now?" Amy asked.

"Because he had to go out with his mom today. He said he'd call me later," I answered nonchalantly.

"You are so lucky!" Amy gushed.

"Yeah, Jennie Pitman, eat your heart out!" Katie enthused.

My heart skipped a beat. "Does Jennie like Avery too?" I questioned. *Did that sound jealous?*

"Oh, I don't know. I just think that you're luckier than she is. That's all," Katie explained. Relieved, I had to chuckle. Being on the pageant circuit did not excite me in the least.

"I wouldn't trade it for the world," I professed whimsically. "That reminds me, how much was the gift certificate?" I inquired.

"Mine was for fifty dollars, Jennie's was one hundred dollars, and Maureen got twenty-five dollars."

"For what?" I asked.

"The Pennsford Mall," Katie stated. *How did I miss the gift certificates?* Not that I was a shopper. Katie knew that, too.

"I honestly don't know how Maureen won second runner-up. I mean she isn't even that cute," Amy stated curtly.

"Yeah, I know what you mean. I don't get that part either," I concurred.

"Told you it was rigged!" Katie whispered intensely, so others remained oblivious to our conversation.

"You keep saying that. So, what's your proof?" I probed.

"I can't tell you how many times I saw Jennie's parents talk to the judges and Mrs. Martin," she stated.

"I noticed that too," I replied. "I saw Mr. Pitman do that before the pageant began."

My parents had absolutely no contact with any of them. We never even discussed the pageant.

"Me too," Amy jumped in.

Joyful screams and splashing persisted in the background as I felt the sun beating down on me.

"Okay, I have to admit it looks suspicious. Let's see," I said slowly to alter the pace of this rapid conversation so that we could organize the facts, "Katie, you got first runner-up. That part I'm cool with; that made sense to me. I think Jennie is very good-looking, but have you ever noticed anything in particular about her body? Seriously, have you?" I searched their faces for confirmation. Please don't tell me that I'm the only one that noticed.

"Are you kidding? She's flat as a board!" Katie replied. *So true!*

"Who does she look like?" I toyed.

Amy and Katie glanced at each other and then back at me with no response. "Okay, guys, think of who was kissing up to the judges."

"Her dad!" They said in unison.

Amy put her hand over her mouth and shouted, "Oh my God! You're right! She *does* look exactly like her dad."

"Which means she kinda looks like a boy," I said restating the obvious.

"How did we miss that?" Katie grieved.

"Case in point," I said sternly. I was Columbo. All I needed was a cigar. "Now, let's get back to Maureen. Amy, you said she's not at all that cute. Do you agree with that, Katie?" I wondered how off-base I was. Maybe people didn't think Maureen was cute. "Now, be honest."

"Yes, I agree with Amy. Maureen isn't even that cute. She's an air-headed, petite blond. That's all. She gives us blonds a bad rap." *Alright, Katie, don't hold back.*

"Okay, why would the judges pick Maureen over, say, Amy?"

Katie shook her head while looking at her friend. "I have no idea," she said sincerely.

"I know why," Amy touted, "because I'm fat. Let's face it." Amy looked sad, like she was about to cry.

"You're not fat!" Katie exclaimed. Amy wasn't fat; pleasantly plump maybe, but not fat.

I gave Amy an empathetic look and gently said, "I mentioned your name Amy, because you are attractive, much better looking than Maureen. Even if you *were* fat—and I'm not saying you are—the judges picked Jennie with her unique body type. In my opinion, your body is more appealing than hers. You even agreed that she resembles a boy." *And her father minus the hairy legs.*

She sat quietly soaking it in while I was soaking up the sun's rays on this scorching summer day. Time to reapply the suntan lotion. I slathered lotion on my exposed skin, noting the distinct fragrance of coconut. Love that smell—the smell of summer!

I watched Katie's wheels turning in her head. I've seen that look before. She was on to something. "Maybe it wasn't about the second runner-up. Maybe it was about the winner. I really think that Jennie was destined to win. I think the second runner-up was arbitrary," Katie theorized, like Kris Munroe of *Charlie's Angels*.

Katie's impressive speculation lead me to question further, "Wow, that's a great point. Why wouldn't they pick someone to make it more believable?"

"Like you?" They both said together. My memory flashed back to the time when Mrs. Martin said I was extremely beautiful. *I'm starting to sense a theme here.*

"What is it with you guys speaking simultaneously so often?" I asked doing my best to avoid their question. "You two are like the twins in *The Parent Trap.*"

They blankly stared at me.

Again, in unison, "The what?!"

I reiterated, "*The Parent Trap.* You know, the movie from the sixties." Crickets.

They shrugged their shoulders and we all sniggered. Leave it to Amy to get us back on point. "Seriously, why didn't the judges pick Christina?" Amy paused. The question hung in the air. "Everyone said she should have won and she didn't even place. What's up with that?"

"Yeah, what is up with that?" I voiced with snark. I, too, can play this game.

"Like I said, Jennie was destined to win. I think she and her parents had an agenda. Maybe they thought winning Miss Blue Lagoon would open the doors to fame and fortune," Katie stated brilliantly.

"But why wouldn't they at least choose Christina as second runner-up?" Amy implored.

"Oh, jeeze," gasped Katie, "because Christina wasn't into it at all. She didn't care about it and told the world so with how she acted. And if you annoyed Mrs. Martin, who always gets what she wants, well . . ."

"Do you know something that we don't know?" I interjected.

"No, I'm totally speculating; I have a gut feeling about this. How could I get runner-up and you not place? It just seems . . . contrived . . . uh, forced. Unless, of course, they judge, in part, on attitude."

Her point was valid. I did have a bad attitude. I did not want to be there. I was embarrassed to draw such attention to myself, and I did think it was kind of stupid for any girl to do, and yet, it was kind of a neat experience as well. Jeez, the deeper truth was that I was afraid. I had stage fright and that was embarrassing, too. In the end, I didn't know how to handle it all with grace. I sabotaged myself.

"I guess it was too obvious that I hated it," I admitted with a shrug. *Oh well. You live. You learn.*

"No, really?" The twins synced their sarcasm.

"Guess that's why I didn't win Miss Congeniality," I fished. Katie and Amy simply smirked at me. "Well, what's done is done. I am okay with not winning. It's my own fault. I should have had a better attitude. If people didn't keep bringing it up to me, I wouldn't have given it a second thought."

"You're a good sport," Amy complimented. *Amy is surprisingly cool. I am beginning to like her.*

"Thanks. That's nice of you to say," I smiled.

"A lot of people told you that you should have won then?" Amy quizzed.

"Actually, yeah, and every time they do, it's like reliving the embarrassment. I realize people think that they are being nice, but

I get mixed emotions. It's a lot to sort through. I wish it would just blow over."

"Let's drop it then," Katie proposed.

Amy chimed in, "I'm hot. Let's take a dip in the pool."

"Cool, let's go!" I said appreciatively. I was sweating from the blazing sun and I needed a distraction. I missed Avery something fierce. He would have made all of this disappear.

The water was cool and refreshing. We swam a little and watched a few kids take turns on the diving boards. One kid, in particular, showed talent. He was doing flips off the springboard. For kicks and giggles, we scored him.

"That's an eight," I cheered.

"Eight for me too," Katie added.

"Likewise," said Amy.

The boy was about eleven years old and he appeared to like the attention from three older girls. He blushed as he got out of the pool.

"Hey, kid, what's your name?" I yelled. "Ted."

I continued to question him, "Are you on the diving team?"

"Yeah," he answered.

Katie whispered, "You're flirting with him!"

I looked at her like she was absurd. *Oh, my gosh, I'm talking to him. That's all!*

"You're pretty good," I complimented. "Thanks!" He blushed again.

"I'm telling Avery," Katie sang. *Telling him what?* Katie continued to sing.

"Will you quit it?" I gritted through my teeth. "I am not flirting with him," I insisted.

"So, do you have any other moves?" I asked while Amy and Katie roared with laughter. They seemed to be especially humored by that question.

"Watch and see," he replied. He performed an inward tuck with minimal splash.

"Impressive," I nodded.

"The kid is good," Amy declared with a distinct nod.

"He's got talent," Katie affirmed.

We cheered Ted on when he popped out of the water.

This cycle of diving, scoring, and laughing continued for about twenty minutes.

Finally, Ted approached us. He stood at the pool's edge, looked down and asked, "Were you girls in the Miss Blue Lagoon Pageant?" We nodded. He looked directly at me and said, "My friends and I think you got a bum rap." *Ugh, did you now? And I was having so much fun.*

"Thanks," I forced a smile. The reminders of this pageant were getting old.

"Gotta go," Ted darted off. Sunning and a show. Gotta love summer! Except for a . . .

"See what I mean?" I chirped. "Sometimes I think this is all a joke and the joke is on *me.*"

Amy pitched the idea of playing cards. "I brought a deck with me. It will keep your mind off of the . . . eh, on fun things." *Thank you, Social Director. Rescue commencing.*

"I'm game," Katie stated.

"Alrighty," I said. "Thank you very much, Amy," I said genuinely as I smiled with my eyes.

We played Crazy Eights as we discussed our budding ninth grade careers. High school would invariably be an adjustment and I wasn't that fond of middle school.

Since I had a poor sense of direction, I shared, "I'm afraid I'll get lost."

"Don't ask an upperclassman for directions. They are notorious for purposely sending you on a wild-goose chase," Amy informed.

"How do you know that?" I asked.

"I have older brothers and they did that to my older sister."

I was beginning to get anxious. I didn't want to miss Avery's call. I got off my towel and started to get dressed.

"You're leaving already?" Katie asked. It was about three o'clock in the afternoon. "That was sudden."

"Yeah, I'm gonna head home. Things to do." *Like wait for my awesome boyfriend to call.*

Amy waved good-bye, "Catch you later."

"Bye," Katie added.

"See you guys later," I said with finality and headed up the hill. I peddled home on my bike eagerly waiting to talk to the guy who makes me forget life's stressors.

Chapter 10

AS I WAS PULLING INTO my driveway, Paul shouted my name. I stopped my bike and watched him run up the street waving his arms. *Oh, my gosh, what could he want?*

I straddled my bike and waited. As I stood there, pictures of his frightful stares flashed in my mind. I wasn't in control of them; they just materialized. My mind did its own bidding and my body followed. My chest constricted. My heart raced, and I found myself holding my breath, fighting to appear unshaken and normal.

"Christina, my mom wanted to give you something. Can you come down to my house to get it?" he questioned almost human-like, so I relaxed a little.

"What is it?" I asked curiously while glancing over to his driveway to see if his mother's car was parked there. Her Barbie-mobile was there.

Maybe his mom got me something for going through with the pageant knowing how reluctant I had been all along. She probably felt terrible because I lost after she acted like I was a shoo-in.

"It's a surprise," he said hastily. *Hmmm, that's awfully nice of her.*

"Let me put my bike away and get changed first. I'll be over in a few," I said, since I might not be able to carry whatever it was while riding my bike and I wanted to be free of my swimsuit.

I walked my bike up the driveway and parked it in the garage noticing my mom's car wasn't in the driveway. Paul disappeared out of sight.

I ran upstairs, took off my bathing suit, washed up in the sink and slid into a fresh pair of shorts and a top. I walked to Paul's house and knocked on the door.

Paul opened the door and motioned for me to come in. I stepped inside the laundry room. He walked away and told me to follow him. Paul stopped abruptly. He looked at me with great intensity. My body automatically tensed.

"It's too bad we don't hang out anymore," he said nonchalantly. His words did not match his facial expression.

"We never hung out," I replied brusquely.

"Yes, we did. Remember we all used to go down to play in your basement?" I vaguely recollected. "You had foam seat cushions down there without the covers on them."

It started to come back to me. Our elementary school hosted a talent show every year that most of the fifth grade class participated in. The girls in my class asked me to be a part of their act. Reluctantly, I said yes.

We mocked The $1.98 Beauty Show that aired on TV. Since the talent on that show was pathetic, I figured my act could be awful and still be in keeping with the hilarity of the show. When it was my turn to perform, I sang "Somewhere Over the Rainbow."

Come to think of it, I lost as a mock contestant that time, too. Two popular girls, Dina and Cathy, pretended to be twins and performed a silly dance as their talent. They insisted on winning.

As soon as the fifth grade talent show ended, I received many compliments on my singing and how pretty I looked in my dress. As I recall, Mrs. Martin was among those who complimented me.

Later that day, after the talent show Paul Martin, my brother, and some other kids from the neighborhood and I were playing outside in my backyard when someone suggested we hang in our basement. In no time, my house was flooded with kids and noise.

Once there, Paul pulled me to the far, dark end of the basement and then pushed me down on some cushions. He thrust his body on top of mine. Terrified, I managed—don't know how exactly—to break away and run upstairs.

Oh, my goodness, I suppressed that memory for the last three years. I forgot it even happened. *Is that why I hated the attention of the pageant? Is that why I decided not to date until I was much older?*

I froze in the threshold of Paul's family room. "Where's your mom?" I asked anxiously, fingers tapping my leg and my heart pounding in my ears. *Oh, my gosh, I can't think straight. I need to get home.*

"Be patient. She'll be here in a minute." Awkwardness overcame me and that's when he turned off the charm and flipped the switch. Angrily, he yammered nonsense, "You know it was my mom's plan that you would win the Miss Blue Lagoon Pageant," he began. "Jennie was to be in second place, the first runner-up, and then Katie.

"My mom already knew that Jennie's parents wanted her to be a beauty queen like her mother, but my mom thought you were much prettier. Did you know that Jennie's parents planted a spy in the pageant?"

Stunned, I shook my head warily. Paul continued like a frothing, rabid wolf, "She volunteered to help out, so she could be on the inside. Remember Mrs. Neumann? She reported *everything* to the judges, including your refusal not to wear high heels and how you insisted on wearing those *stupid stockings.*"

His angry look from Sunday night reappeared. I started to quake. *Where is your mother? Her car . . .*

"My mom was mortified. She was going to insist you wear high heels and not wear the dumb stockings, but Mrs. Neumann said she already talked to you and you were adamant. By then, everyone was saying how you acted like you hated every second of being in the pageant. My mom was FURIOUS. She wanted YOU to win. She liked YOU."

He was getting louder and louder and angrier and angrier. He was so close to me spittle hit my face.

What is happening? I don't underst . . .

"Now, everyone is giving her grief because YOU didn't win. People have been calling nonstop saying that you should have won. They are leaving nasty messages on our answering machine. Some people came to our house. They even went to my mom's work. They are claiming that the pageant was fixed.

"My mom was pissed. She worked so hard on the pageant and YOU messed everything up! My mom is in the hospital now with a nervous breakdown," he screamed at the top of his lungs, "AND IT'S ALL YOUR FAULT, YOU SELFISH WHORE!"

My fault? Selfish whore? I couldn't help it; I was on the verge of tears. "STOP!" I gathered up the courage to shout. "I can't hear any more of this nonsense," I trailed off, covering my ears.

I turned to leave, but he grabbed my arm and twisted it back. It instantly burned.

He wasn't playing. Fire filled his eyes. *Oh my God, what the hell?* I fought for freedom, but he pulled me into the family room and threw me onto the floor. My head banged the edge of the coffee table. He pounced on top of me and pugnaciously held me down.

"Get off of me! Let me go!" I hollered and strained. My head filled with throbbing, searing agony while his heart filled with pure, deranged evil. "What are you doing?!" I barked.

"Shut up, you bitch!" he roared as he smacked me across the face with the back of his hand. My head exploded with stinging pain shooting in every direction.

I can't take this. Am I going to die?

His hands continued to move lightning fast every which direction pressing me against the floor here and there to keep me still. I couldn't get up—I simply wasn't strong enough. This is crazy! *Help me. Someone, help!*

The pain in my head subsided long enough for me to feel my cheek. It burned as if someone touched it with a hot iron.

Instinctively, I knew what he was after. He yanked my shorts down. Then, my underwear.

"NO! NOOO! NO! STOP, PLEASE STOP!" I screamed with as much strength as I could muster.

"Shut up, you stinkin' whore!" He fired back. "This is what you get for humiliating my mom! You are such a loser!" *Did she tell Paul to do this?*

"Noooo, please no!" I pleaded in horror. I bawled hysterically.

Every fiber of my being attempted to fight back. The more I fought, the more my head felt like it was about to explode, the more nauseous I became. I closed my eyes hoping it would end, but to no avail. I didn't give up fighting back though. I persisted. He continued.

I was trapped underneath a monster. The pain in my head, coupled with the helplessness I felt, brought tears to my eyes.

He's actually . . .

"NOOO!!!" I released a terrified and incomprehensible scream while he shattered my insides—my virginity.

I heard him panting and grunting as I screeched in pain, fear and disbelief.

Oooowww!!

I could feel my insides tear as he pushed into me. The most I could do was brace myself until it ended.

Upon completion, our eyes met—his visage shown the face of a gloating feral animal that just killed its prey. My body went completely numb. I never felt so alone, so destroyed. I was decimated.

He relieved me and got dressed. I remained paralyzed with fear and disgust and remained frozen in incredulity.

"Admit it, I was better than Avery!" he taunted.

Avery? What does he have to do with this?

"If you mention one word of this to anyone," he snarled, glaring, "I will kill *you* and *your little boyfriend!*"

My mouth went dry.

"My mom's got connections everywhere—the sheriff, judges, the press, you name it! We can make your life a living hell. I will say it was consensual. It would be your word against mine. And your word isn't sacred. Everyone knows you're a whore. You were flaunting it in this very house, you loser! Get out of here!" Paul bellowed throwing his arm outward from his body pointing toward the door.

I quickly got dressed. A tiny, red puddle on the floor flashed across my path as I tore out of his house. I sobbed uncontrollably.

Of all the things to think, I thought—decided—that I couldn't let my mom see me like this. *My mom invalidated my feelings in the past. Would she think that this was my fault too? What if he tried to kill my mom if she found out? He is obviously capable of committing heinous acts. I should have known better than to trust P . . . I can't say his name, that jackass. He was right, though. Everyone saw me kissing Avery in full display. No one would believe that I didn't want this. It would be his word against mine.* I juddered at the hopelessness and despair of the situation.

I scarpered to my backyard to compose myself. My face still stung from when that jackalope slapped me. *I feel swollen. Am I bruised?*

Mom-Mom told me that my mom didn't miss much, so I had to think fast, but my head felt like there was an electric drill inside it. I couldn't think straight. *What should I do?*

Chapter 11

THOUGH NAUSEOUS AND RATTLED TO my core, I settled enough to formulate a plan. *Mom's car is not in the driveway. I have time.*

I wobbled as I climbed the stairs to the bathroom. I slowly undressed. *Blood. Oh, God.* I threw out all my clothes. *I never want to see them again anyway.* I hated even touching them, as if they were tainted . . . blemished . . . and treacherous. *Ooh, I feel sick. Whaaat . . . ?* I heaved and retched and spewed. Usually vomiting hurt, but it didn't that time. It brought me relief . . . I was relieved to be alone.

Time stood still. The world—my world—was silent. It was black, and it was still. It was the quiet after the storm. I'm not sure how long it took me to move from that spot to the bathtub. It was very fuzzy. My mind was a blur—full of nothingness, but major pounding.

I was bleeding still. And I was so tender. *Oh, no! Is pregnancy a possibility?* I shuddered. My chest seized up with the thought and my breathing was again labored.

I scrubbed every inch of my body raw, but I could not scrub off my memory of his hands on my body . . . or inside me. I could still feel him all over my body and inside me. I trembled.

I completely zoned out.

Without thinking, I robotically grabbed the razor and cut my inner thigh. Nothing else mattered but the cut. It forced my mind to stop thinking of him. Of what he did. It made me stop feeling the pain he caused. This pain I controlled—nothing else, no one else, especially not him.

Zapped of energy and feeling faint, I wrapped the towel around my body. I opened the cabinet door and grabbed a sanitary pad and a Band-Aid.

I gathered up my clothes and shuffled to my bedroom. I dumped the bloody garments in a plastic bag and threw the contents in my trashcan. I forced myself to look at the mirror to see if I could find any bruising or marks that I might have to explain. *Oh, no! They're everywhere!*

Much to my surprise, my cheek was not swollen, but it glowed slightly red.

I eased a long-sleeve navy blue T-shirt over my head. Tender to the touch, my cheek tingled as the shirt brushed over my face. I put on a pair of matching navy lightweight pants. *Do I look conspicuous? Comfortable? Overheated?*

Too numb and too exhausted to cry, I laid on my back in sheer disbelief. I processed the last few hours of my life. He raped me. That jackalope raped me. I felt like hell and I was now damaged goods.

I could no longer see Avery anymore. Paul said he'd kill us both if I said anything to anyone. I couldn't risk that. If he could rape me, he could surely kill me. And he could surely kill Avery. *Aaaahh . . .*

I replayed the hardcore furious look in his eyes. He was out for vengeance. And for what? A friggin' pageant?

I knew from the beginning that pageant was bad news and not for me. *I should have stood my ground and refused to participate,* I thought with anger . . . but it was too late for that. The curtain closed on that possibility. What was done was done. *I want it to blow over.* I remember telling that to Katie and Amy. *Oh, the profundity of those words.*

Despite feeling faint, I rose and put cover-up on my face while sitting at my vanity. I successfully covered the redness on my cheek without any difficulty. The makeup looked natural and healthy. I sat there stunned, staring at my reflection, searching desperately for answers. There were no answers. Only pain.

I folded my arms atop the vanity and rested my throbbing head on them. I felt broken, small and ashamed. For the first time in my life, I truly felt like I lost. From the deepest part of my being, I felt like a loser.

———◆———

"Dinner!" my mom shrilled. I shivered at the sound. Her voice could be so unkind.

My chest pounded, and my stomach cramped. I stood and slowly dragged my battered body across my room into the hallway until I reached the staircase. I gripped the cold railing as I gingerly descended to the bottom of the steps toward the kitchen. *My gosh, the staircase seems so long.* I gently scooted over to my usual spot at the table.

"Hey, Pooch!"

"Hi, Dad," I answered, barely audible and forlorn. My brother, Jared, sat at the table next to his friend, Shawn. *When did they arrive?*

As usual my mom served each of us our meal, first the boys and my father, then me. She determined our portions. I forced myself to eat to avoid drawing attention to myself, knowing my mom harped on me when I refused to eat. Usually, it was easy for me to fade into the woodwork, because the conversation rarely involved me. "What's the matter with you?" my mom asked sounding irritated.

"I have a headache," I replied truthfully.

My mom got up, walked over to the cabinet, opened a bottle, poured out two little round red pills, twisted the cap back on, and placed the container back in the cabinet, closing the cabinet doors. She walked over and handed me the red pills. "Here, take these," she demanded.

"Thank you." *Oh, my gosh, I'll need fifty of them to cure this perpetual pounding.*

The rest of the dinner was par for the course: I washed the dishes and headed back to my room. Still throbbing from my head to my feet, and still ailing from the inside out, I crashed on my bed. It hurt too much to move. *I didn't know my heart, my soul, and my body could hurt like this. This is what hell must be like.*

Eventually, late into the night, the demons that were chasing me lost their battle to sleep.

Chapter 12

WITH THE ARRIVAL OF DAYBREAK, I felt sore all over, especially my head. It was agonizing to move even the slightest bit.

With an incessant sickness in my stomach, I touched the egg-sized bump on the back of my head. Then I went to the bathroom and inspected my face—the redness had gone away. *Whew.*

I walked back to my bedroom to examine myself in my full-length mirror. This time I wasn't so lucky.

I winced at the sight of the black and blue bruises covering my arms and legs. *Damn!*

I convinced myself that I should be fine if I stuck to my original plan. To that end, I grabbed my day's attire and headed straight for the bathroom to take a much-needed shower from having sweated profusely throughout the evening. *Pew, my pajamas stink!* I sniffed myself. *Yuck! I stink!*

The water refreshed me, but the screams of "selfish whore," and "loser" returned, echoing loudly in my brain. The demon that I escaped in my sleep found me once again and called out to me with vigor—it was deafening. He silenced my own good thoughts.

My answer to his condemning words were automatic—I grabbed the pink razor and made an incision near the first. *Ahhhh! Sweet relief.* My head was quiet. A moment of peace.

After I stepped out of the shower and dried off, I took care of my wounds and got dressed. I returned to my room and waited, aiming to stretch the day out as long as possible, in the hope of miraculously regaining my strength. Eventually, I carefully walked downstairs for breakfast.

Per usual, my mom greeted me from her regular spot in the kitchen. "Good morning," she said eyeing me up this time.

"Morning," I mumbled as I was about to sit down.

"Why don't you take some Advil for that headache?" she asked, her eyes boring a hole through me.

"I will. Thanks." How did she know I still had a headache? *What else did she know? Mom-Mom was right.* I slowly walked over to the cabinet where the Advil was stored.

"A boy named Avery called yesterday," she stated flatly. *I wonder when he called.* "He said he'd call back."

Great, I thought sarcastically. A few minutes passed while the TV blared. *Is this what it feels like to have a hangover?*

"Where are you going today?" I was prepared for my mother's routine morning probing, as I sat and forced down my breakfast despite feeling nauseous.

"I thought I would go to the old folks' home," I said unconvincingly, though that was no reflection of my affection for The Manor.

Last year I volunteered at the retirement home as a service project. It was required by school to volunteer somewhere. I enjoyed it so much that I continued to volunteer even after my project was over.

"That's nice, Christina. I'm sure they will love to see you." *Well, that was easy.*

After breakfast, I headed back to my room. I lay down on my bed and considered staying home to nurse my wounds—head and heart, but I knew my mom would get suspicious and probe. After quite some time, I managed to drag myself downstairs and out the door. I peddled for as long as I could until the pain forced me to stop. For a short while, I sat on the curb weeping.

I finally arrived at The Manor and was greeted with cool air in the entranceway. Needing to relieve myself, I headed straight to the restroom. I was surprised by the girl who looked back at me in the mirror. I was not yet familiar with her—she was a loser. I couldn't escape.

My determination forced me to carry out my plan and led me to the reception area. I didn't recognize the woman behind the counter. Initially, I panicked. After composing myself, I announced, "Hi, I'm here to volunteer."

"Are you scheduled to be here today?" *Since when do we have to schedule appointments?*

"No, I'm not. I volunteered here many times before. They said I can just show up. Here's my badge." She took my badge, examined it and handed it back to me.

"Okay, Christina, wait here a minute, please." She walked away and returned with the director. Director Brooks was a sweet, older woman who exhibited a genuine concern for everyone's well-being. I felt calmer after seeing her.

"Christina, it's so good to see you! What brings you here today?" Mrs. Brooks inquired, delighted to see me.

"I am here to volunteer. How can I help out?" I responded weakly.

Mrs. Brooks pondered the options, "Well, let's see. You can go to the REC Center and spend time with residents there. How does that sound?"

"That would be great," although my tone failed to match my response.

"Super, I will call ahead, so they'll know to expect you."

"Thank you," I smiled faintly. I took the elevator down to the floor of the REC room.

Miss Brenda, a heavy-set, middle-aged, black staff member in the REC Center, greeted me warmly, as usual. She was very informal and very caring. I remembered her from my previous volunteer days.

"Christina, it really is you! How are you, honey?" she asked, clearly excited to see me.

"Fine, thanks. You?" It was good to see her welcoming face.

"Better, now that you're here, sugar. Now give me some sugar." She embraced me with a giggle. *You always gave the best hugs—gosh, I've missed you.* Miss Brenda looked me up and down, as she lightly stroked my arms. "Look at you. You're so tan. You're catching up to me," she joked, and we both chuckled. That single laugh turned my whole day around.

She reacquainted me with the residents and newcomers who were playing cards and socializing. I joined in, and we engaged with the retirees until lunch. Today's free-for-volunteers lunch special featured a turkey club served on wheat, white, or rye, plain or toasted. It received great reviews.

I chose rye, toasted. Miss Brenda usually set aside an hour for lunch. "Mealtimes are a time to eat, socialize and relax. You have no business cramming in all that in only a half-hour," she said frequently.

The trauma of what happened yesterday curbed my appetite, but Miss Brenda insisted I eat. She assumed I was trying to watch my figure.

"Girl, you better sink your teeth in that sandwich, or else. I know you white girls are all about your little figures, but you have no business worrying about that now." I knew better than to argue with Miss Brenda. Besides, the turkey sandwich tasted delicious. It was another affirmation that I was meant to be there.

The rest of the day unexpectedly flew by. Miss Brenda gave me another hug good-bye and said, "Now, don't be a stranger, honey." Perhaps she didn't believe me when I told her earlier that I was coming back the next day, and the day after that and so on.

I left the retirement home and peddled home in the blistering ninety-six-degree heat. To alleviate some discomfort from the heat, I rolled up my Oxford shirt and cuffed my khakis.

My mind settled on the time when Avery rode home with me, a mere two days earlier. My heart ached profusely. *I miss him.* I needed a friend and yet, I needed to be far from him. We only had one day together, but I felt incredibly close to him. Too scared to consider seeing him, I forced my thoughts to return to the old folks' home.

When I arrived home, my mom was sitting in the same seat at the kitchen table as she was earlier and informed me that Avery called again. After a closer examination of me, she blurted, "Christina, what happened to your arms?" I momentarily forgot about the bruises.

"Oh . . . uh, I was wrestling." *Keep it simple.*

Keeping her eyes glued on me, she asked "Today?" "No . . . uh, yesterday." I walked away to escape the questioning.

I heard a demanding voice behind me. "Christina, sit down. I want to talk to you." *What? Why are you interrogating me? You're supposed to leave me alone like usual.* I didn't have the energy to argue, so I obeyed and sat down across from her.

"Who were you wrestling with?" *Stick to your story.* "Scott, Katie's brother."

"How old is Katie's brother?" Although my mother met Katie, she didn't know much about her family. "Twelve." That part was true.

With one eyebrow raised, she delved deeper, "Why were you wrestling with him?"

"He's trying to get in shape for the wrestling team at school. It's no big deal," I shrugged uncaringly.

"No big deal?! Have you looked at yourself lately?" My mother exclaimed.

I continued with my charade by replying, "He didn't mean to hurt me. He felt awful about it."

My mother squinted her eyes, "Is something going on between the two of you?"

I snapped, "Scott and me?! No way! He's Katie's kid brother. That's gross!" Scott was a nice guy, but I would never consider going out with him, as he was way too young for me.

Out of the blue, my mother asked, "What about Avery?"

"What about Avery?" I echoed.

"Are you going out with him?" *Where is this coming from? Oh, no! Maybe she heard something.*

"I think he likes me, but I don't want to go out with him." I didn't know which lie hurt more.

"Why not? He seems like a nice boy." I was stunned by her compliment of him, since she rarely said anything nice about anyone.

"He's a player." *That ought to shut her up.*

My mom heaved a heavy sigh, "Oh, Christina, give him a chance." *Is she for real?* Avery must have charmed her, of all people.

"No, Mom. I don't want to date anyone right now. If Avery calls again, please tell him not to call anymore, and do not offer any more information."

She offered to do that when Joel called every day for weeks, but I figured at the time, that I should be mature enough to let him down personally each time he called. This time was different. It was life or death and I wanted to keep Avery alive.

And the award-winning performance goes to—Christina De Rosa!

She bought my stories. I never lied so much. It was draining. I took a shower and relieved my inner torture with pain—pain I controlled. The stinging shower spray reminded me of my cuts and bruises. I grabbed my pink friend and cut my right inner thigh. There was solace in not thinking about anything but the fresh cut.

Burn. Throb. Burn. Throb. That's all my head could handle.

I stepped out of the shower when I heard the phone ring. As I quietly peered out in the hallway, I heard my mom tell him "not to call anymore" and the clunk of the receiver. My stomach dropped, and I forced back a tear.

I lay on my bed and I thought about Avery. When it caused too much distress to think about being separated from Avery, I focused on the old folks' home.

From there, my thoughts veered to the worst moment of my life. When that torturous memory was unbearable, I forced myself to think about the beach, or something peaceful and serene. Dodging the demons was exhausting. I eventually drifted to sleep.

Chapter 13

THE NEXT TWO DAYS I spent at The Manor. The residents noticed I was staring off into space. I forced myself to engage in conversation and games, but I had to constantly be brought back to them and to the present. I was the deeply troubled female version of Walter Mitty.

I apologized over and over to them, but I continued to drift away. The residents were very sweet and caring—they didn't get angry with me; they were simply concerned. I assured them I was fine, but Miss Brenda saw right through my act.

Eating lunch was even a challenge for me. I lost my appetite, but I knew better than not to eat in front of Miss Brenda. I forced myself to eat albeit slowly, one small bite at a time.

My head throbbed. All I wanted to do was lie down. My head felt like a bowling ball with a woodpecker inside of it.

Miss Brenda put down her half-eaten roast beef sandwich, looked me straight in the eyes, and said in her most concerned tone, "Honey, I've been watching you. What's the matter? You can tell Miss Brenda."

I gave her a dismissive wave, "I'm fine. I just have a headache." A persistent pounder.

"Girl, this is bigger than some silly ol' headache. You can't fool Miss Brenda."

"No, really, I hit my head by accident."

"Hit your head! You should go see a professional." *A professional what?*

"No, I'm okay. If it's not better soon, I'll go." My head continued to pound like a jackhammer. I held back my tears, because crying only made the pain worse.

She lifted her eyebrows, "Promise?"

"Promise." I lied and gave her a slight reassuring smile.

I was relieved when Miss Brenda refrained from asking me what I planned on doing later that evening as it was Friday. She used to ask me what activities I had scheduled for the weekend when I volunteered during the school year. Maybe it was because every day is Friday in the summer.

Of course, I didn't have plans. For the last three days, I hadn't spoken to anyone, except my family, Miss Brenda, and old people.

I really was a loser. Even Avery gave up on me. I thought he would have been more persistent. *He did like me, right?*

A few times, in my Walter Mitty fantasy world, I told him about what happened at the jackalope's house. His response was to rescue me by fleeing the state together. Very heroic. Very courageous. Of course, we would live happily ever after.

Back home, after my mom and I shared hellos and pleasantries, she informed me that Katie had called. "What did she say?" I asked, frozen and nervous, bracing myself. *Please tell me you didn't mention anything to her about the wrestling?*

"She wants you to call her back."

"Did she say why?" I winced inwardly.

"No," my mom answered simply, probably wondering why I am asking so many questions.

At the risk of looking suspicious, I prodded, "Did she say anything else?"

"No, just to call her." *Whew!!*

I ran upstairs and called Katie after my shower. I knew I had to nip this in the bud and I seemed to be able to focus better after cutting. It was as if my mind was an overgrown tropical forest and the cutting was my deforestation process.

I sat on my bed, propped up my pillows for support and dialed Katie's number.

"Hello." Katie had an older sister and they both sounded alike on the phone.

"Is Katie there?"

"This is Katie."

"Oh, hi, Katie. It's Christina."

"Hi, Christina. I'm glad you called back."

"What's up?" I asked. My heart pounded, but I put on my best performance to sound nonchalant.

"Well, I was going to ask you the same question." "You were, why?" I scraped my bottom lip.

"Where have you been the last few days? We haven't seen you at the pool," she inquired.

"I've been volunteering at the old folks' home."

"Why?"

"Why not?" I countered.

"Oh, I don't know. Maybe because it's summer and we have the freedom to live a little."

"They are shorthanded, so I offered to help. That's all." Another lie. For a good Italian-Irish girl, I've been lying quite a bit.

"What's going on with you and Avery?" Katie finally asked.

I played dumb, "What do you mean?"

"Are you still going out with him?"

I had no idea how to respond, but I didn't want Katie to keep calling, increasing my mom's chances of asking her about the wrestling. I should have picked someone else's brother. *Too late now, Christina!*

"Well, are you?"

"I guess so." I fidgeted on my bed.

"What do you mean you guess? You are or you're not."

"Why are you grilling me?" I asked annoyed, because I wanted to be left alone. The lying sucked and was sucking what little life I had out of me.

"Because I'm your friend, that's why. Because Avery asked me to call you."

"He did?!" I was surprised, scared, and touched all at the same time. After all, I thought he gave up on me.

"Yeah, he said he tried to call you a few times, but you weren't home." *That's true. I wasn't. Whew.* "So, why didn't you call him back?" *Because I want him alive. That's why!*

"I should have called him back . . . but . . . ," my voice declined. I had very little practice in lying up until then.

"What is going on with you? You were head over heels in love and now you're avoiding him. Did he do something?"

"Did you tell him that I was in love with him?" I said in anger.

"Not in so many words. Listen, I thought you liked him," Katie persisted.

"I did." *I can't deny that.*

"You don't anymore?"

"It's not that simple." I was getting frustrated and it didn't help that I already felt lousy to begin with.

"Yes, it is. Either you do, or you don't," she said dogmatically.

Suddenly an idea popped in my head. "Can you do me a favor?" I asked anxiously.

"Depends."

"Tell Avery that I can't date." *There, that should do the trick.*

"Can't you call him and tell him yourself." Katie was no push over.

"No, that's just it—I can't. I would be *crucified* if I did that." *Trying to keep it real.*

"Are you serious?" she asked incredulously.

At my best attempt to sound convincing, I replied, "*Dead* serious." *Now who's the actress?*

"But your parents never gave you a hard time before," Katie sounded mystified.

"I never dated before," I said in a monotone.

"Oh my God! That's right. I'm so sorry. Are you okay?" The gentler Katie I knew and loved returned.

"Not really. I'm a mess, but you can't tell Avery that. Please tell him that it is in our best interest if we went our separate ways," I eked out, as tears streamed down my face.

Katie was sympathetic, "Christina, I am so sorry. Is there anything else I can do?"

I pictured Katie in her room, twirling the phone cord as she spoke with me. She'd be lounging comfortably on her lime green beanbag chair, placed between her desk and closet. She'd have some cute outfit on and her hair in a messy ponytail. The door would be shut to keep Scott out—she shared a room with her older sister. Her expression would truly be one of deep concern and empathy as she was a terrific friend.

"Yes. Thank you so much. Please don't publicize this. It's painful enough as it is. I don't appreciate being the talk of the town. I have had enough of that . . . for a lifetime." I rubbed my hand on my forehand in a failed attempt to soothe my ailing head.

"No problem. My lips are sealed." I trusted her to honor my request. "Uh . . . so, when are you coming back to the pool? We miss you." *You do? I have to wait until my bruises disappear, so I'll see you next year.*

"I don't know. I guess when The Manor doesn't need me anymore . . ." *I really stink at lying.*

"It's volunteer, right?" She got me.

I bit my lip. "Yeah." *How can I make this work?*

"Can't they find someone else?"

"I guess so, but I like it there. I feel like I am doing something worthwhile." It became clear to me at that moment that I felt safe at The Manor, and that I was lucky to have it in my life.

"Some things never change." *Unfortunately, some things do change, and the damage is irreversible.*

"Hey, I have to eat dinner. Again, I'm very sorry it didn't work out with you and Avery," she empathized. I could hear the care—the love—in her voice.

"Me too," I said sounding very much like Wednesday Addams, the girl from the 1960s show, The Addams Family.

My good-bye with thanks was submerged in tears.

"See you, Christina," she whispered. I gently hung up the receiver, rolled over and curled up in a ball.

I sobbed all night long, my face immersed in a pillow. I cursed God. How could He let something like this happen to me? I was a decent person after all. I asked Him for help, and He said 'no.' Why would He do that? I volunteered, I ate all my vegetables, I excelled in school, and I was nice to people.

Then I remembered that God was only a figment of the imagination. However, the fact remained that I failed to understand why I had to suffer a despicable violation like that. I drowned myself in my despair. Sleep eluded me. Again.

Chapter 14

I SPENT THE FOLLOWING WEEK AT the old folks' home. By the end of the week, my bruises were very faint, but my cuts were always fresh. I wore shorts and short sleeves and I no longer felt faint or nauseous. *Progress.*

My days became routine: I got up, ate breakfast, rode my bike to The Manor, did my thing, rode home, took a shower, cut, ate dinner, did my chores, and went to my room. I avoided friends, and my family kinda sorta avoided me. The Manor proved to be a very good place for me to be. It gave me purpose, and within its untainted walls, I was safe.

Plus, dynamic, loving Miss Brenda was there.

Miss Brenda helped me make a difference in the world. Moreover, she reached out to me for selfless reasons and cared for me unconditionally. I felt special in her presence. I wanted to return the favor, but I found I couldn't. I was depleted, insecure, and exhausted most of the time. I couldn't think straight, my attention span fleeted, and my foggy head resembled Shanghai, China.

Spending time with friends would help—sharing my story would help, but I was bound to silence and solitude.

Bottling up the pain, the frustration, confusion, sadness, anger, disappointment, and betrayal ate away at my confidence and my joy. Believing I was worthless had become the beginning of the end. Volunteering was my only safe haven, and there, for those five hours, I was someone. There, I mattered.

Chapter 15

UPON ARRIVAL AT THE MANOR the following Monday, Mrs. Brook took me aside and informed me that Miss Brenda suffered a horrific tragedy: her son had been killed in a car accident over the weekend.

Stunned, speechless and numb, I listened. "Miss Brenda wanted you to know just in case you volunteered this week. We can make arrangements for you to go to the funeral, but only if you want to. No one would blame you for not going. If you like, I can call your mom to make sure it's okay that you go with us, if that's what you want. It's your decision. You can think about it. The funeral isn't until Wednesday, so you can let me know tomorrow."

"No, I want to go. I don't need to think about it," I said with unwavering conviction.

"Okay, I'll call your mom. Do you want to talk to her?" she said while walking me toward the front desk, presumably toward the phone.

"No, that's okay." I stopped in my tracks. "It's enough if you speak to her." I took a breath and thanked her for her kindness.

"Christina, I understand if it's too much for you to stay today. Miss Brenda won't be in all week. She needs some time to mourn." Mrs. Brook handed me a clipping from the local newspaper.

Jerome Dwight Jones, 17, beloved son of Brenda Jones, died instantly on Saturday from a car accident. Jerome lived his entire life in Pennsford, PA. Jerome was going into his senior year at Pennsford High School. He was an honor student and was a member of the varsity basketball and track and field teams.

The family requests, in lieu of flowers, memorial gifts be made to the Pennsford Athletic Department in the name of the Jerome Jones Memorial Athletic Scholarship Fund. Pennsford High

School, 5045 Providence Street, Pennsford, PA.

Private funeral arrangements will be arranged by Hunsberger and Ryan Funeral Home. There will be a separate memorial service for students and the community held at Pennsford High School Thursday night at seven o'clock.

"Miss Brenda wants you to attend the private service."

Chapter 16

MY MOM DROVE ME TO The Manor the day of the funeral. It would have been tacky for me to ride my bike wearing a skirt, not to mention, disgustingly sweaty. My mom asked Mrs. Brook to look after me and to call her when the funeral was over.

Mrs. Brook drove another staff member, named Mrs. Barrett, and me to the church. The room was mostly filled with black people. Suddenly I felt out of place; I became self-conscious. I felt awkward being one of the few white people in a sea of black people.

The Sesame Street song came to my mind "One of These Things is Not Like the Other." My sense of humor helped me to fend off my anxiety, enabling me to move toward the crowd.

"Would you look at that!" I heard the sweet approval of Miss Brenda. Our eyes met; she was indeed speaking to me. When it was our turn to visit with her in the receiving line, she scooped me in her arms, gave me a squeeze and said, "Honey, look at you all grown up!" She then turned to her relatives with her on the receiving line and announced me: "This here is my friend, Christina. Girlfriend works at the home for free. Ain't that something?" I blushed. *She called me 'girlfriend.'* I instantly felt at ease.

"Miss Brenda, I am so sorry," I muttered, barely audible through the tears.

"Ah, honey, it's okay. My son is with the Lord. Praise God!" She was consoling me. "Gimme some sugar, sugar!" she said as if jovial. I couldn't resist another one of her famous hugs. "Girl, you stayin' for the reception?!" she asked and insisted. I nodded. "Make sure you sit with me."

"Okay," I answered through a shallow breath.

"Lord, have mercy! Girlfriend came!" she exclaimed as I walked away.

Mrs. Brook, Mrs. Barrett, and I took our seats in the back row of the chapel. As expected, Miss Brenda sat front and center.

Wearing a distinguished purple robe and gold scarf draped on his shoulders, Reverend Joe Simms stood at the altar and bellowed, "Ladies and gentlemen, members and guests, we welcome you today on this both sorrowful and joyful day as we are gathered here to bid farewell to our beloved brother, Jerome Dwight Jones.

"It is a sorrowful day because we will miss Brother Jerome. I was fortunate enough to know Jerome and his family on a personal level. I have known Brother Jerome since he was a newborn babe. It was my pleasure and great honor to watch Brother Jerome grow up from being a curious little boy to a becoming a proper young man.

"Brother Jerome probed me about spiritual matters like, 'how can God be three in one; Father, Son and Holy Ghost? Why did the ancients sacrifice animals like lambs and rams? Why didn't they sacrifice camels or snakes?' And finally, 'Will the Eagles ever win the Super Bowl?' " The mourners erupted in laughter. I never knew laughing was acceptable during a funeral service.

After a brief pause, the Reverend continued, "The questions persisted and his faith grew stronger. I will miss those probing questions. I will miss seeing his attentive face every Sunday morning when I look out into the pews. His momma, Miss Brenda, will surely miss every hair on his head and every fiber of his being. But, we must not dwell on what we will miss, but on heavenly matters. Matters that really matter.

"Today is not only a sorrowful day, but a joyful one. We need to focus upward, not inward. For brother Jerome has been reunited with his heavenly father."

"Amen!" someone shouted.

Reverend bellowed, without missing a beat, "This is a time for celebration, not sadness. A time for joy, not sorrow."

"Hallelujah!" shouted another.

"Let us not forget, but always remember, that Brother Jerome is resting in peace with our Lord God Almighty, the Prince of Peace, the Lord of Lords, and our Blessed Savior, our Holy Redeemer!"

Shouts burst like popcorn: "Amen!" "Hallelujah!" and "Praise God!"

"I know those pearly gates in heaven opened wide for Brother Jerome, and for that we must celebrate and be joyful!" the Reverend declared victoriously.

With an affirming nod from Reverend Simms, the gospel choir, all dressed alike in black robes with white stoles, belted out the upbeat, familiar song, "Amazing Grace."

The good reverend took the pulpit one final time. "Our Lord, God the Father, graced us with his only Son, Jesus Christ, who dwells inside those of us who believe. If you are not a fellow believer, come forth to say the Sinner's Prayer so you, too, can live in all eternity."

At the cemetery, Reverend Simms opened with "Ashes to ashes, dust to dust . . ." and the ceremony closed with each attendant placing roses on Jerome's coffin.

I wept when Miss Brenda wailed. Her family embraced her and encouraged her to "let it all out."

Eventually, we all gathered in the reception hall and stood in line to take part in the spread prepared for us buffet style. Before everyone was seated, Reverend Simms gave the blessing.

Miss Brenda insisted I sit with her. The privilege of sitting with Miss Brenda meant I got to butt in to the front of the food line. People stared at me wondering who I was. They dared not say a word because, as Miss Brenda put it, "Make no mind of them. It ain't their business who I break bread with."

Mrs. Brook and Mrs. Barrett sat together on the other side of the room. I piled food on my plate, per Miss Brenda's instructions. She told me that everything was not only delicious, but homemade. *Soul food* was what she called it.

The spread consisted of fried chicken, corn on the cob, buttermilk biscuits, creamy potato salad, green beans and some food I did not recognize. With my plate full of bounty, I followed Miss Brenda to her table. "Can I get you something to drink?" I asked her, hoping I could show her some kindness.

"I would love some iced tea, thank you," she replied appreciatively with a sweet smile. I returned with two iced teas and we dug in. I soon found out how right she was: It was absolutely the best fried chicken I had ever sunk my teeth into.

Somewhere amid the eating, she paused, catching a quiet moment between us, "Here we are again, eating together. Not what I expected this week, but nonetheless. . . ."

At a loss for words, I simply smiled without opening my mouth. Her eyes glistened with tenderness and they shed light on her depth—depth of love, depth of loss, and her depth of faith. I felt terrible for my sweet mentor, but knew I failed to imagine the breadth of her loss. After all, she outlived her only child which seemed cruel and unnatural.

"This is the best chicken I ever tasted!" I replied hardly containing myself, but choosing, quite wisely, to speak of what I knew.

"It's Mrs. Brown's special recipe. It's not a secret, because she tells anyone who asks her, but I tell ya, no one makes fried chicken better than her."

"It's awesome!" I announced before licking my finger. *How dignified.*

"I thought you would like it. You ain't too picky. How do you like the iced tea?" asked Miss Brenda, taking a swig of hers.

"It's a little sweet, but it's good."

"That's called sweet tea. That's how they make it in the South," she informed me.

"Are you from the South? Where about?" I asked.

"Alabama, originally. My momma came up North when I was about ten. Everyone at this church knows how much I like sweet tea, so they made it special for me today. Sweet, huh?" I couldn't tell if she meant the tea or the thoughtful gesture. Maybe both.

"You are surrounded by people who really seem to care about you," I observed.

"There ain't nothing greater than being surrounded by loved ones," she stated.

That's why I help out at The Manor. You make me feel loved, even though you're not family. I wanted to tell her that but couldn't find the words or the courage. *Why is it so difficult for me to share my feelings? I was able to with Avery, eventually. That didn't turn out so great. It could have, if it weren't for, the unspeakable.* I tried to come up with a heartfelt, 'I love you Miss Brenda' without sounding so lame.

"Do you know why I volunteer at The Manor?" I asked her.

"You tell me," she said.

"Because of you."

"Me? Now, I thought you were running away from something," she surmised. *How did she know that?* "I'm right, ain't I?" She saw right through me.

"Well, sort of. But being around you is like being hugged all the time and I really like your hugs."

"Well, I'll be. I like the way you said that," she slowed her speech as if soaking in the thought—being hugged all the time. "That's nice. Really nice. Thank you," she said softly and began to cry.

"I'm sorry Miss Brenda. I didn't mean . . . ," I broke off. I felt horrible because I made her cry. *What is wrong with me?*

"Naw, it's okay. Just thinking about Jerome. He liked my hugs, too," she said with a faint smile. *Of course, he did. Who wouldn't?*

"Brenda, you okay, honey?" someone asked in an amplified voice from the adjoining table.

"Yes, yes, fine. Now, go on about your business. I'm okay," she assured her friend. It was then I noticed that we were having a private conversation among a full table of eight. It was as if the others respected Miss Brenda's unspoken wishes to chat with me alone. I wondered why. "Well, are you going to spill it? What are you running from, girl?" Miss Brenda persisted.

"Miss Brenda, I can't say. I really can't. If I could, I would. You have to believe me." My eyes pleaded with her to trust me.

She flanked me. "Are you in trouble?" That sounded like she thought that maybe I was pregnant or something. *Oh, my gosh! I couldn't possibly be pregnant, could I? It was possible, but how probable,* I wondered.

"No." Keep it simple. I broke eye contact for a moment.

"You sure?" she persisted.

I nodded.

"Okay, I'll drop it for now. But, you can come to me for anything. You hear?" She was offering unconditional, limitless help the day of her son's funeral. *Remarkable human being.* I was feeling the hugs.

"Yes. Got it. Thanks!" I said in earnest then turned to my food.

We talked some more about nothing in particular when she soon signaled to the others sitting at the table that it was safe to converse with us. When they did, they were gracious to include me in the conversation. I could tell that they truly cared for her and were going to be available for her in future days as she walked through the darkness of her loss.

Mrs. Brook came over to me to inform me it was time to leave. Miss Brenda sent me off with one last love-filled, comforting hug and reminded Mrs. Brook that she'd be in next week starting first thing on Monday. I interpreted that to mean she was going to come in early and take an hour lunch. *Nothing like the old folks' home to keep your mind off your troubles.*

We loaded into Mrs. Brook's car and headed to The Manor. The three of us agreed that it was a nice funeral, the food was delicious, and how hard it must have been for our dear friend.

From there, my mom drove me home and I went straight to my room. I had no intention of volunteering without Miss Brenda. Exhausted, I slept.

My mom's scream announcing dinner hours later jostled me. *Ugh, come on. So grating.*

I obediently walked downstairs despite having no appetite. She yelled at me to eat at first but eventually dropped it.

Jared and Shawn drove me crazy with their immature burping and farting noises.

Lunch with adults today at a funeral was better—ten-fold. At a funeral, for pity's sake!

I dreaded dinner every night because my parents tolerated my brother's shenanigans. On the flip side, my mom surprised me by doing the dishes and that gave me more time to myself and to assimilate the day's profound events.

Before nodding off for the night, a plethora of thoughts infiltrated my mind. Most of all, Miss Brenda's belief in God when, *well . . . how could she?*

Hours later, I awoke drenched in sweat, my chest heaving—I was terrified by a nightmare—that jack killed my dear mentor. The dream was incredibly vivid. I had to convince myself it wasn't true. Eventually, I settled down, the demon tired, and already having had its fun, let me spend time with the sandman.

Chapter 17

UPON WAKING UP THE NEXT morning, I decided to go to the pool. Fortunately, my bruises disappeared and my self-inflicted cuts could be explained by me shaving.

Regarding my somber mood—I had reason to be sad. No one could argue with that. At least there was no need to explain why I was black and blue. I would only have to explain why I was blue. A known empathizer, no one would be the wiser as to why I was truly forlorn. Perhaps some would think it had something to do with losing the pageant, especially if they didn't know me well. Others, like Katie, might guess I was depressed because my parents forbade me to date Avery. My mom might think I was sad for Miss Brenda. Most of them would be right to some degree: I was sad about not seeing Avery anymore, and I grieved Miss Brenda's loss. However, I couldn't have cared less about the pageant—that's for certain.

Most of all, I was messed up. I lied to my mom, I lied to Miss Brenda, I lied to Katie, and I asked Katie to lie to Avery for me. I was a big fat liar! And I was a big fat loser! I no longer recognized myself in the mirror.

I yearned to move on without being in such anguish, without continually lying, and without putting myself and Avery in jeopardy. "I will kill you and your little boyfriend!" The terrifying threats constantly replayed in my head. I couldn't shake them. No. Matter. What.

I felt utterly hopeless, yet I forced myself to start my day. I tried to keep moving and to live a normal life. I ate my Rice Krispies and rode my bike to Mom-Mom's. We spoke of the funeral and her knee.

From there, I cycled straight to the pool, avoiding a trip to

Katie's. I flashed my badge and Mrs. Jenski commented that I had not been around in a while. She smiled with approval when I mentioned The Manor and I went on my miserable way. I found a grassy spot on an incline, sat down on my towel and listened to a generic handheld radio with earphones, much like a Sony Walkman.

I tuned out the rest of the world, even in their midst. I lay back on my towel, closed my eyes and listened to the top one hundred hits on my favorite radio station. I became one with my earphones. It was about time I got caught up with pop culture. I was a teenager after all. It was relaxing. Kids did it all the time, but it was hit or miss for me—more like a miss.

I was head banging and toe tapping to the beat of Joan Jett's "I Love Rock 'n Roll" when a tap on my arm startled me. It was Katie. She and Amy were looking down at me. I crouched forward to sit up.

"Mind if we join you?" Katie asked towering over me.

"No, go right ahead," the music still playing in my ears. Bending over, hair falling around her face, Katie smelled like coconut. Even a whiff of it improved my mood. *The delicious smell of summer.* Sometimes, the little things are the cornerstone of peace and tranquility.

"Do you want us to go? Do you need time to yourself?" Katie stooped forward at the waist in an attempt to get closer to get my attention.

Amy tapped me on my shoulder. "Earth to Christina."

Alerted back to reality and in a weak attempt of an apology, I stammered, "What? Oh no. Sorry. I was just listening to music." I yanked my earphones off and switched off my radio. Otherwise, I might have noticed that I was being rude by keeping the music on.

"So, what have you been up to? We haven't seen you in a while." Katie initiated with valid and genuine concern. They both sat down, flanking me.

"I have been volunteering at The Manor," I replied swiveling my head to view them both. Insentiently following the noise, my gaze landed on the pool and its playful occupants.

"You're still doing that?" Katie asked surprised. I nodded. "Then why aren't you there now?" I briefly told them about Miss Brenda and how it was no fun to volunteer without her.

"Are you going back?" Amy inquired arms over her crossed legs bent at the knees.

I confirmed with a nod. I considered saying Miss Brenda needs me, but that sounded arrogant when the truth was that I needed her. "So, what have you guys been up to?" I inquired, reciting my parents' lingo.

"The usual. Nothing really," Amy sighed. She was watching kids fly down on the huge, yellow water slide. The cheers and screams from a skinny, dark-haired girl garnered our attention.

I turned back and teased with a smirk, "Sounds exciting." Then I prompted, raising my eyebrows, "I didn't miss anything?"

Katie drew a deep breath, "That kid, the diver, you know who I'm talking about, right? The one you were flirting with?" Her tone was serious as she waited for a response.

"I wasn't flirting with him, but what about him?" *Why must I feel the need to defend myself as if I would ever entertain going out with a kid that was younger than me? I was just being friendly!*

Katie continued, "He banged his head on the diving board during practice." *Ouch!* I thought about how I banged my head on the Martin's coffee table and that hurt like hell. For days!

I cringed, "Is he okay?" I was truly concerned even though I barely knew him.

Katie's tone lightened, "He was unconscious for a few days, but they say he could be diving again by next summer." I got the chills.

"Really? That's crazy. I'd be too scared to dive after that," I admitted and winced at the thought.

"Me too," Amy agreed, wildly nodding her head.

"Poor kid. That's a shame. He was fun to watch," I concluded. In fact, I secretly hoped to watch him dive today. He was a great distraction.

Precipitously, Amy's eyes widened and she tapped me on the leg when she blurted, "Did you know that Mrs. Martin had a mental breakdown?!"

"Kind of," I admitted with a dismissing hand gesture, hoping to avoid the subject.

Amy beamed back, "Well, she did! They kept it hush-hush, but Paul finally let the cat out of the bag. She was treated for over a week!" Hearing stuff like that was part of the reason why I was avoiding going out with friends. I completely zoned.

Leaning towards me, Katie reiterated, "Christina, did you hear Amy? Mrs. Martin went nuts."

"Ah, yeah. Too bad," I replied nonplussed.

"They say it was because the pageant was rigged like we all thought!" Katie thundered. *I don't know why she's so upset. She did get runner-up after all. Well-deserved too! At least that part made sense.*

"How's Jennie doing? Is she still able to participate in the circuit?" I questioned. There was no reason for her to suffer, too, when she seemed so happy winning.

"Yes, she's allowed to continue because they can't prove that she had anything to do with it," Amy relayed.

"Good for her. I'm glad," I declared sincerely. So sincerely, I surprised myself.

Amy smiled and put her affirming hand on my leg, "You're a good sport, Christina."

"Aaah . . . ," I shrugged.

"Oh, I almost forgot, they were asking about you," Katie informed me.

Bewildered, I crinkled up my face and asked, "Who?" I had no idea to whom she was referring.

"The pageant officials or something. They asked me if I knew if you were coming to the pool, so they could ask you some questions."

I was flabbergasted. "Really? Like what?" I squealed.

Katie shrugged her shoulders. "I don't know. They didn't say. Didn't they call you at home?"

"No." *Why didn't they call me at home? I'm sure they had my info.*

"Maybe your mom talked to them and told them not to bother you," Katie offered. My mom was somewhat protective. *I guess she really did care. Go, Mom!*

Confirming with a head nod, "Yeah, I bet you're right." What could they possibly want from me? The plot thickened. However, I did not dare tell them what You-Know-Who told me about his mom. That would open up a huge can of worms, so I quickly changed the subject and leaped off my towel. "I'm hot. Let's go in the pool."

The three of us welcomed the refreshment the pool offered. I thought of Ted and felt a kinship with him. Diving was his passion, yet he was confined poolside due to his serious injury. I could relate. I, too, felt trapped.

Chapter 18

FRIDAY, THE FOLLOWING DAY, WAS a repeat of the previous day. I went to the pool and hung out with Katie and Amy. We even sat in our usual lush spot, with a clear view of the pool.

It was a gorgeous summer day with blue skies, streaks of white clouds, a gentle breeze, hot, but not too humid, which might explain why it was more crowded. A bounty of kids were playing in the various pools as their moms sat close by watching their precious babies enjoying themselves. *Must be nice to not have a care in the world.*

I longed for the days when I was carefree. Now, all I could think of was surviving each day without feeling like a pathetic loser. Suddenly, I snapped back to my pitiful life sitting with my friends at the pool when I heard a familiar voice and clapping.

"Hey, we should go out tonight!" Amy suggested excitedly.

"Where do you want to go?" Katie asked.

Amy thought for a second, then responded enthusiastically with a suggestion, "How about roller skating? I haven't done that in a while."

Katie turned to me. "Okay, what do you think, Christina? Do you want to go roller skating tonight?"

"Nah," I replied. The mere thought of going out in public made my stomach feel queasy.

"Why not? I know you can skate," Katie stated.

I really enjoyed skating, but I wasn't in the right mindset for a big social outing. What I really wanted to do was crawl under the covers and stay there indefinitely. Instead, I forced myself to look like a normal teenager by meeting up with friends at the pool.

My mouth twitched to the left side. "I don't feel like it." I was thankful for the beautiful day as I cast my gaze toward the pool. Kids were sliding down the jumbo, yellow slide making huge, loud splashes. Even coming to the pool took effort. Everything took effort.

"So, what do you want to do?" Amy asked with an edge in her voice. *Someone's annoyed with me.* She sounded a little perturbed, perhaps deflated.

I shook my head and sighed. "Nothing really," I answered.

Katie gently shook my arm. "Come on, Christina, you need to get out! You need to do something," she expressed emphatically.

"I am out," I argued stubbornly, surveying my surroundings while gesturing toward it to make my point.

Lots of laughter and playful screaming emanated from the pool. One group was playing Marco Polo. At its start, the game was amusing, but now it, coupled with this conversation, was beginning to get on my last nerve. The constant yammering of "Marco" and "Polo" and my friends' push to get me out was becoming increasingly more irritating.

"The pool doesn't count," Katie retorted shaking her head.

I countered, "Why not?" It had to count! I didn't have enough energy for much else. Every minute of the day was a struggle.

"Because, you need to do something different," Katie suggested. "You need to do more than go to the pool and The Manor." More importantly, I didn't want anyone to look deeper into my life.

"Okay. Okay, you are right. I'll see if I am allowed."

Maybe I can somehow get out of it.

Since I had been moping around the house recently, whenever I was home, my mom was delighted to hear that I was going out, especially when the driving arrangements were already set.

Amy called a few other classmates to see if they were interested in joining us. Our mutual friend, Morgan, was on the top of the list.

Morgan was willowy with fiery red hair and freckles, but her eyes made her a standout. They were a remarkable green that were reminiscent of a cat and they drew you in without any reservation. Morgan was extremely bright, athletic, and a friend of mine since fifth grade. Katie, Morgan, Amy and I were in the same class in fifth grade. Morgan was the emcee for our skit in the talent show. She belonged to the other local pool and lived near Amy.

I convinced myself that this idea of Amy's was a good one. I liked roller skating for many reasons. For starters, the rink played decent dance music. I loved to dance and rolling skating was about as close to dancing as we usually got. Secondly, I got to hang out with my friends. Third of all, roller skating burned calories. Not that I was counting them, mind you. I didn't even own a scale. Tonight, I could refuse to obsess about spilling the beans regarding the unmentionable and just have fun.

———◆———

"Whip it" piped through the sound speakers as we rolled around the rink and Katie and Amy checked out the guys. Morgan didn't seem particularly interested in meeting guys, but she played along with Amy and Katie.

I assumed they all knew that I couldn't date because not one of them encouraged me to window shop. They, however, had a great time laughing and getting the attention of a few guys there who attended a different school. I watched the guys fly by my friends who seemed to be enjoying the excitement and conversation. They all were having fun, including Morgan, who swung around my way to chat. Morgan was always one to make sure nobody felt left out. I was enjoying the music when she rolled up to me.

"Hey, why don't you join us?" Devo's new wave song "Whip it" continued to play in the background. I loved the unique tempo created by the synthesizer, electric guitar, bass guitar, and drums. The song was fun to sing, although I had no idea what the lyrics meant.

"I'm having fun skating solo. I need the exercise anyway," I answered, figuring she might find that answer acceptable, because she and her entire family exercised constantly by participating in one sport or another.

"Okay, suit yourself," she said, as she skated away. Katie and Amy were laughing with their new friends when one of them waved me over. I ignored the signal, certain the girls would create some story about my aloofness. The situation made me uncomfortable. Katie skated toward me.

"Hey, I know you're not supposed to date and all, but one of those guys is interested in you."

"That's nice," I stated tonelessly, avoiding her eyes.

She persisted, "He's actually kinda cute. I think he might be your type too."

Indignant, I replied, "Not interested. Nothing personal." It did not feel right at all telling Avery that I couldn't date, then coming here to flirt. Not to mention, inside I was cringing with fright and discomfort at the thought of You-Know-Who finding out.

"I just want you to have fun," she added sweetly.

She's really trying. I feel awful. Now, in more ways than one.

"I am having fun," I insisted. "Don't you worry. I am doing exactly what I want to. Thanks, Katie, for checking in." I did my best to remain composed, hoping my performance was convincing.

"Okay, then." Katie skated away, apparently satisfied with my answer, while Morgan skated toward me. Rick Springfield's "Jessie's Girl" blared on the sound system. *Rick Springfield. I think he's a better singer than actor. Morgan looks super happy for some reason and she's about to tell me why.*

"Wow! That guy is really interested in you," she declared, a little breathless. "He thinks you're really pretty. He won't stop talking about you." *He might think I'm pretty, but I feel ugly.*

"Well, he's barking up the wrong tree. Haven't you heard?" I asked curiously and awaited a response.

"Heard what?" Morgan questioned curiously.

"That I can't date." *That should do it. Then maybe they will leave me alone.*

Morgan raised her chin up, "So, it's true then?" My mind returned to the singer wanting Jessie's girl.

"Yup!" I replied hearing my emotional disconnection. Morgan squinted, "Bummer. What happened?" "Nothing really," I stated flatly.

With tenderness in her eyes and a sweetness in her voice, Morgan persisted, "Christina, it's me. Morgan. You can tell me. You know I don't gossip."

I got choked up. "I know. It's just hard for me to talk about." *Don't spill.*

"Oh, sorry. I didn't mean to pry or push too hard . . . ," Morgan stated soothingly.

"It's okay," I assured her.

"Look, I'm not interested in those guys," she assured me. "We can hang out. I think Amy likes the guy that likes you anyway," she stated with a charming grin.

Taken aback I blurted, "What is it with her?" Amy and I apparently share the same taste in boys.

"What do you mean?" asked Morgan puzzled.

"Oh, never mind," I replied, isolating myself while also keeping myself from hurting Amy with my words.

Thankfully, Morgan blew my comment off. She was always understanding that way. I could be myself around her—terse or soft, she could handle it.

We skated around the rink while listening to "Hit Me with Your Best Shot" and the guy she mentioned kept his eye on me.

Meanwhile, some younger boys were acting silly in the middle of the rink. They were amusing. I chortled, so they hammed it up. They were pretending to hit each other as stated in the song overhead. Perfect timing for some comic relief.

Morgan couldn't resist laughing with me while watching them. "Oh, my gosh, now they're flirting with you, too," she said humored.

"Yeah, they should realize that they don't have a chance in heaven," I asserted. She laughed more, understanding my humor.

"You are too much. Since when do you lead little kids on?" she inquired.

"I'm not. I genuinely thought they were funny—that's all." She smiled a snarky grin, which made me titter. My giggling made her laugh. So, for the next two minutes we were in stitches and chortled at how silly we looked trying not to fall while howling with laughter. It was a much-needed silly cycle and what nights out with friends were for.

The cute boy that Amy liked skated slowly past me. It seemed like he wanted to talk. His friends hung back with Amy and Katie. My heart pounded. Not a confrontation. Please.

For several years I had experience turning boys down, but I hated doing it.

"Hey, Christina, you wanna skate with me?" he asked quite smoothly. *Great, Katie and Amy told new cute guy my name and he's apparently not shy. Now what?_*

"Uh, she's got to come with me," Morgan said, her eyes bulging, sending the clear message, 'Follow my lead.' Rescued. *Man, she's quick on her feet.* She headed toward the bathroom. Morgan wasn't the type who needed an escort to the bathroom, unlike Amy. Fortunately, the music followed us, and the song "I Can't Go for That" by Hall and Oates helped sooth my nerves.

"Thanks!" I said gratefully, once we were safe and sound in the bathroom.

"No problem. I really have to go anyway," she confessed with a giggle and another snarky grin.

"Me too! Good timing! You saved my butt!" What a relief in more ways than one!

After getting out of the stall, she approached me, "Look, Christina, I know it's not my business, but you haven't been acting like yourself all night. I heard about you and Avery. Is there anything you want to talk about?" She was always so genuine.

"No, I'm good," I said, aiming to appear relaxed and at peace.

Morgan wasn't buying it. "No, you're not. Christina, you know I go to Pennsford Swim Club—the same pool that Avery goes to. He is moping around like a lost puppy dog. What happened between you two?"

"I can't talk about it." *I really can't talk about it.* Morgan persisted, "Christina, I'm your friend. You can trust me."

"I know. It's not you. You have to believe me." I didn't want to jeopardize our friendship in any way, but I knew I couldn't tell her about what was really bothering me.

"Then tell me what happened," she insisted.

"Not in here. I hate hanging out in bathrooms. It smells awful." It smelled of stale cigarettes, urine and mildew.

"Alright, let's go." I skated to a secluded corner of the rolling rink. Morgan followed and waited patiently for me to say something. Anything.

When I couldn't find my words, she initiated, "Christina, I have never seen you like this. You seem so scared and sad all at the same time." Morgan impressed me with her astute observation. *Was it that obvious to everyone?* I guessed not. Morgan was always keenly perceptive. I should have known better than to go out with her. She and I were even closer than Katie and I.

"I am sad—sad that I had to break it off with Avery," I finally admitted.

"I'm so sorry. Why aren't you allowed to date?"

"I don't know. I'm just not." At that moment, "You Make My

Dreams Come True" came on.

"Did something happen between you and Avery that your parents found out about?" she pried. *I hope other people didn't come to that conclusion. I never even thought of that.*

Aghast, I jerked backward and crinkled my face, "No, nothing like that at all."

"Then, I guess I don't understand. How come you never said you weren't allowed to date before?"

"Because I was never interested in anyone before, so it never came up." At least that part was true.

Convinced with my answer, Morgan shook her head and replied empathetically, "Oh. Man, that's too bad. What about group dates?"

"No, absolutely not." I didn't want to take any chances. Not with You-Know-Who. I already knew what he was capable of.

"What if we ran into some guys that we knew, or met some, like tonight?"

"Nope. That's why I avoided those guys." *I really hate this. The lies. The deception. I have no life. Why did he have to take everything away?* I started to choke up.

"How would your parents know?"

"They wouldn't, but I would and I don't want to deceive them." I knew Morgan would respect my decision to be obedient to my parents because she was even more of a Goody Two-shoes than I was.

"Well, you wouldn't believe how pathetic Avery has been. I have never seen him like this. The girls are swooning all around him. He's trying to be polite, but you can tell that his heart is broken." I started to cry. "Oh, Christina, I'm so sorry. Maybe I shouldn't have said anything, but I am worried." She put her hand on my back as an attempt to comfort me.

"It's okay," I waved her off. I nodded, but I couldn't manage any more words. My heart ached so deeply. *When will I be able to start living a normal life?*

After giving me some time to return to equilibrium, she continued, "Can I ask you a question?" I nodded. "So, what would happen if your parents found out you dated someone?" I shook my head. I started to shake, thinking about what that jackalope would do if he found out that I told someone what he had done. "Oh my God, you're shaking. Christina, are you okay?"

I was hysterical. "Okay, okay. Calm down. It's okay. You'll be okay." Morgan enfolded me in a comforting hug. "I'll call my dad to come pick us up."

The song "Celebration" by Kool & The Gang filled the room. The music seemed too loud now . . . Knowing my friends, I couldn't leave. I had to stick it out. Girls didn't have short memories when it came to things like this. I don't need any unnecessary conversations about me which might lead to future inquiries, and the ultimate discovery of the cause of my distress. I had to make the most of it. I refused to let Jackalope win this one.

"No, don't. Not yet," I said louder, and more fervently, than I intended. She took one look at my face and knew I did not mean to be offensive. "I don't want to be a wet blanket on this fun night," I insisted in a softer tone. I tried to control my breathing. I needed to pull myself together quickly. I couldn't risk spilling my guts because of all the attention I was getting. A flash of cutting myself passed through my mind. I bit my lip and squeezed my eyes shut.

"All right then. Just let me know when you're ready to leave, okay?" she wrapped her words in a loving tone that oozed comfort and stability. I nodded. "Do you need to go back to the bathroom?" I nodded again and tried to hide my nose leakage.

We skated to the bathroom in silence. I washed my face and blew my nose immediately. I looked horrible. My nose was red, my eyes were blood shot and my eyelids were swollen; it was obvious that I had been crying. We skated back out and sat in the seats outside the rink following its perimeter. Eventually, Katie and Amy found us. A new song broke through, "The Boy From New York City."

"What's the matter?" Katie asked.

I gave her an offhand wave. "Nothing. I'm fine now, really," I assured them. I wanted to be invisible.

"Christina, that guy is like one hundred percent mesmerized by you," Amy informed me. Hearing the lyrics describe this tall, fine-looking guy didn't help the matter at hand.

"He doesn't even know me," I stated in disbelief. I knew I sounded defensive, but I found it very difficult to respond pleasantly.

"Try telling him that," Amy guffawed.

"You did," Katie asserted to Amy. We all dissolved into laughter. It felt so good to let go a little.

"Amy, maybe you need to start playing hard to get," Morgan suggested jokingly. Again, the lyrics were taunting me . . .

Cute guy started to skate over. *Seriously, this song is killing me, the timing is almost too coincidental . . .*

"Everything all right?" He looked right at me. "You okay? I didn't mean to upset you." *Wow, he is brave.* I was impressed. And he was super cute. Totally my type. Katie didn't exaggerate. Morgan began to say something.

"No, it's okay," I said, motioning her off while nodding to indicate my gratitude, "I should handle this." I figured I'd give it a shot. I was feeling stronger and a bit refreshed now. I stood up and the boy followed me as we skated onto the rink. I stopped along the edge of the railing at the perimeter. "I'm sorry, I don't even know your name," I started.

"Kevin. It's Kevin." *This is getting ridiculous.* As I heard The Manhattan Transfer sing, chills were running down my spine. I don't even want to think about kissing. *Don't go there.* Reluctantly, the song transported me back to Avery making me feel so fine when his lips were on mine. *Snap out of it, Christina!*

"I should be the one to tell you, Kevin. I'm not allowed to date—at all. I'm not even supposed to be talking to guys like this. I don't want to lead you on; I don't want you to think that I'm playing hard to get or something because I'm not. I am very flattered, yet upset, that my friends dragged me out here knowing I can't date. I don't think they understand what a big deal this is for me and how much I hate it. Look, I don't want to waste your time. You seem like a really nice guy and all," my voice diminished.

"No, it's cool. I get it. Thanks for telling me. We can be friends, right?"

"Sure," I said with a smile. Saying no to that seemed like too much, and frankly, a little crazy. I knew that I would probably never run into him again. I decided to take that chance. *Will this song ever end with its lyrical jabs?*

"Can I have your number?" he asked as a last-ditch effort. He was nothing if not persistent. And cute!

"No, I'd be in serious trouble for that, but do you come here most Friday nights?" I felt bad, so I tried to make up for it.

"A lot of them."

"Then, I'll try to come here more often. In the meantime, maybe my parents will get cooler and change their minds." *I am getting too good at lying.* I started to feel sick to my stomach from being deceitful, but I quickly argued that it was the right thing to do.

Kevin skated away and Morgan gracefully skated toward me. *I'm so over "The Boy From New York City."*

"What was that all about?" Morgan asked. "Another One Bites the Dust" began to entertain us.

"Just explaining myself," I replied smugly.

"Boy, you're good."

"Too much practice as of late," I averred sadly.

"Guess so." She sounded impressed.

A few minutes later, Katie and Amy skated toward me. "What in the world did you say to him?" Katie asked. *How apropos is this song? Too funny!*

"I told him the truth, that's all," I answered. *Not really, but it will have to do.*

"He said you were really great about it. 'Very cool' were his exact words," Katie informed me.

"He said it was the nicest let down he ever heard, and I don't think he's been turned down much, if at all. What in the world did you say?" Amy requested.

With a demure smile and a wink, I teased "I can't give you guys all my secrets."

I enjoyed being lighthearted for a change, as life had been so agonizing. We all chuckled and ended the evening on a happier and brighter note, the way it used it to be before the unmentionable.

Upon reflection, a little later that evening, I laid in bed feeling spent and somewhat normal—like a regular teenager. I assumed it was due to all the drama. Even though I was an emotional wreck at the rink, it was worth it to go in the end. My friends helped me more than they will ever truly know. The tune "I'm So Excited" by the Pointer Sisters, ran through my head as I dozed off into a rare, but much needed, peaceful slumber.

Chapter 19

THE NEXT DAY MY DAD asked if I wanted to visit his mom in South Philly. I agreed to go, especially since I hadn't seen my Italian Mom-Mom in a few weeks.

I was in better spirits. Listening to The Oldies music station in the car lifted my spirits even more. The '50s and '60s produced great, groovy doo-wops. I smiled as I thought, if I were with Mom, I'd be listening to an AM news radio station with the annoying sound of ticker tape in the background.

We greeted Mom-Mom at her porch door with kisses. She was wearing a blue house dress and slippers that complimented her short white hair.

"How are you, Christine?" she said, squeezing my shoulders. I could feel the love through her thin, bony, yet strong fingers which held me tight.

Sometimes she called me Christine, which totally confused me because she was the one who suggested to name me Christina. For some strange reason, South Philly Italian-Americans had the habit of chopping off the vowels at the end of words. It was nothing personal. That's the way it was in that neck of the city at least.

For example, Mom-Mom's name was Anna, but she went by Anne. For the longest time, I thought her name was Anne. Anne is not a nickname for Anna. Anna makes the name more ethnic, more interesting, and much prettier. Anne is plain. Christine is plain.

The dropping of vowels did not stop with people's names either; the phenomenon occurred with other words too, like saying antipast, instead of antipasto. She also called every type of pasta macaroni, so I never knew what type of noodle I was going to eat. But, that's another story altogether. Mom-Mom did, however, make the best homemade macaroni and gravy—pasta sauce, not to be confused with brown gravy—this side of the Atlantic Ocean. Her Italian dishes absolutely melted in your mouth and burst with flavor and freshness. Just thinking about her food made my mouth water.

"Fine," I answered. "How are you?"

"Good, good. Have a seat. Take a load off," she motioned me to sit down on the couch.

Mom-Mom shut the TV off because, as she put it, "Since the Phillies aren't playing today, there's no need to have this thing on." She was a huge Phillies fan and never missed a game. As a result, I knew a lot about the team.

I found out that Mom-Mom recently went to the casinos in Atlantic City on a senior citizen bus trip. She won again. "I won eighty bucks at the slots!" she said with excitement waving her arms above her head, as if to cheer herself on. Most people return from Atlantic City having won nothing, so she made me proud and I found her enthusiasm endearing. *Go Mom-Mom!*

Mom-Mom offered us a snack. We followed her slow, but deliberate footsteps to the kitchen. I think food was one of the reasons my dad liked to visit his mom. She served the best treats.

We walked through the formal dining room where the ornate gold oil lamp of The Madonna hung—the one with the oil drops that rained continuously throughout when it was turned on. Although the lamp was very gaudy, I found it to be mesmerizing, as I could stare at it for hours, but she rarely turned it on anymore.

From the dining room, we continued to the back of the house to the kitchen that opened up to a tiny fenced-in back yard. The old Formica table was covered with an orange and yellow plastic floral tablecloth. This was the cozy place where we indulged in one of my favorites—chocolate éclairs. With pride, Mom-Mom said, "I bought them fresh from the corner store today." Everything there was freshly baked. I loved how the yellow filling oozed out of the éclair, so sweet, thick and creamy. We never ate pastries like these at home. Yum!

According to my dad, the best junk food in the world was found in South Philadelphia. He'd brag, "The best cheese steaks, the best pizza, the best soft pretzels, and the best hoagies are made in South Philly."

Hoagies had other names too: New Yorkers called them 'heroes,' New Englanders called them 'grinders,' southern Bostonians referred to them as 'spuckies,' while most people outside of Philadelphia called them 'subs,' short for submarines.

The story was traced back to the Philadelphia Naval Yard, otherwise known as Hog Island, and the sandwich itself dated back to the year 1885. I have always been partial to the name 'hoagie,' as a loyal tribute to my birth city.

I loved to get in touch with my Italian roots when I visited my paternal grandmother. It helped me discover who I was to some degree.

After a short time of food and chitchat about the hot weather, my dad's job, my mom, and my brother's activities, and other relatives, we said our goodbyes.

"Now, don't be a stranger," Mom-Mom commanded, with a wink and a squeeze. "Oh, and good luck in high school if I don't see you before you head back to school," she conveyed with a final hug, as she slipped me a twenty. I expressed my appreciation for her willingness to share her winnings, and we were off to the 'burbs.

Chapter 20

$\mathcal{U}$ S PART OF MY ORIGINAL plan, I went to The Manor first thing Monday morning. Miss Brenda radiated her usual warm, friendly self. Well, almost. She refrained from giving me one of her loving bear hugs that I craved. Instead, she waved me over to the square card table for four, but there were only two residents sitting there with her, "Christina, come join us. We're playing Pinochle. I was just saying that we could use another player."

I actually enjoyed playing Pinochle. I liked card games in general.

There were other groups of the elderly sitting at various tables playing card games, board games, or simply conversing. Hanging out with the old folks was more fun than hanging out with my peers at times. Obviously, there was something wrong with me when playing card games with the blue-haired folks was more enjoyable than kicking it with teenagers.

Miss Brenda seemed a bit reserved, but under the circumstances, it was perfectly understandable. Since I didn't know if I should bring up her son's death, I avoided the topic. The last thing I wanted to do was cause Miss Brenda any more sadness.

Every day for the rest of the week, I returned to The Manor to help, but more so, to support Miss Brenda. Each time, she greeted me with her famous bear hug. *'Now that was more like it'* I thought to myself after each and every hug.

Finally, on Friday the thirteenth she said, "You know, you don't have to keep coming around on my behalf."

"No, I want to. Really," I contested.

"Well, I'm lucky to have a devoted friend like you, Christina!" Lucky was a funny choice of words for Friday the thirteenth, but I let it slide, as I didn't think she was the superstitious type. Not that I was either.

I smiled, "That makes two of us."

"Alright then, let's get this party started!" she shouted. Then, she put on some oldies music and everyone perked up, including me. How did she know?

Turns out, the old folks liked the oldies rock 'n' roll too. Some even danced. A few jitterbugged. Most waved their arms, barely moving their hips, although, I spotted some hip action among the more mobile.

Before I knew it, I was dancing among the white-haired. I liked to feel the music and let my body take over. I moved every muscle in my body and it felt invigorating. We all had a ball.

Again, there had to be something wrong when a thirteen-year-old's highlight of the week was getting down with those who could barely get up. But there we were "busting a move like nobody's business," as Miss Brenda put it. I couldn't remember the last time I had so much fun. It was definitely more rejuvenating and more enjoyable than roller skating with the girls. No stress. No lies. No tears. And NO drama!

When I got home that evening, my mom said that Morgan called. Feeling energized from dancing earlier, I dashed upstairs to call her back, skipping steps as I ascended.

"Hello . . ."

"Is Morgan there?"

"Just a sec . . . MOOORRR—GAAAN, phone!!"

"Hello . . ."

"Morgan, hi, it's Christina. My mom said you called."

"Yeah, do you want to come over to my house tonight? My dad said he'd pick up pizzas and make us milkshakes."

I was a sucker for milkshakes and she knew that, especially extra thick, extra chocolatey milkshakes.

"Sure! What time?" I responded quickly, like I was racing the clock on Jeopardy.

"Six o'clock."

"Okay, I'll be there. Thanks!"

My dad dropped me off at Morgan's and said to call him when I was ready to be picked up. Morgan's crew was present: Valerie, Cheryl, Jackie, and Macey. Valerie was a petite strawberry blond with an adorable heart-shaped face, and a cute smile to complement her prominent dimples. We got along, but we didn't have much of a relationship outside the group.

Jackie had a super cute figure, short dirty blond hair, and was always sweet, perhaps a little meek, yet, we only remained acquaintances.

Macey attended the local Catholic school and lived near the rest of the girls. Macey had long, dark, straight hair that she always wore in a ponytail. She was average height and very athletic. I cared very little for Macey, as she was bossy, mean, and wore a facade of being cool and tough. Since Macey grew up with the rest of the girls, she was often part of the crowd—I could hardly contain my excitement when her presence co-existed with mine.

Val followed Macey around like a lost puppy dog, reaching out to her for attention and approval that Val craved, but never received from Macey. I despised watching the cruel display of Macey's constant rejection towards Val. I couldn't be friends with someone who treated people like that.

Basically, I was the outlier of this group, which was fine with me, because I was very good friends with Morgan, the host. She was always the mastermind behind getting cliques together. Morgan and I branched out to different circles, while the other girls, by and large, stuck to themselves.

I always felt welcomed in Morgan's house. Her family was very hospitable and friendly. She had one older brother, one older sister, a younger sister, and a younger brother. Morgan's dad joked that he could never remember our names, but we have all been friends with Morgan for so long that I found that hard to believe.

One day, Mr. Ricci told me that he remembered me because I talked a lot. His nickname for me was "Radio," which both amused and flattered me. Looking back at recent weeks, the name did not fit anymore.

"I see Radio is here," Morgan's dad warmly teased, while giving me one of his famous Italian smiles. "Smile Italian style" was his clever and befitting motto, that I considered adopting as my own. Morgan's dad was stocky, with an olive complexion, dark curly hair, and slightly balding. Morgan giggled at his reference of me. The rest of the gang didn't know who he was talking about at first, but they caught on.

"Oh, you must mean Christina," Macey interjected snidely. Macey was too sly to be blatantly obnoxious in the presence of adults, but her spiteful comments did not go unnoticed by me.

"Hi, Mr. Ricci," I returned with a big smile, instantly feeling welcomed. He nodded.

"Girls, are you ready for your pizza?" he asked. "Yes!" we all answered in unison.

"Oh, too bad. I got hungry, so I ate it," he joked. We knew he was teasing, but his delivery and personality made us crack up all the same. *As long as I have chocolate, I'm good to go! And milkshakes are among my favorite forms of chocolate.*

We crowded around their kitchen table, where I chowed down three pieces of pepperoni pizza, and thanked the Riccis for supplying it. Macey, of course, had to comment on my voracious appetite, as the girls only ate two slices at the most and didn't inhale the pizza with the same velocity or fervor as me. "Christina, you eat like a football player. Maybe next time you should have your own pizza pie," she singularly snickered at her failed attempt at humor at my expense. *Thanks, girls for not laughing!*

We adjourned to the basement, which they called a rec room. They had a full-sized pinball machine and an air hockey unit in one section of the lower level. I walked over to the lounge area, plopped on the sofa, and placed my hand on my belly. I felt as if I had eaten entire Thanksgiving meal. Beyond satisfying!

As I sat and assessed that everyone's mood was lifted from the consumption of pizza, and enjoyment was in the air, I realized that I had a smile on my face. That was the moment when Val pounced on me, digging for gossip.

"So, I heard you went out with Avery. What happened?" Morgan was in the background trying to wave her off, being the protective mamma bear, but Val persisted, and the others joined in and gathered around the sofa, eager to get the scoop.

I heard someone say, "Oh, he's so cute."

"Nothing. I'm not allowed to date. That's all," I said, soporifically, with the intention of communicating that this topic was a tiresome one, so they would drop it.

"Yeah, that's what I heard, too bad," commented an empathetic Cheryl.

"I heard he's been moping around. I see him at the pool

sometimes and he doesn't seem like himself," Val revealed.

"Why would you lead him on like that?" Macey verbally jabbed, with a look of both disgust and self- satisfaction.

"I didn't lead him on. I didn't know I wasn't allowed to date him until after we started going out," I retorted defensively.

"Ohhhh!" they reacted simultaneously.

"Sucks for you, huh?" Macey needled. I rolled my eyes and stifled a nasty response. "Did you kiss this guy?" *You are too much, Macey,* I thought but refused to say. I wanted to be respectful of Morgan and Mr. Ricci. I also wanted them to think well of me—I was fairly certain getting in a catfight after slamming down pizza they generously provided would not help me obtain that objective.

Not only did Macey not know Avery, but she and I weren't even friends. It was *absopositively* none of her business, so I chose not to respond.

"Macey!" Morgan admonished, "Let her be. She may not want to discuss it."

"Girls, your milkshakes are ready," Mr. Ricci called from the top of the stairs. *Whew! Saved by the shakes!*

I managed to get through the night unscathed. *Not too bad for Friday the thirteenth!* I enjoyed my favorite extra thick, extra chocolatey, chocolate shake. *Thank you, Mr. Ricci!* So, the evening was the cherry on top of a good day. *I like cherries too!* My appetite was back in full swing! Later, that night I resisted cutting myself.

Chapter 21

MORGAN CALLED ME THE FOLLOWING day, around noon, to see if I wanted to go out later that night. "Who is in the crowd this time?" I cross-examined her, with a teasing tone. She understood my humor and giggled.

I was her pivotal friend, with whom she could mix and match any friend of hers. Plus, she was aiming to look out for me. She wanted to do her best to make sure that I was okay and I loved her for it.

Tonight, we would hang with Amy, Katie, Erin and Abby. Erin, a dishwater blond, was short, lean, attractive, intelligent, talented, and supercilious. Abby was insecure and very overweight. She was average height, with long, poker straight, dark hair, and small, almond shaped brown eyes.

Abby, the host of the night, had honed in on her skills for entertaining masses of teens. She served good junk food and prepared fun games. We indulged in chocolate ice cream that she insisted we top with potato chips. I was the first to dig in. It was good, but I had tasted better combos, like potato skins and mayo. Or chocolate ice cream and milk, blended.

We played Twister—I had both feet on green, my right hand draped over Amy on blue. Amy had her right foot on yellow, her left hand on blue and her left foot on red. Erin's left hand was on yellow, her right foot was on green and the other foot was on blue, and Morgan had her right foot on blue, her left foot on yellow and her right hand on yellow. I attempted to put my right foot on red, but I couldn't maneuver past Abby's butt, who had her left hand on blue, and her right foot on blue, and her left foot on red.

That's when we all tumbled to the floor, except Morgan, who has remarkable balance and concentration, especially given her tall stature. I laughed so hard I almost peed myself.

It felt good to laugh, and during a quieter moment of the evening, Katie took the time to check in with me, "How are you doing, Christina?"

"I'm good, surprisingly. Thanks for asking." I grinned.

"Yeah, you seem to be doing better than I expected. Anything new?"

"Umm, no, not really. This has been a great party. Abby is the hostess with the mostest!"

"Yeah, she's a good egg. I'm glad you're having fun!"

"Me too. It's about time. Thanks so much, Katie. You, Abby, Amy, and Erin are all friends from the musical, right?"

"Pretty much."

"That's what I thought," I said, tapping my index finger on my cheek. I could picture myself hanging out with this crowd. Things were looking bright.

"Why?"

"You all get along so well, but I didn't remember you hanging out before last year."

I liked this group better than the other group because they were much nicer to each other and me. Unlike Macey. '*Christina, you eat like a football player. Maybe next time you should have your own pizza pie.*' Oh, shut up, Macey!

For the most part, the next few weeks were spent at The Manor. I wanted to spend as much time there as I could before heading back to school, since I had no idea how challenging high school would be, and as a result, would have no idea how often I could visit Miss Brenda.

I was starting my freshman year in high school and my brother was starting his first year in middle school. The two of us were embarking on new stages in our lives, which could make for a very cool and interesting year.

Chapter 22

I
T WAS THE FIRST FRIDAY of September. Miss Brenda and I were eating lunch in the employee lounge when I told her I didn't know when I would be returning to The Manor. Before biting into her ham sandwich, she stated in her sweet demonstrative way, "Honey, you do what you gotta do. Don't worry about little ol' me. I'll be fine. It's you that I'm concerned about." Saying that, she looked up at me and chewed as she waited for my response.

"Me? Why me?" I asked, putting my ham and cheese on a kaiser down.

"Well, it's your path honey," she said after she swallowed. "You think you're on the straight and narrow, sweetie, but you're only headed to damnation." I shot her a puzzled look. "I don't want to sugar coat this any more than I have been." She put her sandwich on her tray and looked at me with a seriousness and a gentleness, and then exploded with some excitement, "Girl, you need Jesus! Plain and simple!" This time the look on my face must have told her she was cuckoo for Cocoa Puffs!

"I know you think this religious stuff is a bunch of hooey, but honey, it's not. If it wasn't for my faith that Christ Jesus is Savior, I would be a mess right now. That's right. My only child is dead, but I have peace of mind knowing that he is in the presence of the Lord God Almighty Himself. And sometime, in the Lord's timing, I will join him. Praise be to God!" She sounded like Reverend Simms.

Again, I sat silently, my jaw agape. "Girl, do you believe that Jesus is your Savior?" I gave her another blank stare. She scooched over a little closer and asked, "Do you believe that Jesus is the Son of God and that He came down to this earth to wash away your sins, so you may be granted life forever?"

"Ah . . ."

"Do you?" she pressed, her gaze unwavering. "Umm, no, I guess not."

"That's what I was afraid of," she said in the same sad tone a doctor delivers bad news to his patient. Miss Brenda paused, gathered a thought in her mind, and looked at me straight in the eyes with more love than I ever witnessed in all my thirteen years. Her eyes welled up and she reached for my hand, "Christina, you need to believe . . . you need Jesus. Without Jesus, there's no real and deep joy, no real and deep peace, no love . . . no life. Do you understand me?"

I shook my head as slowly as I spoke, "Not really."

"You heard of Jesus, right?" she asked in a soft tone. "Yes," I said, feeling the weight of the intimacy and enormity of this conversation.

"Have you ever heard what I'm saying?"

"Somewhat." My mind swirled and searched for answers.

She leaned in closer and gripped my hand tighter, "Why are you resisting his holy presence in your life?"

I bit my lip and cleared my throat, "I guess . . . I don't understand how there can be such a loving God in such a violent messed up world."

"Sweetie, what happened to you?" Miss Brenda asked lovingly. Suddenly, tears fell from my eyes. "Honey, I know something happened. It's none of my business, but—sweet Jesus can help you get through this. God knows I've been through hell and back, but without the Lord, I . . . ," her voice vanished momentarily. "Thank God I had His greatness to help me through the tough times, especially now."

I knew Miss Brenda missed her son terribly, but she was somehow able to hold herself together. Moreover, she was able to love so many people in insurmountable ways.

The loving woman before me continued, "All you have to do is ask Jesus into your heart. Ask Him to forgive you. He knows every sin you committed. And He will forgive you for each and every one. Ask Him to help you to forgive as well. Ask Him to be in charge of your life. Tell Him you know He died for your sins and you will have eternal life. It's that simple! All you have to do is accept Him into your heart."

I was dumbfounded. No one ever explained faith like that to me before, but I was not ready for such a commitment. I had some serious thinking to do.

"When you're ready, Jesus will be waiting with open arms," Miss Brenda assured me and patted my hand. "God bless you, Christina. I will be praying for you," she said closing the topic on her end.

That night I did not reach for the razor.

Chapter 23

I SURVIVED MY FIRST DAY OF high school. Barely.

Homerooms were assigned alphabetically. I about fainted when I saw Avery Evans sitting in the classroom chatting with a friend.

"Everyone take your seats," the teacher directed, gesturing to the last three empty seats.

I scanned the room in a panic trying to find a place, other than the one directly behind Avery.

The teacher looked at me, motioned to that very seat behind Avery, and told me to sit. I felt so flushed, my face burned.

Avery glanced up at me, but he continued to talk to his neighbor. I sat down and tried not to move. *Maybe if I sit still, no one will notice me.*

My homeroom was alive with chatter, but I simply nodded and forced a smile if someone looked at me. My plan of invisibility failed miserably.

"My name is Mr. Sommers. These will be your assigned seats for the entire year," he announced.

No way! I couldn't believe that I had to sit behind Avery Evans every day in homeroom for the duration of the year. At least it beat sitting next to the unspeakable. *Silver lining.*

One of the morning announcements we heard over the loudspeaker was regarding Jerome's death: "If you need help coping with this loss, you are permitted, at any time, to see the grief counselor or your guidance counselor."

Apparently, Jerome was very popular. There was a little buzz in the hallway about his passing, especially among upperclassmen.

First period was Algebra. *NO WAY! Jackalope, the unspeakable, is in here. Not cool. Oh, God. Yes, I am thinking of you.*

I never had a class with him before. *This can't be happening.*

It felt like someone punched me in the stomach. This was my punishment for not applying myself last year in math. I should be in honors algebra, not this class. I had looked forward to skating through this stupid class, but now . . .

"Ladies and gentlemen, my name is Ms. Chandler. You will be expected . . ."

I drifted off to my cousin Emily's story of Ms. Chandler. Emily, Jessie's older sister, had Ms. Chandler in eighth grade who instantly recognized Emily as a relative of my Aunt Irene, whom she taught in Philadelphia many years ago. My Aunt Irene is Emily's mom and Ms. Chandler saw the strong family resemblance. This was astonishing, since my cousin's last name is different from her mom's maiden name.

My daydream was interrupted with a strong tone and a tapping of a ruler on my desk, "Lady Jane, you need to pay attention!" Ms. Chandler annoyed me from the start. She continued, "As I was saying, if you don't do your homework, you get a blue moon." *What the heck is a blue moon?* "Three blue moons and your grade is dropped one grade level." *She's a real peach. More like Homework Hitler.*

The day improved when I discovered that my best school bud, Faith, was in my art class. The class was a mixed group of students from different grades and a lot of them seemed weird, in a nerdy kind of way, not in a fun, cool kind of way.

Faith and I sat together and picked up right where we left off. It was comforting having her in class, because she felt like my intellectual equal, although I knew she was smarter than me. She was very attractive with beautiful, long, wavy, light brown hair and gorgeous gray eyes. She still had that Laura Ingalls Little House on the Prairie look from the day I met her in fourth grade. I wondered why we didn't see each other much over the summers, but my guess was it was due to her parents going through a divorce.

Faith also ended up in my gym class along with Katie and Cheryl. Mrs. Hartzel, our teacher, was huge. She was one of the biggest people I had ever seen in my life—how ironic to be teaching gym and health class. Rumor had it that she just missed qualifying for the United States Olympic swim team in 1956.

My last class was geography. Mr. Nunzio announced that we

were the only honors social science class for our grade. The class was on the larger side and I recognized most of the students from the two former top sections from middle school.

Tammy, a new girl from the Catholic school, who I found out was good friends with Macey, sat behind me and seemed quite anxious. She was particularly squeamish when Mr. Nunzio declared we were the "cream of the crop," which prompted her to share that she was quite nervous to be in class with all "these brainiacs." *It's geography. How hard can it be? He seems cool. No worries.*

The next few days were an adjustment. Academically, my classes didn't seem too challenging, although it was too soon to tell. At this point, school simply existed.

I did my best to avoid Avery and the jackalope, even though it was difficult. I remained quiet in homeroom, since I didn't have any friends to talk to.

As a distraction from Avery, I watched this super adorable, super intellect apply makeup and learned a few things. My guess was that her parents forbade her to wear any makeup, so she took to applying it during homeroom.

I was relieved that Avery didn't say anything to me those first days of school. Unfortunately, that was not the case with the jack. On occasion, he would mouth "loser," or "dead meat" to me, always with a look of hate.

I was able to go to The Manor every day after school, as it was conveniently located next door. After Miss Brenda finished her shift and left for the day, I completed my homework. Later, my dad would pick me up on his way home from work.

I experienced my good days and my bad days that fall. On the good days, I managed to be cut free. That was not the case on my bad days. Sometimes, the jack successfully deflated me with his vile behavior. The razor helped erase that fear and pain, albeit temporarily.

Chapter 24

AFTER THE FIRST WEEK OF school, Avery greeted me. "Hi," I returned meekly. I felt flustered. My heart pounded. I sat down at my desk behind him, shaking. To my surprise, Avery turned around. "Can we talk later, just you and me, say after school?" he asked.

"Oh, sure. I guess so." *Smooth move, Christina!*

"I'll meet you at the smoking lounge outside at 2:20."

"Okay," I replied, barely able to breathe. *What does Avery want? I can't face him. Why did I agree to talk to him? I am such a wimp!*

I rushed out of the room and sat down in algebra class. I zoned the entire period. Ms. Chandler called on me, but I had no idea what she had asked.

"Lady Jane, I suggest you pay attention or you will end up in Siberia."

Every day in algebra, Ms. Chandler yelled at someone and ordered them to go sit in Siberia, which was the most remote place in the room. I failed to comprehend what that was supposed to prove. She treated us like we were in preschool. I rolled my eyes when Ms. Chandler sent someone to Siberia and occasionally, made a smart comment, but I never got exiled there. It paid to have an aunt who was a saint back in the day. *Thanks, Aunt Irene!*

I blankly stared at Ms. Chandler, as she wrote equations on the board. No wheels were turning to fire any neurons in my brain.

I felt someone's eyes penetrating me and instinctively turned toward that direction. It was You-Know-Who—the jack—and he was gloating. My spine shivered.

"Young man, wipe that smirk off your face," Ms. Chandler demanded of Paul. He made an obnoxious sound in reply and she had none of it. "You," she shouted, pointing to You-Know-Who, "go to Siberia!"

"What? I didn't do anything!" The jack yelled slamming his hand on his desk. He glared my way and threatened under his breath, "You are dead meat." *Uh, oh!*

I paid attention after that, and at class's end, tore out of there faster than I can eat pizza.

Art class was fun most of the time. Sitting with Faith while working on our art projects, chatting about the strange characters we shared class with, was entertaining.

One girl's name was Sue and she was a *Doctor Who* fan. I knew nothing of the doctor, except that anyone who liked him seemed totally geeky. Sue believed in freedom of the hair—meaning, she never cut her hair or put anything in it. She wore it plain, hanging straight down. Faith referred to her as "Sue Who." I gave Faith props for her creativity.

Unfortunately, I couldn't focus in art class either. I felt like a train wreck and almost ruined my project. Faith asked me what was wrong, but I, uncharacteristically, blew her off.

My mind constantly returned to the end of the day when I would meet up with Avery. I didn't know if I should. What would I say? I didn't want him in this mess. I fumbled through the rest of the day.

Geography class. Last period. Tammy was getting on my nerves—my few unraveled ones. She constantly whispered that she didn't understand the lesson. I didn't understand what there was to understand. It was geography, not hieroglyphics.

Tammy tapped on my shoulder frequently to ask me questions. I shushed her hoping she would leave me alone. Finally, I snapped, "Tammy, quit bugging me!"

"Jeez, sorry. What's got into you?"

A classmate winked at me, making me feel a bit better for overreacting. Tammy saw the wink, gasped, and threw a little fire our way saying, "What is it with you people?"

I ignored her the rest of the class pretending to take copious notes. When the bell rang, I was the first one out of class. I raced to my locker, switched my books and headed outside to the smoking lounge.

It was strange that we had a smoking lounge, but the administrators designed it to discourage students and faculty from smoking indoors. It failed its purpose, because the bathrooms always reeked of smoke and it was nauseating. Why didn't the administration simply ban smoking altogether?

Avery was already there, when I arrived. He looked as adorable as ever. I practically bit my own lip off from being so nervous.

"Let's go someplace a little more private."

I could not deny his request, so I followed him to the back of the building near the athletic fields. I wanted desperately to hold his hand, to embrace him, to kiss his lips. It was apparent that my feelings for Avery were incredibly strong. I felt irresistibly drawn to him. Interwoven in this feeling of elation was fear. *What if the jack found out? Would he really hurt Avery?*

Avery and I were face to face. He displayed a look of being distraught. I ached for him, along with an intense feeling of guilt, and had the urge to turn away. *Be brave.*

"Christina," Avery paused. "Christina, I really had a great time with you over the summer." I listened, carefully, for the first time all day. "I really liked you. Actually, I still do." *Be strong. Be in control, Christina.*

"Avery, you know I liked you too. I still do. I wish I didn't. That's what's making this so hard for me. My parents would go ballistic if they found out I was even talking to a boy. I don't know what got into them, but you can't imagine how hard this has been for me. I can't even let people see us talking together because I'm afraid it might get back to my parents." I sounded convincing, just as I had rehearsed. I wanted to be able to tell Avery the entire truth, but I just couldn't.

Avery shrugged and suggested, "Maybe I could talk to your parents. Do *something.* I don't know."

"No, that would be a mistake. They are stubborn and steely. I'm hoping this will somehow blow over, but in the meantime, I have to respect their wishes. I hope you understand. I don't like that this hurts you."

"I don't understand. There has to be something we can do," he pleaded.

"There isn't. Trust me. I wish there was," I reiterated.

"So, we can't even be friends?" Avery asked already knowing the answer to his question.

"No, not really. Just know that I truly liked you. A part of me always will," I shared willingly.

"Do you have any idea how bummed out I've been?"

Yes, but I'm glad you are telling me.

"I don't, but I am so, so sorry. This has been torturous for me too. It really has." *You have no idea.*

"Christina, we really had a connection. I never felt like this before. I can't seem to shake it . . . shake you." Avery displayed a look of desperation, which was unnerving.

"Avery, please for both our sakes, you have to move on. We both do."

"Christina, I don't think I can. I tried, but . . . ," his voiced waned as he put his head down.

"Avery, I'm telling you that you have to," I insisted. He lifted his head up, so we were once again eye to eye.

"I see you every day in homeroom and all I want to do is kiss you," he disclosed softly.

"Please don't—don't do this. You are only making this harder for me." He gently took my hands and gazed into my eyes.

"Okay, but one last kiss, please?" he pleaded. How could I resist him with those alluring blue eyes? The jack's threats crept into my head, '*You are dead meat. I will kill you and your little boyfriend.*'

"I can't. It will only make this harder. I'm sorry. I'm so sorry. Please go," I insisted.

I couldn't handle it anymore; I could no longer be brave or strong. The terror of that wicked day replayed in my mind—his accusations, his body on mine, the penetration, the threats, the pain . . . '*I will kill you and your little boyfriend.*' My eyes welled up and I could no longer hold back the tears.

"But . . . Christina. . . ."

I put my hand up in front of my face. "Please," I sobbed uncontrollably. I covered my face with my hands, leaned against the building, slid my body down the brick wall to the ground and bawled. Avery finally walked away.

I sat on the ground for a while until I thought the coast was clear. I needed time to compose myself. I walked to The Manor and freshened up in the restroom. My heart felt comforted as soon as I saw Miss Brenda in the rec center.

"Well, hello, sugar! "She exclaimed. "You look like you've been crying," she said through her hug.

I shrugged. "Allergies," I sniffed. *I really should try out for the school play.*

She motioned toward to the card table, "How would you like to join us in playing Uno?"

I sat down to play and thought that Uno was an odd game for a bunch of white-haired folks, but it turned out to be a lot of fun. Most of the time, they would forget to say Uno when they only had one card left, which made it all the more amusing. We all laughed uncontrollably. I needed to laugh in the worst way. I was incredibly thankful for the old folks' home. It turned out to be my refuge.

Later, I quietly wept in the shower. I tried to control my thoughts—to convince myself that I wasn't a loser and that Avery would not be in harm's way. However, the fear was deep, and it was real, and I was unversed in how to cope with it. With trembling hands, I reached for the pink razor . . . and watched the crimson color swirl down the drain.

Chapter 25

*A*S I SAT IN HOMEROOM, the more anxious I became because I wasn't sure how to interact with Avery.

I wanted to find the balance of friendly and open and distant, which was a contradiction. It was all very confusing. He greeted me warmly with a head nod, "Hey, Christina." I muttered a weak response, aiming to contain my emotions. The announcements started on the overhead speaker.

He turned to speak to me. *I guess he is copacetic with no secret rendezvous.* "Are you okay? I mean, the last thing I wanted to do was upset you," he whispered.

"Uh . . . I'm fine. You?" I glanced around the room to see if anyone was paying attention to our conversation. Thank goodness, no one was paying us any mind.

"I'm okay now that I know you're all right. I still think we can be friends."

I cut to the chase while biting my bottom lip. "I'm afraid we would get too close."

"What if we hung out with other people like in a group setting?" *A totally valid response.*

"We hang out with completely different people," I reminded him, with a hushed tone.

He persisted, "Yeah, but I know my buds wouldn't mind."

The announcements finished. We continued to whisper, despite the volume in the classroom getting louder and louder by the second.

"I'd be accused of using you to climb the social ladder," I replied, raising my eyebrows.

"Is that what this is about?" he questioned with an inquisitive look.

"No, I was just kidding. I joke when I get nervous." I didn't care about social status. Students started to gather their belongings. I looked at the clock. It was almost time to go.

Avery whispered emphatically, "Christina, you can have any guy you want."

I felt my face blush. "If that were the case, we wouldn't be having this discussion," I reminded him.

"You know what I mean," he challenged.

The bell rang. Everyone got up to leave.

Avery grabbed his books and turned around to face me with those ocean blues. "Hey, meet me at the cafeteria by the salad bar after school." That part of the cafeteria was the place where the "A" listers hung out. Since I wasn't part of the "A" crowd, I socialized and ate elsewhere.

"I don't know," I answered, with the scrunched face older people make when trying to read a menu without glasses.

"Pleeeease, Christina," he gently entreated.

"Don't count on it," I replied flatly, though softly. *Man, I hate this.*

"I'll see you later!" Avery waved with confidence and a hopeful smile.

I dreaded first period. I averted eye contact with everyone, to be on the safe side.

Ms. Chandler required every student to solve homework problems on the board. Today, the jack and I had to work side by side. I sloppily zoomed through the problem to avoid any confrontation with him, though he found a moment to be nasty. He leaned over to call me a "loser." A chill ran down my spine, but I steeled myself and shrugged him off.

I deliberately turned my thoughts to more positive things—to Avery. I pictured his Caribbean blue eyes, and gleaming white smile. A warm pleasant tingling sensation filled me. The tingling feeling stayed with me throughout the day.

Fortunately, my art mojo returned, enabling me to create what I envisioned with ease. My art teacher, Mrs. Boyd, was especially impressed.

I entertained the notion of meeting Avery after school. Even if the unspeakable never happened, I would feel awkward around his friends. He said I could have any guy I wanted. Was that true? What exactly did Avery tell his friends about me?

As expected, Avery kept his word, and met me by the salad bar. "Christina, over here." His smile—his excitement to see me and introduce me to his friends made me feel very special. "Christina, you know the guys, right?"

The guys consisted of Joey Glosser, who was in my math class; Peter Brewer, who I shared geography with; and Larry Tomlinson, an honor student. *He is friends with these guys?* I had no clue. How cool.

"Yeah, hi, everyone." I heard lots of greetings in response. The cafeteria was teeming with noisy students awaiting their buses.

"Um, Avery, I can't stay long," I informed him.

"Why? Don't you have to wait for the bus?"

"No, I don't always take the bus home," I replied.

"You don't? So, who drives you?" He knew it would be a long walk home for me.

"Well, I volunteer at The Manor next door."

"You still do that?" he asked with benumbed tone.

"Yes, I really like it. You wouldn't believe how much fun a person can have there. I need to get there soon."

Avery reached for my hand. *Since when do friends hold hands?*

I resisted pulling away, because I didn't want to embarrass him in front of his friends . . . and because it felt so nice and natural. The guys were very aware that we were holding hands, but they were playing it cool for their good friend's sake.

"Can't you go a little later?" He shot me a hopeful, adoring look. Avery was nothing, if not persistent. My heart said yes, but my mind was dead-set against his suggestion. Ultimately, it felt unnatural to argue with him, so I agreed.

"Sure, I can stay for a few minutes." Excited, Avery pulled me into his arms and kissed me. He caught me off guard and completely stunned and electrified me. It was so easy to be with him. It felt as if we never were apart since July. I caught a glance of You-Know-Who—the jack glaring at me. He mouthed the words "dead meat" and I instantly felt twisted up and sick inside. Avery tilted his head to see what startled me.

"What is it with him? I remember him staring at us at his house. Does he like you or something?" Avery asked.

"No," I turned away from Paul and whispered to Avery, "He hates me."

"How could he hate you?"

"I have no idea, but he does."

"Well, he gives me the creeps." *You and me both.* "Hey, you're shaking. Don't let him bother you."

"He hangs out with my brother. I'm afraid he'll say something. Please—please, promise me you won't go near him or say anything to him. It will only make it worse."

"Make what worse?" Avery asked.

"He's crazy. That's all. Trust me—stay away from him. He is wildly nuts." Avery pulled me closer and kissed my forehead and held me tight.

"This is your idea of not getting close?" I added, sweetly chiding him.

"Well, I said we could hang out with my friends and here we are." *Yes, here we are. And hell is on its way.*

Later that evening, I tried to wrap my head around what happened with Avery. Technically, I didn't tell Avery what actually transpired—you know, the unspeakable. However, Creepoid—I decided to call him that because he was downright creepy—would think I did, or at the very least, feel threatened that I will say something someday. Who knew what could cause him snap? What could trigger him to hurt Avery? Or me again? I second guessed everything I did and said. *I hate living like this!*

I loved being with Avery. He made me feel so safe, so secure, and so special. I was a mess when I wasn't with him. Why did he have to be so persistent? So sweet? So supportive? And why did he have to possess the most bewitching blue eyes that melted my heart?

Clueless, I pondered my future. Should I continue with the pretense that my parents forbade me to date? I refrained from telling anyone what happened that unspeakable afternoon, so no one knew that I was tainted goods. If I kept my dirty secret, maybe I could have a relationship with Avery after all. And that would be wonderful.

Even though I was in a quagmire, I resisted cutting. I forced my thoughts, instead, to wander to my conversation with Miss Brenda.

About God . . . Jesus . . . how she claims Jesus gets her through even the toughest of times. If she can handle losing her only son, then I should be able to handle my problems, which paled in comparison. However, I couldn't bridge that gap yet. I still felt alone, confused.

Chapter 26

DURING MY NORMAL MORNING ROUTINE at my locker, I felt a stare. Unnerved at first, my heart rested when I learned that it was Avery. He was beaming. He looked like he won the lottery.

"Good morning!" he said as chipper as ever.

"Good morning," I replied, with a genuine smile. "To what do I owe this visit?" I asked playfully.

"I couldn't wait to see you!"

"You are too much," I tittered.

He raised his eyebrows up and down. "Too much that you won't kiss me?" he gambled.

"Since when do you ask?" I giggled. He kissed me on the cheek. "Is that the best you can do?" I smirked, not knowing what possessed me to unloose my chains.

Avery leaned in to kiss me and said, "Well, in that case . . ." he brushed my hair away and caressed my lips with his. I could barely concentrate to get my necessary books for the beginning of the day. I floated, truly lighter, to homeroom. That's a real thing. Jane Austen was right. We agreed to meet at the cafeteria again after school.

I walked toward algebra class, when Creepoid snuck up from behind me. He growled directly in my ear dripping with evil disdain, "So, Loser, where's Golden Boy?"

The hair on my neck stood on end. "Relax! I haven't said a word!" I gritted through my teeth, not even bothering to turn my head. I wanted to say, 'Get the hell away from me!' but thought better of it.

"You're dead meat if you do, *bitch!*" he ferociously threatened millimeters from my face, emphasizing the word 'bitch.' I winced at the smell of his rancid breath and shuddered.

"Get away from me!" I yelled uncontrollably, finding my voice. It came out louder than I expected, and everyone in the hall stopped to see the commotion, as I was walking into the classroom.

All eyes were on me. My heart beat with rage and my face burned with embarrassment. Ms. Chandler approached, "Is there a problem?" She searched my face for a clue.

Creepoid raped me and threatened that if I told anyone he would kill me and my boyfriend. Does that constitute a problem?

"No problem," Paul inserted. Ms. Chandler waited for my response.

"Mm—mm," I shook my head. After studying us for a second, she moved on. Feeling the eyes follow me, I took my seat and looked downward.

"Okay, class, it's time to rotate. Those of you in front, move to the back. The rest of you move forward." I moved to the back of the row. The rest of the period flew by, without me paying attention to one word.

Although a few classes came and went, I was still a bit shaken from the early morning verbal altercation. I hoped gym would take my mind off of Creepoid. While I was changing into my gym clothes in the ladies' locker room, Katie bounced up and told me she heard that I was back with Avery. Locker doors slammed shut. "Yup, you heard right," I told her with confidence, pep, and sheer happiness. Thinking of Avery improved my mood.

"So, what about your parents?" Katie asked.

"They don't know. I'm holding my breath. It's nerve-racking." At least that part was true. I shut my locker.

"You're going out with Avery, right? As in Avery Evans?!" Faith asked in disbelief, leaving no breath in her lungs. "When did this happen?" she asked, seemingly disgusted for some unknown reason.

"Good question." I thought about the answer. "Recently," I teased, with a tilt of my head and a shrug of my shoulders. By then, we were sitting in our rows on the gym floor.

Mrs. Hartzel announced that, due to the beautiful weather, we would be going outside for gym class to play flag football with the boys. There was a lot of murmuring, because this was the first time we combined classes, and the tension between the sexes was evident.

"Come on, ladies, hustle!" Mrs. Hartzel yelled.

"Hey, there's Avery," Katie pointed out. "There, on the field." I followed the direction of her finger.

"I can't believe you didn't tell me you were going out with Avery," Faith said incredulously, nudging my ribs. "Faith, I told you, it just happened, as in today."

"That's not what I heard," Katie alleged.

"What did you hear?" Faith asked.

"I heard that you two were making out in the caf yesterday after school," Katie purported.

I felt embarrassed by the accusation. "We were not making out," I declared, defending my reputation. Faith shot me a dirty look, communicating that she doubted me, so I staunchly asserted, "I swear. We weren't making out. Katie's sources are wrong."

"Since when do you swear? You don't even believe in God," Faith questioned.

"Just a figure of speech," I quietly replied.

"Now you're swearing and making out in public," Faith shook her head in disapproval. At that very moment, she reminded me of Sister Mary Margaret, the critical penguin with perfect grammar.

"Ladies! Stop chattering and play ball!" our teacher yelled over the ruckus of the classes and through the breeze.

Avery swaggered in my direction. As luck would have it, we were on the same team. "Hey, Christina, I didn't know we had gym at the same time," he stated flirtatiously.

"Me neither." He ran toward our opponent and stole one of his flags. "Nice move!" I praised.

"Hey, thanks!" He smiled.

I tried to steal flags from our opponents, but I wasn't quick enough. I figuratively patted myself on the back for trying. I paused to soak in the beautiful weather and fresh air, here and there, when I could. *Boy, how I love this.* Gym was definitely a positive distraction that assuaged my anxiety, albeit temporarily.

Avery kept an eye on me, yet managed to play a good game, while I simply worked up a sweat running in, what felt like, circles. The other girls had about as much success as I did. The whistle blew signaling that class was over.

"What class do you have next?" he whispered, as he jogged by. *He can even jog with a swagger.* I found myself whistling at him, before I even consciously decided to.

"Lunch," I answered, with a smile large enough to be seen from Mars.

"Me too. I can't believe we've had lunch together this entire time. I'll see you then!"

"Uh . . ." I hesitated, "I'll see you later." I didn't plan on seeing him at lunch, as I figured he sat on the popular side, which would explain why we never ran into each other.

"Oh, I almost forgot," Katie informed me, out of breath, from running to catch up with me, "I heard about your run-in with Paul Martin in math class." *Jeez, you hear all the scoops.*

"What run in?" Faith asked, as soon as she caught up with us. *Does she like Creepoid?*

"Oh, it was nothing," I said dismissively. *I don't want to relive it. Please drop it.*

"Nothing?!" Katie raised her voice. "Are you kidding me? I heard you screamed at Paul to get away from you at the top of your lungs."

"That would be true," I admitted, saying each word at half-speed to give myself time to create a logical reason for yelling at Creepoid.

"Why did you yell at him?" Faith quizzed with no sign of empathy.

I found myself walking slower, as if my mind needed that energy to produce an answer for these two, and quickly. "Hmm . . . because he was bothering me! He keeps staring at me. It's agitating. He gives me the creeps," I attested, fists clenched. Quite naturally, my pace quickened as I spoke.

"Maybe he likes you," Faith offered. It was a valid supposition, but somehow, I felt accused and not reassured. *She doesn't mean it that way. No, she's too sweet. Isn't she? Now, I'm second guessing Faith.*

"Noooo, he doesn't," I insisted, after considering her words for a moment. A moment was all I needed to give them. "Trust me, he does not. No way. No how." I stressed, ready to punch a wall.

"You and Avery," Faith said, switching topics abruptly, and ignoring my obvious frustration and obvious moment to be a consoling friend, "Who would've thunk?" she considered, shaking her head dubiously . . .

"Well, it's not too far-fetched. We went out for a fleeting moment this summer," I replied, still sounding angry. *I think she's insulted me three times, and ignored me just as many, but who's counting?*

"That's what I heard, but I didn't believe it," she confessed, "and I felt rather insulted." Katie and I shared a confused look.

Oh, this is about your hurt feelings, not my fear for my safety. Why didn't you say so in the first place, Faith? What in the world has come over you? We crested the hill and entered the school. "Why not?" I investigated minimally, hiding a subcutaneous boil, which was a risky move, as I might have bubbled over a nice steam of anger that she was clearly unprepared to wear to lunch.

"I thought it was a rumor. I figured you would have told me," she said, holding the locker room door for us.

"Oh," I began to reply, my anger lessening a bit. I might understand her feeling left out of things, "I would have, but I didn't see you all summer and it was over way before school even began." I snapped my fingers to emphasize the fleeting moment. "I didn't see any point in mentioning it." I swapped my gym shirt out for my magenta top.

"Christina, it was worth mentioning. I feel like a fool now for telling people that it wasn't possible that you two got together." She said this, hanging her head like a toddler might when denied ice cream or candy. I failed to understand this feeling she had, and I had too many of my own to sort through. I was overwhelmed.

"Faith, I didn't tell you because I was still upset from the whole thing. It hurt too much to even think about it." That was the truth, as much as I could share of it.

"I can vouch for that," Katie chimed in. She was becoming a dear friend to me.

"So, am I forgiven?" I asked with a softer, sweeter tone. I think the sweetness from Katie helped me be gentler with Faith in that moment. I faked some of my kindness—and need for forgiveness too—assuming it was the best thing to do to help us all move forward.

"Forgiven," Faith answered, with a satisfied smile.

Avery was hovering and scanning the cafeteria. Having been able to get close to him unnoticed, I was able to catch Avery off guard thus startling him by tapping on his left shoulder, "Looking for someone?"

He jumped. "Oh, hey! Whew, man, how'd you sneak up on me like that?"

"I'm better at this than flag football, so it seems." He brought out my happiness, and thus, my silliness.

"Yeah," he replied with a smile. "Glad we were on the same team. I thought we could eat lunch together. What do you think?"

"Ah, I don't know. I don't usually dump my friends like that." I hated to miss an opportunity to spend time with him, though nervous about it too, but hated to hurt my friends more.

"Well, I could sit with you at your table," he said raising his eyebrows.

"You and a bunch of girls? I don't think so," I replied, vehemently shaking my head.

"Why not? You hung out with the guys yesterday."

"True, and it was awkward for me," I admitted. "What? I didn't realize. You seemed fine."

"It was okay." Lunch always went by so quickly, I didn't want to spend the time talking about it, especially when I was carrying a load of books that were feeling heavier as each second passed. "I'll meet you later, after school—just you and me. How about that?" I suggested.

"Promise?"

"Promise," I affirmed.

My relationship with Avery was the talk of the lunch table. It was almost surreal. The girls couldn't believe I gave up eating with Avery to sit with them, including Faith. At least I had them on record for saying that, for future references. You need that with your friends, for the moment they flake.

I really enjoyed spending time with him. I felt safer. Happier. I smiled just thinking about him. I finished eating my childhood favorite sandwich, peanut butter and jelly, and quickly scanned the table. On impulse, I announced, "Since nobody minds if I eat elsewhere, I'll catch you all later . . ."

"You don't have the guts to do that," Faith taunted. I thought it was just her way of dissuading me from sitting with them.

"Watch me." *Oh, I am getting my voice back. Perhaps a new one. A bigger one.* I grabbed my books and my Chips Ahoy! chocolate chip cookies and left. I couldn't believe what I was doing.

The serving lines separated the two lunch rooms, so this was an effort. Plus, to find him—that might prove excruciatingly difficult and somewhat embarrassing. I nearly backed out and turned around, but there he was, where we met yesterday, waiving me over.

"Christina, over here!" he shouted. I think they heard him in Beijing. My face flushed. I walked over and the guys made room for me to sit next to him. Everyone was gracious.

"So, what made you change your mind?" Avery asked.

"It was sort of a dare," I answered, as I plopped down on the hard, plastic, backless seat.

"Are we really that scary?" Joey said, before stuffing his face with a huge bite of his bologna sandwich. He chewed and a dab of mayo could be seen on his bottom lip.

"Well, yes and no," I hedged, and started eating my chocolate chip cookies.

"What do you mean by that?" Peter inquired, after taking a sip of his chocolate milk.

"You guys aren't scary per se, but it is intimidating coming over to this side of the lunch room . . ." Instantly, I had to think of a good reason why, " . . . because I've been so used to eating on the other side." *Lame! I'm a goof!* I tried to distract them from my nerdy reply by taking a swig of water.

Undeterred by my lack of wit, Avery declared, "Looks like you won the dare," and he put his arm around my shoulder and gave me a quick squeeze. *Phew! Crisis averted.*

"Yeah, how 'bout it?" I affirmed with a smile, as he drew me closer. We spoke for a few more minutes until it was time for fifth period. Everyone stood up to leave.

"I'll meet you here after school then . . . okay?" Avery stood up as he kissed me. Once again, I was magically transformed. I needed a moment to recover. I lost sense of time for a second or two. "Christina, I said I'll meet you here after school, okay?" he repeated.

"Oh, yeah, uh-huh. I'll see you after school." Suddenly, I remembered I had to get to class, and floated away . . .

Anxious to see Avery, I counted the minutes until school let out. I darted out of geography, weaved through the maze of people in the halls, arrived at my locker to switch out my books, and then headed to the caf as fast as I could without running. As usual, Avery stood there alone, looking as irresistible as ever. *How did he get here before me?*

He called me over, we kissed, and all was right with the world. "Wanna go for a walk?" he asked.

"You read my mind," I said. "Lead the way." We meandered, hand in hand, like we did that starlit summer night after the pageant. We found a secluded spot under a tree. "How did you find this place?" I asked, putting my purple backpack down on the ground.

"Oh, just lucky, I guess," he said slowly. Something was on his mind. I was mesmerized with him. He wrapped his arms around my waist, so I wrapped my arms around his. We started to kiss. His lips were very soft and gentle, yet I felt electrified. "I've been waiting for months to kiss you like that," he shared in a sultry voice.

"So, what took you so long?" I laughed. "Just kidding!"

"Sit down. I want to talk to you about something," he said in a serious manner.

"Okay," feeling both curious and anxious. We sat down under the tree. I sat Indian style. Avery leaned in, with both legs bent at the knee, with his feet flush to the ground. His elbows rested at his knees, his hands clasped.

"I heard you yelled at Paul Martin today in math class," he stated, in a concerned tone. At least someone cared, unlike Faith, who made me out to be the bad guy.

"Yeah, I did," I admitted.

"Why? What happened?" Avery asked tenderly.

"He keeps giving me evil looks," I told Avery the truth, but not the whole truth. I hugged my knees close to my chest.

"Yeah, I noticed that too. Like at his house the night of the pageant, then the next day when I took you home. He seemed pissed off for some reason, like he was mad at you. Did something happen between you two?" Avery delved deeper. *That would be an understatement.*

"No," I lied. I didn't think it was prudent to tell Avery the truth about the unspeakable. I feared he would reject me because of what happened. I couldn't take that chance. Not to mention, I cherished our lives.

"That doesn't make any sense. Joey told me that Paul stares at you in class and you have no idea why."

"Nope, none," pursing my lips together, as if clueless.

"Are you sure?" Avery pressed.

"Why are you so concerned about this?"

"Because that a-hole is messing with my girl. That's why!" Avery exclaimed. *My girl. I like the sound of that.*

"Avery, just let it go. Maybe he'll back off now."

"And what if he doesn't? I can't stand around while that jackass torments you."

Then I got an idea. *What if Avery threatens Creepoid to leave me alone?* This having nothing to do with the unspeakable act. Just that Creepoid had been making an ass out of himself and people have noticed. *I tell Creepoid that he better stop threatening me or he will get his butt kicked.* Guys hated to be beaten up, according to my brother. In fact, my brother was never beaten up, but the possibility terrified him. *Avery could take Creepoid, not that I want him to fight, but Avery would be a threat to him.* My head was spinning for sure while considering this scenario.

"Christina, you okay?" Avery asked.

"Yeah, just thinking." The wind was taking hold of my hair, so I pushed it back behind my ears.

"About what?"

"About why he's psycho towards me."

"Do you think you know?"

"Maybe." I bit my bottom lip. "I heard that Mrs. Martin went to a psych ward for about week due to an emotional or mental breakdown. Something to do with the pageant," I planted.

He nodded, "Yeah, I heard something about that."

"Well, people accused Mrs. Martin of rigging the pageant because they thought that I should have won. I know it's crazy. Like, who cares about a stupid little poolside pageant?" I shook my head and rolled my eyes. I could vaguely hear students clamoring in the distance yet felt confident that no one else could possibly overhear our conversation.

"Are you saying that Paul is taking this out on you?" *Don't say his name!*

"Bingo."

"That's crazy!"

"I know, but it seems to fit. He started acting angry and nutty the night of the pageant. You remember the evil stares, right? Well, he didn't act like that before the pageant."

"Ooh . . ."

"Plus, Katie told me that some official looking people at the pool were asking her questions about me regarding the pageant. They wanted to ask me questions, but no one ever contacted me. We think it's because my mom told them to get lost. They can't question a minor without parental consent, I guess."

"All this for a pageant!" Avery exclaimed. "I know, crazy, huh?"

"Well, they are right, you know," he said. "Who? About what?"

"The people who thought you should have won. I am one of them!" he declared with a glint in his eye.

I smiled a shy smile, "I wish I never agreed to do that stupid pageant in the first place." I put my head down.

Avery gently lifted my chin. "If you didn't do it, we might not be together," he pointed out. I laughed, because he was probably right. He lay back on the ground and pulled me down with him. We kissed. Then Avery leaned forward. "I oughta kick his ass."

"Whatever you do, do it publicly and off school grounds," I paused. "Just in case he goes ballistic. You don't want to get suspended," I said lightheartedly.

"Yeah, right," he agreed. Then the light bulb went off. "You want me to beat him up, don't you?"

"I want him to leave me alone," I corrected. *But, yes, now that you mentioned it, I would love it if you gave him what's coming to him without you getting injured.* "But," I cringed. "I don't want you to get hurt. I would feel terribly guilty if you got hurt."

"I'm flattered."

"You should be," I nudged him flirtatiously. We kissed for a minute, as if nothing else mattered, even in my completely messed up world.

"Hmm, I think I missed my bus," Avery assumed.

"Oh," I cracked up, "sorry!"

"No, you're not."

"You're right, I'm not. At all. I'm actually glad," I managed to say, in between chuckles. He joined me, as we rolled on the ground with laughter. I enjoyed making him laugh.

"Do you want to go to The Manor with me?" I asked.

"I don't know." He paused. "Do you have to go to the old folks' home?"

"No, not really. Why?"

"Why don't I walk you home?" He paused. "I can drop you off before your house, if you're worried about your mom seeing us together."

"I suppose I could. Okay, let's go!"

"Hey, what's the hurry? We don't have to go yet."

"Oh, right. Don't you need to call your mom first to let her know that you'll be home late?"

"Nah, as long as I'm home in time for dinner, it's cool."

"Oh, okay."

"So, I guess we have plenty of time to kill," he figured. *That wouldn't be my choice of words exactly.*

"What did you have in mind?" I asked.

"This," and he kissed me tenderly, yet passionately. We stopped for some air. "So, what should we do about Paul?"

"You mean Creepoid?"

Avery cackled at the nickname. "Yeah, him."

"I don't have a clue. What do you think?"

"I'm going to tell him to leave you alone, or else. I will let him know that I have eyes and ears in the school, so I will know if he's staring at you, much less harassing you."

"Sounds like a plan . . . ," I paused. "Except, he lives on my street too, remember?"

"He'll get the picture," he said confidently, with a nod.

"Since when are you such a tough guy?" I inquired. I had a right to know after all.

"Since now. Ever since I found out my girlfriend is being harassed." I smiled. I loved the fact that he said girlfriend. *Girlfriend.* "What?"

"Nothing," I blushed.

"You're looking at me funny."

"No, I'm not." At least I didn't think I was, but I couldn't help it.

"Yes, you are. Spill it," he teased.

"Okay, okay," I hesitated. "I . . . I like how you called me your girlfriend," I confessed, grinning.

"Oh, that. Well, you are, aren't you?"

"Yes, it's just that I'm not used to being someone's girlfriend."

He cocked an eyebrow. "Seriously? You never had a boyfriend?" Avery leaned on his elbow.

"No, never."

"Wow!" Avery stated, apparently astonished.

"Is that a bad wow or a good wow?" I was curious. "I'm just surprised. Do you have any idea how many guys would love to go out with you?"

"Seriously?" I toyed with him.

"Yes, seriously."

"You *have* to be kidding."

"No, I'm not."

"Then how come I don't know about them?" I claimed ignorance. Keeping up the pretense.

"Christina, *everyone* knows you turn down guys all the time."

"They do?" *This is news to me.*

"Yeah!"

"But I don't tell anyone," I stated innocently.

"You don't, but they do."

"Why would they . . . ?"

Avery cut in, shrugging his shoulders, "Embarrass themselves like that? Good question. I don't know." "So why did you... . . . ?"

"You mean, why did I take a chance on you?" He read my mind. Again.

"Yeah, why?"

"Because," he hesitated, "I couldn't help myself. You looked so great in your bathing suit!"

"Get out of here!" I shoved him playfully.

Avery's arm collapsed beneath him. He righted himself and rested his elbows on bent knees. "No, I won't," he kidded. "I never saw you in your bathing suit before. I was mesmerized." He literally said mesmerized. He could understand how I felt about him then. "I figured it was worth a shot. That I couldn't do any worse than I did the time I asked you to dance."

"Oh, you remember that?" I cringed and bit my lip.

"Yeah, you ran away. I tried to find you, but you disappeared."

"Oh, my gosh! That's right! I ran outside," I exclaimed, putting my hand over my mouth, as I recalled the memory.

Avery's eyes pleaded with mine. "Why didn't you want to dance with me?"

"Because you were going out with Amanda."

"That's just it: we weren't going out," he said flatly. "You weren't?" I asked, puzzled.

"No, I know people thought we were. Amanda's sidekick made it seem like that, but we weren't going together."

I tilted my head and squinted my eyes, "Then why did you go to the dance with her?"

"I didn't," he shook his head.

I turned my head slightly, "I thought I saw you with her."

"You may have, but we didn't go to the dance together."

"I remember hearing that you two were each other's dates."

"Oh, I believe you. You see, Amanda and I did go out for a very short time."

"Why did you break up?"

"Because there wasn't any chemistry. We were friends after that. That's it," he gave a dismissive wave.

"Ohhhh!" *That's it! That explains why I never saw you two being affectionate with each other.*

"You're giving me another funny look," Avery informed me.

"This entire time I thought you two were this big item last year and you weren't. I wondered why I never saw you two all cuddly and stuff."

"Oh, that. Well, we were only in middle school for one. Secondly, Amanda was against any public displays of affection. She also didn't talk much. Again, no chemistry," he shrugged.

"I've never been big on public displays of affection either," I apprised him.

"You could've fooled me!" he hooted.

"What? I'm not . . ."

Avery chimed in, "Christina, you act like no one else is around when we are together. Like you don't care what anyone thinks."

"I do?" I questioned, incredulously.

"Yeah, you seem so cool and confident."

"I do?" I repeated in disbelief.

"Yes! You do!" Avery exclaimed. This conversation had a familiar ring to it. "That's what's so cool about you."

"Okay, but just for the record, no making out in front of an audience," I avowed. Avery smiled. "What? I'm serious!" I smiled back, hitting him on the leg.

"Alright, I get it." He offered me a comforting hug and ended with a sigh.

"What?"

"It's just that you give off cues on what you want me to do," he enlightened me.

"I do? Really?"

"Yeah, you do. Maybe they're subconscious, but I sense how you want to proceed." *How interesting.*

I praised him with a wink and a pointed finger, "Darn you're good."

"Actually, we have a good connection, but I do think you might confuse the heck out of someone else though."

"I think you're right. I must confess that." We shared a good laugh.

Avery stood up. "It's getting late. I think I better walk you home."

Avery helped me up by lending his outstretched arm.

We both started laughing for no apparent reason and then, like a good romantic comedy, gazed into each other's eyes and kissed again. It was long. It was sumptuous—and it was heavenly.

"Your kisses," I shook my head, smiling, reliving the sensation. Avery looked tenderly into my eyes. Then I continued, "they blow me away!" I stated breathlessly.

"You have the same effect on me, but . . . ," his voice faded.

"But, what?" I asked curiously. By then we were walking with our hands entwined together.

"I . . . ," he suddenly stopped talking.

"You, what?" I questioned, frantically, wondering if I did something wrong.

"I can't get enough of you," Avery admitted, turning his body to face me. He seemed almost exasperated. Like there was something he was hiding or frustrated about. My heart was racing, as I felt exactly the same way. "I really like you, Christina." By this time, we were walking in the woods. We stopped and kissed each other. It was very endearing and romantic.

My French lessons infiltrated my thoughts, my speech. "Je t'adore. Avery, I adore you." We continued to walk, holding each other's hands, talking about anything and everything. It was sunny and about seventy-five degrees. The air was fresh; the azure sky, cloudless.

We continued to walk toward my house, when we both spotted Creepoid riding his bike. I started to judder.

"Christina, I know, I see him too. I'm going to talk to him." I squeezed Avery's hand, unintentionally, after Creepoid shot me one of his wicked looks. "It's okay. I'll handle it." Avery gently squeezed my hand, reassuring me that everything would be fine.

"Avery, please be careful." I nervously put my hand over my mouth.

"Christina, he's right in front of your house. What about your mom? Aren't you worried she will see us together?"

"Right now, I'm more concerned about what's going to happen between you and . . . ," my voice disappeared as I couldn't say Creepoid's name, but Avery knew exactly what I meant.

"Maybe, you should go inside," he suggested.

"No!" I raised my voice, quivering. "I'm sorry, Avery, but he really scares me." We stopped walking. My chest felt tight.

"Christina, I know he does. That's why I want to put an end to this."

"What are you going to do?" I asked, breathless and afraid.

"I don't know yet. Just follow my lead. Okay?"

"Okay," I replied weakly. Together, we walked toward Creepoid. He shot daggers at us with his eyes. "Slumming again, Avery?" the jack intimated, as he threw another dagger at me.

"What's your problem, Paul?" Avery confronted him.

Me? I don't have a problem." *Yeah, right?!*

"You seem to have a problem with Christina and it needs to end. It's time for you to leave her alone," Avery demanded.

"And what are you going to do about it if I don't?" Creepoid provoked.

My heart hammered out of my chest.

"You really have to ask?" Avery stood his ground fearlessly. *Go Avery!*

The jack taunted, "I thought you had better taste in dogs, Avery." *He called me a dog! That jackalope coward!*

"Okay!" Avery swung hard—I mean really hard and slugged Creepoid square in the face.

BAM!

He didn't see it coming; we heard the smack of Avery's fist to Creepoid's face. The jack screamed in agony, then held his nose. Blood streamed through his fingers and down his chin. He glanced at his hands.

"I think you broke my nose!" the jack blubbered. He desperately attempted to gain his composure, but it was obvious he was shaken. Avery shook out his swinging hand, cuffed it and massaged it with the other. *One shot. That's all it took? That's my guy!*

I sensed Creepoid was trying to figure out if I told Avery what really happened, so I shook my head when Avery wasn't looking in my direction. This appeared to settle the jack down quite a bit.

"If you stay out of my business, I'll stay out of yours," he weakly bargained, hunched over, dripping in blood.

"I want you to leave Christina alone! Stop harassing her! Stop staring at her! In fact, don't even look at her! Got it?!" Avery shouted with a massive amount of authority. Creep—the jack—nodded.

"If you so much as look in her direction, we'll have words—and you won't like it!" Avery threatened.

"Yeah, I got it. I got it." Creepoid said, utterly humiliated.

"That includes math class. Don't mess with her. You mess with her, you mess with me. Now get away from her house! Don't ever be around here either!" Avery commanded. *My hero!*

The jackalope left, defeated, his tail between his legs.

Chapter 27

THE NEXT DAY AVERY WAS waiting for me at my locker. He was flipping through a notebook to pass the time. "Good morning!" he beamed when he saw me.

"You're so chipper this morning. You must sleep soundly," I smiled, as I took my heavy backpack off my shoulder and placed it on the floor.

He replied, his face joyful, "Like a baby."

"Lucky you," I said with a half-sigh, half-yawn.

"Don't you sleep well?" he inquired.

"No, not really—not lately anyway." I was still having nightmares on a regular basis, but perhaps that will change. I hoped.

"That's too bad," he stated in a sincere tone.

"No, biggie. I'm used to it." Avery held out his hand, which reminded me that he hurt it.

"How's your hand?" I asked, gently taking it in mine.

"A-okay. Thanks. It doesn't hurt anymore." I latched onto his other hand, recalling our public display of affection conversation the day before, noticing he preceded with caution. His neglecting to kiss me created a void, so I kissed him. Avery shot me a confused look at first, but after a moment of contemplation, he leaned in close enough to kiss me, but instead whispered, "I thought you didn't like public displays of affection."

Motionless, I softly replied, "I said 'I didn't want to make out in public.' If the display isn't over the top, I am good with it."

"Oh," he moved a hair closer for effect and uttered, "this should be an interesting journey."

Resisting the temptation to kiss him, I whispered with playful allure, "If you weren't so adorable, it wouldn't be such a problem."

"Ooooh, so it's my fault now," he teased, almost too softly to hear, and so close I could feel his breath tingling on my neck sending blissful shivers down my spine.

"Yes . . . it . . . is. It most certainly is," I blushed. I grabbed what I needed out of my locker and we walked holding hands to homeroom. We listened to the announcements as I watched Miss Intellect put on her makeup. Lucky for her, she didn't need much to enhance her natural beauty.

Buzz.

Avery and I collected our books and stood up. "Time for class," he stated, as he lightly pressed his cheek to mine. "I'll see you at lunch—and, oh," he imparted with a wink as he met me eye to eye, "I got your back, Christina." *Oh my gosh, I'm in Casablanca.*

So far it was true—he did have my back. Creepoid avoided me the entire first period and now had his own problems with which to deal—the chatter regarding his two black eyes and bruised nose.

Joey affirmed me with a polite nod and turned away. I guess he knows. And I, finally without much effort, was able to concentrate on the entire math lesson.

Faith fired a million questions and comments at me during art. With a twinge of disapproval, she launched, "I can't believe you left like that during lunch yesterday. Was it worth it?"

"Yeah, I think so," I reacted, before fully processing her question. The mere thought of Avery tempted me to daydream as I was getting out my drawing.

"Are you going to eat with Avery from now on?"

As I took pencil to paper, I relayed, "Oh, jeez, I don't know. Maybe. It was definitely fun."

"I thought you weren't allowed to date," Faith countered, with a bite that I didn't understand, as she stared at her art project.

"My parents don't know." I furrowed my brow.

"So," she alleged, drawing out her words sort of like a teacher aiming to highlight a point they want the students to remember, "you are lying to them?" It was Sister Mary Margaret all over again. *Will Faith correct my grammar next?*

"I haven't lied to them yet, technically," I quipped, with a bit of teenage snarkiness.

"Christina, it's a lie of omission. Fess up—you are lying," she retorted, emphasizing each syllable. Faith was a devout Catholic. *Is a lie of omission a Catholic thing?*

Truly perplexed and annoyed, I asserted with a raised voice, "Why are you giving me such a hard time?" I slammed my pencil on the table for emphasis. I didn't know such behavior was in me.

"I'm not," Faith relayed, in a matter-of-fact manner, as she shrugged her shoulders and flagrantly dismissed me with her hands.

"Yes, you are," I insisted. "You really are." I was feeling more agitated with each sentence that disdainfully escaped her lips. I picked up my pencil and shot a quick glance around the room, hoping to find that no one noticed our loud disagreement. A few students were looking at us. No such luck there, though we escaped our teacher's discipline.

Exasperated, she blurted, "I guess I can't believe you didn't tell me any of this. You used to tell me everything!" She was pouting like a spoiled toddler.

"It's uncomfortable for me to talk about. That's all. It's *not* you." I tilted my head down, trying to get a handle on the drawing at hand, hoping the trying conversation would end.

"Why?" she asked curtly.

"I don't know. It just is," I relayed in staccato, revealing my frustration, without looking up.

Faith leaned forward over her artwork, stretched out her arms and insisted, "You do know why—tell me."

Wanting desperately for Faith to drop it, I asserted myself once more, "I don't want to make a big deal about it. That's all. I hate drama. I hate unnecessary attention. Look around, Faith. People will now make judgments about us."

"Telling me makes it a big deal?" she pressed undaunted.

Abruptly, I again put my pencil down but with control this time. I looked Faith square in the eye and shared, "I also don't want anyone—you—to feel like I'm rubbing it in their—your—face that I have a boyfriend and they don't. Maybe I will unintentionally make them sad or upset."

"What makes you think that I don't have a boyfriend?"

I raised my eyebrows and smirked, "Do you?"

"No, but you shouldn't assume that I don't," she confirmed flatly.

"Why is it okay for you not to confide in me, but I have to confide in you?" I questioned testily.

Emphatically, unapologetically, and quite boisterously, Faith declared, "Because that's the way it is."

"What sense does that make, Faith?"

All she could offer was a smug shrug. We didn't speak much after that. You could have cut the tension with a saw—a power saw at that—so I focused on my drawing.

I was too angry to bother to start a new conversation. It was just as well, as I was able to channel my anger-fueled energy into my art piece. I felt more and more distant from Faith by the second. *Why is she being so hostile?*

I couldn't wait to meet Avery for lunch. I surmised I wouldn't be missed by Faith.

———◆———

Avery was waiting for me at his table. The guys said, "Hi," as if our lunch ritual had been going on for years. *They are so nice.*

"Any problems today?" my boyfriend inquired, as he pulled his sandwich out of the plastic sandwich bag.

"Not really," I replied, with a scrunched face.

"That doesn't sound too convincing."

"Faith is acting strange," I grumbled, while opening my lunch bag.

"Strange, how?" Avery probed.

"She's badgering me with questions about you and isn't satisfied with any of my answers. She tells me that it's okay for her to be closed-mouth about her life, but that I need to tell her *everything about me and my life.* What's up with that?!" I flung my arms forward with my palms turned up and then clasped them together and continued, "I really don't understand why she is fussing about this."

"Girls!" Peter said with a major eye roll. Avery shot him a disapproving look.

"That's fine. He's right. It's a total waste of my time and energy. I don't get it." I shook my head. "She's never acted like this before," I said, before taking a sip of my water.

"Someone's jealous," Peter sang between chews.

"Well, maybe. She told me that she was mad because I never told her that we dated over the summer," I recapped.

"Why didn't you?" Joey asked. He stopped chewing and eyeballed me.

"In terms of this past summer, it was too upsetting to talk about, actually."

"Oh, you mean after you dumped Avery?" Peter jabbed. *Aren't you inquisitive and sensitive?*

"I didn't dump Avery," I shot back. Avery echoed the sentiment with me.

"Hey, give them a break," Joey inserted. "Your parents said you couldn't date, right?"

"Right!" Avery and I both replied together, which made us all pause and then burst with laughter.

"You two are scary together," Peter stated wide-eyed, flinching.

"Anyway, I didn't say anything to her about us. I'm not the type to go blabbing about my personal life. At moments, yes, and to friends, yes. But I don't talk just to talk—and I certainly don't write it in the sky or paint it on a billboard."

"You're not like that?" Peter questioned, giving me a side-ways glance.

"No, I really don't blab—not about things that actually matter or affect someone else," I replied, with the conviction of a judge about to rap her gavel giving her final judgement.

"Interesting," Joey said, slowly enunciating each syllable, with the contorted look of a mad scientist and his fingers intertwined and rubbing each other, like irritated snakes. He brought us all down with hilarity.

"Enough of me," I segued in much better spirits, "what else is happening at this table?"

"Joey likes Mindy," Peter blurted. Joey turned beet red.

Mindy ranked the most popular girl in our grade.

She was attractive, intelligent and athletic—the perfect package deal on paper. I was friends with her back in fourth grade, but I haven't hung out with her since.

"Oh, who doesn't?" I quipped, assuming all the guys were gaga for her, but also making sure they knew that the topic was safe to discuss with me.

"I don't. Never did," Avery averred.

"Good answer," I teased with a wink. "Is she dating anyone now?"

"I don't think so," Peter responded. Joey's face was still crimson.

"Don't all girls keep up on the dating scene?" Peter inquired.

Everyone's eyes were wide and peering my way, anxiously awaiting my profound analysis of my kind: the unpredictable, and often overly dramatic, female teenage population. I took a moment to smile at the thought that I was about to speak for all of us.

"I don't pay much attention to that kind of stuff, unless it's obvious. I mean it. I don't blab. Do you believe me now?" I directed my question to Peter.

"Yeah, I guess so," he replied. "You'd be the first and only girl to be like that ya know?"

"Yeah," I softly replied, nodding, "I do. And it can be a lonely place . . ."

Peter sat back, folded his arms, nodded and smiled approvingly. "Whaaat? Who knew Christina was so cool?" Peter affirmed, giving a lift to the mood.

"I did, of course, Peter," Avery joked, puffing out his chest, like a proud athlete awaiting a medal to be hung around his neck. Again, this created a volley of laughter.

"So, Joey, are you going to ask her out?" I was curious and tired of being on the hot seat.

"Are you kidding? I can't ask her out!" he thundered.

Surprised, but unintimidated by his remarkably loud and passionate response, I followed up, "Why not?" Joey was this cool kid, with somewhat of a bad boy reputation.

"Because it's Mindy," Joey whispered, lowering his head.

"So?" I returned.

"He's chicken," Peter declared, as he crumbled up his lunch bag.

"Wait. Scared? Why? You're cool; she'd be lucky if you did," I stated wholeheartedly.

"Because she's all that and I'm not," Joey stated, hanging his head. His hue was returning to its normal shade, but his demeanor screamed insecure.

"Whaaat? Who says you're not all that? What trash are you listening to?" I fired.

"I guess I did," Joey replied, submissively.

"Well, you should change your self-image then," I suggested, lightly thumping the table with the bottom of my closed fist.

"Just like that, huh?" Joey asked, as he snapped his fingers. I could tell that he was frustrated at my words, but that he was also considering them. Avery and Peter's heads turned left to right while they followed our verbal volley.

"Yeah, sure. You're a nice guy. And funny. Anyone can see that after a few minutes of hanging out with you," I assured him. A red hue reappeared on his face and he momentarily broke eye contact. He looked at his lunch. "Joey, if you really want to go out with her, then ask her out. If she says no, then it's her loss. If you still like her after a while, ask her out again. No big deal," I claimed. "What's that saying? 'The answer is always no if you don't ask, but if you do . . . ' Something like that."

"No big deal for you, because you don't have to worry about getting rejected," he countered defensively, firmly tossing his apple to his lunch bag.

"True, but you shouldn't worry so much about what other people think," I suggested. "Even if she does say 'no,' that doesn't mean that she doesn't like you."

"Heh? Now, you lost me," Joey said, shaking his head, as if to shake out this information that didn't seem logical to him.

"You lost me, too," Peter admitted.

I raised my eyebrows and pursed my lips in Avery's direction, pleading for assistance. I bit into my turkey sandwich.

"Yeah, Christina turned me down last year," Avery added to make my case.

"You did?" Joey asked. Avery and I looked at each other.

I nodded in affirmation. "Yes, I did," and took another bite of my sandwich.

"Why?" Joey asked, perplexed. What's that saying . . . ? *Girls want him and guys want to be him. Seems to fit.*

"Because I thought he was dating someone else," I replied, half chewing my food, with my hand covering my mouth. If Avery was willing to take the hit for being rejected by me, the least I could do is make a point that things are not always what they seem.

"Amanda, I bet," Peter guessed, with a pleased smirk on his face.

"Exactly," I answered, impressed with myself for proving my point.

"And here you are now," Peter said, gesturing with his hand at both Avery and me.

"And here we are now." I turned toward Avery. Our eyes met and danced in the affirmation that persistence can win out.

"But—there are many reasons that a girl will say no when she wants to say yes," I quickly added. They waited for me to continue. "Maybe they are not sure you are serious—that you are teasing them; making fun of them. Maybe they know that their friend has a crush on you and they are trying to be loyal, even though every part of them wants to go out with you. The sky is the limit and you won't know unless you ask, but I know that probably sounds like a bit of a reach for you." *Like a crow trying to fly with a condor.*

Joey leaned toward me and whispered, "Could you talk to Mindy for me?"

"I don't know if that's such a good idea. I haven't talked to Mindy in years," I replied.

The thought of talking to Mindy, at the very least, was not appealing. Mindy was fun and friendly back in fourth grade, but she morphed into this creature that I no longer recognized. Not only was she no longer nice, but she seemed to believe that she was a queen and the rest of us were her equerries. In addition to that, she seemed to think it was our honor to be blessed with such noteworthy positions.

"I just want you to get a feel for what she thinks about me," Joey said, with a bit of insecurity that I wasn't used to seeing in him. He munched on some chips while waiting for my response.

"Yeah, I get that. But I still think it's better if you ask her directly. I always appreciated that."

"Yeah, but we've already established that you're not the average chick," Peter argued, flattering me.

Wide eyed, I tilted my head forward toward Avery with my hands on my hips, and teased, "Did he call me a chick?" I paused for emphasis and repeated, "Did he call me a chick?"

"Yeah! Don't call my girlfriend a chick," Avery jested playfully, to which we all got in a good laugh.

Before the laughter fully ceased, Joey leaned toward me while speaking in a soft tone, keeping the question asked a second time between us, "So, can you talk to Mindy for me?"

"Okay, I'll talk to Mindy," I whispered back. "but, you know, she may not be honest with me either. Girls can be tight-lipped, especially with those outside their close circle of friends. Me approaching her is kind of random."

"She's in our geography class, Christina," Peter quietly reminded me.

Oh my gosh, you popular, cute guys need my help. I can't believe you are asking me. Talking is one thing. Inviting me into your lives is . . . wow. How did this happen? This is only my second time sitting here. You guys are adorable . . . and not so intimidating. I misjudged you.

"Oh, right," I replied, realizing I don't have an out. *Okay, I'll help him out. What am I getting myself into?*

"Avery, why aren't you in honors geography?" I asked, in an effort to change the subject, putting the pressure on someone other than myself.

Avery answered matter-of-factly, "I didn't get recommended."

"Apparently a lot of people didn't, because there's only one honors geography class."

"Christina, why are you in regular algebra?" Joey asked me. *I opened the door to that one.*

"Because, I didn't get recommended for honors."

"Yeah, but you don't seem to belong in our class. You're the smartest one in the class by far," Joey stated.

"It is kind of weird, but it's nice to be able to coast without any effort," I admitted.

"She means no offense," Avery assured Joey. Avery looked at me like I was being insensitive.

"Oh, of course not. Jeez, not at all, Joey," I apologized, not realizing prior to my response that it could seem insulting or arrogant to those who struggle with the subject.

"Are all your other classes honors?" Joey questioned.

"Yes," I said, drawing out the word, so that I had time to think, and—or—keep my mouth from uttering another insult by accident.

"Mine too," Peter said, "but we only have geography together."

The bell rang, interrupting the conversation, as was the case every day at lunch, and per the usual, we all jumped to attention and gathered our books.

"I'll meet you here after school," Avery said, with an added hopeful ring to his statement, which was music to my ears.

"See you then," we both exchanged, giving one another a quick kiss, like a married couple with a polished routine of habit, and departed.

———◆———

That little peck of a kiss will have to sustain me for nearly three hours. I wondered why I told Avery I didn't like public displays of affection. He was doing fine before I opened my big mouth. I made a mental note to clarify things even better later.

I waited to talk to Mindy after geography class, but she was arguing with someone, so I left. I asked Peter to tell Joey that it wasn't a good time for me to talk to her after that class and that I would do it when the timing was right—seemed right. *Is there a good time to do this?* I felt bad that Joey's nerves could not be eased today, but he'd have to wait.

Chapter 28

*A*VERY AND I MET AFTER school and sat under the tree. It was quickly becoming our tree.

He caressed my cheek and smoothed the hair away from my face. He leaned in, our eyes met and he kissed me. It was unhurried, gentle, and fabulous.

Time stood still and I was completely lost in the moment following his lead. It wasn't before long that we were lying on the grass adjacent to each other.

After a graceful shift of his body, Avery was straddling on top of me. He was careful not to crush me making sure I was comfortable. With reassurance, our lips collided, our tongues danced together. My arms clung loosely around his neck while his hands wandered, affectionately caressing most of my body.

Every now and again, Avery released sensual expressions that drowned out the cars driving in the distance.

"Ah, Christina!" he passionately murmured repeatedly.

Shifting to free myself from the cold, hard tree roots beneath me, I too shared in the audible utterances of sheer pleasure initiated by him. "Oh, Avery!" I exclaimed, staying in the here and now of our intimate moment together.

Kissing Avery was surreal. He made me feel safe, secure, adored. I was able to let my guard down, too, able to lose myself from the summer horror that still plagued my thoughts on a continual basis. Altering my mind to the present moment of bliss, our interlude continued to transform my mind and body for a treasured amount of time.

Abruptly, he paused. "Christina," he said, in a breathy voice that caught me off guard, but without alarming me. After an intentional delay, he cupped his hands around my face and gazed into my eyes.

I could tell he wanted me to really hear him. He declared in a sultry tone, "Christina, I love you!" I heard the words and I truly felt them.

Without hesitation, I responded automatically, "Oh, I love you too!"

However, an instant later, I questioned our professed love for each other. It seemed too soon. I panicked. I no longer felt safe, secure. I felt suffocated, like I couldn't breathe. Physically, my body promptly reacted by tensing up. I froze. I couldn't move. I felt paralyzed.

My abrupt statuesque like figure was, naturally, a cause of concern for Avery. "Christina, what's the matter?"

"I . . . umm, maybe we're moving too fast. I'm only thirteen." I felt like I was acting too grown up for someone who was barely a teenager. After all, I only recently changed my mindset to date and everything was happening so fast. It was simply too much, too soon.

As Avery glided off of me, he reacted surprised, "You are?"

Unsure of what he meant, I sat up, cocked my head and asked, "I am what?"

"Thirteen?" That's what he got out of my statement? *Goodness.*

"Yes, I turn fourteen in November." Saying it out loud made it even worse.

My gut told me that I was way too young to be in a serious relationship. I questioned my choices and doubted myself that perhaps I should have waited to date after all. It was all so complicated. So many thoughts and feelings flooded my mind. I tried to remain present with Avery. That seemed to ground me.

"What day?"

"The twentieth," I answered, a smidge deflated by his questions. *Is he avoiding the topic? This very serious topic.*

"Wow, I'm almost a year older than you," he said with an excitement that I didn't understand, but that was clearly genuine. "I turn fifteen February tenth."

I nodded, "I know. I remember. You have the same birthday as my brother." We were having this casual topic about birthdays, but my mind, in the background, stayed on more serious matters.

"Cool," he replied, calmly nodding his head. He said it sweetly, with a smile, and he shifted back into a Romeo sort of mood. His glittering blue eyes bore a hole into mine and it felt as though he was looking through me. I remained breathless and confused.

I loved being with Avery; I even think I loved him, but we needed to take things slower physically. Even though my virginity was stolen, I craved some sense of purity in my relationship. I still desired to wait to have sex until I got married, but if we continued like this, I didn't have a chance of that.

"I'm really sorry, Avery," I gasped, swallowing the tears from the deluge of mixed and confusing emotions that were suddenly in the forefront of my mind.

"Hey," he stated, with urgency, "what's wrong?" Then, in his next breath, he added some of his unique humor to release the tension, "Do you hate being only thirteen that much? It's really not that bad—this, too, shall pass."

"I can't do this," I shook my head in doubt and fear, followed by a shallow, nervous chuckle.

"Do what?" he asked, while gently using his index and middle fingers to raise my head so he could see the face I had been hiding.

"You know!" With my eyebrows raised, I stared at him with bulging eyes and nodded, like he should have known what I was talking about. My words dangled in the air while he searched his mind to unravel my code. At last, I saw his baby blues light up with comprehension.

"Ooooh, I don't expect you to have sex with me right here, right now."

"You don't?" I asked puzzled, although extremely relieved.

"No, I don't," he affirmed tenderly. "I think we should wait until we're both ready."

"Whew!" I sighed. "Avery, don't get me wrong. I absolutely love being with you. I'm just not ready to . . ."

"I know what you mean. Sometimes I think I should wait until I'm married. Crazy, huh?"

"No, not at all. That's how I feel!" I practically squealed with excitement. I reached out and squeezed him, releasing all my concerns.

After embracing, Avery clenched his hands around my upper arms, nodded, and looked straight into my eyes. "Then we should slow it down a bit," he concurred, as he soothingly rubbed his hands up and down my arms from my elbows to my shoulders. I was so comforted and elated that we shared the same views on sex, that I could barely contain myself.

"You are the best boyfriend ever!" I exclaimed and planted one on his lips.

"You can be so confusing," Avery shook his head, rolled his eyes, and laughed. He readjusted his sitting position and outstretched his legs.

"I don't mean to be," I said ardently. "I really, really don't."

"I know. I know. That's one of the many endearing things about you." He paused a moment to gather his thoughts. He panned the sky, left then right, and seemed to find answers in the clouds. "I know this is new for you Christina, but it's new for me, too."

"It is?" I tilted my head to listen closely. I wanted nothing to distract me from his explanation, from knowing him.

"Yeah, sure. This is the first time I had a girlfriend that I liked enough—felt close enough to even consider having sex with."

"So, you've considered having sex with me?" I don't know why I sounded so shocked. *Do guys think of anything else? Ever? How do they get any work done?*

"I'm not going to lie, but that doesn't mean I will, you know, go through with it." I stared blankly at him, not sure what he meant by that, as if to say I didn't get a choice in the matter. For some reason, I let it slide, as a moment of silence passed us by. With his head down, and while yanking out blades of grass, he shared, "I'm still a virgin, too." He assumed I was a virgin. Of course, I let that go uncorrected. I must have looked surprised. "What? You're surprised that I'm a virgin? Did I disappoint you?"

"Disappoint? No," I replied, shaking my head. "Quite the opposite. I'm relieved. It kind of takes the pressure off."

"So, you're okay with all of this?" Avery questioned, searching my eyes—my face, looking to see that they didn't contradict my words. He was very astute and thorough.

"Absolutely. I prefer it."

With a certain amount of conviction and finality, he exclaimed, "Good!"

However, I couldn't help but address one more weighty matter, before branching off to a much-needed lighter topic.

"Avery, I just need to say one more thing. I need to clarify something." I took a deep breath. "I made a mistake."

"I'm listening." He tilted his head slightly toward me to hear my confession.

"About public displays of affection . . ."

Avery stretched out the word, "Yes . . ." I could tell he thought trouble was coming and was bracing himself. He encouraged, "Go on."

There was a pause, as I gazed upward to formulate my thoughts. "I want to be able to kiss you longer than a peck on the lips. Like how we were together before I said anything. Except I don't want any more public makeout sessions like we had at the party that night we first got together—and how about not kissing me when adults are around? So, is that okay with you?" I exhaled.

"Umm, yeah, totally!" Avery said in agreement and I sat there relieved.

"Great! Then we're on the same page?" I asked, looking for any physical signs that could indict his face for betraying him.

"Absolutely!" After gazing into each other's eyes, we kissed. It was soft and tender. He then calmly broached the silence. "Christina, I have a favor to ask you." He shifted, nervously, and sat on his knees.

"Yeah," I waited patiently for him to find his courage and his words.

"Uh, don't tell the guys that I'm a virgin, okay?" Avery asked anxiously, running his fingers through his flaxen hair.

"Why not?" Even though I didn't understand his request, I felt like he needed to be heard.

"I never told them I wasn't, but I'd like to keep them guessing. I get that it could sound stupid to you," he added, "but, it kinda isn't to me, as dumb and ridiculous as that sounds."

With a warm smile and by resting my hand on his shoulder, I assured him by saying, "Your secret's safe with me."

"Ah, thank you. Very much," and he went back to sitting with his legs stretched out in front of him, his arms propping him up from behind. He seemed as relieved as me at that moment.

"Can you do me a favor too, in that vein?"

He looked my way for a moment, asking me to complete that thought with the tilt of his head. He then returned his sights to the woods.

"Can you keep our relationship private too? At the very least, don't tell your friends anything that isn't true or let on that something is true when it isn't?"

"You mean don't tell them we've had sex when we haven't," Avery summarized. He grabbed his knees and tittered. *He's sharp, this one. He really is.*

"Um, basically," I scrunched my nose while nodding my head.

"I think I can manage that," he said playfully, looking my way. Instinctively, I shot him a disapproving look for my dignity's sake, as I felt like I needed reassurance. "I won't say a word. I promise," he avowed with absolute conviction that steeled me.

"Thanks. I appreciate that."

The rest of the duration under our tree was spent mostly snuggling, intentionally keeping things between us much less intense. We talked about lighter subjects until the sun glowed less bright, telling us it was time to get home for dinner.

———◆———

We ambled through a somewhat dense, but small, patch of woods, holding hands on our journey home. The temperature was crisp and the sky clear for a late fall afternoon. Avery turned slightly to my right when he asked, "So I take it that your mom doesn't know about us?"

"No, I guess not. She didn't say anything." *Well, at least that wasn't a lie.*

"Would it be okay if I called you tonight? Maybe I could say I needed a homework assignment or something?" *My mom was supposed to go ballistic, if I dated anyone. How could I make a smooth transition out of this one?*

"For what, gym?" I retorted sarcastically, followed by a snigger. "I don't think that's a good idea," I advised, unable to find a transitional idea of any kind in that split-second. After meandering down the narrow path a few steps further, we came upon a clearing, when I asked him, "Do you lie to your parents a lot?"

"No, not really. I don't need to. You?" he volleyed. *Only in life or death circumstances.*

"No." I lied. So ironic. Up until the unmentionable I had no reason to lie.

Avery nodded toward me. "Hey, would you be able to call me?" He continued to gesture with his hand, "I mean, if that's okay with you, of course."

I hesitated, "Ah, I guess so." Expounding further to protect his feelings, I added, "I have a phone in my room. I can talk privately, but the walls are thin."

"Okay, I'll get the picture when you start whispering," he quipped, having a knack for humor and its timing. We laughed together. "You're looking at me funny again."

I hesitated and then tittered, "Oh, it's just that I never called a guy before."

"Never!" he exclaimed, quite shocked, which, I admit, was one hundred percent flattering.

"No, never!" I smirked, shaking my head. "I told you I never had a boyfriend and I was too afraid to even hang out with guys as friends."

"Why?" he asked, as if I had told him I was going to dye my hair hot pink.

"I'm not really sure; it's just how I've been. In some ways, I am old-fashioned I guess."

"What do you mean?" he asked, in a hushed voice having an instinct that it might lead to more intimate, hard to divulge information.

"Okay, but promise not to laugh." I turned to examine his face. I needed to determine if he was taking this seriously.

"I promise." he said, with sincerity. I waited. "I do. I promise," he insisted.

"Okay," I took a moment to gather my thoughts, and then I spoke with purpose, aiming to carefully select every word. "I had this notion that I should wait to have a boyfriend until I was closer to being ready to get married." I studied his response. No shock on his face. *Good.* That's reassuring.

My eyes searched upward to capture my private thoughts. "I thought that dating should be a courtship—old-fashioned, yes, I get that. Umm, therefore," I hesitated, rebooting my courage, "I figured that I was too young to date; I mean, I don't want to get married until after college, so dating made no sense."

Still, he was with me, and seemingly unruffled. *Wow!* "I kept boys away at arm's length . . . until this summer. Everything changed when we took that walk together. I threw away those old-fashioned ideas. I adopted a new set of ideas for me . . . for us . . . because you seemed worth it." It took some guts to share my last sentence. *Go, me.*

With an inquisitive expression on his face, Avery cocked his head in my direction, "How so? How did you change it?"

"Well, I still want to wait to have sex until I get married, but I figure I can date a little in the meantime, knowing it most likely won't lead to marriage." I sounded like a girl from the 1950s.

"Wow! Okay." I could see Avery inwardly processing my absurd views of dating.

I cringed, "Okay, now you're scaring me. Did I freak you out?"

"No, it's just very conservative thinking, that's all," He replied, in a forced casual tone.

I nodded with fervor. "I know. Oh, I definitely know that."

"Was it your parents' idea to wait to date?"

"No, I came up with the lame idea on my own. Like I said, I'm old-fashioned." *I belonged to the poodle skirt era, not the "Modern Girl" by Sheena Easton era.*

Avery's smile shined brightly, "The more I get to know you, the more fascinating you become."

"Yeah, right," I said sarcastically, playfully bumping into his left shoulder.

"No, really! It's like you are so sweet and sexy at the same time. You boggle my mind," Avery guffawed, shaking his head.

"In a good way I hope." I winced.

Avery asserted, "In a very good way. You're very intriguing. I'm honored that I was the one who changed your mind about the dating thing."

"You should be," I teased nudging him again.

I saw the wheels turning in his head. "So last year when I asked you to dance at the dance, you told the guys and me that it was because you thought I was at the dance with Amanda." There was a chill in the air that went right through me.

Trying to sound as diplomatic as possible, I embellished, "Right. I didn't want to hurt Amanda's feelings and I didn't think it was right for you to dance with someone else when you were spoken for. I didn't want to be the other girl, so to speak."

Avery probed, "What if you knew Amanda and I weren't together? What would you have done?"

Embarrassed, I covered face and giggled. "I think I would have said no because I was too terrified to date at that point. It wasn't anything personal."

After Avery contemplated his thoughts for a brief moment he said, "This makes me think that you should have a heart-to-heart discussion with your parents about your views on dating. They might respect it and trust you dating guys. They should know that you have a good head on your shoulders—that you won't let any boyfriend take advantage of you. It's such a relief for me to know what your stance is, because I can be true to myself now. We can hold each other accountable."

Confused, I asked, "What do you mean by 'hold each other accountable'?"

Avery let out a deep thoughtful sigh. "Well, you know, we can support each other, like, look out for each other. Make sure we are doing the right thing," Avery dithered. "Basically, make sure we don't have sex. Make sense?"

I beamed and threw my hands over my mouth. "Wow! Now you blew me away. I'm so glad we had this discussion. Yes, it makes sense." *Perfect sense.* "Maybe I can talk to my parents after all," I exclaimed with new excitement for this relationship and for this wonderful solution to my . . . lie. *This may work. What a perfect solution. Yes! Thank you, God!* I was starting to seriously reconsider the existence of God.

Avery slung his arm around my waist as we continued our journey toward my house. We remained silent for a while, yet the silence exuded an air of comfort. I sifted through our most recent conversations, since they were rather intense and revealing. I assumed Avery needed to do the same.

"Can you call me tonight if everything goes well with your parents?" he asked with anticipation.

I shrugged my shoulders and grimaced, "Uh-huh, if it's not too late."

"You can call as late as ten," he clarified, with certainty. I was surprised his parents would allow such a late phone call. I didn't even talk to my girlfriends after nine o'clock.

Needing reassurance, I turned to Avery and asked, "You're sure your parents won't mind me calling that late?" He cupped my hand into his and assured me with his ocean blues, "No, not at all." Then he nodded, with a confident smile. "It should be fine. Trust me."

"I do trust you." I grinned in return, and we continued to walk with our fingers intertwined.

Before we reached my house, he stopped unexpectedly and turned to me. "Christina, I will watch you from here and wait until you get inside. I don't want to jeopardize your chances of dating . . . me."

I smiled sweetly, "Thanks, for walking me home." Our youthful eyes united.

"Christina, whatever happens, remember, I will always love you!"

My heart thudded. Even though he said he loved me earlier, it surprised me to hear it again so soon afterward. With a natural ease that amazed even me, I replied softly, "I love you too, Avery."

Astonishingly, on this delightful day, no one was around, allowing us the freedom to part with a quick peck. I dashed the rest of the way home fueled by the comfort and knowledge that I was loved by my dream of a boyfriend, and that I no longer had to continue in the charade that I wasn't allowed to date. Now all I had to do was wait. The catchy jingle from the classic Heinz ketchup commercial lingered in memory as I anticipated the resolution.

———◆———

Since I didn't go to The Manor, I still had homework to do, so I decided to do it immediately, and breezed right through it, including the dreaded book report on a book I barely read.

As usual, dinner was uneventful. My brother's friend, Shawn, ate dinner with us. Again. They both left to have a catch in the backyard.

While my mom and I were in the kitchen alone, I casually addressed her as I loaded the dishwasher, "By the way, Mom, if a guy named Avery calls, let me talk to him, okay?"

"I thought you said that you didn't want to talk to him," she questioned, while scrubbing the last bit of spaghetti sauce that spilled on the stove.

"I do now. We had a misunderstanding," I clarified, "but we worked it out. It was my fault, really. I totally misjudged him."

"Oh. Do you expect him to call tonight?" She turned from the stove to face me, sponge in hand.

Feeling pressure from a very minor inquiry, I responded, "No, not tonight, but, yes, he will be calling sometime soon." I was not used to sharing much with my mom. It felt a bit awkward, to say the least.

My mom pressed, "Is that why you haven't been going to the retirement home?" *She does notice things.*

"Yeah. I've been spending time with him after school. He's a, umm, a good guy. He's different . . . it's been . . ." I was at a loss for the right word, ". . . great." *For a lack of a better word, but it gets the job done. Let's hear it for honors English class!*

"So, when do I get to meet him?" she asked, arms crossed, head tilted, looking straight at me. I knew right then that she meant business.

I wasn't expecting that response, but I suppose I should have. *Of course, she would want to meet him. Duh!* I replied, while wiping the table, "Ah, I don't know. Soon, maybe. You'll like him," *You'll think he's cute, too.*

I heard a distinct yell from the family room. My dad leaned forward on the couch and turned toward the kitchen.

"Pooch, did I hear that you have a boyfriend?" *Please don't let this be an actual problem.*

Turning to face my dad, "Ah, yeah, Dad," I answered. My response sounded more like a question.

My dad followed up, "What's his name?" *Play it cool.*

"Avery Evans," I replied flatly, trying to contain my delight in going out with him. I didn't want to appear like a pathetic love-sick teenager causing my parents to have concerns. Then they would really be up in my business and I couldn't chance that.

The door to the laundry room slammed shut. My bratty brother's sing-song voice could be heard from the hallway, "Christina has a boyfriend." Then, he bounded into the family room with his baseball and glove. He must have overheard our conversation; so much for privacy. *Oh, great. Here we go. That's all I need now. More grief from my annoying baby brother. Just ignore him. At least Shawn went home. Finally.*

Without missing a beat, my dad continued with the inquisition, "What grade is he in?"

"My grade. I've known him since fourth grade. We were in the top section together in middle school." What a welcoming change it was to be able to answer questions honestly.

"Oh, good, so he's intelligent. No idiots for my daughter," he winked and showed off his Chicklets with his affable grin.

"Yes, he's smart, Dad. I think you would like him." *How could he not?*

"So, when do we get to meet him?" my dad asked, working his way back to my mom's inquiry, in a not so demanding manner that I appreciated.

"Yeah, uh, I don't know. I don't want to scare him off. I don't want you two to intimidate him."

"You're not embarrassed by us, are you Christina?" my dad asked in jest, raising his eyebrows.

"No, it's just that we just started to hang out." I was trying to sound lighthearted and not give away the fact that I wanted this conversation to end. I wasn't ready to put my relationship with Avery on display for my family. Again, too much too soon.

"He's probably a nerd," Jared interjected before he headed upstairs, getting a good punch in before the buzzer.

I was in too good of a mood to let my brother spoil it for me, so I remained quiet, despite my temptation to scream at him. Instead, I merely glowered at him indicating I had enough of his sophomoric attitude. My grimace made him stop a few steps from being out of sight on the staircase. "Who would want to go out with you? Ewww, ser-i-ous-ly!" he taunted. He had the potential to be funny, but for all his effort on this night, he missed, for I refused to dignify a response.

"Alright, that's enough," my dad directed at my brother. "Get upstairs and do your homework." *Looks like I won that round.* Then he turned to me, "Well, I'd like to meet him whenever you're ready."

"You could invite him over to dinner," my mom added. "That might be nice, don't you think?"

"You really want him to eat with us?" I pressed. "You are serious?"

"Oh, Christina, don't be so silly," my mom replied, with a wave of her hand, "Of course, he can eat with us. Let me know what he likes."

"Let me ask him if he wants to." *Please don't let this be a big deal.* Until now, my mom minimally showed interest in my life.

"Let me know," my mom instructed. Then she joined my dad in the family room to watch *Entertainment Tonight,* leaving me to finish the dishes.

At last, after drying the pots, and desperate to sneak in some privacy, I seriously contemplated calling Avery. As I sat up in my bed, with one hand on the cradle of the phone, I started to dial with my other hand. I was a little apprehensive to call, as I never called a boy before. I never even considered calling a boy until today. I was so used to being on the other end—the one receiving the phone calls.

Bur-ring, bur-ring . . .

"Hello," Avery answered. A comforting sigh escaped from within when I recognized his voice. I saw him a few hours ago, yet nonetheless, I was flush with emotion.

"Avery, hi, it's Christina." *Whew! I was able to get the words out. That wasn't so bad.*

"Hey, Christina!" He exclaimed, with sheer excitement, and without hesitation, he eagerly asked, "Did you talk to your parents?"

"Yes, and we're cool!" I blurted with enthusiasm, like a toddler seeing Mickey Mouse for the first time in person at Walt Disney World.

"WAIT. You mean you're allowed to date now? Just like that?" He sounded beyond thrilled. Hearing his response was icing on the cake. I could only imagine his face with a big ol' toothy grin on it.

In the moment of triumph, I bounced on my bed and I squealed, "Yes, isn't that great!" I was such a cliché and I didn't care.

"Yeah, that's the best news I've heard in . . . *forever,*" he agreed. "Does this mean I can call you? Anytime?" he asked, encouraged.

"Sure, that won't be a problem. I checked. You are in the clear." *All systems go!*

"Do you have any restrictions?"

"Nothing unusual. At least none that I know of. They didn't say. In the end, they were kinda relaxed about the whole thing."

"I knew it would work out."

"What? No, you didn't," I protested, arms crossed as if he was in the room to see my cute protesting stance.

"It just had to work out," he stated, with the conviction of Reverend Joe Simms.

"If you couldn't get through to your parents, I was going to talk to them myself," he declared. "And I believe that I could have persuaded them in five sentences or less."

I howled with laughter to the point that my stomach hurt. His comment made me completely forget that I was aiming for temporary anonymity. "You're kidding, right?" and I giggled some more. *He wouldn't, would he?*

"No, I'm serious." He couldn't help but laugh with me. Laughter can be so contagious. "I really am though," he managed, in between bursts of chortle. "I totally would have spoken to them. I wouldn't have given up without a good fight." True enough. *It is one of 763 things I deeply like about you.* He continued, with a more genuine tone, "Christina, I really care about you. I think about you when we're not together. I can't imagine my life without you." Silence. He sounded incredibly sincere. Again, Avery shared his heart with me and I was speechless. "Christina, . . . are you there?"

"Me too," I said quietly. "Does this mean that you'll eat lunch with me from now on?" I laughed heartily at my own interjection of good humor—so much so, my mom told me to keep it down. "Oh, before I forget," I said, lowering my voice, "my mom wants to have you over for dinner."

"Cool. When?" I admired his confidence.

"You really want to meet my parents?" I shook my head and made an arm gesture in my otherwise empty room.

"Sure, why not?" *Are you fearless?*

"Just don't mention the fact that I couldn't date before because it was awkward enough to bring up the subject. They might get defensive. I don't want to offend them or to push my luck." *Brilliant, if I do say so myself.*

"No problem—parents love me. I've got this," he asserted confidence and ready to hurdle any and all obstacles in his path, like Carl Lewis.

"I bet they do," I chuckled. "I gotta go. It's getting late." I found myself smiling, as if he were in the room.

That's what he did for me over and over—he made me smile. He. Made. Me. Smile. As a result, this unexpected, quickly developed, and deep friendship became my new lifeline. Talking to him at night became a new, profound help. For the first time since the incident, I felt relaxed before bed.

Many nights since the aforementioned, I woke up in the middle of the night from my nightmares, making it even more challenging to fall back asleep. Proper rest eluded me on occasion for several nights in a row. After those consecutive sleepless nights, I felt sluggish, irritable, distracted, and I suffered a never-ending pounder. That night, talking on the phone with Avery was the commencement of many peaceful nights, and my urge to cut vanished.

"Night, Christina. See you tomorrow." I could hear him smiling through the phone. It was such a pleasant, soothing sound. A smile adorned my face as I dozed off in a deep slumber.

Chapter 29

THE FOLLOWING MORNING AVERY MET me at my locker. He impressed me with a not too long—but long enough to fill me up for a while—smooch. Our PDA conversation was a success.

If I had any serious religious convictions, I would have believed that God gave me a perfect boyfriend to make up for the hell He let me suffer with Creepoid—or Jackalope—but since I still didn't believe in God, I had no right to swear. Faith made that abundantly clear a couple of days ago.

Instead I stated, "Yum! Perfect!" smacking my lips together. Avery laughed and brightened the moment again with his dashing smile.

Hooray! Mrs. Hartzel announced, "Due to the warm, sunny weather, we are combining the boys' and girls' gym classes again." Another round of flag football in the fresh air. On that note, I ran outside with the other girls to be personally greeted by the most attentive, awesome boyfriend ever.

"Hey, Christina, we're on the same team again," my guy said, cheerfully, his blue eyes glistening in the sun.

This was my lucky day. The word 'lucky' reminded me of Miss Brenda, because I remembered seeing her last month on Friday, the thirteenth. That was the day we got down to the oldies at The Manor. I wondered how Miss Brenda was doing, as I hadn't seen her in a week. I had hoped she didn't feel like I abandoned her. I figured I could visit her today after school.

Avery gave me some helpful tips to assist in my game. I played a little better, which continued my good fortune for the day. The whistle blew indicating the game was over and it was time to head back to the locker rooms. As expected, I agreed to meet Avery for lunch again.

At lunch, Avery and I greeted each other with another perfect kiss. I sat down with Avery and Joey, immediately noticing Peter's absence. Upon questioning Peter's whereabouts, I was informed that he was at the library studying. Avery emphasized that Peter took his grades very seriously. I figured as much, as he always seemed like the intense studious type to me. Eventually, the three of us started to talk about weekend plans, or lack thereof.

"So, what are you guys doing this weekend?" Joey inquired, as he took out his bologna sandwich.

Avery turned to me while he was rummaging through his lunch bag, "Oh, right, today is Friday! What do you want to do, Christina?"

As I took my tried and true peanut butter and jelly sandwich out of the plastic sandwich bag, I answered, "Well, I thought I would visit the old folks' home, since I haven't been there all week."

"Are you visiting your grandparents?" Joey asked.

"No, I volunteer," I answered, before taking a bite of my sandwich and chasing it down with water.

"Oh, cool," Joey said. I was surprised he thought that was 'cool' and thankful that he dropped the subject.

"We can do something afterwards," Avery suggested, and then bit into his appetizing chicken salad sandwich on a croissant.

Why can't my mom make sandwiches like that? As much as I liked peanut butter and jelly on plain white bread, chicken salad on a flaky croissant would have been such a treat.

"Sure," I replied, lightheartedly, not having any idea what to do later.

"How 'bout if we see a movie tonight?" Avery asked, delighted with his suggestion.

"What movie?" I returned, and continued to eat my humdrum sandwich, while eyeballing Avery's sumptuous delight. Months had passed since I had been to the movies, so the idea was appealing.

"I can take a look at what's playing when I get home today after school and give you a call after you get home from the old folks' home."

Avery didn't seem to mind me going to The Manor today. I

guess he figured we would be seeing each other later tonight. *I get the best of both worlds.*

"Hey, Christina, don't forget to talk to Mindy today, okay? Maybe we could double date," Joey suggested, as he grabbed his red apple. Avery shot Joey a look like he was crazy for thinking Mindy would go out with him. "What?" Joey asked, noticing Avery's face, before taking a big bite out of his juicy apple.

Crunch.

"Don't get your hopes up, buddy," Avery responded, chewing on his delectable crescent sandwich.

Gesturing towards both of us, Joey retorted, "Anything's possible! Look at you two!" He continued to munch on his apple.

"I'm afraid to ask," I commented, rolling my eyes.

"You know, Christina, you're known to blow off guys," Joey responded quickly.

"Nice save," I observed, as everyone knew Avery was part of the "A" crowd. Me dating Avery messed up the social order, despite the countless offers I had to date.

"So, you'll talk to Mindy?" Joey persisted.

"Peter told you I tried yesterday, right?" I hoped, wincing.

"Yeah, yeah," Joey said, listlessly.

"I'm not so sure you two would make a good couple," I regretted saying aloud as soon as the words left my mouth.

"Why?" Joey asked, with a furrowed brow.

"You need someone . . ." I was thinking about how Mindy was arguing after class, how she was always surrounded by her posse, how she was practically revered. Like the other day she was freaking out on her friend after geography class. I continued, "less intense."

"Like you?" Joey asked, sincerely.

"Don't let her fool you. Christina, can be very intense, trust me," Avery winked at me lightheartedly, and I giggled in response to his good-humored verbal jab.

"What's that supposed to mean?" I asked, shoving Avery playfully, still amused by his comment.

"Like you don't know," he teased, with a raised eyebrow.

"Hey, tell me," Joey said curiously.

"Never mind," I said, giggling, giving Avery another good-natured shove.

"Why is it okay for Avery to go out with someone intense, but it's not for me?" Joey asked.

"Honestly?" I asked.

"Yeah!" Joey replied.

"Promise you won't get mad?" I winced.

"Promise," Joey assured.

"You're more fragile. Avery is very rare in my estimation." *Oops! That came out wrong.* I made him sound like a wimp, but that's not what I meant at all. After getting to know Joey, he seemed like a teddy bear, instead of the tough guy I thought he was. To be fair, I'm not sure anyone could handle Mindy, including Avery.

Barely containing himself, Joey leaned towards me. His eyes widened and he yelled, leaving his jaw hanging, *"Are you kidding me?!"*

Without hesitation, Avery came to my rescue by pointing his finger at Joey and rebuked him, "Hey, you promised Christina you wouldn't get mad."

"Yeah, but you were the biggest baby when she dumped you this summer," Joey justified.

Avery exclaimed, "She didn't dump me!"

Simultaneously, I said, "I didn't dump him!"

"Whatever!" Joey replied in a huff. He rolled his eyes and crumbled up his lunch bag.

I eyed Joey firmly, "Look, I didn't witness how Avery was after we broke up this summer, but I can tell you that he's been my rock all week." I boldly defended my position. "I know you know at least part of what I'm talking about," I said to Joey, referring to what he witnessed during math class. "Relationships can be like roller coasters, even in a week's span. I think you would be better matched with someone more . . . subtle to smooth out those bumps." *Did I salvage that one?* I truly thought Mindy would rip his heart out. I honestly didn't understand what guys saw in her, other than her decent looks. *Does he not see how nasty she can be?*

"Well said," Avery quipped. *At least he gets what I'm trying to say. I like him more and more.*

"What are you talking about?" Joey asked, with a confused contorted face.

"Okay, how can I put this?" I stood up to the plate a second time. "You're a nice guy, Joey. I wouldn't want to see you frustrated on a continual basis. Basically, you need a girl who is simple and sweet," I stated, feeling both exasperated and concerned. Avery nodded his head in agreement, as he threw his trash away.

"What? Like 'simple' as in 'stupid'?" Joey said, defensively. *Oh, my gosh! He thinks I think he's stupid. I know he's not. Why did I open my big mouth? I don't want to see him get hurt. Think quick, Christina!*

"No, I mean simple as in uncomplicated. And sweet because you deserve someone who would treat you as well as you would treat them." After getting to know Joey, I imagined that he would treat his girlfriend with the utmost respect and kindness.

"So, you don't think Mindy is sweet then?" Joey lobbied.

"No, I never said that. I don't think she's simple. You need both sweet and simple." I emphasized 'simple' so that I wouldn't insult Mindy, even though I definitely didn't think she was sweet. I felt victorious, but drained. Feeling parched from my tête-à-tête with Joey, and noticing the time, I took a swig of water and collected my trash.

Joey leaned forward, slammed his arms on the table, and practically whined, "Can you please talk to Mindy today?" *Did he hear anything I said?* Unfortunately, I saw heartbreak in Joey's future.

"Alright, I'll talk to Mindy!" I was frustrated simply talking about Mindy. I couldn't imagine going out with her. I mean, I really couldn't imagine going out with her—or any girl for that matter. They are all annoying, including myself.

I started to feel sorry for Avery having to put up with me. As if on cue, Avery gently placed his hand in mine and gave me a reassuring look that he instinctively knew I needed. All was wonderful in my world.

Just then the bell rang, signaling the end of lunch. Saved by the bell!! I was glad to finally be done with that exhausting conversation. I meant well, but not so sure how I came across.

"Christina, meet me here after school, okay? I want to say good-bye to you before you leave for the old folks' home." I nodded, completely lost in the moment, completely zapped from the Mindy conversation with Joey.

Joey began, "Christina," He continued, as he bobbled his head, "don't forget, you know. . . ."

I nodded to Joey, gave Avery my final mid-day kiss to hold me over until after school. Wooooooowwwwww!!!!!! I floated away to class.

———•———

I approached Mindy after geography class. Her Majesty was surrounded by her ladies-in-waiting.

"Mindy, can I talk to you privately for a sec?" I asked. She nodded the silent signal and her court vanished.

"I'll catch up with you guys later, 'k?" Mindy promised. "So, what's up?" She asked curiously.

"Well, first of all, I was wondering if you were dating anyone." I didn't want to tell Mindy that Joey liked her if she already had a boyfriend.

"No, why?" she asked, tilting her head.

"Well, I know someone who is interested in you."

"Yeah, who?" She asked. I paused for a second and considered not telling her right away but didn't feel like playing games.

"Joey Glosser."

"Really?" she responded. I couldn't ascertain from her response if she was the slightest bit interested.

"Yeah, so would you go out with him if he asked you?"

"You're going out with Avery, right?"

"Yeah. . . ." I didn't know what this had to do with Joey liking her.

"Hmm," Mindy paused, "maybe we could double-date or something."

Not expecting that answer, I stood there, dumbfounded, "Oh, sure. I'll pass it along."

"Great! I'll be outside by the field hockey field, just in case. See you later then, Christina."

"Yeah, see ya, Mindy." *Well, that wasn't so hard.*

I met the guys at the caf after school. Before I launched into my conversation that I had with Mindy, I made sure I got my fix first. *Yes, his kiss does the trick. Amazing. Okay, time to focus.*

With a bright smile on my face, I blurted, "Well, Joey, you'll be happy to know that Mindy said she would go on a double date with you, Avery and me." The guys congratulated him, slapping him on the back.

"Really?!" Joey said, excitedly. "Who brought up the double date?"

"She did."

"Oh," he appeared dejected, as he lowered his head.

"What's the matter? I thought that's what you wanted," I reminded him.

"Well, not for her to suggest it."

"What difference does it make?" Peter said, stealing everyone's thoughts.

"I don't know. I guess it doesn't make a difference." I could see the wheels spinning, but I didn't know what was going on in that brain of his.

"Dude, you should ask her to go out with us tonight," Avery said. He looked to me for approval.

I gave them the reassuring nod. "Sure, maybe you could ask her in person. You might have time to catch her at the field hockey field before your bus comes."

The guys encouraged him to go. He bolted.

"Why do you think he didn't want Mindy to suggest the double date?"

"Who knows?" Avery grimaced, "But at least she sounds interested."

"I guess so."

Before leaving for The Manor, I waited to find out what happened between Mindy and Joey.

Upon Joey's return, I asked, "So what happened?"

"We're going to the movies with you guys tonight," he responded, a little out of breath.

I turned to Avery and asked, "So, what's the plan, Chief?" *I probably should've said, "Great! What's the plan?" but I'm not certain it is 'great'.*

Joey turned to Avery, "Yeah, Avery, what is the plan?"

We could hear the rumbling of the buses, which distracted us to Joey's dismay.

"Uh, I don't know yet. I'll call you later." He gave me a quick kiss and ran for the bus.

———◆———

It only took a few minutes to walk to The Manor, as it sat adjacent to the high school.

"Well, I'll be. Look who's here. It's none other than Christina.

How ya doing, honey?" Miss Brenda asked.

"Great! How are you?"

"You do look good. Now give me some sugar, sugar." Miss Brenda embraced me with one of her famous hugs. "So, how's school?" We sat down with the residents to resume our conversation.

"School's okay," I said casually.

"We sure missed you around here." The residents in company nodded their heads in agreement.

I looked around the room, "So, did I miss anything?"

"Well, let's see. . . ." Miss Brenda went on to tell me about the various illnesses and conditions, but nothing uncommon or earth shattering. I suggested we have another dance party like we did a few Fridays back.

"What are we waiting for then?" Miss Brenda asked, while she walked over to the stereo. "Let's get this party started!"

The residents got up slowly when the music started. This seemed to be the highlight of their week. I got the impression that Miss Brenda didn't want to do this too often because it would lose its appeal, or worse, cause too much excitement for their fragile hearts. After much butt bumping, arm waving, and fancy footwork, we crashed. All of us, including me. The dancing was a huge success. The residents were all alive and kicking. Maybe not kicking, but there were definite signs of life. After Miss Brenda left, I did my homework, while waiting for my dad to chauffeur me home.

———◆———

"So, Pooch," my dad inquired, "what are you doing tonight? Anything?"

"We're supposed to go to the movies."

"Who? You and what's his name?"

"His name's Avery, Dad."

"So, you are going with Avery?"

"Yeah, and another couple."

"What are you going to see?"

"I'll find out the details when I get home." *This should be interesting. It'll be our first 'official' date.*

The arrangements were made via Avery. His dad was going to pick me up and drop us off at the movies. Afterwards, we were supposed to go to a nearby diner. Then Joey's dad would pick us up at the diner.

Fortunately, my parents had no problem with the arrangements. In fact, my dad slipped me some money. "Just in case," he said, with a wink.

"Thanks, Dad," I responded, grateful for the cash. "Call me if you have any problems. Okay, Pooch?" "Okay, Dad."

I anxiously waited for Avery upstairs in my bedroom.

Why am I so nervous? It's new. That's gotta be it.

It seemed so grown up to be going out on a date, rather than hanging out and playing video games, except for the fact that we had to be chauffeured. And Mindy would be with us.

Fourth grade was the last time I hung out with Mindy. Since then, she turned out to be the most popular girl in our grade. In contrast, I was far from being considered popular.

I actually didn't mind that Joey was coming with us, since he was easygoing.

The doorbell rang and subsequently, I heard my dad answer the front door.

"Christina!" he yelled. I walked down the stairs wearing my new favorite Gloria Vanderbilt jeans, a brightly colored aqua shirt, with a thick black belt hung low below my waist, covered by a matching jean jacket. When I reached the landing, I introduced Avery to my parents, as my mother entered the foyer.

As expected, Avery was very courteous and polite. Since we didn't want to keep everyone waiting, we left rather abruptly. I was pleasantly surprised when Avery opened the car door for me. *I think this date feels different for him as well.* I slid in next to Mindy who sat next to Joey. Avery sat up front.

"Hi, Christina," both Mindy and Joey said in unison.

"Hi, guys." I was so nervous I failed to spit out their names.

Avery introduced me to his father, saying, "Christina, this is my dad. Dad, this is Christina."

I muttered an insecure, "Hi."

"Hello, Christina, it's nice to finally meet you. I have heard so much about you."

Mr. Evans' tone and comment instantly put me at ease. "Nice to meet you, too!" I managed vivaciously, hoping to recover from my meager 'hi'.

At the movies, Joey and Avery insisted on paying for Mindy

and me, respectively. Avery gently led me inside by the hand. Our friend and his date followed. Avery had the concession stand in his sight.

"So, what's your pleasure?" he asked, making this date thoroughly official and officially good. "Popcorn?"

With a scrunched-up nose, I replied, "I'll pass on the popcorn, but thanks anyway."

"Something else then?" Before I could answer, he got it, "Wait, I know—you like chocolate!" I smiled with delight. "Which one then?"

"Umm, Reese's Peanut Butter Cups, please." *Peanut butter and chocolate. Two great tastes that taste great together—that's always a 'yes' for me.*

"Would you like a drink with that?" the counter lady asked, in her penguin-like work clothes.

"Root beer, please." Avery got a Coke and Jujubes. Mindy and Joey got their bag of popcorn and sodas.

Avery whispered in my ear, "Hey, for the record, is this considered public, even though it's in the dark?"

"Somewhat private, if we sit all the way in the back," I answered.

"Let's sit in the back then, 'k?" he grinned, his eyes as big as saucers.

I nodded and followed Avery down to the very last row in the back. The lights were dim, but there was plenty of light to navigate the stairs. At least we sat in the middle of the back row. Mindy sat next to me. The girls were flanked by the guys. It felt uncomfortable sitting next to Mindy.

I had to remind myself that I was on a date with Avery Evans and just doing Joey a favor! Avery wasted no time slipping his hand into mine. I turned my head to face Avery. He leaned over and kissed me. *Back to cloud nine; I like it.*

Avery whispered in my ear, "You okay?"

"Couldn't be better," I smiled brightly.

The theatre grew darker, the volume louder, as we were taken out of our own lives and into those on screen. It proved to be a super escape from teenage life in Pennsford, even though *Grease's* sequel wasn't as good as the original.

Grease 2 didn't have the catchy songs that the original *Grease* did. I didn't expect the songs to be replayed on the radio like the original. The first Grease movie soundtrack was incredible and was still played on the radio.

Olivia Newton John was adorable and sweet in the original. Her songs continued to soar on the top ten music charts, like "Physical," which climbed to number one.

I was never crazy about John Travolta, but he was, no doubt, a phenomenal performer. His looks never appealed to me, especially the huge dimple on his chin.

However, the starring actor, Maxwell Caufield, was gorgeous in *Grease 2*. I drooled each time Maxwell filled the screen. I hoped it wasn't obvious. The actor's boyish good looks reminded me of Avery. I would definitely watch the movie again simply to see him on screen. He alone made the movie worth seeing.

Before heading to the diner, Mindy and I used the restroom. While we were each in our individual stalls, Mindy asked, "So how long have you and Avery been going out?" *AWKWARD! I just want to pee. Can't I have a moment to myself here?*

Pause.

"A few days."

"Didn't you two go out in the summer?" *Why? Are you writing a book?*

"Yeah." I wanted to keep it simple with Mindy, since I didn't like or trust her.

"So, what happened that you stopped going out?"

Enough of the questions. Let me relieve myself in peace.

"I wasn't allowed to date."

The poorly timed rapid-fire interrogation continued, "So how come you're here now?"

"My parents changed their minds."

"What prompted them to change their minds?"

I wondered why she was drilling me. *Enough already!* "I don't know. They just did," I said, trying not to sound annoyed. By then we were both out of our separate stalls washing our hands at the sinks provided.

"Lucky for you then, huh?" she smiled.

Something didn't seem right about the Mindy inquisition, or even her smile, for that matter. I have been questioned before on the very same topic, but this had an edge to it. Something was out of sync, yet I couldn't quite put my finger on it. As a result, I felt very unsettled.

I added this to the long list of reasons why I hated public restrooms. At last, we left and found our dates waiting for us in the lobby.

"Ready, girls?" Avery asked.

"Yes, let's go," I said almost too quickly. We walked hand in hand, while Mindy and Joey had a noticeable distance between them.

We were seated at a booth in the diner. Avery motioned for me to slide in first. Then he sat next to me—right next to me. I noticed because, again, the distance between Mindy and Joey was the other extreme. I moved over a little to lessen the glaring difference. I gave Avery a reassuring smile. Likewise, he smiled back.

"Christina, order what you want, okay?" Avery encouraged.

"Okay, thanks," I answered with a smile.

Joey told Mindy to do the same. The waitress came over, clothed in her uniform, a short red dress and white frilly apron. She took the pen out from behind her ear and asked, "What can I get you folks?"

Avery nodded in my direction, "Christina, you order first."

"I'll have an extra thick chocolate milkshake, made with chocolate ice cream, please." *I was high maintenance when it came to my chocolate shakes. I am flexible, but not with my shakes. Life is too short.*

The waitress turned to Mindy, "Okay, doll, what would you like?"

"A Diet Coke, please," she said with finality.

"And you, young man?" the waitress said, looking at Joey through her reading glasses, that hung halfway down her nose.

"A milkshake sounds great. I'll have a vanilla one."

"What would you like?" the waitress asked Avery. "The same as her," Avery said, motioning to me. The waitress repeated the order and asked if she missed anything, then left.

Our conversation landed on *Grease 2,* of course, and I was smart enough to keep my intense attraction to Maxwell to myself. *Yes, we were on a first name basis.*

Joey debated if he would have rather seen *E. T.* for the tenth time. I found it endearing how he liked it so much. The temptation to tease him was unbearable. He was such an easy target for me.

I said, playfully, "I thought that only girls and little kids watched that movie ten times," knowing that all walks of life found *E. T.* irresistible.

"What can I say? I'm a sucker for cute, little aliens with glowing fingers," Joey responded like a good sport.

Mindy didn't seem too impressed. Instead she stared at Avery and tried to make small talk with him.

Out of the blue, Mindy asked, her eyes focused on the boy next to me, "So, Avery, are you trying out for the baseball team in the spring?"

I was completely unaware that Avery played baseball.

"I plan on it." Avery turned to me, switching the conversation in my direction, instead of back to Mindy, and asked, "Christina, are you going to play any sports?"

I was not athletic per se, but I could usually hold my own without looking too pathetic.

I shrugged, "I have no idea. I haven't given it any thought."

"What position do you play, Avery?" I asked.

"He plays first base," Mindy answered, before Avery had the chance. *Interesting how she knew that. Is she marking her territory?*

"Oh, I like to play first and second base myself," I commented, ignoring her rude behavior.

"I didn't know you played softball, Christina," Joey stated, clearly interested.

"I used to," I clarified.

"When did you play?" Avery asked.

"Back in sixth grade. Faith and I were on the same team.
I played second base. Faith played third."

"Interesting," Mindy said insincerely. *Do the guys notice her insincerity?*

"Joey, you strike me as a baseball player. Do you play?" I asked.

"Yeah, I play left field." *Yeah, he's out in left field alright, not having a clue about Mindy,* I thought, worried for him.

"Joey is an incredible baseball player. He had the most RBIs last season," Avery bragged for Joey's benefit to impress Mindy, but she didn't even blink an eye, as she continued to stare at Avery.

"That's impressive!" I praised, to fill the obvious void.

Mindy chimed in, "Avery, didn't you have the most base hits?"

"Ah, yeah, I did," he said, reluctantly.

"So, Mindy, what position do you play in field hockey?" I asked, to take the heat off of Avery.

My stomach was tied in knots for Joey, because it was obvious—like, painted in the sky obvious—that Mindy was interested in Avery, and suggested the double date to get closer to my guy. I was hardly jealous, but extremely annoyed. No. In all honesty, I was pissed, because Joey was fond of Mindy, yet she was using him to be close to Avery. That was cruel. Even vicious. *She is a snake. A viper.*

I was not overly concerned about Mindy sinking her teeth into Avery, because I sincerely believed that Avery was never interested in her. I also figured if I acted nonchalant, then Mindy would think I was clueless to her antics.

I waited in anticipation for her next move, while I also waited for my extra thick, extra chocolate milk shake. *Oh, I won't get sucked into your games, Mindy. I have the patience of a saint. Gosh, maybe I do believe in God. May God grant me my shake and I will remain civil.*

"I play forward," Mindy answered.

My move. "That must be how you stay so trim," I said sincerely. I figured flattery would get me somewhere with someone like her.

"It helps," she said, flipping her hair with a flare of conceit.

I tried to think of a topic to get Joey involved in the discussion. *Move two.* "Mindy, you and Joey are both athletic and play sports. They are two pretty cool things to have in common." I looked at Joey, then back at Mindy.

Dead silence. *Ok-ie-do-kie.*

Then I thought of another topic. *Movies. How appropriate, since we just came from watching one.*

At that moment our order appeared, three shakes and a Diet Coke. Maybe there is a God after all. The tune from Sesame Street sang in my head, "One of these things is not like the others." *Okay, Christina, act civil. You promised.*

"Christina, ordering a milkshake was a great idea!" Joey said spiritedly, sipping on his shake. "I didn't think it would be this good."

"I can't resist chocolate shakes. When I was eight years old, I made myself a waffle topped with chocolate ice cream and maple syrup and drank a chocolate milkshake with it," I recollected. "I'm completely and utterly addicted. I confess it." I shot Avery a glance and tapped his thigh with my left hand. It was my version of a wink. He got my double meaning, that he, too, was my addiction.

With a repulsed look on her face, Mindy countered, "That sounds disgusting!" Despite her outburst, I smiled a toothless grin as I was happy to be enjoying my milkshake, yet, withheld a snicker, as I promised I would behave. I understood where she was coming from, but it was scrumptious, one of the best breakfasts I ever had. *Cheers to you, God!*

"I can't wait to try it, but I'll have to try the vanilla version of that!" Joey said, heartily.

Mindy contorted her face. *Now that's attractive!* Clearly, she didn't have an open mind to turn junk food into a major meal, or maybe the combination of maple syrup and chocolate ice cream grossed her out. Needless to say, I appreciated Joey's enthusiasm and vote in my favor. *You're alright, Joey.*

The waitress came over and asked if everything was okay. We all concurred.

"The shakes are great! Thanks!" Avery responded.

"Glad you're enjoying them," she replied. "Did you need a refill, honey?" she asked Mindy.

"No, thanks," Mindy responded, with her arms folded, looking disgruntled. *What's the matter, Mindy? You're upset that you didn't steal my boyfriend right from under me? Get you own and stay away from Joey. He's too decent of a guy for you.*

The three of us polished off our shakes and Mindy sipped the last of her Diet Coke. Joey left the table for a moment to call his dad, leaving Avery, Mindy and myself behind. The three of us sat there soaking up the awkwardness.

My only entertainment was the song that came back to my mind, *"One of these things is not like the others. One of these things just doesn't belong."* I couldn't help but smile. I thoroughly enjoyed my shake and held up my end of the bargain by biting my tongue many times. *I will have to explore this God thing later, but for now I am open to possibilities.*

Joey returned. "He'll be here in a few minutes. Did I miss anything?" The lack of response continued the thorny silence.

"I'm glad we all got to see *Grease 2* together. I think it was a fun movie. Thanks for inviting me!" Mindy eventually said with kindness that surprised us all. I panned Mindy and Joey, and finally laid my eyes on Avery.

"Oh, um, yeah, it was fun. Thanks for coming," Avery said, graciously. It was clear he had to push the words past his lips. He was too sweet, because she truly was a pain in the butt. Honestly, I couldn't figure out for the life of me what her appeal was. *Does Joey see it now? Is he finished with her?* I was keeping my fingers crossed.

We waited outside for Joey's dad to pick us up, except it wasn't Joey's dad that came. Instead, it was his brother, Sam. I have to admit, that made me a little nervous to have his brother drive, because I heard he was reckless and a little wild. I wasn't sure if my parents would approve, but I tried not to show my concern. I didn't want to be a worry wart or a total nerd. I held my breath and hoped for the best.

It helped to know that I lived the closest, but I was surprised when we pulled up at Mindy's house first. Mindy bid her thanks, yet couldn't get away fast enough, even with Joey by her side. My heart ached for him.

Sam couldn't help but comment when Joey climbed into the front passenger seat. "Nice girl!" he said, breaking the tension in a sarcastic tone, which clearly communicated what we were thinking all night long. *Joey is fortunate to have you as a brother.*

"Yeah, I'm glad that's over," Joey replied.

I was afraid to say anything unsure of how he might react.

"What was *that* all about?" Sam asked.

"She has the hots for Avery! I knew it. I just knew it!" He yelled, as he spoke vehemently with his hands. *I wonder if he's Italian with all those hand motions.*

"That's why she suggested going to the movies as a double date," grumbled an astute Joey, as he gritted through his teeth. *Oh, nice insight, Joey. Whew . . . Crisis averted.*

"Wow! That must have been awkward," Sam paused, "for all of you!" He bent over laughing. "She's a peach, Joey. What were you thinking?" He continued to chuckle very hard, hitting the steering wheel with his hands. *Keep your eyes on the road, Sam!*

For a special effect, I snapped my fingers. "Darn, this blows my chances of joining the girls in the 'A' crowd!" I whined sarcastically. "I'm just kidding!" I quickly followed to reassure them, just in case they misunderstood me. We hooted with laughter.

Joey turned around to the backseat, looked at me, and stated, "Christina, now I understand why you're not friends with her." He continued, "And don't say it!"

"Say what?" I teased.

"You know, I told you so," Joey conceded.

"Joey, I can't tell you how sorry I am. That was rotten of her. I can't believe how well we all handled the situation, by the way. We, as in, the three of us," I said, giving us each a proverbial pat on the back.

"We should just blow it off. Act like nothing happened. No reason to dignify her actions," Avery advised.

"Yeah, right!" Joey and I said together followed by a high-five between Joey and Avery.

Sam changed the subject and said in a singsong voice, while raising his eyebrows, "Christina, do you have an older sister?"

"Uh, no, but I do have an older cousin." She's Jessie's older sister.

"Cool, how old is she?"

"Eighteen. She's a freshman in college."

"Suh-weet!" Sam said, excitedly. "Does she look like you?"

"Uh . . ." I thought for a moment, "yeah, only thinner and taller."

"Seriously?" Sam exclaimed, practically jumping out of his skin. *The wheel, Sam! The wheel!*

"Seriously!" I replied. blinking furiously and pursing my lips for added drama. "You goof." I paused to contemplate my next statement. *Oh, what the heck!* "Her name is Emily O'Ryan. She graduated from Pennsford last year."

"Oh my God! She's hot!" the crazy driver said, excitedly. I thought he was going into cardiac arrest. Little did he know that she was studying abroad in Belize.

"Do you mind?" Joey broke in, sounding annoyed.

"We'll talk later, Christina," Sam said with a wink. I had no idea what he meant by later, so I kept quiet.

Sam pulled into my driveway based on Avery's directions. "It was nice seeing you, again, Christina. Maybe I'll see you around," Sam said, as if it were wishful thinking on his part.

"Will you quit it?!" Joey demanded, accenting his exasperation with a punch to Sam's arm.

"Whaaat?" Sam responded, as if he didn't get Joey's inference. Big brother teased like an expert.

"Bye, Christina," Joey said sweetly.

"Good night, guys." I led Avery to my side entrance.

Avery began apologizing, "Hey, I'm sorry about tonight. It turned out to be a mess on our first official date. I hope you'll give me another chance at a first date."

"It wasn't your fault. I just feel bad for Joey."

"Oh, he'll get over it. Mindy, that is. After seeing her like that, how could he continue to like her? You *warned* him."

"That I did, but I had no idea she was interested in *you*." *Guess I wasn't that swift either, because it took me long enough to figure out that Mindy was interested in Avery. How could someone be so bold?*

The car's headlights flashed.

"Sorry," he whispered in my ear. After a quick kiss and a final good-bye, I glided into my house as he jogged back to the car.

Chapter 30

MY DAD PREPARED HIS USUAL weekend breakfast of homemade buttermilk pancakes and crispy bacon.

I could smell the tantalizing aroma as it made its way up to my bedroom. I couldn't wait for my taste buds to appreciate my dad's latest culinary creation.

I quickly dressed and raced to the table. "Dad, thank you! This is delicious!" My mouth applauded every flavor—every ingredient— enthusiastically.

My dad asked me how my date went, but I was wholly disinterested in divulging anything private in front of my brother.

"It was okay," I sighed, pouring maple syrup on my pancakes.

"What movie did you see?" my dad asked, before taking a bite of his pancake.

"*Grease 2*," I replied, while adding more syrup to my pancakes.

"Isn't that rated R?" my mom asked, with an accusing tone, as she put down her coffee cup.

"No, it's PG," I huffed. It seemed like she was always picking a fight with me.

"How did you like the movie?" my dad asked, redirecting the conversation.

"It wasn't as good as *Grease*, but it was still entertaining. The main actor is super cute."

Jared rolled his eyes and made strange noises while inhaling his breakfast. *He's so immature!*

My dad chewed his pancakes and took a drink of orange juice. "Your boyfriend . . . uh, what's his name?" He hesitated in the middle of a thought.

I decided to come to his aid. "Avery."

"Right, Avery. He's nice-looking," he stated as a kind of a

question.

"If you say so, Dad," I teased, before taking a bite of pancake.

Jared looked at each of us, then burst, "You gotta be kidding me! This conversation is so weird." He slammed down his glass after finishing the last of his orange juice and then shoveled the last bite of pancake down his gullet.

My dad continued without pause, ignoring Jared's outburst and very obnoxious chewing, "Well, he seems like a decent guy."

"He is. He really is," I smiled in agreement.

"I'm outta here!" Jared announced loudly, grabbing a piece of bacon off his plate. *Good! What is wrong with him? I don't get him at all.*

"Where are you going?" my mother asked Jared in a curious tone.

"Shawn's," he said curtly and took off. Either he couldn't tolerate the conversation, or the fact that he, for once, wasn't the center of attention.

My dad resumed his inquiry, "So why was last night just okay?"

"Because we doubled with Joey and Mindy . . ." I waited for a response before proceeding.

"Yeah," my dad replied. My mom sat and listened without interrupting, while eating her breakfast.

"Well, it turns out that Mindy likes Avery. She completely ignored Joey and flirted with my date the entire night. It was so awkward. I feel bad for Joey because he really likes Mindy." I took another bite of my mouthwatering pancakes and dabbed the side of my mouth with a napkin to remove the unwanted syrup.

"How do you know she likes Avery?" my mom asked, raising her one eyebrow.

Exasperated, I threw my napkin down next to my plate and returned, "Mom, didn't you hear anything I just said?!"

Fwoosh.

"Christina," she leaned in and said quite calmly, "you could be reading into something that isn't even true."

"Mom, you weren't there. It was SO obvious! I don't even think she tried to hide it. She's a real jerk." I raised my voice in my defense and brusquely ripped into a piece of bacon. *Life is better with bacon.*

"So how did Avery handle it?" my dad inquired.

"He tried to deflect the conversation from himself to Joey. Joey was a good sport about it too, considering. He didn't give Avery a hard time about it. We would have had fun without Mindy. She ruined the entire evening. I don't see how anyone could like her. She was like a wet blanket. The guys and I had milkshakes and she drank a Diet Coke." I rolled my eyes, as I chowed down my pancakes. *I bet Mindy isn't enjoying a fabulous breakfast like this!*

"Christina, maybe you should order Diet Cokes too," my mother suggested in a judgmental manner.

I glaringly turned my head toward my mom. "You criticize everything I do . . . and say!" I gritted through my teeth with my mouth full of pancakes.

"Now hold on—you're the one criticizing Mindy for drinking a Diet Coke."

Snarling inside, containing some of it, I replied, "You missed the point. We were enjoying a fun, fat drink and she's all worried about calories!" My mother frustrated me to no end. I looked at my dad for reinforcements. "Dad, do you think I should be so self-conscious and insecure that I won't even allow myself the simple pleasures in life like a milkshake?" I took a swig of my orange juice after taking a few more bites of my pancakes.

"No, Pooch, I think you have a healthy attitude about food for a girl your age. I also think you're misunderstanding your mother. She has your best interest in mind. Give her a break." *My dad, forever the diplomatic one! I love him for that!*

The phone rang. My parents waited for me to answer the phone, even though they were closer.

"Hello."

"Christina?"

"Yes."

"It's Avery." I turned my back to my parents.

"Hey. What's up?" I asked cheerfully. It's astounding how easy my mood swung from one end of the spectrum to the other.

"Do you have any plans for today?"

"Nada." *Now, I'm speaking Spanish. No idea why.*

"I thought maybe we could hang out together." *I'm all yours.*

"Sure, what did you have in mind?"

"I'm open to suggestions," he said graciously.

"I'm flexible." I wasn't a dare devil, but I did have time on my hands.

"We could hang out at my house."

"Okay."

"Let's meet at half-way on our bikes."

"When?"

"The sooner the better." *I like the sound of that.*

"Hold on." I placed my hand over the receiver.

"Mom, I'm going over Avery's, K?" She nodded, while sipping her tea. I lifted my hand from the receiver. "Okay, I'll meet you in twenty." *I'm outta here! ¡Adiós!*

I rode my bike to our meeting spot to find Avery in his Levis and T-shirt straddling his bike. It was another beautiful day; the birds were chirping and the morning air was a little cool, but I could tell it was going to heat up.

Avery greeted me with enthusiasm, "Hi, Christina!"

"Hi, Avery!" I replied with equal excitement.

"Glad you could make it!"

"Me too!" Even though I just saw him last night, we really didn't get a chance to enjoy our time together.

"You ready?" he gestured with his head.

"Yeah, let's go!" I started peddling.

"All right, let's go!" He turned around on his bike and waved his arm for me to follow his lead.

We talked while we rode to Avery's house. I could hear the distant roar of a lawnmower.

"I think Sam has a thing for you," Avery began.

"Sam? Sam who?" I asked bewildered. At first, I didn't know who he was talking about, but then I recalled the drive home from the movies.

"Joey's brother. He drove us last night."

"Oh, right. Last night. Wait. What? Why do you think *that?*"

"He wouldn't stop talking about you the whole way home." Avery slowed down his pace to allow himself to successfully carry on a regular conversation, so I followed suit. "Joey had to remind him that you were my girlfriend. Do you know what Sam said to that?"

"Uh, no, what?" I turned slightly to Avery but was careful to peddle straight ahead. *It's harder than it looks to talk and ride bikes.*

"He asked Joey why he couldn't find a girlfriend like you." Aw. My cheeks warmed up, but I didn't want to discuss Sam's possible interest in me, especially not with my boyfriend.

"Do you know if Joey still likes Mindy?"

"That's just it. He doesn't. He and Sam are on a quest now to find themselves girlfriends like you." *What?!*

"Really? Why?" I let out a giggle. I was both flattered and baffled.

Avery turned to me with a big grin on his face, "Guess they realize how lucky I am."

"No, I'm the lucky one." I honestly felt very fortunate in that regard.

"I think we're both lucky," Avery concluded. I tittered. "Oh, yeah, even my dad said you were nice."

"Wow, I didn't expect that. I barely said a word," I reminded him.

"I know. That's the weird part. Mindy was kissing up to him and he didn't like her at all." *Ha, ha! Take that, Mindy!*

"I wish everyone else could see right through her like your dad. I can't believe Joey is over her already. I mean I thought he really liked her."

"That's Joey for you. He is so easygoing. He gets over things quickly. He's not about to waste his time on someone who acts like that." Avery paused to catch his breath. "I think he's going to interview girls to see if they like milkshakes." *WHAT?!*

My laughter made me lose control of my bike and started to swerve. "You're kidding, right?" *Please tell me he's kidding. They would think he's a weirdo.*

"Yes, but he likes how you're able to be yourself. I probably shouldn't tell you all this. You might go for Joey," Avery was silent for a few seconds. His baby blues narrowed slightly, "I noticed how you were complimenting him last night too."

I gasped inwardly, "I only did that because I was trying to . . ."

Avery cut me off, "I know why you did that and that was very nice of you. We should agree not to double date with other couples until they are officially a confirmed couple."

"Sounds like a plan," I wholeheartedly agreed.

Moments later we arrived at Avery's. He told me he'd be right back and walked to another part of the house. I could hear the mumbled conversation.

"Hey, Dad, where's Mom?"

"Upstairs putting clothes away."

"Christina and I are going downstairs to play video games."

"Christina's here? Tell her to come in here to say hello."

Avery walked back to the kitchen to get me. "My dad wants to see you."

"Okay," I said, sheepishly. I walked over to the living room with Avery to where his dad was sitting in a chair with the newspaper on his lap.

"Hi, Mr. Evans," I greeted him, cordially, with a smile.

"Hey, Christina, how are you?" He sounded delighted to see me.

"Fine, thank you!" I replied cheerfully, piggybacking on his dad's exuberant greeting.

"Did you enjoy the movie last night?" he asked in a non-intrusive manner.

The mention of the movie made me smile, "Yes, I did actually."

He creased his brow, "Avery tells me it was some night."

"Yes, it was," I nodded in affirmation.

I heard light footsteps approaching when Avery's mom sweetly called out, "I thought I heard talking . . . Oh, hello, Christina, how are you?"

"I'm doing well, thank you. How are you?" As she answered, I realized I forgot to ask Mr. Evans the same question. I bit my lip for being impolite.

"Boy, it's a shame what happened to Joey last night. Maybe you two could throw a little gathering here tonight? Avery, you could invite your friends and Christina could invite hers," her eyes glittered.

"Uh, it's kind of last minute," Avery said, the corner of his mouth lifted.

"Oh, Avery, you don't have to plan ahead all the time." Mrs. Evans turned to me and asked, "Christina, what do you think?"

I crinkled my nose, "Honestly, I'm not so sure. Our friends don't exactly hang out together." I cringed inwardly at the thought of our friends attending the same party.

"That's precisely my point," Mrs. Evans clapped her hands together.

Avery shook his head in disagreement, "I think we had enough matchmaking to last us a lifetime after last night's fiasco." I couldn't help but laugh. We needed a break since the eruption of Mount St. Mindy.

"Well, then, Christina, why don't you have dinner here? Hang out for the day," Mrs. Evans suggested.

I looked to Avery for some guidance. I felt like an eight-year-old on stage in a spelling bee. *What is the right answer?* His mouth turned upwards and he nodded.

"I just have to check with my mom."

"Avery, let Christina use the phone." My mother didn't understand why I had to stay at Avery's house all day and cautioned me to not be a nuisance, yet in the end, she acquiesced. Christina, you may go on to the next round. *Congratulations!*

Chapter 31

*J*UST LIKE THAT ONE DAY in the summer when we hung out in Avery's basement, our time alone was spent playing video games and kissing, but this time we kissed way more than we played video games. *I'm guessing I'm not a nuisance.*

Avery assured me his parents couldn't hear a thing, because the basement was virtually soundproof. In middle school, he convinced his parents to buy him an electric guitar that he played all the time, but they couldn't take the noise. Not that Avery wasn't a good player, mind you, but the constant noise was too much. It was a win–win situation, and now he gets to have all his gatherings in the basement. His parents trusted him to stay out of trouble and they got peace and quiet.

Aren't they suspicious of us, though? They had to be somewhat suspicious of our behavior. We barely came up for air. We kissed on the couch. On the floor. With me on top. With him on top.

"I like you on top of me on the couch," Avery said, so seriously, while sitting next to me on the floor against the couch. He announced it like it was critical research for his federally funded grant.

"Well, I like you on top of me on the couch," I simpered. "So, we both like the couch. I think because it's softer. What do you think?" I asked with my brow raised.

"Let's test it out again to be sure!" he suggested with a wink. We climbed on the couch together. I ended up underneath at first. Avery laid on top of me, gazing at me with his gorgeous ocean blue eyes. I started giggling.

Avery carefully hoisted himself up. "What's so funny?" he chortled.

"I am glad we can just be ourselves," I exhaled.

"It's great, isn't it?" Avery beamed. "No games." I nodded in comprehension. *No games. Just us.*

Avery gently lowered his body on mine and leaned in to kiss me softly. I melted. It wasn't the first time that day I felt all gooey inside. I lost count of my melting sessions as I found myself in a perpetual heavenly state. *If there was a heaven, it would surely be something like this.*

We continued to kiss. The kisses were soft and sensual. It wasn't the first time he stuck his tongue in my mouth searching for its partner, and once again I didn't resist. We kissed more passionately, more forcefully, uncontrollably. I was feeling restless and excitable. He didn't stop. My heart raced, my chest pounded. I felt lightheaded. He moved his hands over my body, his skin touching the fabric of my clothes. I liked the new sensation.

"Oh, Christina!" Avery moaned. He slipped his hand up my shirt and gently caressed my bra.

"Oh, Avery!" I uttered passionately. Our tongues parted as he moved his lips to my neck. I moaned. He kissed my ear and sucked on my ear lobe. He hesitated.

"Oh, don't stop," I encouraged. Things quickly heated up. "Oh, Avery!" I cried with passion. "Avery!" My body thrusted.

"Oh, Christina, I love you!" he bellowed.

"I love you too, Avery!" I felt Avery against my body and my body told me to do one thing, but my mind suggested another. Then, I thought I heard something. I swiftly jerked upward.

"I heard something," I gasped. I yanked my shirt down while Avery leaped off of me. I swung my legs over the edge of the couch.

"Avery, honey, can you come up here?" Mrs. Evans shouted down the stairs. My heart hammered through my chest. *Did she hear us?* I couldn't shake the feeling that Avery's mom heard us.

"Okay, Mom," Avery responded. "I'll be right back!" he assured me and dashed away. My face burned red hot from embarrassment. I imagined his mother hearing us moan and pledge our undying love for each other in the heat of passion. I was utterly mortified. I wondered if I could somehow sneak out undetected. But how?

Avery bolted down the stairs a minute later and exclaimed, "Boy, *that* was close!"

"You mean she didn't hear anything?" I asked, desperately

needing reassurance.

"No, thank God!" he exhaled, as he sat dangerously close to me on the couch.

"What did she want?" My heart nearly pounded out of my chest.

"Lunch. My mom wanted to know if we wanted to eat lunch." *That sounded innocent enough.*

"Oh, what did you say?"

"I told my mom I would check with you first."

I scrunched my nose. "Oh, I am kind of hungry." I had worked up an appetite after our steamy interlude.

"Great, let's get something to eat!"

Still not convinced Mrs. Evans didn't hear us, I held up my palm. "Whoa! Wait a minute, Casanova, I think she heard us."

"She didn't," Avery said emphatically, and shook his head.

I squinted in his direction. "How can you be so sure?"

"I just am."

My shoulders slumped and my mouth straightened "I don't think I can go up there right now."

"Why not?"

"I am so embarrassed," I buried my face in my hands.

Avery leaned in, placed his hand on my leg and rubbed my back with the other. With a soothing voice he said, "Christina, I told you she didn't hear us."

"Why can't we just eat down here?" I pleaded, blinking back the tears.

"Now *that* would look suspicious," he said convincingly.

"Eating down here looks suspicious, but the fact that we're getting it on down here doesn't set off any detectors?"

Avery's mouth turned upward. "You are so funny."

"I know. I'm a riot," I smirked as I rolled my eyes.

"I thought you were enjoying yourself earlier," he teased.

"I was—too much maybe," I confessed. I shouldn't have let myself go like that. I was super aroused. I never felt like that before and the possibility that we were overheard made me want to crawl under a rock. Never had I been so embarrassed and I wasn't ready to show my face. What if I looked guilty? I had to trust Avery. Harping on it would only make matters worse and would make me look guilty. *Breathe.*

"I know it was intense, but we can take a break and get something to eat," he urged.

"You're hungry, aren't you?"

"Yeah, I worked up an appetite." *He didn't just say that, did he?* "Come on, let's get something to eat!" Avery pulled me off the couch. I conveniently fell into his arms. Our eyes locked and we started kissing again. I couldn't resist those dreamy blues framed by his long dark eye lashes.

"Maybe we shouldn't be alone after all," I concluded.

"Come on, let's eat!" He took my hand and led me upstairs. I found myself drifting once again.

———————

Avery's parents were in the kitchen. The food was spread out like a buffet on the counter. Mrs. Evans was making her husband's sandwich. "How's chicken salad?" Mrs. Evans asked, looking in my direction. "It's Avery's favorite, so I make it quite a bit."

"That sounds great! Thank you very much!" *I can't wait to sink my teeth into the sandwich. His looked so scrumptious yesterday at school.*

"We have croissant rolls," she offered. *Score!*

"I love croissants!" I stated overjoyed with excitement. This was a change from the norm at my house.

"You can make your own sandwich if you like." Mrs. Evans suggested. After we made our sandwiches, Avery and I sat down to eat our lunch along with his parents in the kitchen.

"Oh, my goodness, this is so good! Your chicken salad is delicious, Mrs. Evans," I said, smacking my lips and rubbing my stomach, demonstrating how passionate I was when it came to food.

"I'm glad you like it, hon. I thought we could have a barbecue later for dinner. Christina, do you like burgers?" Mrs. Evans asked.

"Yes, burgers would be great!" *My kind of family! I could get use to this!*

"With a chocolate milkshake, right?" Avery joked.

"Cute," I sneered. "Very cute."

"I wonder if Joey started his interviews?" Avery teased. I felt my cheeks burn slightly.

"Joey has a job interview?" Mr. Evans inquired with a raised eyebrow.

"No, he liked how Christina ordered a milkshake last night compared to Mindy's Diet Coke, so I told Christina that his first line of questioning for any new girlfriend of his would be if they like milkshakes. He's making this a prerequisite."

With a creased brow and a slight panic in her voice, Mrs. Evans asked, "Joey isn't really going to interview girls, is he?"

Avery shook his head and took a deep breath. "I hope not. I was only kidding. But I'm telling you, he was really impressed by Christina ordering a milkshake." *Enough with the milkshake talk already. Now I want one.*

"I like to see a girl with a healthy appetite," Mr. Evans commented.

He glanced my way at that moment when my mouth was full to capacity. I imagine I looked like a chipmunk, cheeks stretched to their maximum. Impersonating Disney's Chip and Dale was not my intention.

Mr. Evans continued, "Young girls worry far too much about their weight these days. They seem to think that it's the only component to a woman's beauty."

"Gosh, if they only had perspective," added Mrs. Evans.

"It's what's inside that counts the most." Mr. Evans nodded in agreement.

I said with an extra amount of fervor, "My dad said the same thing!" *I like this guy! He reminds me of my dad. Maybe that's why I light up every time he speaks to me.*

I changed the subject, "Avery, do you have a baseball and an extra glove?" Talking about last night reminded me of our conversation about baseball.

"Yeah, why?"

"I thought we could play catch after lunch. Get some fresh air."

"Christina, you play baseball?" Mr. Evans asked.

"No, softball, but I didn't think he would have a softball."

"Don't you have a softball, Avery?" Mr. Evans asked.

"I think so," Avery replied. "We can play catch with a softball instead." We finished lunch and helped clear the table. We walked in the garage to find the ball and gloves.

"Are you sure you want to play catch?" Avery asked incredulously as he was rummaging through boxes filled with sporting equipment.

"Yes, don't you? It's good practice."

"Girls play catch?" he asked with a twisted mouth, still hunting for another glove.

"Yes, and some of us even order milkshakes," I winked.

He chuckled. "Do you play catch with you brother?"

"No, we don't get along. I throw with my dad."

"How come? What's up with your brother?"

"Typical sibling stuff, I guess. But he is a tremendous athlete. He teases me for my lack of athleticism."

"I've seen you in gym. You're not that bad." *Gee, thanks!*

"Thanks, but you're also not my baby brother," I sighed deeply. Thinking of my brother made me a little sad because we never got along. He was only getting more annoying as he aged, which I thought was impossible.

"Good point. I'd much rather be your boyfriend anyway. Ah, here, you take this glove."

We walked to his backyard and started throwing the ball back and forth to each other. It was refreshing to be outside on such a perfect autumn day. It was just warm enough to wear shorts, but Avery and I were both wearing jeans and short sleeve shirts. *We're even dressed alike.*

"I catch better than I throw," I warned. Apparently, I threw like a girl, whatever that means. I am a girl. I can't throw any other way!

"I can help you with that." he offered. *Ooh, this guy.*

It usually took a few throws in the beginning to warm up before I started to throw the ball with accuracy. Since I lacked strength, I never managed to throw the ball hard, fast, or far. I was okay with that, because I lacked the competitive edge.

We tossed the ball around for a while. We practiced our fielding and caught pop ups for variety.

"You should go out for the softball team in the spring, Christina."

"I can't think that far ahead. What about you? Do you think you'll join the baseball team?"

"Probably," he shrugged. *I wouldn't mind watching Avery in his baseball uniform sliding into home. He would look good in anything. Or out of anything.* My mind drifted and I began to feel flushed and breathless. *Boy, it's hot out!*

The mere thought of *Fantasy Avery* caused me to fan myself. "Hey, let's go for a walk," I suggested, as I needed to cool off. Pronto.

"Okay." We tossed the ball and gloves and off we went.

We held hands, as we strolled around his neighborhood. We strode toward an enormous house with an impressive gray stone front. "I love stone houses. They are so beautiful," I said in awe, staring at the house after a moment of silence.

I didn't mind the quiet; in fact, I liked it more than I thought I would. It gave me clarity and peace. It also provided breathing space. I was getting overheated moments before simply visualizing Avery playing baseball or out of his uniform. I had it bad! Taking a walk was the perfect distraction.

"That's Joey's house," Avery informed me.

"Really? Wow! It's beautiful—and huge. I didn't realize how close you two lived to each other."

"Yup, we've been friends since before kindergarten," he said proudly, with a toothless grin.

I shook my head in disbelief, yet was impressed.

"Wow! I can't imagine being friends with someone that long," I stated slack-jawed.

"I remember when you moved here in fourth grade. Didn't you get most talkative?"

I hid my face, "I did. You remember that?" I wasn't even the most talkative, but somehow, I managed the illustrious title. I will never be able live that down. It will haunt me forever.

"Yeah, you should have been voted best looking," he complimented.

"That wasn't one of the superlatives," I replied red-faced.

"It should have been," he said with conviction as his eyes danced in the sunlight.

"Then you would have been voted best looking guy, hands down," I declared, with a distinct nod. I had the hots for him back then. No one compared to Avery, even my friend's much older sister thought he was adorable, in his white knee-high socks and shorts back in fourth grade.

"Guess we make a great pair!" he surmised.

My mouth opened to a wry smile. I never considered our looks as a reason for our compatibility. Truth be told, Avery's stellar looks intimidated me. Secretly, I feared people were passing judgment on me. Because I fell short of the female version of Avery's handsome good looks, I ranked lower in social status. Yet, none of that seemed to matter when Avery and I were together, or even when we hung out with his friends. It was all so easy.

"So. what's Joey up to today?" I asked.

"I don't know. Do you want to see if he's home?"

"No, I don't want to bother him."

"Are you kidding? He wouldn't mind. You should knock on his door to see if he's home. I'll wait here," Avery suggested.

"Yeah, right! Like that would ever happen!"

"Why not? It would be funny."

"Avery, what's got into you? That's cruel," I said dismayed. *What if Joey thought I was interested in him, even for a moment? I couldn't do that to him or his brother or anyone for that matter.*

"Nah, he would just think I put you up to it anyway."

"So why bother then?" I asked perplexed.

"I was just messing with you," he swayed back and forth.

I winced, "Well, I wouldn't do it anyway."

"I know you wouldn't. Your jaw dropped when I asked you to call me the other day. You lead such a sheltered life." I didn't understand where this conversation was coming from.

"Until recently," I teased, testing the waters to see where this conversation was headed.

"Guess I corrupted you." There was silence. Avery looked at me with a big grin on his face. "You're not disagreeing," he teased.

"I'm not agreeing either."

"So, which is it? Do you agree or disagree?" he asked cocking an eyebrow.

"That depends on your level of experience. You know I never had a boyfriend, so I couldn't have corrupted you. Likewise, if you are just as inexperienced, then I suppose it was null and void of corruption."

I shot back to the moment in his basement earlier, when Avery had taken it up a notch in his physical prowess. Even though I was a willing recipient, I wouldn't have initiated any of that. I couldn't help but wonder what, if any of that, was as new to him as it was to me. He didn't seem like a novice, but what did I know? I was a rookie after all.

"Are you asking about my experience with girls?"

"No, that's your business, not mine," I pressed my lips together tightly, as if to keep myself from taking back the words that just left them.

Avery squinted his eyes, as he methodically lifted his head and down, "Interesting. I feel like I should tell you."

"That's up to you, but I'm not asking, just for the record. To be honest, I'm not sure if I want to know," I turned away from him.

He taunted, "But what if *I want* to tell you."

Okay, I'll bite. "Let me guess, you are somewhat experienced."

"How did you know?"

"Because you seemed to know what you were doing since you first kissed me." I enjoyed every moment in the moment, but . . . . the aftereffects in the basement . . . I was still reeling over the thought of his mom possibly being an observer in our throes of passion.

"I fooled around a little, but it was nothing serious."

"What do you mean it wasn't serious?"

"I wasn't going out with any of the girls."

"Oh, well, that makes it better," I said with a hint of sarcasm. *I noticed he said girls as in more than one. I'm not sure I like the sound of that.*

"What I mean is, it never amounted to anything more physical, because I wanted it to be special, to mean something." He gathered his thoughts. I remained silent. "Like when we're together, it's different . . . because I really care about you," he paused and looked right at me. "You're not saying anything."

"I don't understand how you can be so nonchalant about something so intimate," I said earnestly. I felt ashamed for fooling around in his basement after all.

"Christina, I love you," Avery declared once again and very sincerely. "I don't take our relationship lightly. I am seriously in love with you. I just want us to be on the same page."

"What page is that?" I dared to ask.

"I'm sensing that you regret our time in the basement earlier," he said.

"Why do you think that?" I did feel guilty, but I didn't want him to know how I truly felt. My feelings were all over the place. I loved being with Avery, but I also felt reckless and I didn't like that feeling. It felt wrong.

"Because you keep suggesting to do things out in public."

"Oh, that. Well, I did want to get some fresh air," I rationalized, as it was partially true.

"Christina, are you're afraid to be alone with me now?"

We stopped walking. He turned to me, put his hands in mine, and peered deeply in my eyes. I resisted the urge to run away this time. I didn't want to tell Avery the truth about the unspeakable, yet I didn't want to lie. My eyes welled up. "I . . .," my voice dwindled. "I love being with you, Avery. I think I like it too much. I love kissing you, but I think we got carried away. What if your mom didn't interrupt us? What then? I don't want to start something we can't stop on our own." I put my head down and stared at my Nikes.

"We won't. I promise," Avery said confidently, enunciating every single word.

I turned to him and asked him in a small, choked-up voice, "How do you know?"

"Because I've been able to stop in the past."

"But you said yourself that those girls didn't mean anything to you, that you wanted it to be something special."

"I will stop because you are special and I respect you too much to continue," he assured me.

"How am I different from the other girls then?"

"I love you, Christina. I was never in love before and I never told anyone that I loved them until now."

"I must seem so silly to you." I looked down at the ground. I was still wearing my sneakers.

"No, you seem so sweet to me." He gently raised my head with his hand. My mouth tilted upwards, my eyes still watery. He kissed me softly. "I love you, Christina. I will never hurt you," he promised.

"I love you too, Avery!" I embraced him. "Let's go back inside."

———◆———

"I forgot how good you were at video games," he complimented me on our third game of Asteroids. He beat me at every game, so I hardly felt like a worthy opponent.

"You still have me beat," I squirmed in my seat trying my best to manipulate the joystick.

"I'm sure I play a lot more often than you do," he answered in staccato because of the movement and jolts of his arm.

"I don't play much. The last time I played video games was here." I reminisced back to that special day we shared together before the unspeakable happened and ruined my summer, my life.

"That was the best day I had all summer. The night before was the best night I ever had." *Aw! You're so sweet!* Every aspect of my body tingled.

"Really? Me too!" I nudged him playfully.

"Today is the best day of my life so far." He stopped playing Asteroids, turned me toward him and looked directly into my eyes. His sincerity was palpable. "I know what you're thinking." I needed to process the day when it was over before I made an assessment, as I was still feeling guilty for fooling around on the couch before lunch. Avery understood how I felt. "It's not so much what we do, but being able to spend the entire day with just you." Avery knew exactly what to say and how to say it. He seemed a lot older than fourteen. I couldn't picture other guys in our class saying things like that, but then again, I wasn't privy to those conversations.

"This day definitely ranks up there as one of my best days," I said softly.

What he asked next, surprised me. "What was the best day of your entire life?" His question had weight and I wanted to answer it well, but nothing came to mind. I felt like there had to be some special day.

"Actually, I'm drawing a blank." And then, my black and white mind found the color.

"My tenth birthday," I blurted. "We had been living in our new house for a year. I was in fifth grade then and my mom and my cousin, Emily, planned a surprise party for me. My mom bought all my favorite junk food and Emily invited my neighborhood friends. It was great. We ate Doritos, cheese puffs, corn chips, potato chips, pretzels, chocolate cake and drank soda. We never served food like that all at once before . . . or since, come to think of it. Gosh, I really am Italian loving my food." *My Italian Mom-Mom would be proud.*

Avery waggled his eyebrows. "Sooo, you like surprises?"

"I liked that one. How about you? Do you like surprises? Have you had any?" I asked, putting down the joystick. *Clearly, we're taking a respite from Asteroids.*

"I guess it would depend on the surprise. You surprise me all the time and I like you."

"How do I surprise you?" I leaned back. "Are you serious? You are not just flattering me, are you?"

"No. No. I am serious. Listen, you like to play video games, for one, and you're good at them. You like to play softball and you're good at that too. You're easy to talk to and you're easygoing around my friends." My stomach fluttered. *This is so surreal.* Just when I thought things couldn't get any better, he launched into the most endearing speech. Then he added for humor's sake, "And we can't forget how you order milkshakes when other girls drink Diet Coke." We shared a laugh together. "They're not big surprises, but they're still surprises."

I felt compelled to share my thoughts after his charming discourse. "You surprise me too, Avery. You seem a lot older than fourteen, like way more mature than I ever expected. You say the sweetest things and I can't believe how open you are. Seriously, I would never have the courage to say half the things to you that I do if you didn't share your feelings first." *And I'm a chick. Usually girls are more forthcoming with their feelings than boys.* "I feel like I can tell you anything." Well, almost anything. I still couldn't tell him about the unspeakable. *I will take that secret to my grave.*

"I'm glad you feel comfortable with me now. I know it wasn't always the case." I could see the wheels turning in his mind. "It's strange because you always seemed confident in class, yet you never initiated conversation with guys on your own. Why?"

"Oh, I thought I told you why," I squinted, with my chin tucked in.

"No, you didn't. And don't tell me you were shy, because I don't buy that excuse."

"Avery, I was scared, that's all," I said timidly, not understanding his line of questioning. *What does he want to know exactly?*

He glanced at me sideways. "Scared of what?"

"Scared of boys." *Looks like I had reason after all, even though it wasn't you I needed to be afraid of.*

"What were you so afraid of?"

"I didn't want to get hurt I guess."

"Did someone hurt you before?" The unmentionable crept into my mind again and I began to tremble. "Christina, you're shaking. Are you okay?"

"Yeah, I'm fine." Although I sensed his concern, I wanted him to stop asking me those questions. I couldn't risk telling him what happened. There's no telling what Creepoid would do.

"Who hurt you?" He asked me in a soft, concerned tone.

"No one," I lied. "I don't want to talk about this anymore," I said, swallowing my tears and the emotions that churned them.

"Christina, you can tell me."

"Avery, just drop it, okay?" I commanded.

"No, I'm not going to drop it," he said, forcefully. "I want to help you. I know you're hiding something. You said yourself that you could tell me anything. Now's your chance." *How did he know I was hiding something?*

"Please, Avery I don't want to talk about this." I started to cry, so I put my head down. He gently wiped my tears away.

"Oh, Christina, I'm really sorry." Avery lifted up my head and kissed me tenderly on the forehead. He then drew me closer and held me in his arms. I cried on his shoulder while he rubbed my back. My emotions ran through the entire gamut—from fear to sheer pleasure, from torture to ecstasy, from anxiety to serenity. It felt good to cry, to let it all out.

I pulled away still sobbing and bowed my head. "I'm sorry." I felt terrible for crying, for ruining a great day.

"It's okay." Avery embraced me again, trying to comfort me. "Shhhh. It's okay. I'm so sorry I upset you. I didn't mean to hurt you. I love you, Christina. Please forgive me," he said soothingly in my ear. There was a momentary pause.

"It's okay. I love you too," I cried.

Avery's hands caressed my face and moved a strand of my hair behind my ears and off my wet cheeks. Our lips found each other. We kissed passionately. I eased myself down on the floor with Avery clinging on top of me.

A part of me wanted desperately to tell him what happened, but I couldn't. Instead, I wanted him to fill the void I felt—the unworthiness, the guilt, the shame. I wanted him to stop the pain, the anguish, the torture I continued to suffer day after day, as I unwillingly and uncontrollably relived that real-life nightmare. I wanted so much to give myself to him completely, hoping that maybe he could erase that horrific scene on that summer's day in the Martins' house.

I needed to get lost in those moments with Avery. I was driven to remain focused on the present, to force myself not to drift to the unpleasant past.

I slid my hands up his shirt and pressed my hands on the small of his back and held him lovingly close. "I love you, Avery," I whispered.

"I love you too, Christina!" Avery hushed in a sexy voice. He kissed me feverishly along my neck, nestled by my ear, and back down my neck, along my clavicle to my chest.

I melted by the second. Chills ran through my body. My mind was free of thought and I was free of pain. We breathed heavily, panting. I felt like I was going to explode. Every fiber of my being was relishing his touch, our closeness.

He inched my shirt up and kissed my belly button. I flinched and practically yelped when his lips caressed my stomach.

Unexpectedly, Avery abruptly stopped. With a deep sigh, he said, "I'm sorry I can't do this." His face revealed his shame. I knew that look all too well—I saw it every day in the mirror.

"What's wrong?" I asked, stunned, feeling rejected.

"I don't want either of us to regret this." I leaned forward. We both sat up facing each other. "I promised I would stop if . . .," his voice dissipated. I caressed his face with the back of my hand.

"But . . .," I weakly attempted to plead with him. Realizing Avery was right, I leaned in and squeezed him tightly. At that moment I was extremely grateful for Avery's better judgment. "Thank you," I whispered.

We held each other tenderly for what seemed like an eternity. The security I felt in Avery's arms prevented me from ever wanting to release our embrace.

A knock on the basement door interrupted the moment. "Avery, Christina, it's dinner time," Mrs. Evans called down to us.

"It's time to eat. Will you be okay?" he asked tenderly, his eyes filled with concern.

"Yes, I'm fine." There was silence. "Avery . . .," I waited for his response.

"Yeah?"

"Thank you!" I hugged him again. He stood up and pulled me up in his arms. I wanted our time alone to last forever. I totally and implicitly trusted him and that thought brought on tears. I felt so emotional, so vulnerable. It was good and it was new, but it didn't replace the reoccurring nightmare. Nothing could.

Out of nowhere, Avery licked me on my cheek like a dog. Shocked and humored by his antics, I threw my head back and asked through the laughter, "What did you do that for?"

"You needed a laugh." I chuckled again. "See, it worked!"

"Where do you come up with this stuff?"

He shrugged. "I don't know. It just came to me."

———◆———

We ventured upstairs to discover an empty kitchen.

"They must be outside." When we ambled outback, we found Joey standing by Mr. Evans at the grill. *I forgot it was a barbecue.*

"Hi, guys," Joey waved to us casually. Avery and I greeted him together.

"How long have you been here?" Avery asked surprised.

"I just got here." he answered. "I stopped by to see if you wanted to hang out." Joey glanced in my direction and then back to Avery. "Your mom invited me to stay for dinner."

"I didn't think you two would mind," Mrs. Evans said. Honestly, we didn't mind. We sat around and talked after we loaded up our cheeseburgers. Joey couldn't believe I spent the entire day at Avery's house.

"Don't you two get sick of each other?" Joey asked, with a pained look of being constipated. Avery and I turned to each other. I noticed his parents also exchanged looks. We both shook our heads. "So, what did you do all day?"

Ah, we made out mostly. We almost had sex. Avery licked me like a dog. It was just your average day.

"We played video games, we played catch, took a walk," Avery was about to continue when Joey interrupted.

"You played catch?" he said with a confused look in my direction.

"Yeah, I like throwing the ball around. It was my suggestion," I said, somewhat defensively. Avery's longtime friend slowly nodded approvingly.

"Hey, are you guys doing anything tonight—like, later?" he inquired.

"No. Why?" I answered.

Joey shrugged, "Ah, I was hoping to hang out with Avery."

"It's not too late to invite a few people over," Mrs. Evans suggested, pressing her lips together, her eyes dancing with delight. *She is so cute!*

"Yeah, Avery, let's have a party!" Joey shouted like a second grader getting his first dog. I blushed thinking of Avery licking me like he was my pet dog.

"I don't know. It's last minute," he replied.

"I can make a few calls at my house," Joey suggested, practically panting like a dog. Again, my cheeks warmed up recounting Avery's pet-like impulses. Little did they know what went on in the basement earlier.

Avery addressed me, "Christina, what do you want to do?"

"I think a party sounds like a great idea!" I got caught up in Joey's enthusiasm.

"A party it is then!" Avery declared.

Chapter 32

E SETTLED ON THE DETAILS and split the calling list.
Joey ran home to call the guys. My job was to call the girls.
Seemed fair enough. Virtually painless thus far.

First on the list was Morgan. I asked her to make some calls,
since I was at Avery's. She was copacetic with calling most of our
friends. Then I called Faith, but I was informed that she was at her
father's bachelor pad, so she wouldn't be able to make the party.

The three of us agreed not to call Mindy and her posse, which
put my mind at ease, because it was well out of my comfort zone
to hang out with them.

Morgan called back and she was able to get in touch with a
bunch of people who would be able to attend. I didn't know
whether to feel comfort or worry, so I decided to go with the flow.
Fingers crossed!

Joey said the guys would be coming, yet I had no idea who that
entailed, as boys rarely elaborated on the specifics, and I didn't
want to press. I wondered what Joey told the guys. I hope they
weren't expecting Mindy and her crew.

Avery, Joey, and I set out the snacks, paper plates, napkins, drinks
and cups. Just before eight o'clock, the guests started to arrive.
Larry, Steve, and Tom were the first to show up. Like Larry, Steve
and Tom were known for their acumen and they all excelled at
sports. Also, like Larry, Steve was good-looking, but Tom was what
I considered average-looking.

Avery and I greeted everyone at the door, while Joey stayed
downstairs in the rec room to keep the guests down there. We told
the guys to join Joey downstairs.

Morgan came with Erin, Abby, Amy, and Katie. Shortly after, Val,
Cheryl, Jackie, and Macey arrived together. They thanked Avery

for inviting them before they headed down to the party room.

Next Peter, Matt, and John arrived. John was a soccer player and had the soccer thighs to show for it. *Okay, I noticed.* We had gym class together and I found him quite intimidating, especially the times he came charging at me when we played against each other. Matt and John were both attractive and smart.

Finally, Adam and Doug came together. Katie liked Doug. A lot! Doug's younger brother was on my brother's baseball team. Katie would come to the games hoping Doug would be there. She used to flirt with him like crazy. Doug was a cutie pie but reminded me of a male version of a blond bimbo. I didn't know Adam, but he seemed nice enough.

At a quarter after eight, Avery and I decided to join the crowd downstairs. And boy, was it crowded! *Man, we can throw a party together in no time!*

I quickly surveyed the guests. There were four distinct cliques. The girls, for the most part, stuck to themselves, each clique unto itself. Group one included Katie, Amy, Erin, and Abby. Group two consisted of Valerie, Cheryl, Macey, Jackie, and Morgan, who wanted to talk to the group she didn't come with. Altogether, I counted ten girls, including myself.

Peter, Larry, and Doug were playing video games, while the rest of the guys were in the room with the pool table. I noticed that there were ten guys and ten girls. All the boys were deemed popular, but the girls were not considered popular. Unfortunately, the social statuses were glaringly different.

"Do you mind if I join the guys in the pool room?" Avery asked out of consideration.

"No, it's okay. Have fun!" The host gave me a smooch on the lips and off he went. I walked over and sat next to Morgan.

"Thank you so much for calling everyone!" I said appreciatively.

"No problem. It was easy. You two look like quite the couple," she stated, her chin slightly tucked.

I tilted my head back and shared, "Yeah, I can't believe I spent the whole day here."

"You spent the whole day here at Avery's house?!" A wide-eyed Morgan bellowed. Katie and Amy scurried over when they heard Morgan shouting. "Oh, sorry!" She apologetically placed her hand over her mouth.

"What did you do all day?" Katie leaned in and asked quietly. I blushed and could feel my face burn a bright red. The four of us giggled.

"Was it just you two?" Amy asked.

"For most of the day, until Joey showed up for dinner. Mrs. Evans thought it would be a good idea for us to have a party to bring our friends together. It's kind of a long story," I waved my hand airily.

"I have time," Morgan said expectantly, leaning back and folding her arms. I shared with them how we all went to the movies last night and how Mindy ignored Joey and paid attention to Avery. I told them about the milkshakes, of which Morgan and Katie totally appreciated the significance, having known me well since fifth grade.

When I finished sharing, Amy admitted with a frown, "I don't get the milkshake thing."

"Christina loves to eat—especially loves chocolate shakes—and she's not too timid to eat in front of anyone, including boys. And she couldn't care less about the calories, unlike Mindy, who ordered a Diet Coke," Katie quickly surmised.

The light bulb went off over Amy's head. "Oh! Now, I get it!"

"I missed you guys!" I said puckering my lips.

"Ah, we missed you too," Katie returned sweetly.

"So, what's it like being Avery's girlfriend? What did you do all day? Do you get along with his parents?" Amy shot me one question after another, like a tennis ball machine.

"Okay, well, in a nutshell, it's awesome being Avery's girlfriend. He is unbelievably sweet!" I gushed. I couldn't hide my intense like for Avery.

"And he's a great kisser!" Katie teased.

"Katie!" Morgan admonished.

"No, no, it's okay. They got the deets over the summer. Kissing Avery was a major topic of conversation, one that I tried to avoid, but failed miserably," I said, admitting defeat.

"Go on," Amy encouraged, with the rolling of her hand.

"We played video games, played catch, took a walk, ate lunch, dinner, planned this party. And yes, I do get along with his parents. They are very nice. In fact, it was Avery's mom who suggested, as soon as I arrived, that I stay for dinner," I summarized quickly, while making eye contact with each of them. I couldn't help but try to gauge their responses.

Valerie bounced into our conversation. She had something to tell us and she clapped to emphasize the excitement of her impending news, "I can't believe I am at the same party with Joey Glosser!"

"I take it you like Joey?" I asked. Val nodded frenetically, every bit of her was oozing lust for Joey.

Forming her hands like she was praying, Val asked, while clapping frantically, "Can you like fix me up with him?"

"Ah, I can't make you any promises," I winced, thinking about Mt. Saint Mindy, as I didn't need another eruption.

"Oh, pleeeessssee!" Val begged, clasping her hands together, fingers intertwined. She bounced them, and her knees. *If I'm not careful, she'll launch out of this room with that boundless energy.*

I cringed under the pressure, "Err . . . my last attempt to match-make crashed and burned. I'm still reeling over it."

"I will do anything!" she said. Her bounce became a jump—the one jump turned into 2 jumps which turned into three. Her eyes entreated me like a puppy's when begging for that treat you're withholding, until it sits as commanded. Once more, the dog simile put a smile on my face.

"Anything, Val?" Morgan replied, with a slight close-lipped smile. "That's risky," especially with this one," she added, winking my way.

"If you weren't so cute," I said to Val, pinching her cheek like I was her Italian grandmother.

"Thank you! Thank you! Thank you!" she said, while grabbing both of my hands with hers.

"I'll see what I can do. Again, no promises! And you can't be mad at me for the outcome, promise me." She agreed. *She is adorable. I hope this goes well.* With that, I headed over to Avery and told him that Val had the hots for Joey. Avery called his best man, Joey, over.

"Yeah, what's up?" Joey asked, with nonchalance. I held my breath.

"Val likes you," Avery stated to the point.

"Oh, okay," Joey shrugged. Not the response I had hoped for her.

I begged the question, "So, are you interested?"

"Uh, I hadn't really thought about it."

"Well, think about it, okay?" I said. "Please," I smiled at him. "She really is sweet. Look how cute she is," I indicated in her direction with a slight head bob.

"Yeah, sure." Joey walked away with his hands in his pocket. *Nothing says 'not interested' like hands in the pockets. Bolting from the conversation does as well.*

Avery stole a moment to give me a kiss and by the time I returned to being a proper hostess, I noticed that Erin and Amy had jumped into a pool game with the guys, while Morgan casually watched.

"Hmm, will you look at that? This party isn't a complete flop after all," I concluded.

"No, but it sure is a different kind of party," Avery stated. I could only imagine as he was used to the Ring of Fire girls setting different people ablaze with their cinders of cruelty.

"I better go talk to Val. I don't want to leave her hanging."

As I walked over to Val, she pounced on me like a wild African cat, before I even got the chance to speak, "So, what did he say?"

"Well, he's thinking about it," I said, slowly drawing out what little information I had, while aiming to gently give her a small clue that there wasn't a hopeful outcome.

"Thinking about what?" she crinkled her forehead. *Jeez, she doesn't get this.*

"You. It's not that he didn't like you. He just never thought about you like that." *Honest and painless.*

"Oh, okay. That's better than a flat-out rejection, huh?" Val asked, her energy clearly diluted.

"Yes, it is," I bobbed my head.

"Thanks for trying, Christina. That was nice of you." I nodded. "So," she added, "what's it like going out with Avery?"

"I should just get a tape recorder and tape my response," I stated in weariness. *I need to hide my feelings better.*

"Oh, sorry. I was just curious." *You and everyone else.*

Macey, Jackie and Cheryl leaned in to hear what I had to say. I figured I should tell them to spare myself from having to repeat the response to the ever-popular question of the night.

"It's okay," I put my hand on her arm.

Abby popped over. "What's going on?"

"Christina was just about to tell us about her and Avery," Val explained.

"Oh, cool, I'm listening," Abby said, leaning forward, while slapping her hands on her thighs.

"Well, Avery is very sweet for starters. We talk about anything and everything." The girls literally cooed. "He's very good to his friends."

"So, you've been hanging out with his friends?" Cheryl asked.

"Ah, yeah. Joey mostly."

"He is so cute!" Val could barely contain herself.

"He is actually. Joey's a real sweetheart," I affirmed.

"But not like Avery," Abby added.

"No, not like Avery," I blushed a little. "Avery is amazing. He acts way more mature than you'd think." "How so?" Macey snarled.

"Well, he tells me things that take a lot of courage. He's just so open and honest," I shared.

"Like what kind of things does he say?" Jackie asked curiously, at which time Morgan joined our group. "Uh, it's personal. It's not for me to say."

"He told you he loved you, didn't he?" Abby prodded. I blushed big time and put my hand over my mouth. "Oh, my gosh! He did! I was right! Look at her blushing!" Abby cheered, pointing at me with one hand, as she touched her nose with the other.

"I'm not saying anything," I declared, feeling hotter by the second. *Why did I have to be so obvious? I would totally lose at playing Poker.*

"Oh, you don't have to. It's written all over your face," Macey sneered. *What is her problem?*

"All right, girls, give her some space. Break it up," Val said. "She said she didn't want to talk about it." Val winked at me and whispered, "We'll talk later in private." I thought Val was a cutie, but she wasn't someone I would confide in.

With a huge grin on her face, Macey clapped her hands together and yelled, "I think we should play spin the bottle." I ignored her.

Morgan grabbed me by the arm and pulled me away to a more private location.

"Yes?" I asked, eyebrows raised.

"Are you two really in love?" Morgan probed. I grimaced. "Aren't you guys going a little fast?" I remained silent. "Look, Christina, I'm genuinely concerned."

I glanced at her sideways. "Concerned about what?"

"You getting hurt. You doing something you'll regret. I saw how close you two are. You guys are acting like a married couple!" she whispered vehemently.

"What? We are not!" I said offended. "It wasn't even my idea to host this party!" I retorted in my defense.

Morgan drew a deep breath and calmed down. "I know, but still. Please tell me that you'll be careful," she insisted.

"Yes, Mom. I'll be careful," I answered with a sarcastic tone.

"Don't you want to wait to have sex until you're married?"

Morgan restated a previous conversation between the two of us. I did in fact tell her that I wanted to wait. And at the time, I did want to wait.

But now, I was so confused. I loved being with Avery. If he didn't stop earlier today, I may have . . . But Avery did stop. He said he wanted to wait and I told him I wanted to wait too.

Then again, what's the point? It wasn't like I was a virgin.

Morgan broke my thought process. "Christina!" she yelled in a whisper. "You told me you wanted to wait," she hesitated. "Oh my gosh!" Morgan didn't dare say the Lord's name in vain. "You didn't? Did you?" Her eyes were as wide as the ocean is deep.

"No!" I said, emphatically. "Of course not!" I snapped back.

"I'm telling you. You two seem awfully intimate." Morgan had always been very intuitive.

I assured her, "Don't worry. Avery wants to wait until he's married too."

"Did he say that?"

"Yes, he did, as a matter of fact," I pursed my lips and folded my arms. She didn't need to know how close we were earlier to doing the deed. I was open with her, but not that open. My sexual relations were just that, mine.

"Oh, all right then. You're usually such a good judge of character. I was just concerned."

"Oh, don't be. I'm fine. Really," I waved her off, dismissively.

We both looked over to a lot of commotion. It appeared that Macey rallied up the troops to play the ever famous, spin the bottle.

"Figures Macey would suggest something like spin the bottle," Morgan grumbled, as she rolled her eyes.

Macey stood on a bench with her hands cuffed around her mouth and shouted, "Okay, we're playing spin the bottle!" She threw her hands in the air and pumped them.

The guys were hovering around her, practically salivating. She was in her glory and it was probably the only time she would ever get any action. Avery made a beeline to me.

"Avery, I don't want to play," I said desperately. Avery grabbed my hand and held it securely.

"Me neither," Morgan added.

"Everyone has to play," Macey declared.

I started to tremble, thinking of the last time I was forced into a situation. "Christina, it will be okay. I'll sit right next to you." Avery's words somewhat comforted me.

"But . . ."

Then chanting began with lots of overhead fisted air pumps. "Spin the bottle! Spin the bottle! Spin the bottle!"

"Please, Avery don't make me play," I pleaded, still shaking. I was terrified to kiss anyone but Avery.

Val shouted, "Morgan, come join us!"

"I'm not playing!" Morgan refused, arms crossed, shaking her head.

Macey swayed her forefinger back and forth and sang, "Uh, uh, uh! Everyone has to play!"

Morgan continued to shake her head. Her eyes were pleading with us. "Avery, please, we don't want to play," I said on Morgan's behalf as well.

Macey taunted, "Morgan, don't be such a baby,"

Finally, Avery stated, "We're going to sit this one out."

The group followed Macey's lead and started chanting with more fist pumping, "Everyone plays! Everyone plays! Everyone plays!"

Avery turned his back to the group and said to Morgan and me, "Look girls, maybe the bottle won't land on you."

The intense chanting continued. "Everyone plays! Everyone plays! Everyone plays!"

"Don't worry. I have a plan," Avery winked at us. "Follow me." We followed Avery over to the group.

"Okay, everyone needs to sit boy girl, boy girl," Macey directed. Avery motioned to Morgan and me that he would sit between us. Joey sat on the other side of me which put me more at ease. Avery reached for my hand. Then he whispered something to Morgan.

She nodded.

"What did you say to her?" I asked.

"I wanted to make sure she's okay." I liked how Avery not only looked out for me, but for my friends too. I wondered what Avery's plan was.

Macey stated, "The rules are that you have to kiss on the lips." I squirmed. "Okay, who's going first," Macey asked. We all agreed that Macey go first since she organized it. She was more than happy to comply. "All right, I'll go first."

Macey spun the bottle. It landed on Steve who was sitting adjacent to her. She leaned over and kissed Steve smack dab on the lips. Steve spun the bottle. It pointed to Cheryl. He gave her a quick peck on the lips. Cheryl twisted the game piece. It rested in front of John. Their lips collided by accident because John awkwardly jerked forward. John gave the bottle a whirl and it landed on Erin. They kissed. Erin rotated the beverage container, which pointed to Joey. Val was beside herself when Erin and Joey kissed. When Joey spun the bottle, it landed on . . . Avery dashed his hand forward to push the bottle before it settled on me. Avery endured a lot of grief for that.

"Yo, Avery, you can't do that! It landed on Christina!" Soccer Thighs remarked flagrantly. *He is always so intense!*

"I can do anything I want. It's my party." *Yeah, you tell him, Avery!*

"Boooo . . .!" the crowd yelled fiercely. Avery literally got booed at his own party, followed by chanting, which was led by none other than Macey. *What's her deal?* "Christina! Christina! Christina!"

I translated that to mean they wanted me to kiss Joey. I felt very awkward sitting next to him at that moment.

He glowered by the second. I felt kind of bad for Joey. He was jilted by Mindy last night and now me, sort of. It wasn't anything personal. It's just that he wasn't Avery. Surely, Joey could understand that.

The chanting continued. "Christina! Christina! Christina!"

If it was up to me, I would have never invited Macey. She was always stirring the pot.

Avery whispered in my ear, "It's up to you, Christina." He lovingly squeezed my hand.

"All right! All right!" I exclaimed.

"Yay...!" The crowd cheered.

I felt Avery staring him down, all the while holding my hand. Joey leaned over to kiss me and gave me the slightest little peck on the lips. I realized it was my turn to spin the bottle. The bottle landed on Avery! I was so relieved and we didn't even cheat that time.

A soft chant continued in the background. "Christina. Christina. Christina."

Avery and I leaned in at the same time and kissed. It was tender and sweet.

"Ahhhh!" the group expressed, adoringly. Avery spun the bottle. I couldn't believe it landed on me!

"You have to be kidding me!" Adam shouted. *Why is he so upset? It's not like we rigged it this time.*

The group chanted "Kiss! Kiss! Kiss!" *Look what Macey started!*

Avery whispered in my ear, "Let's give them a show!" I nodded. This time our kiss was bolder, more passionate, and lingered.

The crowd went wild. "Wahoo! Go, Avery!"

I blushed beyond belief. I felt my face turn beat red and I instinctively covered my hands over my face. Avery put his arms around me and we laughed. He kissed me quickly, yet tenderly, on the lips and told me it was my turn to spin.

This reminded me of the episode on The Monkees, when Davy Jones played spin the bottle and the bottle always landed on him. Oh, how I was in love with Davy Jones back then. He was the epitome of cuteness back in the '70s. My childhood crush, prior to Avery.

I gave the bottle a quick spin and it fell on Morgan. It was so close to landing on Avery. I spun it again and it landed on Larry, who was sitting next to Morgan. I had to lean across Avery to kiss Larry who pecked me on the bottom lip. The game continued. At one point, Val and Joey kissed. Val giggled and turned a bright shade of red. Joey didn't seem to mind the kiss, as he was able to test the waters. Katie and Doug kissed too. Katie was rather aggressive. Doug blushed in that case. We finished the game and Morgan managed to survive without having to kiss anyone, and she was the only one who didn't get a turn.

A relieved Morgan exhaled to Avery and me, "Phew, I'm glad that's over!"

Tom yelled from the pool room. "Yo, Avery, you playin'?"

"I'm gonna play pool, okay?" Avery kissed me a short-term good-bye.

Morgan walked over after Avery left. "You're right," Morgan said. "Avery is sweet. You two are too much though. You should have seen his face when you had to kiss Joey. It was intense."

"Avery's protective of me."

"No, really?" Morgan said dripping with sarcasm.

Katie bounded over and stated, excitedly, "You throw the best parties, Christina! I can't believe I got to kiss Doug."

"Katie, you practically tackled him," I recounted.

"Oh, he loved it!" she teased, waving her hand.

"Maybe you should play hard to get," Morgan suggested. Morgan must be the expert on playing hard to get. She sure did practice what she preached.

"Too late for that!" I exclaimed. The three of us cracked up.

I flopped back on the couch and exclaimed, "What a day! My head is spinning!" Just then I heard a somewhat familiar voice.

Sam roared from across the room, "Christina!"

"Who is *that?*" Katie asked.

"Joey's brother, Sam."

"I think you have another fan. Only you, Christina." Katie winked at me as Sam hurried toward us with a mega smile on his visage.

"Hi, Sam," I said, nonchalantly. "What possessed you to crash this party?"

"Moi?" asked the guy who badly impersonated a Frenchman. "I did not crash zee party."

I had to ask. "Sam, are you drunk?"

"No, just high on life!" He paused, then fired thoughts and questions rapidly. Apparently, he and Amy shared the same tennis ball machine. "I like this song! Who's your friend? We should dance!" Sam pulled Katie out on the dance floor. "Hey, you're the chick from the beauty pageant. I remember you!" He shouted over the song, "Apache" by Sugarhill Gang. Fortunately, Katie didn't seem to mind dancing with Sam.

"Let's go dance!" I dragged Morgan out on the dance floor. It didn't take long before the room turned into a fun dance party thanks to Sam the Man. That's what I started to call him, because I liked to dance.

We danced to the next song "I love Rock 'n Roll," by Joan Jett and The Blackhearts. Avery joined us and we danced to "You Dropped a Bomb On Me" by Gap Band.

When the slow song "Open Arms" came on by Journey, Avery and I were like two suction cups stuck together. Jeffrey Osborne sang another slow song, "On the Wings of Love" which sent shivers down my spine, because that's exactly how I felt at that very moment. It was as if no one was in the room with us. We kissed tenderly, then it started to heat up between the two of us.

Avery whispered in my ear, "I wish we were alone right now." I smiled. We continued to embrace each other even when the tempo picked up with "Get Down On It" by Kool and the Gang. I pulled away when "Freeze-Frame" came on by J. Geils Band and danced wildly.

"Christina, you are one crazy chick!" Sam shouted over the music. I shot Avery a look I knew he would understand.

"Don't call my girlfriend a chick," Avery teased.

"Sorry!" Sam apologized, playfully.

Morgan and Katie giggled. We all continued to dance to songs like "I'm So Excited" by the Pointer Sisters, "We Got the Beat" by The Go-Go's, "Whip It" by Devo—one of my lunch time juke box middle school favorites—, and "Making Love" by Roberta Flack. Avery and I found ourselves kissing on the couch once again.

"Get a room!" yelled Sam the Man from ten feet away. We ignored the suggestion and went on with our business.

A moment later, Sam the Man sat down next to Avery. "Ahem," he interrupted.

"What?" growled an annoyed Avery, without looking back at him. I heard giggling in the background.

The interloper tapped Avery on the shoulder. "You're ignoring your guests."

"What do you care? You crashed the party," Avery joked. I rested my head on his shoulder. I was getting tired, as it was getting late.

Joey's big brother gave us a big bear hug and stated, "You two are annoyingly cute."

"You are just annoying," Avery jested.

All of a sudden, Sam the Man jumped up and blurted, "Okay, I'm outta here! Nice talking to you!" And the big, goofy guy crashed the party on the dance floor. Hands swayed, heads bobbed. Dancers were singing, smiling, and laughing. A little while later, the party started to wind down. Someone shut the music off. A bunch of us were just sitting around. Avery and I were sandwiched together with no room to spare between us.

"I need a ride home," I realized.

"I can give you a ride home," Sam the Man offered.

"Thanks, but I'm out of your way," I yawned in response.

"You can get a ride with us. My dad is driving. He should be here any minute," Morgan offered.

"Oh, great! Thanks!"

"Why don't we give these two love birds some privacy?" Sam the Man suggested. "Ladies, come with me." Everyone funneled upstairs.

Avery tilted his head back against the couch, "Wow, what a night!"

"I know. It turned out better than I thought it would."

"I really had fun," he said, his eyes glinting in the dim light.

"Me too," I smiled in between yawns.

"I love you, Christina," Avery said as he kissed me.

"I will always love you, Avery," I replied softly. "I better get going. Thanks for such a memorable day."

"The best day ever!" Avery grinned and winked.

"The best day ever!" I agreed, and we hugged each other.

Avery held my hand as he guided me upstairs. I thanked his parents for being such gracious hosts and departed.

BEST. DAY. EVER.

Chapter 33

I SLEPT IN BUT WOKE UP with a smile on my face. I had this strange urge to go for a jog, so I laced up my sneakers shortly after breakfast and set out for a run.

It was another gorgeous day in Pennsford. The sun warmly greeted me. The air was crisp and the sky was vast, blue, and cloudless. Running felt good—natural—and I wondered why I didn't do it more often.

I started out slowly and methodically as I approached the dense woods. Dodging the trees kept my speed to a minimum as I followed the sinuous dirt path and jumped over the fallen tree branches. I listened to the crunch of twigs with each step, the rhythmical beat of my heart, and the flapping of birds flying in the trees above me as they chirped greetings to each other.

Hundreds of thoughts infiltrated my mind at once. I thought about the day before as there was much to process. Most of all, I couldn't shake the idea that I almost slept with Avery, or, at least, that I wanted to. *What is the point in waiting? It's not like I am a virgin.* My stomach dropped forty feet and my body shuddered.

For fleeting moments at a time, I would forget that I wasn't a virgin anymore. It didn't seem fair. It didn't seem right. *It wasn't my choice.* I tried not to allow my mind to go down that path of thinking, because it would always lead to that horrific day at the Martins'. But when my mind recalled that violent day, no matter what technique I used to distract myself, the horrible nightmare would come flooding back with a vengeance.

This time was no exception. I was robbed of my innocence in the most violent manner. Visions of that crazed monster glaring at me with such hatred caused me to scream silently from within. Thoughts of the unspeakable caused me to gasp for air. I stopped dead in my tracks, slumped over, heaving my next breath while swallowing the bile in the back of my throat. I dared to stand up straight, to face my fears.

The woods enveloped me. The trees swirled around me, suffocating me. Only narrow rays of sunshine broke through the tower of trees. It was dark and eerie. Just like my thoughts. Just like my perpetrator. I had to break free . . .

I sprinted out of the woods and onto the street. The sun, warm and bright, welcomed me back to safety. The bright yellow star also brought a rush of hopeful memories of the last thirty-six hours that made me beam.

I reflected on my catch with Avery and taking a walk on his street. I relished all the times he told me he loved me and how I reciprocated.

My friends—I thought of them too. I wondered if Joey and Val hooked up. I assumed Katie and Doug didn't. I thought about how Sam the Man seemed to be having fun with my friends. I was grateful for the goofy giant crashing the party because he made it more fun.

I pictured us playing spin the bottle and thought of my panic and relief.

Kissing Joey wasn't too bad. Larry's kiss was awkward. It was a near miss as if it didn't count, but it counted. It had to count.

Then I found myself laughing out loud when I remembered Avery licking me. He had a knack for knowing exactly what to do and when to do it.

I flashed back to the moments before he licked me too, like how he tickled my belly when he kissed it. A chill ran through me. I continued to recount our most intense moments together. The urges to be more intimate became more intense with every movement. Every kiss, every touch was like a slice of heaven.

I was scared of this strong desire that had grown inside me. My emotions were like a pinball, bouncing off the many walls of the board. At times, I felt like I was racking up crazy points; at others, like my ball was out of play.

One minute, I was enjoying an innocent game of Pac-Man with my sweet boyfriend, and the next, we were on the verge of having steamy sex. I moved from laughter to tears. I felt exhilarated, embarrassed, guilty and shameful. The run helped me sort through the pinball machine of emotions that I carried like a backpack with me.

I kept a decent pace, running through the townhouses behind my housing development, while memories of the previous night played like a movie in my mind, and before I knew it, I was home. I was upstairs in my bedroom when the phone rang.

"Hello," I answered.

"Hi, Christina. It's Avery."

"Hi, Avery. What's up?" I answered, casually.

"I just got back from church. Are you doing anything today?"

"Nope. What about you? Are you busy?" Please say no.

"No, I was hoping we could hang out together."

"What did you have in mind?"

"I thought we could play softball. Joey and I talked about getting a game together. What do you say?"

"Would I be the only girl?"

"We usually don't play with girls, but we know you can play, so you can join us."

"Okay. Where should I meet you all?"

"Meet me at the same spot. I'll walk, since you left your bike over here."

"Oh, right, I forgot about my bike."

"Don't forget your softball glove." *I completely forgot about my bike.*

———•———

I met Avery at our usual rendezvous location with glove in hand.

"Hi," I said, blushing at my secret thought-life. *My goodness if he only knew.*

"Hi, Beautiful." He gave me a kiss on the lips, instinctively causing my lips to curl upward as my cheeks heated up from his compliment.

"What? No licking today?" I teased, batting my eyelashes.

Jerking his head backward, he chuckled. "Only in private."

"Well, we better get some private time today," I hinted, with a flirty smirk, my eyes dancing.

"I'll see what I can do," he winked.

We arrived at Joey's hand in hand. The guys were already there warming up. Joey's backyard was huge, like Veteran's Stadium, where the Philadelphia Phillies played. Okay, maybe not *that* big.

We picked teams. I was on Avery's team, of course.

Dreamy Eyes turned to me and announced, "We're in the field first. You play first base. I'm playing second."

"I thought you liked playing first."

"I do, but I think you're better suited for first." *He'd know.*

We started to play. My teammates didn't wing the ball to me, like they did to each other, but I was able to play the base effectively, by making all the possible outs. It was our turn to bat.

Peter taunted, "She can catch and field. Let's see if she can bat."

"Ladies first," Avery gestured to home plate. *Even here, he's a gentleman. My gosh, sometimes I can't believe he's real. Someone pinch me.*

"Are you sure?" I asked, knowing that the better players bat first. Technically, I should have batted last.

"Batter up!" someone yelled from the field. *Jeez! Testy. It's just a backyard game of softball, although it is the size of a professional ball field.*

"Sink in!" Sam the Man yelled, as third baseman. All the fielders moved forward.

"Gee, thanks!" I replied, realizing that they weren't expecting me to hit the ball far.

The pitcher lobbed the ball over the plate. I swung hard and dumped it between the shortstop and the left fielder. I got on base and my teammates cheered me on. I think I surprised them. I know I surprised myself.

Avery shouted, "Way to go, Christina! Great hit!"

I inched away from first base toward second to get a head start in case Avery got a hit. He stepped up to the plate. The pitch was fast and hard. He swung, connected—you could hear that wonderful cracking sound of the ball hitting the bat. We rounded the bases. Avery was on my tail like lightning. He nearly passed me. I struck home plate with Avery inches behind me. Avery hit a two-run homer!

Our teammates high-fived each other and congratulated Avery and me on scoring the runs. Avery swung by me and put his arms around me. He gave me a big kiss on my cheek to celebrate our success and lifted me off the ground, sending shivers down my spine.

"Is there anything you can't do?" Avery asked, beaming from ear to ear. I returned the smile. I didn't want to entertain that question, because I knew all too well that I got lucky with my hit as the opposing team went easy on me. Nonetheless, we rejoiced together.

I whispered in Avery's ear, "Let's go have some private time."

"But we just started playing."

"I know. I thought we could quit while we're ahead," I suggested with a flirtatious grin.

"Let's stick it out. I promise we'll have some alone time later," he proposed, and kissed me tenderly as if he was sealing his promise. My insides turned to mush.

I can work with that I thought to myself hoping the kiss would hold me over. "You have a deal." We shook on it. Joey complimented me after we finished playing,

"Good game, Christina!"

"Yeah, you can play softball with us any time," Steve encouraged.

"Thanks for letting me play," I said, appreciatively.

"Avery said you could play and he was right," Joey commented.

"See, I told you," Avery interjected. My stomach growled ferociously, like it was ticked off at me because I didn't feed it. "Was that your stomach?"

"Uh, yeah. I didn't eat lunch."

"I'm hungry too. Let's go get something to eat," Avery said. "Hey, guys, catch you later!"

Lucky for us, his mom still had some chicken salad left over. Soon after lunch, we found ourselves making out on the couch in the basement . . . again. *Finally, some alone time.* Avery pulled back from our interlude. "Thanks for playing softball." He sat back and continued with pride and a flicker in his eye, "You were great! The guys were really impressed!"

"You must be my lucky charm," I teased. "I'm surprised you all let me play."

"You heard Steve. You're like one of the guys now, except I would never kiss one of them!" he declared.

I shuttered at the mere thought. "I hope not!" He gently brushed a stray wisp of hair out of my face and kissed me again. Once again, I found myself getting lost in Avery's luscious kisses.

"I better get going," I said abruptly.

"Why don't you stay for dinner?"

"I would, but my parents gave me a lecture this morning about overstaying my welcome. Sorry."

"Okay, I'll ride back with you," Avery stated.

As we rode back to my house, we talked and joked around. We were never in short supply of conversation. When we arrived at my house, he said, exuberantly, "This had to the best weekend I have ever had!"

His childlike enthusiasm and honesty made me laugh. It flattered me too. "I know. It was awesome! I'm so glad we were able to spend the entire weekend together. I hate the thought of heading back to school."

"We'll see each other tomorrow, slugger," he reminded me.

I ribbed him after nodding. "That's true, but it's not the same. Avery, thanks again for such a great weekend!"

I looked around to see if the coast was clear, making sure nobody was around. I kissed him good-bye and waved to him as he rode away. My heart ached as I missed him instantly.

Chapter 34

*A*VERY WAS LEANING AGAINST MY locker first thing Monday morning. We both smiled brightly and greeted each other with a kiss. We talked about our incredible weekend together. I couldn't get enough of him, but I also didn't want him to get sick of me. To that end, it was better that we didn't have health class together.

I walked into math class. Joey was sitting at his desk across the room and mouthed, "Hi."

Val came in and told me that Avery and I hosted a great party. I wanted to find out if anything transpired between her and Joey, but class was starting. I tried to observe any communication between the two that might reveal their status. Nothing. I doubt they even glanced in each other's direction.

Later, Katie leaned toward me and whispered during health class, "Christina, what a great party you and Avery threw Saturday night. I had so much fun."

"Anything in particular you care to share?" I hinted, raising my eyebrows.

She shook her head and said, "Are you going to have more parties?" I shrugged. "You and Avery are too cute together!" she gushed.

Faith exclaimed, "Sounds like I missed the social event of the year!"

"It wasn't the same without you!" I said, trying to sound empathetic to her absence. The truth was Faith and I didn't attend many parties together anymore. We were more like best friends in school, but not out of school. I went to her house a few times and we hung out at middle school dances, but that was it.

"I take it you will be eating lunch with him again today?" she inquired. I nodded.

———◆———

Avery and I exchanged the usual hello kiss in the caf. This was my chance to ask Joey about Val.

"So, Joey, you said you would think about going out with Val. What did you decide?" I asked, while getting out my sandwich.

"She seems nice enough, but I'm not interested. Sorry," Joey answered, then took a bite of a granola bar.

I shrugged, "Oh, okay." I didn't want to push it and took a bite of my turkey on rye.

"Christina, you were really great yesterday playing softball," Peter complimented, before laying into his ham and cheese sandwich.

"Thanks a lot! It was fun! It was really cool of you guys to give me a shot." My mouth spread across my face, and I proceeded to munch away at my lovingly crafted sandwich.

"You would think that these two would get sick of each other," Joey said under his breath. We could practically hear the rattling in his baffled brain trying to wrap his head around this boyfriend-girlfriend stuff Avery and I shared.

Avery put his hand on my lap and smirked, "Don't mind him. He's just jealous."

I turned to Avery and bit my lower lip, "Maybe I should eat with my friends."

Joey leaned forward and reached out to me, "Christina, I was just kidding. Really. You should stay."

"Yeah, you're one of the guys now," Peter declared. It seemed as if I won Peter over, but not Joey, who I once thought was a bad boy, turned sweet. I was confused with his erratic behavior toward me.

"See, I told you," Avery reminded me of our previous conversation the day before, after playing softball. Their comments helped me to feel better, enabling me to reconsider leaving their table. Besides, returning to the girls' table would be like admitting defeat.

"Christina, what's up with your friend Macey?" Joey scowled.

Peter nodded in agreement, "Yeah, she is obnoxious!"

"Wait a second. You guys seemed to be going along with her antics," I responded. The chanting echoed in my memory.

"You mean the chanting after Avery cheated when he moved

the bottle?" Peter jabbed. I winced, looked down and took a swig of water. "We were just going along with the crowd," Peter explained.

"Speak for yourself," Joey huffed, and crumbled up his wrapper and threw it in his lunch bag.

"Well, the truth is she's more of an acquaintance. She's friends with Val, Cheryl and Jackie," I answered, eyeing up my Double Stuf Oreo.

"Is she friends with Katie?" Joey asked.

"No, why?"

"I think Sam likes Katie," Joey stated.

"Oh, really?" I sang, raising my eyebrows.

"Yeah, since you're taken," Joey nodded, and smiled a toothless grin.

I gave him a sideways glance. "Do you know something I don't?"

"Like it isn't obvious?" Joey answered with a contorted face and flailing hands.

"Not really. I thought people were just messing with me by saying he was interested. In fact, he barely spoke to me this weekend," I answered innocently, before taking a bite of my heavenly cookie. *No matter what, chocolate makes life so much better!*

"Only because he doesn't want to dis Avery," Joey disclosed. I looked at Avery, who was enjoying his hoagie. "Why do you think Avery came out to dance with you when he was playing pool?" Joey toyed.

In his own defense, Avery interjected, "I wanted to dance with Christina." *Pee-yew! I could smell those onions!*

"Whoa!" Peter held up his palm to me and asked, "How do you know Sam?"

"He drove us home from the movies Friday night," I responded.

"Just from that?" Peter said, shaking his head with a confused look. "It seemed like you two went way back."

Joey chimed in, "They met at the Martins' the night Avery and Christina hooked up."

Suddenly, I felt sick to my stomach. Picturing the Martins' house made me feel nauseous and the heat rose to my cheeks. I put down my Oreo. *Guess there are some things my favorite cookie won't cure.*

"Christina, are you okay?" Avery asked. I shrugged, shook my head, and wrapped my arms around my stomach. "Guys, cool it. You know Christina didn't do anything wrong. Just leave her alone, okay?"

He lovingly squeezed my hand. *Thanks, Avery.*

I sat there, willing the horrid thoughts from that wicked afternoon at the Martins' to escape my mind. *Focus on pleasant things, Christina. You can do this. Think of the beach, the waves crashing on the sand. Laughter. Seagulls flying overhead. Digging for sand crabs . . .* My mind snapped back to reality upon hearing a familiar voice and feeling a hand on my thigh.

"Hey, Christina, are you all right now?" Avery persisted, in a concerned voice.

In a split second, I regained my composure. I smiled within, placed my hand on his, the one resting on my thigh, and turned to him in a soft tone, "Yeah, I'm fine. Thanks."

And I was. Eventually, I managed a real smile, upon gazing into his worried eyes.

He released his hand and pulled me into a side hug, which brought on tiny giggles on my behalf. That boyfriend of mine always knew exactly what to do or say.

I settled back into eating my stuffed wafers by separating the chocolate ends and scraping the middle goodness off with my teeth. Double Stuf. Double the deliciousness. While I was dissecting my tasty treat, I sensed a stubborn stare in my direction.

Joey turned to me and asked, "So, Christina, is Katie dating anyone? Sam wants to know."

"Not that I'm aware of," I replied, scraping away at my delectable delight.

Joey probed, "Did she mention Sam at all?" He took a bite of an apple but kept his attention on my response.

"Nope. Not at all, but she did say she had fun."

"Yeah, it was a good party," Peter affirmed.

Joey looked at Peter and said, "You're stoked because you got to kiss Erin."

"So did you," Peter smirked, throwing his trash into his lunch bag.

It was disgusting how Joey carelessly spit out the juice from his apple as he goaded Peter. "Yeah, but that wasn't the highlight of the party for me."

I missed eating with the girls. At least they didn't spit.

Yuck!

"What was it then? Kissing Christina?" Peter taunted. *Why bring me into the conversation?* I felt more uncomfortable by the second. Most notably were the bats flying in my stomach. I hated being the center of attention like that, so I shied away from Joey, and I regretted not leaving earlier.

Avery stepped in, "Dude, chill. That's my girl you're talking about. Man, one stupid game of spin the bottle and you guys are going nuts. Relax."

With that said, the conversation totally veered in a different direction. I, too, veered. I didn't know what to make of Joey being hot and cold towards me. He made me uncomfortable, as if I offended him. I wracked my brain to think of a time that I may have said something to hurt his feelings, but nothing significant came to mind.

The bell rang. Everyone stood up and grabbed their books.

"Christina, I'll meet you after school, okay?" Avery said. I hadn't returned from my private getaway.

Avery repeated with more volume, "Christina, I said I'll meet you after school, okay?"

"Oh, okay." We kissed good-bye. I walked mindlessly to class, with my eyes burning from the lingering scent of onions.

I met Avery after school at our usual secluded spot under the tree. Without much hesitation, we began kissing each other while lying on the grass. *Whew! The onion smell was gone!*

My mind was on overload from the past few days, being jam-packed with activities. I couldn't switch off the plethora of thoughts that bombarded me. It was as if my mind was being attacked like a participant in dodgeball. As much as I ducked or held up my arms to protect the balls from pelting me, they still came at me hard and fast. As a result, I felt very restless and confused.

I thought about how I originally wanted to wait to date until I was closer to the age of being married. How I never kissed a guy until Avery. How I loved being with Avery, yet I couldn't shake the fact that I was only thirteen. I didn't want to get a bad reputation, but I wondered if it was too late. I thought about how Joey was friendly one minute, then attacked me the next. Everything was blissful when Avery kissed me, so why did I react so abruptly?

"Avery, stop a second. Please stop."

"Hey, sweetness, what's the matter?" He asked in a caring tone.

"I . . ." I hesitated, not exactly sure what my problem was. "I don't know how to put how I feel into words."

Avery pulled himself up and leaned against the tree. "It's okay. I'm listening."

I sat beside him, looking upward pleading for the sky to be my Cyrano de Bergerac. It worked. "I don't want to be that girl."

Avery crinkled up his nose. "What girl?"

"The one guys want to go out with because she puts out," I blurted with a tinge of both shame and embarrassment.

"Oh, *that* girl!" He got it. "You're not that girl," he said definitively, shaking his head.

It made it more humiliating to have to support my statement with evidence. "Yes, I am."

He tilted his head. "Why do you think that?"

I felt uneasy, because I was about to broach an awkward topic again. "Well, I hope I'm wrong but . . ." I forced myself to complete the unnerving, possibly arrogant, sentence. It was the only way to peace. ". . . it has to do with our conversation at lunch today."

"Oh, jeez. What about it?" Avery said, bracing himself.

"It sounded like Joey and his brother . . .," I couldn't get the words out.

"Oh, the fact that they both like you." I winced. It pained me to hear it confirmed out loud.

"Yeah. It's not like Sam even knows me. His first impression of me was the two of us making out. Apparently, I made quite the impression that night—and that makes me feel kinda sick inside."

Avery waved his hand in a dismissive manner. "Sam's a goof. You can't go by what he thinks."

"And what about Joey? I know he's your friend and all, but . . ."

Avery cut me off before I could finish. "Joey is plain jealous. That much is obvious."

"You mean he isn't interested in me," I asked for clarification.

"No, I think he likes you, but he also sees the fun we have together. He wants that for himself. You can't really blame him, just how he handles it."

"Except I practically hyperventilated when I had to kiss him. I didn't mean to hurt his feelings. It was nothing personal. It's just that it wasn't you. I thought he understood that."

"No guy likes to get his ego bruised."

"I bruised his ego?!" I gasped and threw my hand to my mouth, completely dumbfounded. "I had no intention of doing that!"

"You didn't exactly jump his bones, like Katie did with Doug."

"You noticed that?" I cringed.

"You couldn't miss it! I take it she likes Doug?" Avery concluded.

"Yeah, she's had a thing for him for a while now. I'm sure he knew before she pounced him."

Avery squinted his eyes. "Do you think she would go for Sam?"

"I don't know. He's not really her type."

"Who's your type?" Avery asked.

"You," I stated emphatically.

"Anyone else?"

"No. How about you? Who's your type?"

"You and nobody else," he replied ardently.

My teeth anxiously scraped my bottom lip. "What about all the other girls you fooled around with?" I was surprised I said that and feared I sounded jealous.

"I was just experimenting," he said casually.

"What?" I shoved him playfully.

"Experimenting. I didn't want to feel like an inexperienced fool when I started dating the girl of my dreams."

"And that would be?" I sang, batting my eyelashes.

"As if you don't know," he smirked.

"I don't. You did go out with Amanda."

"Yeah, and she turned out to be way different than I expected."

I glanced at him sideways. "How so?"

"I already told you. She didn't talk and there was no chemistry between us. Not like you and me."

"Tell me about it," I said, not realizing at first that I spoke aloud.

"Christina, the truth is, my friends do like you and I've accepted that. It doesn't change how I feel about you and it won't change how I act around you. I hope it doesn't change how you feel about me or how you will act around me."

"It's awkward. That's all. One minute Joey is saying hello to me and the next, he's attacking us."

"Yeah, he was annoying at lunch today. He's not usually like that. I'm sorry about that. He's a little ticked off because I've been spending so much time with you."

"Ooooh, that makes sense. That clears up some things. Maybe you should spend some time with him after school. I can always go to the old folks' home," I suggested, gazing downward.

"Christina, I know what my options are and I want to spend every minute I can with you. Don't you get that?" he gently lifted my chin up.

"Yeah, I do." Because I did. I really did. "I really do."

"You're blowing your friends off at lunch, right?"

"Well, yeah." Sort of. They hardly seemed to miss me, or maybe they were understanding, as they admitted they would do the same if the situation were reversed. It was not as if I ditched my best friend, who I've known since kindergarten and played with every day since.

"But you still see them and talk to them, right?" he caressed my cheek, while he brushed back a ringlet and placed it behind my ear.

"Yeah," I replied nearly breathless, as I tingled all over from his gentle caress.

"It's not like we're severing ties to everyone else. We're simply spending more time with each other." Good point. I noticed it got quieter in the distance.

"Avery, I think you missed your bus again."

"Yeah, I did. That means I have more time with you," he grinned, like a little boy receiving the Atari gaming system for his birthday.

"So, you're not getting sick of me?"

"Now that you mention it," he teased. I shoved the joker and started to tickle him. "I'm kidding. I'm only kidding," he surrendered. I rested my head on his shoulder and we sat quietly for a few moments. Then Avery carefully adjusted his body, looked into my eyes with such intensity, as if he was trying to reach the deep recesses of my soul, and affirmed in his husky seductive voice, "Seriously, Christina, I love you. I know I told you that before, but I don't think you realize how much I really love you. Sometimes I can't believe it myself. Like, how it happened so fast. I didn't think it was possible at our age, to be so in love, until I fell for you."

I was deeply touched, and therefore, rendered speechless, like it was the sweetest sound I ever heard. The mellifluous boy before me held my hand and then, lightly stroked my face. My pulse quickened. The serenade continued, his baby blues glistening, "I love how you laugh. I love your smile. I love how you order milkshakes. I love how you shake when you have to kiss someone other than me when playing spin the bottle. I love how you're not intimidated to play softball with a bunch of guys. I love how you don't want to come between my friends and me. I love how you appear confident when you're really not. I love how you volunteer at the old folks' home. I love so much about you.

Tears gathered in the corners of my eyes, after hearing the most touching profession of love that ever existed.

With our eyes still locked and my heart beating faster, I leaned into him. "Avery, I am crazy in love with you!" We hugged each other tenderly. I laid my head on his chest and snuggled in his arms. It felt so comforting being in Avery's embrace—so peaceful and blissful. I was with Avery and nothing else mattered in my crazy mixed-up world.

Chapter 35

"HEY, BEAUTIFUL!" AVERY RADIATED JOY, as I walked up to my locker first thing Friday morning. I looked around as if to see to whom he was speaking.

"Who me?" I teased.

"Yeah, you!" he replied, with a cute nod of his head. He seemed to be able to wink at me with a gesture. Then he greeted me with his routine good morning kiss that always managed to elevate my spirits to a level I only recently discovered.

We walked to homeroom together and listened to the morning announcements, which included the home football game. "Hey, let's go to the football game!" A gleeful Avery suggested.

"Okay. I'm game. No pun intended," I joked.

"Cool." The bell rang. The essence of his eyes glistened brightly against his royal blue Izod. We parted ways but his image was seared on my mind.

———— ◆ ————

Avery picked me up to go to the football game. I followed his lead into the car as he slid next to Peter. Sam the Man was driving again, with Joey in the front passenger seat.

I wondered if our chauffeur was going to be hanging out with his brother the entire time, or if he would hang out with guys in his own grade.

My silent inquiries were answered upon our arrival. Sam the Man darted away, as he barked instructions about our ride home. I assumed Avery and Joey knew the drill.

It was a brisk autumn evening. With clasped hands, Avery and I rambled along the grassy section of the football stadium outside the enclosed football field, as the guys hung close. I searched for a friendly face, not knowing if any of my friends would be in attendance.

People of all ages and sizes ambled in all different directions. They resembled an ant colony. Everyone seemed to have a mission and destination. Not everyone had jackets on. Some people wore only sweatshirts. I was wearing one underneath my jean jacket. Avery was also wearing a jean jacket and jeans. We matched, but not on purpose; never on purpose. That would have been too corny.

We meandered along, pushing through the crowds. I was surprised to see so many people. There were tons of adults. Since my parents never missed one of my brother's sporting events, I assumed they were parents of the football players. Morgan spotted us and came over with Erin, Katie and Amy.

While everyone was exchanging their hellos, Morgan clarified, "Katie told me you would be here with Avery. Otherwise, I would have invited you to come with us."

Before I could respond, Sam the Man appeared out of nowhere.

"Hey, look, the gang's all here!" Sam the Man announced, with a grin that extended from here to the sun.

"I thought you were hanging out with your friends." My lips tightened and my cheeks puffed out.

"Moi? I wanted to make sure your first high school football game was a good experience."

"I'll pretend I didn't hear that," Avery sneered.

The incredibly wise and experienced upperclassman announced, "The game is about to start. Why don't we go find a spot in the stands? You can see the plays better from the seats."

"Sam the Man has a plan in the stands," I couldn't resist. We all shared a brief laugh, but in truth, he did have a solid idea. I knew Sam and Peter were excited about their prospects and I also knew my friends would appreciate the mixed company. As we approached the bleachers, the Pennsford Cougars reached the forty-yard line after the kickoff. But the real entertainment was in the stands.

Avery and I watched as Sam the Man entertained the girls. Basically, he was showing off for Katie. Katie didn't seem to mind, as she always had a fantastic sense of humor. At least, she always laughed at my silly jokes.

From the looks of it, Amy loved Sam the Man's silliness too. Erin acted like she was above that sort of folly. Morgan was always good for a laugh, but she also managed to strike a delicate balance by engaging in conversation with everyone.

Peter struggled to hold Erin's interest. Having hinted to Morgan that Peter could use some help, Morgan immediately went to Peter's rescue by keeping the conversation going.

Joey watched the game, exchanging comments with Avery. Although content, I wondered when and if Avery and I would have some alone time. I halfheartedly watched the Cougars crush the Pythons' offense and Sam the Man put on his own show for the girls. I watched the cheerleaders. I watched parents cheer for their sons. I watched little kids bug their parents for snacks. I watched teens flirt with one another. I watched spectators watch the game. I watched people walk up and down the stands. After a half hour of watching a lot of nothing, I heard a lot of shouting.

Joey yelled, "Yes! Go, go, go!"

Avery cheered, "All right! Yeah, Cougars! Way to go!"

The crowd roared, jumped up, and pumped their fists in the air. Sam the Man performed a silly dance and spun around. We scored a touchdown! Everyone was electrified. The kick was good! Spectators threw their arms up in the air.

We earned the extra point. The score was Cougars seven, Pythons zero.

Avery and I left for a few minutes to grab a hot cocoa and when we returned, Sam the Showman was still in entertainment mode. *Where does he get the energy? I am exhausted just watching him.*

After 120 minutes, the final score was Cougars fourteen, Pythons three. To celebrate, Sam suggested we hit the Pennsford Diner to keep the party going. Amy frowned. "My dad is supposed to pick us up here."

"So, see if he will drive you to the diner," the showman suggested.

We all met at the Pennsford Diner. It pleased me to no end to witness my friends and Avery's friends getting chummy.

"So, Christina, are you going to order a chocolate milkshake?" Joey asked, displaying steeple fingers. I did appreciate his humor, but I was much too cold to indulge in that chocolatey goodness.

Erin did her best to avoid Peter. Peter got the hint. I felt bad for him, but I didn't like Erin much anyway, so I felt relieved that she wouldn't be hanging out with Avery and me when Peter was around.

The showman worked his magic with Katie. She laughed at his crazy antics, but I wasn't completely convinced Katie was into Sam the way he was into her.

"Excuse me, guys. I'll be right back," I said.

"Hey, wait up!" Katie shouted. I waited for her to catch up to me and we entered the lavatory together. She proceeded to talk while we were in separate stalls. "So, what do you think about Sam?"

"Funny, I was about to ask you the same question, Katie," I smirked.

"I think he's a riot. Do you think he's interested in me?"

"Uh, yeah!!" I said as if it was common knowledge.

"Would you go out with him? I mean, if you weren't going out with Avery."

I exhaled deeply, "I really don't know, because I am dating Avery, and I just can't think like that right now. But, he can't be all bad if he's making you laugh."

"I know. I can't remember the last time I laughed so hard." Flush. "You don't seem like you're enjoying yourself tonight," she observed, as we approached the sinks.

"Yeah, I guess I'm concerned about people getting their feelings hurt. Now I have it on both sides, the guys as well as the girls." I reached for a paper towel to dry my hands.

Katie's eyes widened, she nodded and said, "Oh, you mean Erin and Peter." Katie was as perceptive as ever.

"Yeah, Peter is pretty cool once you get to know him. I don't want anyone blaming me for rejection or failed relationships."

"Nobody's going to blame you for anything. You take things to heart way too much, you know," Katie said incisively, with the wave of her hand. "People make their own choices. Other people's relationships can't be your fault, one way or another."

"I know. I know," I rolled my eyes. *But . . .*

Katie raised her eyebrows. "So, things with you and Avery are okay then?"

"Oh, yeah! No problems. He's easy!" I smiled, just thinking about him.

She gave me a sideways glance. "So, we're not in the way of you two?"

"No, I came with the guys, but his friends might think that I am between Avery and them."

"You mean Peter and Joey?"

"Yup. Sam the Man went off to be with his friends until he saw you."

Katie tilted her head and pressed her lips together. "Why don't you come over to our side of the table to give the guys some space?"

"I might do that. Thanks for that idea."

I walked back to the table and must have had a strange look on my face while I contemplated the switcheroo.

"Something wrong?" Avery asked.

"No, not at all. Let's switch seats, so you can be with your friends," I smiled assuredly.

That seemed to be the solution. I was able to relax while watching Sam the Showman entertain the girls. He thoroughly enjoyed being the life of the party while Joey and Peter appreciated a chance to hang with Avery. And just like at lunch, they periodically invited me into their conversation. Thanks to Katie's simple suggestion, a happy medium was created and everyone appeared content.

Chapter 36

THE NEXT DAY, AVERY AND I met at the usual corner. This time I arrived first. After waiting two minutes, which felt like a lifetime, I greeted my man with a smile that made my cheeks hurt. "Hi, Avery, how ya doing?"

Avery returned, with a smile equally bright, "Great, now that I'm seeing you, beautiful! Have you been waiting long?" I shook my head in response. He leaned over, still straddling his bike, to give me a peck on the cheek, as few people ventured outside this brisk morning.

I resisted the urge to pounce Avery once we were alone in his basement. Instead, I struck up conversation while sitting next to him on the couch. "How's Peter doing? He didn't say much on the way home from the diner."

"He's okay." He shrugged.

"You sure? He seemed a little bummed. I thought he was disappointed that Erin didn't show any interest in him."

"Oh, that. He'll get over it." Avery waved his hand indifferently.

"You think so? That's good to hear."

"At least he tried. He doesn't talk to girls much." Avery was right. I recalled how Peter rarely interacted with girls, except for me at lunch. Although attractive, he was too studious and uptight about his grades and never talked to girls, unless he had to in a group setting to work on a project for school. However, he was good at sports, so the cool jocks liked hanging around him. As a result, Peter became popular by association.

Avery continued calmly, kind of deep in thought for a Saturday morning, "I think you helped him become more assertive."

"I did? How?" My eyes narrowed in disbelief.

"Because you're so easy to talk to. He got used to you, you know, talking to you and all, so he's not so afraid to talk to girls anymore."

"Wow! So glad I could help," I said, knowing it wasn't anything I did intentionally, but it made me feel good inside knowing that I impacted someone's life. "Ave," I said seriously.

"Yeah?" he answered attentively.

"Oh, nothing." At times I felt guilty for having such a wonderful guy when most girls didn't. I kept worrying that it would end in a blink of an eye, like it was too good to be true, but I couldn't tell Avery that.

"What? You can tell me," he assured me.

"I feel so lucky that you're my boyfriend." I nestled my head under his chin. Avery put his arm around me.

"Yeah, I know what you mean. Sometimes I feel like this is too good to be true."

Upon hearing those familiar words, I jerked my head up and exclaimed, "You do? That's exactly what I was thinking!"

The deeper connection I felt with Avery spoke to me so intensely that I threw my arms around him. We started to kiss. We shifted positions enabling Avery to be on top of me. He whisked a ringlet out of my face. Avery kissed me along the side of my neck. I giggled in response. He tenderly kissed me along my clavicle as he placed his hand up my shirt to caress my back. My body tingled with pleasure.

That was the moment I realized I had always been on the receiving side during such risky moments, while Avery's parents were right upstairs. I wondered if any of that mattered to him.

Just then he carefully lifted the front of my shirt and started caressing my left breast with my bra securely fastened in place. Patiently, I waited all week for us to be alone in his basement, to relish in such sensual delight.

Yet again, my conscience advised me to stop, while my body begged for more. As my mind was plagued with this dichotomy of guilty pleasure, Avery inched his way down my rib cage and nuzzled into my mid-section. I practically leaped out of my skin as my body burned for more. Uncontrollably, I panted Avery's name and repeated, "Oh, Avery!"

My mind was adrift. When I realized what he was doing, I jerked forward, breathless, gasping for air. Avery stopped abruptly.

"I'm sorry, Christina. I should have stopped sooner. I'm so

sorry!" Avery pleaded.

I hurriedly yanked my jeans up and zipped them. I felt so foolish for getting swept up in the moment as I clearly wasn't ready for that next step in our physical relationship. I deceived myself and led Avery on. *What am I doing! I can't keep doing this!*

"It's okay. It's okay. I thought I was ready. I'm sorry." I sat there for a moment in shear disbelief, my head hung low.

Avery leaned forward, lovingly, placed his arms around me, and drew me closer. I settled in his arms, while feeling ashamed. I didn't want to be *that* girl. The one who is easy. The one with the bad reputation.

Even if no one knew what happened in the Martins' family room, I craved some sense of purity in my life. I was terribly confused. Since I was already impure, what difference did it make?

Without realizing it, I started to cry. The memory of that horrid day in the Martins' house crept back in my mind and took permanent residence. I couldn't shake it no matter how much I tried. I felt helpless, hopeless and undeserving. I pulled out of our embrace and sobbed, burying my face in my hands.

"Christina, I am so sorry. It won't happen again. Please forgive me," Avery implored, as he tenderly rubbed my back. I couldn't speak. Avery softly placed his hand on my chin, prompting me to raise it. He lovingly wiped the tears from my cheeks. "Please, Christina, forgive me."

I could barely look at Avery. I felt guilty, because I put myself in vulnerable situations. It was my fault. I was the weak one. I felt sickness in the pit of my stomach. I felt unworthy of a boyfriend like Avery. He was so sweet, so tender. "Christina, please say something."

I shook my head and stammered, "It's n-not your f-fault. It . . . is . . . mine." I sniffled, trying to compose myself in between gasps of air. "I'm not m-mad at you. I'm . . ." I gasped, " . . . confused." I continued to tremble trying desperately to pull it together.

"What are you confused about?" Avery said, trying to make sense of it all.

I wiped my nose and took a deep breath. "I'm t-torn. P-part of me w-wants to be with you in the w-worst way, but an-no-ther p-part of me thinks it's w-wrong."

"I know. I feel the same way. I keep thinking of my Sunday school teacher. How she would be disappointed in me if we actually had sex. I think I would I regret it in some ways. Not because of you, but because of my pledge."

"W-what pledge?" I wiped my nose again.

"We all pledged in Sunday school that we would wait until we were married to have sex."

My eyes narrowed, my brows furrowed. "R-really?" My body started to return to normalcy.

"Yeah, Joey was there too. He goes to church with me sometimes. He's already hinted about the pledge."

"Oh." Then I realized what that meant. My mouth twisted as I barely formed the words, "You mean he thinks you and I . . ." I clasped my hand over my mouth and that pit in my stomach returned.

"Yeah, but I told him we didn't and to mind his own business."

My eyes were glassed over and I tilted my head. "Does he believe you?"

"I think so." Avery didn't sound very convincing. I hunched over and wrapped my arms around my nauseous stomach.

We sat quietly for a few minutes until Avery broke the silence. "Christina, I am crazy about you! But, I don't want to hurt you or our relationship in any way. You have to believe me," he pleaded. I raised my heavy head and turned to him. He continued, "This is as hard for me as it is for you."

I believed he struggled with all of this, but in no way did I think his struggle was as severe as mine. He didn't have Creepoid screw up his life.

"I believe you." I could see the wheels turning in his adorable, yet distraught little head.

Avery squinted. "Do you go to church?"

"No."

He creased his brow. "What religion are you?"

"I don't really have one." I attempted to explain to Avery how I didn't necessarily believe in a God. He was taken aback by my statement, as he failed to grasp how that was possible.

"So, what is preventing you from having sex then?" he asked curiously.

"Morals." I simply stated. He just stared at me. "What? I'm still a good person," I tried to convince Avery as well as myself.

"I know you are. I'm surprised you don't even believe in God," he said, stroking the nape of his neck.

"What's wrong?"

He raked his fingers through his hair. "Nothing," He said unconvincingly.

"Avery, tell me. I know something is wrong." *I'm panicking here!*

"Have you ever gone to church?" He continued to comb his hair with his fingers.

"Yes, when I was little; before we moved here."

Where is this headed? You're freaking me out!

"What did you learn?"

"I don't remember much."

He leaned closer. "Do you know anything about salvation?"

"A little." I recalled Miss Brenda's speech, which I had thought about from time to time, but never made any definitive conclusions.

"What do you know?"

I bit my lip and started to wriggle in my seat. "Avery, what are you getting at? Just tell me what's wrong. Please!"

Avery held up his palm. "Okay, okay." He looked me straight in the eyes and proceeded holding my hand, "You see, I believe that Jesus is the son of God. He died on the cross for our sins. If you believe that and ask for forgiveness of your sins, as well as asking Jesus into your heart, then you have eternal life."

I raised my eyebrows. "And if you don't . . ." *I'm almost afraid to ask.*

"If you don't, you are damned to hell for all eternity." Avery wrung his hands. His story matched up with Miss Brenda's.

"So, you think I am going to hell?" *What the hell was hell anyway?* "You think hell is real?" *A guy in red with pointed ears and horns holding a pitchfork in a fiery inferno?*

"Yes, just like I think heaven is real. It says in the Bible, 'For God so loved the world, that he gave his only begotten Son, that whosoever believeth in him should not perish, but have everlasting life. For God sent not his Son into the world to condemn the world; but that the world through him might be saved. He that believeth on him is not condemned: but he that believeth not is condemned already, because he hath not believed in the name of the only begotten Son of God.' That's John 3:16-18."

I looked at Avery blankly. "You memorized that?"

"Yeah, it was part of a Sunday school lesson."

"What does it mean?" *I feel kinda stupid for asking.*

"Well, if you accept Jesus as your Savior, you will live forever. If not, you go to hell."

I licked my lips before scraping my bottom lip. *I have to ask.* "What is hell?"

"Simply put, it is separation from God, forever." My jaw dropped and I shivered automatically. "Why don't you come to church with me tomorrow?"

I was very hesitant but curious. Since Miss Brenda talked to me about this, I couldn't quite shake it. I felt like there was more to it but nothing really stuck, although it did resonate. "Oh, I don't know," I cringed. "It's been so long. I'd be uncomfortable." *I hate the kneeling part.*

"I'm sure it will be okay with my parents," he said excitedly, "and don't worry. There's nothing to be scared about. I will be with you the entire time."

I nodded, not knowing what else to say at that moment.

Maybe there's something to this God thing after all.

———◆———

Pennsford Methodist was a white brick church with a tall white steeple at its apex. It adorned stained glass windows and prominent white pillars. It was a beautiful piece of architecture.

It reminded me of the Roman Catholic Church I attended. While I got confirmed as a member there, I had learned next to nothing about God and the Bible.

Upon entering the Sunday school classroom, I was greeted without hesitation by a twenty-something-year-old woman. "Hi, welcome! Is this your first time here?" Her eyes were affixed on me.

"Yes," I nodded.

"Well, I hope you are comfortable and find a home here. It's good to have you." *Wow, how nice. Didn't expect that.*

"Thank you."

Then she looked at Avery and said, "You look familiar. Is this your first time in this class?"

"Yes, but I've been going to this church since I was born."

"Ah, that explains why you look so familiar. Well, welcome to the high school Sunday school class!"

I spotted Erin sitting across the way. She came over upon seeing us and asked about Joey. "Ah, he's at church with his mom," Avery informed her.

"Oh, right. Well, it's good to see you here, Christina," Erin said and walked back to her original seat. We took our seats at a nearby table and others joined us while waiting for the class to commence.

Two extremely attractive adults stepped up to the front of the room: one man and one woman, both young-looking. I guessed them to be in their mid-twenties. The couple introduced themselves to the newcomers as Brett and Fran Newbury, and explained that they were husband and wife, and have been teaching Sunday school together for over four years, and that this was their second year at Pennsford Methodist.

Previously, they served in Virginia, which they called the Bible Belt. They said that they were in full-time ministry, but I didn't know what they meant by that. They used terminology with which I wasn't familiar, but I sat and listened.

They said that they didn't have any children of their own, but rather thought of their various ministry groups as their children, including Pennsford Christian Academy, the local Christian school, where they were both employed. I didn't even know there was a local Christian school. Based on their cheers, I surmised a few students from the class attended the Christian school.

First, they started by singing songs using the overhead projector so we could follow the words. Mrs. Newbury sang, while her husband played the guitar. I felt very uncomfortable singing songs I never heard before. I looked around the room to find that I was the only one not singing, but nobody said anything.

After the worship concluded, they asked us to think about our biggest fears. Instantly, I thought about Creepoid coming after Avery and me. I shuddered at the thought of it. The Newburys instructed us not to disclose our fears to each other, but to share them with God through prayer. They quoted all sorts of passages from the Bible and told us to look up the references with them.

A few people had their own Bibles. I didn't realize that people owned Bibles. I thought Bibles were only used in the church and owned by the church. I doubted I had ever even touched a Bible. I was afraid to touch one for some reason.

As a group, we looked up a few verses on being afraid: "Casting all your care upon him; for he careth for you" (1 Peter 5:7), "Cast thy burden upon the Lord, and he shall sustain thee: he shall never suffer the righteous to be moved" (Psalm 55:22), and "Be careful for nothing; but in every thing by prayer and supplication with thanksgiving let your requests be made known unto God" (Philippians 4:6). Avery shared a Bible with me that was provided by the church.

At the end of the class, we settled on the verse, "And fear not them which kill the body, but are not able to kill the soul: but rather fear him which is able to destroy both soul and body in hell" (Matthew 10:28).

Mr. Newbury clarified, "Christians shouldn't fear anyone but God, because no one except God can destroy the soul. God is the only one to be feared. Only God has the power to destroy both body and soul. Once you accept that Christ is Lord and Savior, your soul will live forever."

Shortly after, Mr. Newbury ended with a closing prayer to wrap up the Sunday school session and then we left to find Mr. and Mrs. Evans in the sanctuary for the church service.

The service was much different than Catholic Mass.

Hooray! No kneeling! Maybe that's just a Catholic thing.

There were a bunch of other things that were different too—things that I liked better and I felt a lot more comfortable at this church. The people were friendly, as they took the time to speak to you, and the service was more straight forward. I never understood all of the motions we had to go through at Mass. I knew they were symbolic, but they just seemed awkward—like I was going through the motions for the sake of going through the motions.

Again, I heard the message about salvation, with an invitation to say the sinner's prayer like I did at Jerome's memorial service.

It seemed this God, that I didn't quite believe in, was out there in a big way, very close, and tracking me down. *These words seem like they are for me. Just for me. They can't be. Does anyone else feel this way?*

"Ave, what is this sinner's prayer people keep mentioning?"

"It's when you admit your sins, ask for forgiveness and accept Jesus as your Savior. By doing so, you live forever in heaven with Jesus."

"That's it? That's all you have to do to live forever?" I questioned.

He nodded.

I heard that before, but it took a few times to hear it to finally grasp the concept. I bit my lip and rubbed my hands together, feeling compelled to say the sinner's prayer. The verse, "Jesus saith unto him, I am the way, the truth, and the life: no man cometh unto the Father, but by me" (John 14:6), echoed in my mind, but I wasn't even sure how I knew it.

The lighting in the sanctuary hit Avery's blue eyes in such a way causing them to twinkle. "Christina, I can come down with you to say the sinner's prayer, if you want me to."

That seemed like a decent proposal. We walked down the aisle together. Although the minister was talking with some people, he immediately excused himself to talk with us.

He bowed to Avery in a proper, but not regal sort of way. "Hello, Avery, it's good to see you. I don't believe I have had the pleasure of meeting your friend." He gestured toward me, extending his arm in my direction.

Avery introduced us, "This is Christina De Rosa. She wanted to say the sinner's prayer." Then Avery looked at me and said, "This is Pastor Boyle." He exuded warm understanding eyes and a sincere smile.

"Indeed. Well, Christina, allow me to ask you a few questions before we proceed, okay?" I nodded. He continued, "Have you said the sinner's prayer before?" I shook my head. "Do you believe Jesus Christ is Lord and Savior?" I nodded. "Do you recognize that you are a sinner?" I nodded. "Do you want to repent? By repent, I mean to ask God to forgive you, and to promise not to sin again. Repentance means a change of mind. So, you want to change your sinful ways to do what is pleasing to God. Is that what you want?" He waited for an answer.

I mustered up a, "Yes."

He took my hands in his, bowed his head, and closed his eyes. In turn, I bowed my head and shut my eyes. He began, "All right then, repeat after me: Jesus, I need you."

I echoed, "Jesus, I need you."

"I repent for the life I've lived apart from you."

"I repent for the life I've lived apart from you."

We got into a rhythm, yet I repeated every word with conviction.

"Thank you for dying on the cross to take the penalty for my sins."

"Thank you for dying on the cross to take the penalty for my sins."

"I believe you are God's Son and I now receive you as my Savior and Lord."

"I believe you are God's Son and I now receive you as my Savior and Lord."

"I commit my life to follow you."

"I commit my life to follow you."

"Amen."

"Amen." Suddenly, I felt as if a weight had been lifted off of me. I opened my eyes to see Pastor Boyle looking down at me, with the ends of his mouth forming the beginning of a smile.

He shook both of my hands together, released them, put his hand on my shoulder, and announced, "Congratulations, Christina, by the grace of God, you are saved. If you have any questions, please don't hesitate to come see me, okay?"

"Okay. Thank you." I smiled. *Well, that was easy. And not at all corny like I thought it would be. Maybe that's because I needed it.*

"It was an honor meeting you, Christina. You are always welcome here."

"Thank you!" I smiled even brighter than before, as if to celebrate a deeper joy than I ever experienced.

"Thanks a lot Pastor Boyle!" Avery said appreciatively.

"My pleasure, Avery. Have a great week you two!" He turned on his heel and waved good-bye.

We told Avery's parents what happened and they were thrilled beyond belief. Mrs. Evans gave me a big, excited hug.

"We should celebrate! Why don't we go out to lunch?" Avery's mom proposed, holding back tears of joy. She paused briefly, her visage aglow, as her right hand crossed over on her heart, and asserted with delight, "We'll buy you a King James Bible. It's so beautiful. It's like reading poetry."

———

Over the next few weeks, I attended church with Avery every Sunday. We studied Matthew, chapter six. I was like a sponge. I found the passage fascinating. Life couldn't have been any better; I was learning a lot about the Bible and I was incredibly thankful for such a tremendous boyfriend to share in my spiritual growth!

I continued to visit The Manor on Fridays after school. Miss Brenda shrilled, and squeezed the life out of me, when I told her I was saved. After I told her how and when, she wasted no time celebrating. It started with her hugging me with an embrace so hard I truly lost my breath. It continued with her shouting, "Lord, have mercy! I have been praying especially hard for you ever since you walked through those doors that summer day. Miracles never cease. Thank you, Jesus!" She openly praised God in front of everyone. I never saw someone so elated in my entire life. Miss Brenda said that my salvation was cause for true celebration, like none other. That night we danced to the oldies.

Every other week from that precious day, we enjoyed our oldies dance party at the Manor. The residents came to life on what ironically became known as "Oldies Night."

I relived my salvation celebration on those Friday dance nights. It was later in life that I would realize what sincere and profound love it was for Miss Brenda to pray for me for months on end. That act—that free act of thoughtfulness—has taught me more than many an academic lesson. That free love of hers was priceless.

Occasionally, I had nightmares about the unspeakable, but I no longer woke up in a pool of sweat. It was clear to me in that alone how powerful God was working in my life. *I wonder if Sister Proper English would notice my transformation. Do nuns have some sort of X-ray vision into one's soul?*

Nevertheless, I experienced a greater sense of peace that surpassed all my understanding. "And the peace of God, which passeth all understanding, shall keep your hearts and mind through Christ Jesus" (Philippians 4:7).

Chapter 37

*A*VERY AND I GREETED EACH other with the usual, but always wonderful, morning kiss at my locker. In homeroom, we listened to the announcements, telling us to vote for one girl to represent our class on the homecoming court. The top two will be chosen.

"I know who I'm voting for," Avery hinted, raising his eyebrows up and down wearing a clown-like grin.

"Oh, no, please don't," I pleaded.

"Why not?"

"You know I hate that kind of stuff."

He protested, "Oh, come on. You're the prettiest girl in our class."

"You're a little biased."

"Who are you voting for?"

"I don't know yet." I had to think fast because we needed to write a name down right away and turn it in. *Oh, the pressure!*

I picked an attractive Indian girl named Anita Patel. Her skin was medium to dark brown. She had shiny straight black hair, and equally attractive brown almond-shaped eyes framed with dark eye lashes. She was a natural beauty with full lips and a round-shaped face requiring no makeup. Anita stood a slender five feet four inches. She was my idea of beautiful, but she was more of a wallflower. As a result, I doubted many others, if any others followed suit in voting for her.

"So, who did you vote for?" Avery asked again.

"Anita Patel."

"Interesting choice. I would have never thought of her."

"And—who did you vote for?"

"You'll never know," he teased with a big grin on his face.

"Avery!" I hit him on the shoulder.

He toyed with me by putting his finger to his lips, winked and whispered, "It's a secret ballot."

———◆———

Friday, the first day of October, Avery and I were talking to each other in homeroom when they announced the homecoming results.

"The two freshman attendees are . . . Mindy Roberts and Christina De Rosa..." *What?! This can't be! How in the world?!*

"Christina, you won! Congratulations!" Cheers roared throughout homeroom. I wanted to hide. *How in the world did this happen? This is a drawback of dating him. Grrrr!*

###

Later in the day, I walked in the girls' locker room for gym class and overheard a couple of girls chatting. I didn't know them well, but I recognized their distinct voices. "I can't believe Christina won," griped a girl in a plaid miniskirt and cute heels.

I pictured her eye roll. *Oh, my God. Help me.* I stopped and hid behind the wall. I couldn't make myself small enough.

"I know, like, she's so not, you know, cool," the other chimed in, mimicking a Southern Californian valley girl accent.

"And did you see what she wore the other day? A plain purple T shirt and Levi jeans," Miniskirt volleyed back. They snickered. *Hey! What's wrong with my purple tee?*

"Like, really. How plain! Mindy is all like, you know, why couldn't it be one of us?"

I made a mental note to boost my style of attire.

"Mindy said she is such a pig too!" *What?! Oh my gosh . . . Why in the world . . .? NO!*

"Like, oh my gosh, like, isn't she in our gym class too?" added Valley Barbie. *These chicks are nasty. Don't they have anything better to do?* I wondered what everyone else was saying behind my back. Literally behind my back!

"Oh, yeah, oops! I wonder if she heard us. We better go," I held my breath until they left, and then I cautiously made my way to my locker. It was easy to track them—the click clack of their heels against the concrete locker room floor gave them away. I prayed the entire way for them not to see me. *Thank you, God. Thank you.*

Katie sat next to me against the wall, as we awaited our turn to kick during kickball. "Hey, Christina, congrats!" Katie exclaimed. I gave her a look that said, 'you have to be kidding.' "Or not. Oh, I should have guessed. Not your thing, huh?"

I glared at her, shook my head, and huffed. "Mindy said I was a pig," I whispered.

"To your face?" Katie inquired aghast.

"No. No. I overheard her posse talking. Let me just tell you—they were vicious. I really wish I wasn't here right now."

She gave me a convincing wave, "They're just jealous."

"Now everyone thinks I'm a pig."

"No, they don't. What's that supposed to mean anyway?"

"I think it's because I ordered a milkshake on our double date."

"Ohhhh! Well, you are a hearty eater," she ribbed with a chuckle.

"Thanks a lot!" I said with notable sarcasm.

"At least it doesn't show. They wish they could indulge and still look like you. That's all. Don't worry about it." Katie said empathetically. She pointed to direct me, "You're up."

It was my turn to kick the ball. I thought I heard oinking.

"Oink! Oink!" I most certainly heard oinking.

Flustered, I completely missed the ball. *How embarrassing!* The pair of piglets cackled their butts off. They were happy to be burning calories at my expense.

My gym teacher let me try again. I kicked the ball and someone caught it in the outfield. *Oh well. At least that was a good kick. I saved face.*

Again, I heard cackling and more oinking. I never asked to be on the homecoming court. I never wanted to be on the homecoming court. I knew better. I couldn't take the gossip, the teasing, the name calling. It was horrible. Girls were so cruel.

I tried my best to shrug it off, to act like I didn't care, but I did. Ow, I did. *I'd like to shove a Diet Coke up their little oinkers.*

Getting changed, the oink sounds continued. Here an oink, there an oink, everywhere an oink, oink. It was awful. I couldn't wait to get out of the locker room.

I raced down the hall to lunch and distinctively heard more pig noises. Everywhere I went people were oinking. Oink, oink.

I sat down gingerly next to Avery at our lunch table. Joey and Peter were there too.

The same two girls from gym class suspiciously circled our table.

They were eyeing me up and cackling. I braced myself for what was to come and intentionally turned away from their direction.

"Oink, oink," one of them said, while they both sniggered and walked away.

"What was *that* about?" Peter asked. I cringed and deeply exhaled in frustration.

"Nothing I care about. Just ignore them," I answered, shaking my head in annoyance.

"Come on, obviously that was directed towards someone at this table. What gives?" Peter persisted.

"Mindy told her friends that I was a pig," I answered in exasperation.

Peter naively asked, "What? Why would she say that?"

"I'm not really sure," I shrugged. "I just don't need this today."

"I bet it has to do with the time we double-dated and you ordered that milkshake," Joey offered.

Ding, ding, ding! You are the winner for answering correctly regarding this strange turn of events in my life. Ordering the milkshake would forever be embedded in his memory and seems to have a lasting impact on others like Mindy and her piglet posse.

"Yeah, that's my only guess," I agreed, "but I don't know. I mean, it's so stupid. And how long has it been since then? Who acts like this?"

"Oh, her for sure. She was freaked out by that for some reason. Avery and I had one too. Girls are so strange," Joey said, shaking his head.

"Not all girls are strange," Avery flashed a reassuring smile.

"Thanks," I sighed softly, returning a half-smile.

"Oh, maybe they're jealous that they didn't win that homecoming thing," Peter surmised with a pleased look on his face.

"Yeah, I bet that's it!" Joey concurred, enthusiastically. I didn't know boys talked about this kind of stuff. It felt a little awkward and yet it was helpful.

"Yeah, that's it, Christina. That's exactly it! Jeez, and you didn't even want to win," my guy added. *These guys are great. I had no idea. What was I so afraid of?*

"Really? You didn't? That's cool," said Peter.

"Why?" Joey asked, nonplussed.

"I really don't like that kind of attention. It makes me very uncomfortable," I answered candidly.

Joey remarked, "You are different, Christina. You're all right."

"Thanks, guys," I returned, with a toothless smile. Their help—their encouragement was greatly appreciated and cherished.

"Well, who did you all vote for?" Peter asked, scanning everyone.

"Sorry, Christina, I voted for you," Joey confessed, as if he had wounded me.

"Me too," Peter said, contorting his face as if he was ashamed. "Actually, I think everyone in my homeroom voted for you," Peter surmised, in a sheepish grin. "Sorry."

"Mine too," Joey added. "Avery, who did you vote for?"

"Christina, of course," Peter replied in Avery's stead.

"I will never tell," Avery winked in a mischievous way, his mouth spread from ear to ear.

Joey implored, "Dude, give us a break. Tell us."

"No, it's a lose-lose situation. If I picked Christina, she would be mad, because she told me not to pick her. If I picked someone else, well, you know . . .," Avery justified.

"Christina, would you be mad if Avery picked someone else?" Peter asked. "You didn't even want to win . . . and you did anyway."

"Well, truthfully, that depends," I answered.

"Depends on what?" Peter asked.

"Who it is and why," I replied, with my lips pursed.

Peter begged, "Come on, Avery fess up!"

"Why do you care?" Avery asked. *Someone's getting peeved.*

"I'm just curious," Peter explained. "So, tell me. Who did you vote for?"

"Drop it, Peter, okay?" Avery advised firmly.

Peter sighed and backed off like a scared puppy dog. "Who did you vote for, Christina?" Peter asked.

"Anita Patel."

"Are you friends with her?" Peter asked.

"No, I just think she's beautiful in an unassuming way."

"She isn't bad, but I would have never thought of her," Peter said.

"Hmm, me neither," agreed Joey.

———◆———

That afternoon, I went up to my room and prayed. I was told

that prayer is a two-way conversation between God and me, so I tried it. I prayed that the teasing at school would stop. I prayed that I would get through the homecoming events with comfort and ease—without embarrassment. I prayed that if Avery put someone else's name down besides mine for the homecoming court, that he didn't like her. I prayed for Miss Brenda to feel loved and comforted. I also asked God why He let her son die. That's just too hard for me to comprehend.

After dinner, I readied myself for a date with Avery—we were headed to a party at his buddy, Doug's. I was somewhat anxious because I had no idea what to expect.

For a change, I decided to tease my hair. I usually didn't do much with my mane. It was so thick and long and I didn't like spending too much time on it, but after hearing the piglets' comments, I thought I'd primp.

I put on a hot pink, off the shoulder shirt, and paired it with my black leggings. This outfit screamed for my big gold hoops and long necklaces, my flat heeled punk black boots and my fashionable pink bow for my big hair. I was all set! I felt very confident knowing my outfit was the epitome of style. *No more plain, purple T-shirts and jeans!*

The doorbell rang. I heard Avery talking to my father. I meandered down the staircase. As soon as my dad laid eyes on me, he complimented me, "Hey, Pooch, you look great!"

"Yeah, you do look great!" Avery echoed. *My two biggest fans!*

"Thanks!" I said with a smile as big as my hair. *Whew.* And off we went. Avery, me, and Madonna.

I slid in the back seat after Avery. Katie was in the front seat with her man. Joey sat on the end on the other side of Avery.

"Wow! Look at you!" exclaimed Katie. "I haven't seen you styling since last year."

"I'm making a comeback," I teased.

Katie quipped, "Oh, there's lots of teasing going on here—first your hair, now me." We shared a good laugh. *Maybe this will be a good night after all.*

"Boy, I'll say," Sam added. Katie hit him on the shoulder. "What?!" Her boyfriend didn't know when to shut up.

I wondered how Katie felt going to a party hosted by the former object of her lust.

We arrived at Doug's, and cars were parked everywhere, even on the grass. Avery and I walked together, holding hands, providing me with the extra security I needed. People crowded in every room of the house. Some were guzzling beer and wine coolers while others were dancing to Crosby, Stills and Nash singing "Wasted on the Way." My nervousness caused me to unintentionally squeeze Avery's hand.

He turned to me. "You okay?" my security blanket asked, rocking my hand.

"Uh, I'm not used to this. The crowd, the noise, the drinking." *I feel like a fish out of water.*

"Don't worry. Just stick with me and you don't have to drink." *Good, because I wasn't planning on it.* "Do you? I mean, I never saw you drink before," I said meekly.

"Yeah, I drink, but I don't get drunk." *Interesting.*

"You didn't have alcohol at your party."

"I never have alcohol at my parties. My parents would freak." Freak. That's the second time I heard that word today. I casually looked around the house.

"Where are Doug's parents?"

"Out of town."

As we were talking, guys greeted Avery with a high five, they turned to me, nodded and shot Avery an approving look.

Katie perused the room. She turned around and walked over to me.

"I feel so out of place. I've never been to a party where people drank," she stated.

"I know what you mean. It's my first time too."

She shrugged, "Guess we'll have to make the most of it." *Whatever that means.*

The two couples hung out for a while talking. Sam the Showman cracked jokes. I prayed he didn't drink, as I wanted to remain in one piece on the way home.

The two popular girls from gym class and lunch circled me again. "Oink!" *Boy, do they have nerve!*

"What's with the oinking?" Sam asked. *Oh, jeez. Here we go again.*

I asserted, "It's for my benefit."

"I don't get it."

"It might be because I drink milkshakes. Dunno for sure, but it is getting tiresome."

"That's stupid!" Sam the Man declared. I love this guy!

"Yeah, well, they won't leave me alone."

The big guy had a crazed look on his face. Apparently, Avery read his mind. "Don't even think about it, Sam," Avery said sternly.

"What?" Sam asked with a mischievous twinkle in his eyes, all the while feigning his innocence.

"I know you too well," Avery said with an arched brow.

I didn't know what was going on, but I was curious. The girls cackled their way over to their puppet master. Sam watched them—studied them as if deep in thought. I had the urge to drink a chocolate milkshake.

"Ave, let's get some fresh air," I suggested, as I couldn't take the party noise or the oinks anymore.

"Okay." He turned to Sam, "Don't do anything I wouldn't do," he warned.

"What's the fun in that?" the goofy giant replied.

Katie and I looked at each other with question marks floating over our heads. We had no idea what was transpiring, but we both knew something was up.

Avery and I departed outside, where it was peaceful and dark. Apparently, they kept the party enclosed to minimize complaints. Playfully, I swung Avery's arm. We walked around the corner to where Doug's house was out of sight and out of mind.

Avery brushed my hair back off my shoulders. He broke the silence by saying, "Your hair is crunchy."

"I sprayed it." *Well, that's an understatement. I have an empty can of hairspray to prove it.*

"Oh, I like it better the other way . . . but you still look nice. You always look pretty." I made a mental note of his disapproval.

"Thanks." I think. *Well, I can't please everyone. So much for trying!*

Avery peered into my eyes and kissed me softly, sweetly. My body became covered in goose bumps in response. I found my way back on cloud nine. His kisses were so incredible that they transported me to a place far away.

We kissed again and it was over the top fantastic—tongues danced together, hands wandered aimlessly.

A few cars drove by, but we ignored them. We were enraptured. But all good things must come to an end, and thus we found ourselves back at Doug's house.

"Anything interesting happen while we were gone?" I asked.

"Not unless you call guys walking in a stupor interesting," Katie answered.

"Not really."

Katie and I wandered around the house attempting to appear independent and undaunted. We ambled downstairs. As soon as we appeared, the two popular girls oinked. We pretended to ignore them and acted like we had a purpose being there. After an eternity, we climbed the steps back into the kitchen where Avery, Sam, and Joey were gathered.

"So, did they?" Sam asked. *Did who do what?* I stood there quizzically.

"Yup," Katie affirmed with the smack of her lips. Sam the Man's face became red hot with anger, the wheels were turning in his head.

"Any friend of Avery's, who's like a brother to me, is a friend of mine." Then he turned to Katie and asked, "Can I get you a drink?"

"Sure," Katie answered with a wink. Sam straightened his shirt, stretched his neck and was off with the utmost look of determination and clenched fists.

As my friend poured Katie's drink, he glanced upwards and his eyes opened wide as they peered beyond the kitchen. I instinctively followed his resolute eyes.

The two populars sashayed towards us, like they owned the place. Upon entering the kitchen, the girls squeaked, "Oink! Oink!"

Sam, pumped for a fight, raised his voice to the guys, like when the quarterback calls a play to his teammates, "Remember the Jones twins?"

Without hesitation, Joey shielded Katie, likewise Avery shielded me, and they quickly told us both to "move away."

We obeyed, and like a perfectly timed pass play, Sam maneuvered and tossed. Liquid arched through the air and landed squarely on both miniskirts. NIAGARA FALLS! OH MY GOSH! They were soaked! Their perfectly coiffed hair was ruined. It was beautiful. Almost graceful. Definitely memorable. Touchdown!

"AHHHHH!!!!" both popular girls screeched. "You idiot!" one of them squealed. *Ha, ha! She totally sounded like a piglet.*

"So sorry! I must have tripped over my *piggies. Oink, oink!*" explained Sam, the super soaker.

"Umph!" One of the girls shrieked and stomped her feet.

Triumphantly, head high and shoulders back, Sam the Man winked at me as he strode away laughing toward the front door. Katie quickly followed. The rest of us boarded Sam's victory train.

"Ahhhh!!!!" yelled the girls. We left hearing lots of squealing and laughter, leaving the piglets in the wake—or monsoon.

"Let's go get some shakes!" Sam the Super Soaker shouted.

Chapter 38

IN THE CAR, ON OUR way to the diner, Katie, not being shy, asked her boyfriend, "Who in the world were the Jones twins? And what did you do to them and why?"

"What did I do to them? They were two punk kids who picked on Joey when he was in kindergarten, so I filled two ginormous water pistols with red Hawaiian Punch and sprayed them both simultaneously, until the guns emptied. They ran away crying like the big babies they were. Wimps. They could dish it out, but they couldn't take it. Waah!" the Super Soaker wailed. Joey remained torment free from that day forward. The Jones twins have since relocated. *Wonder why?*

Moments later, we were all sitting around a table at the diner, discussing our orders. Avery, Joey, Sam the Man and I affirmed that we would, in fact, order a shake. Sam turned to his girlfriend, "So, what are you ordering?"

"A chocolate shake sounds great!" Katie rhymed. She glanced my way with a wink. *What a sweet friend. Katie, not the milkshake.*

Sam turned to Joey and exclaimed, "You were right! Girls ordering shakes is a turn on."

Again, we chortled at Sam's silly sayings.

"Sam!" Katie playfully slapped him on the arm. Avery's eyes turned green with jealousy. All of a

sudden, it got tense. Very tense. Everyone stared at a stewing Avery. *Do I see smoke coming out of those ears?*

"Yo, I didn't mean anything by it. I swear! It's all in jest. We all need a good laugh, A." There was an uncomfortable silence lingering at the table, along with a chill in the air. "Dude, I mean it! I'm just messing around."

"Seriously, Sam, no more jokes. Christina is *my* girlfriend. Got it!" Avery said emphatically.

"Yeah, I got it. Sorry!" I didn't understand what that was all about. It seemed like Sam was referring to Katie not me. Was there something I missed?

Joey got up and walked away towards the restrooms. Sam abruptly excused himself, leaving Katie with Avery and me which felt awkward. A moment later, Katie left me alone with Avery, giving me the opportunity to get to the bottom of Avery's outburst.

"What's going on with you?" I asked.

"Nothing."

"Avery, that wasn't nothing. You practically bit Sam's head off."

Sounding exasperated, "Christina, you wouldn't understand."

"Try me."

Avery shook his head. "It's hard having a girlfriend who everyone wants to go out with." *I can relate. Jennie, Mindy, Val...*

I leaned in toward him, "Avery, I'm not going anywhere. I am not interested in anyone else. You have nothing to worry about. *Really.*" I placed a hand on his arm for reassurance.

"It's not that I would blame you if you did dump me for someone else." *Where is this insecurity coming from?*

"Avery, is that what this is all about? You think I'm going to dump you for someone else?"

"Well, kind of." He shrugged. *That's ridiculous!*

"Who do you think I would dump you for?"

"I don't know. Anybody . . . Joey, Sam."

"What?" I said, incredulous. "First of all, Sam has a girlfriend, in case you forgot." *Plus, I'm not interested in him like that. At all.*

"You looked at him like he was your hero after he splashed the girls." *Wow, you don't miss much.*

"No, I appreciated the fact that he completely embarrassed them, putting them in their place. Something I couldn't do for myself."

Avery continued in a serious tone, "It wasn't his place to do that."

"Whose place was it?"

"Mine, I guess."

"So, why didn't you do something?" I asked, curiously.

"Because they're girls. I didn't want to look like a bully." Okay, that sort of made sense, but those girls were the real bullies.

"Hmm," I paused and pondered. "Avery, don't you think the

situation is hard enough on Joey as it is? I mean not only are you, his best friend, going out with someone, but his brother is too."

Avery blurted, "I think he still likes you." *Still? Are you threatened by Joey?*

"Well, I don't know about that. He hasn't done anything to give me that indication. You have to trust Joey and me."

"It's not just Joey. The guys keep telling me that I'm the luckiest guy because I'm going out with you." *Honestly, I had no idea. They seemed so cool when I was around—more accepting me than wanting me.*

"The girls tell me the same thing and I'm not flipping out on them." *They just drool at the subject of Avery.*

"Christina, I love you. I don't even look at other girls." *I believed him. Wholeheartedly.*

"Avery, we have to trust each other, okay?" *Don't you know that I live and breathe for only you!*

"Yeah."

"Now, please play nice." I smiled, tilting my head toward him, "Okay?" I waited for a confirmation like a teacher admonishing her pupil.

"All right, if I have to." Avery smirked, like he was a little boy who had to share his toys.

"You have to." I affirmed with a wink.

A minute later the gang returned. The tension noticeably lessened. All five milkshakes were served. Perfect timing because that conversation worked up my appetite. *Life really is better with milkshakes!*

Avery turned to his best friend's brother and slapped him on his back, "Sorry, Bro."

"Don't sweat it," he forgivingly waved Avery off. Sam the Man held up his milkshake and toasted, "Here's to friendship!"

"Friendship!"

The powerful word 'friendship' echoed along with the clanking of the milkshake glasses. *Now, that's a good word. Life is good.* Before taking a sip of my shake, I silently thanked God for answering my prayer, as I was sure that he used a new friend to end the humiliating pig noises, and he gave me others to carry me through it. That's what friends are for—to protect, love and support each other no matter what. This night, albeit different and strange, had unified us and will certainly be one I remember fondly.

Chapter 39

THE ENTIRE WEEK I HELD my breath in anticipation of being teased, even though the two popular girls hadn't said one word to me since Sam the Super Soaker splashed them with the sodas. They deserved it, although my attitude didn't seem very Christian. Yet, what did I know? I was finding my feet with this new faith. At least Sam's plan worked. No more oinking. *You can exhale now, Christina! Thanks, again, God!*

On Homecoming Saturday, I found myself on the homecoming court float, waving to the spectators during halftime as we circled the football field. I was forced to wave—or else—feeling like the most awkward princess in a Disney movie. It was surreal.

I wore my stone-washed Jordache jeans, a fitted gray and hot pink blouse with thick horizontal stripes, paired with a thin hot pink belt. As usual, I didn't bother with my hair because it was too cumbersome to "do" twice in one day; my efforts for nice hair had to wait until the eight o'clock dance. That's where the action was going to be. So, I kept it very simple—long, curly ringlets flipped to the side.

Mindy was wearing a high-necked, light pink and white, vertically striped, puffy shoulder blouse that flared at the bottom, and a tight short black skirt. She complimented it with several gold and pearl bracelets and large gold and pearl stud earrings shaped like flowers. She looked like she was ready for the 1982 runway at Fashion Week in Paris.

We sat side by side on the back of a 1967 metallic coal Ford convertible Mustang. I didn't plan on matching my transportation, nor did I desire to look like a mere peasant compared to the queen next to me.

The tension was thick between the two of us. The pony car

jerked and Mindy and I bumped each other—her face thrust on the side of my head. She opened her mouth to speak and I fully expected a royal British accent. Instead, she calmly exhaled a compliment, "Nice earrings."

"Thanks," I replied politely. *Is she playing nice? Something's not right.*

"This is so queer, isn't it?" Mindy said, to my surprise. *Is she kidding? She lives for this kind of attention.* No way was I convinced that she wasn't relishing every moment of her fifteen minutes of fame.

"Totally," I answered. *I couldn't agree more with your statement, although I'm not buying it.*

"Hey, I'm sorry about what my friends did. They were just jealous. I mean, who wouldn't want to act like Mickey Mouse and Goofy waving to everybody? I feel like I'm on a stupid float at Walt Disney World."

She was being decent, although I still had my suspicions. *I'll play nice. I'll put my toe in and test the temperature of this tempest known as Mindy.*

"Really. I would gladly trade places with them." *God knows I tried.*

"I know you would. I wish we could trade places," she taunted.

Hmm, these waters seem cold based on her tone and the vibe I'm getting.

Okay, I'll bite. "You do? Why?" I asked, reservedly. *Please God, don't say what I think she's going to say.*

"Oh, you know," she said slowly drawing out her words, "Avery." She gushed saying his name and didn't even attempt to hide it. "I would love to go out with Avery."

My body convulsed when those words hit my ears. *You what? Nah, she didn't just say that? That's nuts and her brand of rotten made me speechless.* I had no words.

So I carved up all I could—I replied, meekly, "Uh, we're exclusive." Unfortunately, it sounded more like a question than a statement. We continued to wave to the spectators like Disney characters in a parade at my favorite theme park.

"I know. I would want him all to myself too." I felt squeamish. *Why was she telling me this? Am I a mouse dangling from a cat's mouth right now?* We drove around the field and continued to wave to onlookers as I tested the tempest's waters. *Ahhh! They're freezing!*

The most I could do was to try to understand this dreadfully mean character next to me. That was my only defense—to determine who she really was, so I pursued it. "Why are you telling me this?" Hoping the waters would warm up.

"Consider it a warning." *Come again? The waters suddenly turned frigid.*

I needed clarification, so I took the bait. "A warning?"

"Yeah, I see no reason in playing games," she answered smugly. *Wrong, this is a made-up Mindy game and I'm a pawn!*

I remained perplexed, angry, and silent.

"Yeah, it won't be such a surprise to you when I steal your boyfriend." *WHAT!??? Holy crap balls!*

"You can't be serious!" I said, imitating a blown gasket. *Something tells me that this tempest turned temptress doesn't play fair.*

"Watch me." *What a bitch!* I couldn't wait to get off the ridiculous so-called float. As soon as the Mustang stopped, I took off in search of Avery. Instead, I found Morgan wandering around alone.

"Morgan!" I screamed. I was fuming, smoke was oozing from my ears. My actions got the better of me. I wasn't doing a good job of looking like a saint, but rather like a crazed girlfriend. Morgan would know how to handle this without it blowing up in my face.

"Hi, Christina." I grabbed Morgan and abruptly pulled her away from the crowd, to prevent anyone from overhearing our conversation.

Wide-eyed and with full intensity, I looked Morgan straight into her cat-like eyes as I blurted, "You aren't going to believe what Mindy just said to me." I couldn't contain the smoke and the fumes emanating from my body.

"What?"

"She said she was going to steal Avery from me!"

"She actually said that?" Morgan cast an incredulous look, as if to suggest that I was bonkers.

I delivered Morgan the blow by blow account of the conversation. "No way! Wow, that's bold! Who does she think she is?" *Apparently, some sort of royalty immune from the consequences of unscrupulous behavior.*

"I know! Avery's freaking out because the guys are saying he's lucky for going out with me. He was mad at Joey for liking me and . . ." I stopped. So many thoughts ran through my head.

"And what?" Morgan urged me to continue.

I shook my head and divulged, "It sucks being popular! I never asked for this, Morgan. I hate it!" I probably appeared pathetic, complaining about being popular, when it was every girl's dream. Every girl's dream, but mine.

Then at the snap of my fingers, my arch enemy became the tempest turned temptress, Mindy, the most popular girl in our grade.

Morgan suggested, "Maybe you should tell Avery what Mindy said."

"You think?" I asked earnestly, squishing up my nose.

Morgan nodded, "Yeah, then he'll know exactly what her motives are. He won't be able to play dumb."

I spotted Val a few yards away. It appeared as if she was looking for someone, and my money was on Morgan.

I put my hand on Morgan's arm and quickly added, "Don't mention this to anyone, okay?" I didn't want my business out in the open and I knew most people would blab, but I trusted Morgan implicitly. She was a safe and sure bet.

"Sure, no problem," she assured me by crossing her heart with her right index finger. "Your secret's safe with me."

Chapter 40

I PRAYED TO HAVE FUN AT the dance as I waited in my bedroom for Avery to ring the doorbell. The last
dance I went to was in eighth grade when I ran out on Avery after he asked me to dance. As I recalled, I didn't have much fun at that dance.

This time, I worried about Mindy's threat and I feared being a crazy, jealous girlfriend, but I couldn't help myself. Even though Avery repeated for the tenth time that he didn't like Her Royal Highness at all when I told him about her malicious plan, I couldn't shake feeling insecure. I just knew that I wanted to be with Avery, as he had a way of making me feel better.

Ding dong.

I felt like running down the stairs, but I didn't want to plunge to my death as I was unsteady in my high heels.

"Christina, Avery's here!" my dad shouted. Incredibly anxious, I carefully descended the staircase wearing a knee length, flared, layered, royal purple, sleeveless dress, with a sweetheart neckline. It was my turn to feel like royalty, as I wore my hair in a chic chignon, with loose spirals framing my face, as well as showcasing my faux pearls. The overall look I created unintentionally added a few years to my age.

"Wow! Christina, you look beautiful! Bea, are you going to see the kids off? They're all dressed up for the dance."

Avery's protuberant eyes were burning with desire. Uttering not a sound, he complimented me profusely.

My mom came running holding the camera.

"Okay, I'm here," she said, a little breathless, as she arrived in the foyer. "Christina and Avery, why don't you go in the living room so I can take your picture?" We finally left after my mom snapped a few photos.

Since I liked Mrs. Evans, I readily complied when Avery told me she wanted us to stop by his house for more pictures.

Avery insisted his dad drive, instead of Sam the Man, to keep it low profile. My date wanted to avoid making a big deal out of the dance, as his mom would have insisted on taking pictures of everyone if we went with the gang.

When we arrived at his house, Mrs. Evans was in the driveway, ready with camera in hand. "Christina, you look absolutely beautiful!" Avery's mom gave me a hug and was extra careful with my dress. "I knew you would." She stepped back and took me in. "What a gorgeous dress! You're so, so beautiful! Thank you for coming here so I could take a few photos. Now let me take your picture!" Avery and I smiled again for more pictures. At last, we were off.

The gymnasium was transformed into a festive dance floor. It was decorated with streamers and balloons. A table tempted us with punch and baked goods. A huge disco ball hung from the ceiling. The DJ played "My Sharona!"

"Come on!" I pulled Avery onto the dance floor with Katie, Sam, Joey, and Peter. The song "My Sharona" reminded me of our middle school years when it constantly played on the jukebox during lunch —a time when life was much simpler.

"Thank God you showed up!" a relieved Katie said to me as she hated being the only girl.

We moved our bodies to the beat of "We Got the Beat." Comical and fun Sam the Showman roamed all over the dance floor, flinging his body this way and that. Katie playfully rolled her eyes. Morgan, Val, Cheryl, and Jackie joined our group.

Next, the DJ played "I'm so Excited." We continued to dance, taking turns in the middle of the circle we created. Adam and Doug joined us as the song transitioned to Michael Jackson's "Beat It." We were having a blast, and it showed because we drew quite the crowd. "Rock This Town" by Stray Cats came on next, followed by Toni Basil's "Mickey."

Afterward the tempo slowed down. I recognized the first few notes of "Endless Love."

Brooke Shields starred in the movie that featured the song, but I never watched it due to its adult rating. I was told many times in the past that I looked like Brooke Shields. Other than both of us having long brown hair, I failed to see the resemblance. Maybe if I wore Calvin Klein jeans I would look more like her.

The crowd broke up while Avery and I slow danced together. Katie and her senior class boyfriend moved to the music next to us.

"I love this song," I confessed, whispering in Avery's ear.

"I forgot to tell you. You look beautiful."

My heart smiled. I wanted to kiss him right then and there, but it went against my no public display of affection rule to kiss in front of adults, and there was no shortage of chaperones looking on. Swaying to the music, we drew closer. I relaxed in his embrace and closed my eyes while I savored the enchanting moment.

A tap on my back startled me. I opened my eyes to discover Mindy standing there asking to cut in. At first it didn't register what she was doing. Avery gave me a blank stare. I knew it was proper to concede, so I did the polite thing and moved away from Avery. Flabbergasted, I walked off the dance floor.

I don't know why I was so shocked, because *Her Royal Pain in the Butt* did warn me, after all. *Oh, she messed up my perfect Avery moment. Watch out, Mindy! This war is not over!*

I quickly found Peter and pleaded with him to cut in on Mindy and Avery. "No way!" he reacted.

I recalled Avery saying how shy he was. Then I told him what Mindy's plan was. He appeared to be bothered by her scheme, but nonetheless refused. Feeling defeated, I struggled not to stare at my boyfriend and Her Royal Annoyance, while they danced together.

When the tune changed to "Ebony and Ivory," Avery left Mindy stranded in the middle of the dance floor and came toward me with a purpose. He held out his hand, "Christina, do you want to dance?"

My heart was refueled as my date led me to the dance floor. Shortly after, Mindy cut in. Once again, I reluctantly stepped away from my man as my heart sank. To my surprise, Peter rushed over to cut in. My pleasure and gratitude spilled out in a burst of laughter. I noticed Morgan and the others cheering on the perimeter of the dance floor.

My zany upperclassman friend yelled at Mindy, "That'll teach you to mess with us!" Katie giggled as she danced with her bold, boisterous boyfriend.

Mindy looked absolutely pissed! Her Royal Vexation may have won one battle, but my friends helped me to, once again, take the lead in this boyfriend war.

Avery and I swayed to the music. Katie winked at me and her dancing partner gave us the thumbs up. What a blessing it was to have allies. The DJ put on "Kids in America" and we got our beat on.

The next slow song, "Open Arms," brought on the last eruption from Mount Saint Mindy. As the song commenced, I glanced around the room for her. I spotted her next to Peter across the dance floor, and, by the looks of her body language, she was yelling at him. Her hands were flailing and her mouth was wide and tense. She came toward us full of anger, looking for a fight. Gritting her teeth, she glared at me and demanded, "I'm cutting in!"

Aghast but calm, I simply looked at her and replied, "No, I don't think so."

Shocked, with fists clenched, she replied emphatically, "But you *have* to. Rules are rules!"

To that I said, "In that case, rule number one—don't steal someone else's boyfriend." I followed it more intensely with, "Go find your own!"

She tried to form words but failed pathetically. Stomping her feet like a spoiled toddler, she stormed off.

Avery and I both heaved a sigh of relief. We heard cheers of approval and Sam the Man roared, "That should teach her!" *I love you, Sam, for your loyalty and bluntness!*

At the refreshment table, Mindy's two animal impersonators walked up to the snack table. Sam the Super Soaker immediately recognized them and warned, "You say it and I spray it!" The girls ran off with a befitting squeal.

The rest of the evening was fun and trouble-free. No more Mount St. Mindy eruptions interfered with our gala event. Instead, Her Royal Malevolence and her court of swine laid low the remainder of the evening.

Chapter 41

MY BIRTHDAY WAS AROUND THE corner—on November twentieth I'd celebrate becoming fourteen. In some ways I felt so young, like adulthood was miles and miles away—too far to be seen—yet, in other ways, I felt ready for it. Part of me was afraid to grow up, and another part of me wanted freedom and money—the ability to do whatever whim I possessed. However, I learned that without responsibility, one may not enjoy certain liberties.

I thought about Avery when I wasn't with him. When we were alone together, we were always tempted to expand our physical relationship, but somehow resisted. Avery wanted to stay true to the promise he made last year at Sunday school. Knowing I needed to honor his pledge didn't make it any easier.

Then I reminded myself that we were still young—very young. I constantly found myself bewildered as to how intimate Avery and I were despite our youth. We got along so well. We snuggled a lot when we were alone. We talked about everything, and we constantly laughed together.

Instead of having the usual party for my birthday, my parents agreed to have Avery over for dinner. Typically, he didn't spend much time at my house. Rather we spent most of our time alone in his basement or eating with his parents when it was mealtime. The day of my fourteenth birthday happened to be on a Saturday. Avery came over and we hung out in my basement. We couldn't keep our hands off of each other but knew we had to remain quiet. Unlike Avery's basement, my basement was not soundproof, but at least it provided some privacy.

The steps that led down to the basement were bare, so we were warned by the creaks if anyone was coming down. We made ourselves comfortable on the old blue couch. I never realized how comfortable the couch was, but then again, I was always comfortable with Avery.

While we were kissing, Avery broke away and said, "I have something for you." He eased his body off of mine and grabbed his jean jacket that was draped over the arm of the couch. He scavenged around in the jacket pocket and, eventually, pulled out a small box in shiny, purple gift wrap with a gold bow and handed it to me as if it were on a silver platter. "Happy birthday, Christina!"

My heart filled with joy and my cheeks filled with a warm glow even before I opened it.

"I wrapped it in purple because it's your favorite color." I noticed! *Nice attention to details!*

I wasn't expecting him to get me anything. I gently unraveled the gorgeous wrapping paper. I peeled the tape off and was so careful. I was able to save the paper in one untorn piece. *This will be my memento.*

I opened the box and pulled out a fourteen-karat gold charm bracelet with two charms—the letter C and a delicate rose.

I gasped and covered my mouth with my shaking hand, "I love it! Thank you!" *Best boyfriend ever!*

"Each charm represents your name. C for Christina, and a rose for De Rosa," he smiled proudly.

"I never owned a charm bracelet before. It's beautiful!" I was incredibly touched—tears welled up in my eyes. "It's perfect! Thank you so much!" Avery secured the shiny jewelry on me, and with a few flicks of the wrist the bracelet sparkled even more as it jingled playfully.

I kissed him to show my deep appreciation for my wonderful birthday present. We got lost in the intensity of the moment and soon entered dangerous territory.

His hand slid up my shirt. My fingers ran through his light-colored, wavy locks. Our tongues connected to one another. He broke away to relish kisses on my neck. I leaned backwards as he leaned toward me cupping my breast. I desired to shout his name, but all I could do was moan, praying the sounds of passion fell on deaf ears.

He started to unbutton my jeans. I jerked his hand away and cried breathlessly, "Not here, not now." He moved his hand and pulled up my shirt. "No, Avery!" I whispered firmly. "We can't do that here!" I couldn't bear the thought of being seen or heard, but not enough to stop. I wanted it as badly as he did, but the timing was off, way off.

"Dinner," my mom shouted from above. Startled, he sprang to his feet and I yanked down my shirt. We were panting from exhaustion and shaking from fear. I covered my face with my hands, so he put his consoling arms around me. No words were needed between us—we both knew what the other felt and what they would say. The battle for sexual purity was excruciating.

Our fingers were intertwined together as I lead him up the creaky stairs. I prayed that our secret was still ours.

With pride, I showed my mom and dad the new birthday gift glittering on my wrist. They seemed particularly impressed by the thoughtfulness of the charms.

For the special occasion, my mother served homemade mushroom soup for starters, followed by thick, tender, juicy steak, accompanied by homemade garlic mashed potatoes topped with brown gravy and green bean almondine.

Avery sincerely praised my mom's cooking, "Mrs. De Rosa, this is the best steak dinner ever!"

Did my mom just blush?! Never, in all my fourteen years, have I seen someone have such an effect on my mom.

My dad and I followed suit with the compliments, but my brother remained noticeably silent, even though his plate was practically licked clean.

To finish the meal outdone by all other meals, and in honor of the self-professed chocoholic, my mom served her decadent homemade chocolate cake and they all sang "Happy Birthday to You." Even my mom knows that life is better with chocolate.

My fourteenth birthday was extra special having shared it with my knight, who came bearing shining jewelry, which solidified, without a doubt, that Avery was the best boyfriend anyone could ask for. I found myself mesmerized with the shiny charm bracelet thinking how thoughtful and perfect the gift was, and how thoughtful and perfect he was.

Chapter 42

ONE DAY, AFTER THANKSGIVING BREAK, we had a big geography test. I caught Tammy cheating off of me. Again! I reiterated that I was not the best geography student. Case in point, I only recently found out that Belize was, in fact, a country, but she argued, "You get A's on everything!" This was true, but it was sheer luck and I didn't want any part of cheating. Ever!

I flashed back to the time when a girl in my fourth grade music class copied off my test. The day the teacher handed back the tests, she stated that she witnessed a student cheating, so she gave the culprit a zero. There was a big, fat zero on my test. I approached the teacher to defend my case, but she refused to listen. Looking back, I should have persisted. If I took the test again, she would have seen that I knew all the material. The other girl received one hundred percent! I was furious! Stupid teacher! It made my blood boil.

The next day, before Mr. Nunzio passed back the tests, he announced to the class that he witnessed some people cheating. *Not again!* He said, "I will give the culprits another chance on the test if they admit to their offense today."

With apprehension, I approached Mr. Nunzio after class, and told him what happened to avoid another false accusation. He affirmed my innocence. Relieved, I thanked him and departed.

Two mornings later, I arrived at my locker where there appeared to be a lot of commotion. I noticed a strange look on my guy's face. "Hey, what's wrong?" I asked. He touched my shoulder and stepped aside—the word "NARK" was splattered across my locker in red spray paint. To my dismay, people pointed and snickered.

"Do you know what this is about?" Avery questioned. I turned crimson with embarrassment, matching my lettered locker. Without speaking, I robotically gathered the books I needed, like C3PO, and put the others away.

Immediately, I reported the vandalism to the principal's secretary. I refrained from divulging my perception as to why it happened because, I figured, matters could get worse. They told me they suspected who the guilty parties were, would handle the matter, and for me not to worry as I did nothing wrong. I politely thanked her and quivered as I walked away wondering when I would stop being violently and verbally attacked by fellow students. I was a walking target, and it was unnerving, to say the least. I never knew when or how the serpents would strike next. *Please God, make it stop! I can't take any more of this! I'm scared!*

I couldn't wait to talk to Miss Brenda about the locker incident after school, even though it wasn't Friday. "Mmm, mm, mm!" she said, as she shook her head. "Girl, sounds like you are being tried!"

"What do you mean tried?" I asked, completely clueless.

"I mean, it's up to you to do what's right in the face of evil," Miss Brenda stated, like this was common knowledge. I still had no idea what she was talking about.

"But I didn't do anything wrong," I insisted. "I'm nice to people. I'm just trying to live my life. I don't get how people are so nasty— period, much less to me, someone who doesn't bother anyone." My brother's face flashed across my mind. *He doesn't count. That's a sibling thing.*

"Girl, you always do something wrong. We all do. We're human. All of us are sinners!"

Still nothing registered. "I don't get it!" I said feeling defeated, shaking my head. "Why is this happening to *me?*"

"The devil. He's trying to tear you down. Fact is, you did nothing wrong. Honey, you chose to follow God. Oh, that makes Satan plenty angry. That's what happens when you first believe. He comes at you, hard and fast to keep you down, especially the special ones . . . and you are special. Make no mistake about that, sugar." Miss Brenda always had a way of making me feel that I was more than I believed I was. *I love you. Thank you for being in my life.*

I gestured for help, "So what am I supposed to do?"

"Bounce back. Get right back up. Tell them to bring it. They will back away 'till the next time."

"They? Who? My classmates?" *What in the world is she talking about?*

"Satan and his crew. They'll get tired and go find someone else to attack."

Attack! She gets it. Her understanding brought such comfort. I was so glad to have her as a friend.

When I got home, I looked up Deuteronomy 31:6 like Miss Brenda told me to. It read, "Be strong and of a good courage, fear not, nor be afraid of them: for the Lord thy God, he *it is* that doth go with thee; he will not fail thee, nor forsake thee." *God will never leave me! Wow! Cool.* I could breathe again.

Later that night, I prayed for Satan and his buddies to bring it on. I was ready for a fight. I knew I had to get back up once I fell down. I thanked God for Miss Brenda. I felt like I could talk to her about anything—almost anything.

I still didn't tell anyone about the contemptible day at the Martins'. Without fail, I shuddered every time I thought about that attack, so I tried not to think about it.

The graffiti was nothing in comparison, although it was public humiliation. At least no one knew what Creepoid did to me. Thank God I didn't get pregnant. I couldn't bear the thought. God protected me from a worse fate. *Thank you, Lord, that I didn't get pregnant!* I read Deuteronomy 31:6 over and over until my body fell into a slumber.

I woke up in the middle of the night, panting in a sweat. I had a horrific nightmare.

I dreamed that I was in the high school, but it was presumably night, as it was frightfully dark. I wandered around alone for reasons unknown. All of a sudden, an angry mob came towards me with lit torches. The fire was blinding. The mob was chanting, "Nark, nark, nark!" It was then I realized they were after me. They tried to burn me alive. As I fled for my life, I screamed, frantically searching for a friendly familiar face amid the darkness and terror.

Mindy appeared, leading the popular pig-squealing girls in the rank, chanting, "Oink, oink!" I spotted Tammy who was yelling, "Nark!" My fourth-grade music teacher shouted, "Cheater! Cheater!"

Then I saw *him*! Jackalope's eyes were ablaze with fire like the torches. He was screaming at me, "You stupid whore! You ruined my mom's life! I should have killed you when I had the chance!" Surrounded by the murderous mob with no conceivable way out, I crashed into my traitorous locker—betraying me with the letters N-A-R-K in red, dripping with blood.

I woke up, all sweaty and shaken from the terrifying nightmare. Knowing I could visit Miss Brenda for help, I prayed myself back to sleep:

Dear Lord,

Please God, protect me. I'm so scared and tired. Right now, I just want to go back to sleep. I need my rest. I need to be alert for classes tomorrow. Help me to fall back asleep after that terrible nightmare. Please stop the nightmares. They seem so real and they really shake me up. I can't take any more of this. Please make it all stop . . . Please God . . .

I told Miss Brenda the next day about my dream, except for the part with Creepoid. "Lordy, Lordy, that's some dream," Miss Brenda acknowledged, shaking her head.

Then she slapped her knee and encouraged, "Girl, you gotta keep fighting back. It ain't easy, but the Lord is on your side. Have faith. Don't give up! Jesus is your rock. He'll get you through this, whatever it is." She emboldened, "Repeat this verse, Psalm 18:2, 'The Lord *is* my rock, and my fortress, and my deliverer; my God, my strength, in whom I will trust; my buckler, and the horn of my salvation, *and* my high tower.' "

While wringing my hands and clenching my teeth, desperately, I asked, "What do I do other than read and pray?"

"In this case, prayer is the answer. Not much else you can do with a dream. The more people praying for you the better! Ask your sweet boyfriend to pray too. And keep repeating the verses I told you about. Here, I have another one for you, Isaiah 41:10, 'Fear thou not; for I *am* with thee: be not dismayed; for I *am* thy God: I will strengthen thee; yea, I will help thee; yea, I will uphold thee with the right hand of my righteousness.' These words are your arsenal. Use them to fight back. You got this, honey." *Thank you, Miss Brenda! I love these verses.*

She paused, looked me over carefully, and finally asked the dreaded question, "Is there something else going on?"

I hesitated, as if to ponder the question, completely unsure how well she could read between the lines. "No, there isn't," I answered, shaking my head, feeling an icy chill run through me. *God help me! I'm tired of lying.*

It followed that I read and reread the verses she gave me so often, I memorized them without effort. I almost missed the great change that had taken place in me—cutting hadn't crossed my mind during this awful time. Praying did. Reading verses did. That was progress. That was victory.

Chapter 43

IN EARLY DECEMBER, MY FRIENDS and I were gearing up for the holidays. Avery and I decided we would go shopping with Sam the Man and Katie. It was great not having to rely on our parents to drive, allowing us a little more freedom and, in some cases, but not all, convenience.

Much to our dismay, the upperclassman parked his car in the boonies. We dared not complain, as we were appreciative for the ride. I pictured him to be the type to follow people to their cars, practically taunting them. I was wrong. Our driver wasted no time finding a parking spot on the other side of the world, far away from the entrance to the mall.

"Mall drivers are crazy, especially this time of year. I'm not taking any chances getting my car hit," reasoned the zany driver himself, as he parked in a remote location. *Do they offer shuttle buses from here?*

The Christmas decorations adorned the mall inside and out— Christmas trees in shop windows, bright, colorful lights, poinsettias, red ribbons, green wreaths, banners spewing festive well-wishes. We were all caught up in the festive mood of Christmas. Everything seemed fun, everyone seemed to be of good cheer.

Katie and I were frantic about what to get our men. We didn't want to seem too mushy or over the top, but enough to know we cared. It was hard to find that delicate balance. At some point, we figured we would have to split up from the guys.

It was nice having Katie date Sam. Katie and I got along well when we hung out together, and her goofy boyfriend was always good for a laugh. They were the perfect couple with whom to double date.

"Ladies, why don't we catch up later," suggested Sam the Man, to my relief, as well as Katie's.

We planned on meeting later at Friendly's. The guys went off together, while Katie and I headed for Modell's Sporting Goods.

I decided to get Avery a Philadelphia Phillies baseball cap since he played baseball and was a huge Phillies fan. There were all different variations of Phillies hats, but I decided to go with the classic red one with the white "P" on the front. I knew I had to get something else, but what? I settled on a Phillies T-shirt.

Even though Katie knew Sam the Man also played baseball and was a Phillies fan, she didn't want to get her man the same thing for Christmas. We were off to find a department store or clothing store for young men.

As we walked out of Modell's, I heard an unfamiliar voice shout, "Christina!" I turned around to see a super hot teenage boy waving at me. At first it didn't register who he was.

As I squinted to get a better look, Katie nudged me, "That's the guy from the skating rink."

"Oh my gosh, you're right," I replied and bit my lip, as I watched the guy walk towards us, my adrenaline pumped.

"You don't remember me, do you?" asked the boy.

"Uh, yeah, you're the guy from the roller rink," I said with a warm smile, forgetting his name.

"Right, I'm Kevin."

"Yeah, hi, Kevin. This is Katie," I motioned. "She was there too. At the skating rink."

"Yeah, I remember you," Kevin said to Katie. "So, I guess you two are buying Christmas gifts?" We nodded.

"Me, too. Oh, here comes my friend, Collin."

"Hey, Collin, what's up?" I asked, trying to catch him off guard. Sam's silliness was wearing off on me. Collin gave me a confused look.

"Yo, what's up?" he replied.

After a good laugh, Kevin explained who Katie and I were and mentioned not seeing us at the rolling rink since the night we met. Can we say awkward? I provided him with some lame excuse.

I looked at my Swatch watch, "Sorry, but we gotta go. Shopping awaits," I declared.

"Oh, sure, sure. See ya later!" Kevin said, enthusiastically. We said our goodbyes and went our separate ways in pairs. I considered telling Kevin that I was shopping for my boyfriend, but I didn't feel like explaining the sorted mess, or at least the fake version of the story. What were the chances of bumping into him again? So I let it go.

Katie bought an expensive collared Izod shirt, on sale, for her man, and we met up with the guys at Friendly's. Avery and I greeted each other with a little kiss, despite our rules against PDA, while Sam the Showman pretended to molest Katie. She laughed it off, being her usual easygoing self.

"What a nut!" I exclaimed, in reaction to the scene the goofy giant created. We were seated after a twenty-minute wait.

"Let me guess," Sam fished, "you're ordering a chocolate milkshake."

"I don't know. It's freezing out." I turned to my boyfriend. "What do you think, Ave?"

"Go for it!" Avery encouraged. Then he whispered in my ear, "I'll keep you warm." Naturally, I blushed and Sam went crazy.

"Hey, no secrets! Didn't your mother teach you that it was rude to whisper?" our elder averred. I rolled my eyes and smirked. *But it's okay for you to go all gaga with your girlfriend outside the restaurant?*

"Just ignore him," Katie suggested, giving him a playful little shove. She continued with a cute grin and wiggled in her seat, like a happy toddler, "I think I'll have a chocolate shake."

"Me too," Avery and I said at the same time. We looked at each other and chuckled.

"I'm in too," Sam the Man made it unanimous. We had a good time eating our cheeseburgers with fries while sipping our shakes. The guys generously handled the bill.

When we were almost to our car in the lot, I heard, "Christina," this time from a familiar voice.

Once again, I turned around to see Kevin. Only this time, he was with his friend. I felt the blood drain through my face. Even though I was holding Avery's hand, I hoped I could get by without providing Kevin with the dreaded and dishonest explanation. Maybe if I acted chill this would blow over.

"Oh, hey, Kevin, Collin. This is my boyfriend, Avery and this is Sam."

"I thought you weren't allowed to date, Christina," Kevin recalled. Boy, was he bold? *Guess I owe him an explanation after all.*

Great.

"You're right. I wasn't, but my parents changed their minds." *Okay, that wasn't so bad.*

"How do you know each other?" Sam asked eyeing us up, suspiciously. Katie shoved Sam the Man again.

"We met at the roller skating rink over the summer," Kevin replied.

"Well, we have to go. See you around Keith!" Sam waved, and walked off abruptly, with Katie in tow, causing her to stumble.

"It's Kevin. Yeah, later," Kevin stated firmly, obviously annoyed. "Bye, Christina!" Kevin said sweetly, then walked away with Collin. I waved goodbye. Avery shook his head. I squeezed Avery's hand, to ensure him that he had nothing to worry about. I loved him and no one, including a random guy I met roller skating—even if he was super hot—would come between us. After all, I barely knew Keith . . . I mean Kevin.

"That guy's got it bad!" Sam the Man declared, shaking his head. He turned to me and added, "Christina, I never met anyone who attracted so much attention."

"Look who's talking!" Katie ribbed, raising her eyebrows at him.

"Moi?" responded Sam the Man as he attempted to portray an innocent Frenchman. Katie defended me, by explaining that I let Kevin down graciously over the summer. The fact that I needed someone to plead my case wasn't a good sign, yet I remained quiet, confident that I was innocent of any wrongdoings where Keith, I mean Kevin, was concerned.

Chapter 44

CHRISTMAS ARRIVED, BUT I DIDN'T get to see Avery until the day after when the Evans family picked me up for church. Even though I wanted to hear more about God, I was anxious to spend some time alone with my guy.

During Sunday school, we discussed how Jesus was the Son of Man, the Messiah—and how the Jews missed the mark with Him, because they were awaiting a powerful king that would destroy the Roman government that ruled them. Most people back then didn't recognize Jesus as Savior because he didn't forcefully overthrow the government, as they expected. Instead, he was born to a simple carpenter and talked about entering the kingdom of God by believing in Him, while teaching love and forgiveness.

We read Luke 6:37, "Judge not, and ye shall not be judged: condemn not, and ye shall not be condemned: forgive, and ye shall be forgiven."

I wondered if I would ever be able to forgive the unspeakable act. After some discussion, Matthew 6:15 was recited by Erin, " 'But if ye forgive not men their trespasses, neither will your Father forgive your trespasses.' " *So, this is saying if I don't forgive Creepoid, then I am not forgiven? How can that be? That's not fair! I never did anything even remotely despicable and I get to suffer a double whammy—I suffer from the ongoing torment, and I'm not forgiven because I can't forgive that jackalope! How can I forgive him? He destroyed my life! He stole my virginity! I hate him for it! I will hate him forever! I will never be able to forgive him!*

I snapped back to reality when I heard the words spoken by Avery, "Christina, are you all right?"

I nodded and a forced smile appeared on my face. He gently reached for my hand and held it. Instantly, I felt better, but I knew it was only temporary. I knew that, all too soon enough, I would once again be tormented by that evil act, haunted by his menacing threats and awful accusations. *Why does it haunt me so when my life is so good?*

After church, we went to Avery's for lunch. We ate ham sandwiches from the leftovers and then retreated to our usual spot in the basement. I handed Avery two red gift-wrapped boxes, each topped with green bows. He opened up the smaller box first and acted like it was the greatest gift he had ever received, "Hey, this is great! I needed a new baseball cap. Thanks!" I smiled in response. He tore open the gift wrap of the other box. "Awesome! A Phillies shirt! Yeah! This is so cool! Thank you!" He leaned over and gave me the sweetest kiss. "I love both gifts! Thank you so much!" I smiled with ease because his enthusiasm was so contagious. *You make my day!* His enthusiasm was gift enough.

It was my turn to open up the small shiny red gift-wrapped box, adorned with swirly gold ribbon. *Do the best things come in small packages?* I tore open the tiny, felt, black box and found a beautiful fourteen-karat gold, Christian cross charm with seven minuscule diamond chips. The charm was exquisite. Both my jaw and stomach dropped as I gasped for air taking in its beauty and his generosity.

"Oh, it's beautiful! Thank you!" I leaned over to kiss him.

"I figured it would be the perfect gift for Christmas and it goes on your charm bracelet." I couldn't stop staring at the charm. It was somewhat of a déjà vu from my birthday. "Here, let me help you put it on." He carefully put the new charm on the treasured bracelet that I proudly wore every day.

"I really, really, really love it! Thank you!" I flicked my wrist once the charm was on the bracelet and watched it dance in the light. "I love the way it sparkles!"

"They're real diamonds!" Avery beamed with pride.

Real diamonds?! GENUINE DIAMONDS! This is too much! I love it!

"Wow, it's stunning!" I couldn't help but think how the gifts I gave Avery paled in comparison. "You really know what to get a girl." I was so impressed with the cross and it truly was the perfect gift for me, having recently made a commitment of faith. *How thoughtful. A great reminder of the greatest gift anyone could receive!*

"No, I know what to get YOU! I had to get the cross with the diamonds because it reminded me of you."

"Of me? Diamonds?" I said, perplexed.

"Sure, it matches your sparkling personality." I smiled, despite his obvious confusion with someone else.

"You are so wonderful!" I gleamed. We embraced and kissed each other softly, romantically, and ever so dearly. Avery put his hands on my cheeks and leaned his forehead on mine.

"I love you, Christina," he said in an irresistibly charming manner. My entire body tingled in response to his affirming words.

"I love you too, Avery," I echoed.

Avery touched my soul so deeply, and yet so lovingly. I felt adrift and sighed, as if to take in the wonder and beauty of our relationship. Oh, how I loved Avery. Everything about him caused me to internally burst into glee . . . his gorgeous ocean blue eyes, his luscious lips—especially when they were on mine, his fair hair, his athletic build, the way he looked at me so endearingly, the way he spoke to me so sweetly, the way he touched me so tenderly, the way he chose gifts for me so thoughtfully. I was truly in love.

He brushed the stray strands of hair away from my eyes and drew me closer. We kissed unabashedly. I slumped back into the couch and scooted myself downward, as Avery leaned on top of me. My fingers frolicked in his thick hair and my body moved with his.

Avery nimbly unbuttoned my maroon cardigan. He repeated the motion with my white silk blouse. I surprised him with a new lacy white bra that opened in the front. As I dressed earlier that morning, I was hoping I would be in the exact position in which I found myself. Some things were predictable. Our routine on the couch was one of them.

Despite the allure, Avery never once unhooked my bra. Rather his fingers lightly caressed the lacy material. I relished every moment of every kiss, every caress. "Oh, Avery," I sighed with delight.

After a brief interlude, Avery shot me a satisfying look—his eyes filled with lust. We reached into the depths of each other's souls, drinking it all in—the powerful connection between the two of us, the love, the tenderness, the passion. Unable to contain it, we resumed positions and let our teenage bodies run amok.

My thoughtful boyfriend had a knack for giving pleasure. My body quivered with delight and screamed for more. I became more adventurous, more daring as I wanted to please Avery in return. Our bodies yearned for each other. It was becoming more difficult to stop, but somehow—I don't know how—we managed to stop.

Our escapades always left me with daydreams of making love to Avery. I imagined making love to him would erase that horrific moment in time at the Martins' house. That moment was terrifying and painful and disgusting and I didn't want to get suffocated in those thoughts yet again.

I envisioned Avery being tender, affectionate, loving as our bodies united. I imagined the two acts would cancel each other out—the unspeakable one at the Martins' and the enchanted encounter with my sweet boyfriend. I could start fresh, anew and create wonderful new memories with Avery, but I didn't dare. I didn't want to disappoint my special guy.

I felt that I should support his pledge of purity, although one couldn't call it purity, but abstinence. I felt obligated to support his pledge of abstinence. In my heart, now as a believer, I knew he was right. Avery said it would be a wonderful gift he could give his future wife someday. That hopefully, she, too, would have the same gift to give.

That's where I would disappoint. I had already done the "dirty deed." In my case, it was, without exaggeration, "dirty." Honestly, I wasn't even sure if I could go through with having sex at this point in my life, even with my amazing boyfriend, as magical as I imagined it would be.

Anytime Avery skated on thin ice, I became very skittish. He thought I was trying to be chaste. I didn't dare clue him in otherwise. Avery was best left in the dark, as I needed to keep him safe from Creepoid. I still couldn't take any chances, because it wasn't worth the risk.

As I pondered this scenario, I realized that Avery's life—his abstinence—mattered too. My mind needed to be on what Avery needed. I needed to put both selfish emotions of anguish and desire aside to create space for Avery's needs, but most importantly I needed to do God's will.

Chapter 45

"SEE YA, DAD," I WAVED, as I rushed out the door to go to Jackie's party.

"Have fun, pooch! You too, Avery. Happy New Year!"

"Thank you, Mr. De Rosa and happy New Year to you too."

Since my mom was nowhere to be seen, I turned my head back and yelled, "Bye, Mom!" Silence.

Avery slid into the car first, next to Joey who was next to Peter. I was practically sitting on top of Avery, but he didn't seem to mind. Katie sat in the passenger seat up front with her man. "Bet you're glad your girlfriend isn't a chubber, Ave, seeing that she's sitting on you."

"Keep your eyes on the road, Sam, and your comments to yourself," Avery suggested boldly, considering Sam was our ride.

On our way to the party, my mind wandered to an earlier private conversation when Avery mentioned that Peter's new love interest was Amy. *So, Peter likes Amy. This could be fun.*

The party was in full swing by the time we got there. There were tons of teens, including the usual suspects, and I assumed Morgan performed her magic to draw quite the crowd. I told Avery I would catch up with him later. He reminded me not to mention that Peter likes Amy. My lips were sealed.

"Hi, Morgan. You did a great job with the invites!" I congratulated her.

She gave me a dismissive wave, "You know me. I got connections."

"So, does Amy have her eye on anyone or is she waiting for Mr. Right to walk through her doors?"

"Amy? She likes Alex Touey last I heard." Morgan popped a chip in her mouth. "Why? What's up? What did I miss?"

I rolled my eyes and stuck my tongue out in disapproval. "Is Alex here?" I couldn't imagine being at a party with Alex. *Blah! Gag me with a spoon!*

"I doubt he's coming. He hangs out with the burnouts."

I contorted my face, "I know. What does she see in him?"

"Beats me. Amy's odd that way. But I see you brought the 'A' crowd. I'm impressed," she teased.

"Well, I seem to make a scene at the other parties, so we decided to be low-key tonight."

Morgan chortled, "Yeah, like beverage shooters." Morgan knew about Sam the Man drenching the popular girls at Doug's party. "Jackie's mom would freak if there was a mess to clean up," Morgan warned. "Just a head's up 'cause I care." *Okay, then, so why have a New Year's Eve party at your house, Jackie?!*

I glanced around the room. Everyone was having a good time chatting, laughing and eating. "You know I don't instigate things. Plus, I'm not so . . . so controversial with you guys."

Morgan guffawed. "Controversial. Is that what you call it? Interesting choice of words."

"For lack of a better word," I responded breezily.

"Well, I'm glad you came."

"Thanks. I can't take all the drama." *At least not when it's directed at me.*

Morgan changed the subject. "Hey, did you ever find out who spray-painted your locker?" Surprisingly, that drama didn't last long at all. For the most part, I heard a few whispers and saw some pointing, but that was it. *Guess my prayers worked! Thanks again, God.*

"No, but they painted it right away and told me not to worry about it. Something about having an idea as to who did it."

"Who do you think did it?"

"Not sure, really," I shrugged.

Morgan pressed, "So did you nark? I never did get the story."

I did my best to explain what I suspected, "I didn't want to get in trouble for cheating when I didn't cheat, so I explained to Mr. Nuzio that I didn't cheat. The person who cheated shouldn't have blamed me for anything. Mr. Nuzio already knew who the culprit was, but he was waiting for a confession. I made sure that he didn't think I allowed someone to cheat off of me. Can you believe someone would cheat off of me?" I asked incredulously. "I don't even study."

"You still get good grades," Morgan stated.

"Guess I'm lucky."

"It's not luck. I've had classes with you. You're smart."

"But *far* from the smartest," I said, dragging out the word far.

"Yea, well, we all are far from that. Puh-leeze." She continued, "So, what did you get on the test that involved the cheating?"

"An A," I said, casually tilting my head.

Morgan reaffirmed, "See what I mean? You get good grades. Stop acting like you don't! Jeez, you downplay so much. Just enjoy what God gave you already."

I meekly replied, "Morgan, the test was easy. The whole class probably got an A."

Morgan smirked and with utter confidence challenged me, "I doubt that, since someone felt the need to cheat."

Good point! Never argue with a redhead. "Okay, okay. You win."

She nodded, paused for a moment, and then asked, "And will you try to accept your God-given gifts? It is sweet on one hand, but on another, it's annoying. It's like you want to walk around blind to yourself. It's not bad to recognize God gave you brains and looks—the key is to not live for them or let them be what defines you."

Her words made me quiet. Since those two sentences were a lot to soak in, a lot to wrap my head around, I had to set aside time to ponder them later. Now was not the time. I nodded and smiled with my eyes to show my appreciation. Morgan was a tough cookie with high expectations. She was a good friend to challenge me—I knew that.

The top one hundred hits from the radio were playing when Ave and I met up. George Benson sang "Turn Your Love Around."

Jackie was the hostess with the mostest. She constantly made sure there was enough food and drink, which must have cost a small fortune, by my estimation. Beer flowed freely from a keg in the kitchen. Jackie's parents were divorced and Jackie's mom essentially let her have full reign of the house—less a huge mess, I guessed. However, this was the first time my friends hosted a beer party—it surprised me.

I couldn't help but wonder why Amy was interested in Alex Touey, considering he had such a bad reputation. I didn't expect

Amy to be into a "bad boy." And wow, would her mom flip if she knew. *Is she rebelling?* My curiosity got the better of me. When we had a second alone, I asked her.

"Isn't it obvious?" she asked.

"No, not really," I stared blankly, shaking my head, racking my brain for a valid reason. Nothing came to me. Nada, zip, zero, zilch . . .

"He's so hot!" She replied, holding the potato chip bowl, eating the chips one by one.

"That's it?! He's hot?" I replied, not buying her shallowness. Barf! He was greasy and I wanted to dip him in Clorox. I made a point not to stick my tongue out this time, although I felt a gag stuck in my throat. *Yes, he was that bad.* "Well, I didn't want to prejudge him. Joey Glosser had a bad reputation and you even said he's the nicest, kindest guy, except for Avery, of course."

"That's true, but Joey wasn't known for doing drugs," I reminded Amy.

"Didn't Joey hang out with Alex?"

"Oh, yeah, he did," I confirmed. That fact was long forgotten. Amy's face lit up.

"Do you think he could possibly mention something to Alex?" *Oh, no! Not again!*

"Is Alex here?" I asked.

I noticed the song changed to "Why Do Fools Fall in Love."

Alex Touey burst through at that very moment, as if on cue. Wearing a jean jacket and chains on his jeans, he staggered and looked disheveled. His motley crew trailed behind, looking much the same.

Amy sported a look of both embarrassment and astonishment. Dazed, she handed me the bowl of chips and said, "He's totally wasted. What should I do?"

Having never been in her situation before, I could offer her not one piece of advice. I was surprised he showed up too. I could feel bile inching its way toward the back of my throat.

"Yo, you got any food?" Alex Touey beckoned to no one in particular. I assumed he had the beer munchies and I shook my head again in disbelief.

Amy looked baffled and remained standing frozen in front of me. Sam the Man stood up, just to be a presence. Alex looked up at Sam the Man and said, "Dude, you're tall. You're like a giant or something." Then the light bulb in his wasted head went off. "Your Joey's brother, right?"

Sam the Man didn't respond. He simply glared down at the scum bags with his arms folded. I must say that he looked quite intimidating. I gulped. Down went the bile. Joey, the aforementioned, was somewhere else in the house at that moment. No way was I getting him involved in this mess.

Alex looked over to Amy and said, "Yo, is this *your* party?"

Amy stood with her jaw hanging, speechless and motionless like a statue. Alex persisted, sounding confused while he scratched his greasy head. "Duuude, aren't you Amy? Is this *your* house?"

Amy finally snapped out of it and offered a shaky, "No, this isn't my house. Jackie lives here."

Alex nodded and shouted, "Cool. Cool . . . cool. Happy New Year!"

"Alex, let's check out the rest of this pad. This place looks monster big, man! Let's roll!" Trevor Murphy yelled.

"Yeah, yeah, yeah. All right. Catch you later, Amy," he said, with a wink and a click of his tongue. Off they went, Alex and his motley crew, to check out Jackie's mansion.

"What was that about?" I asked anyone in hearing distance.

Amy answered quickly this time, "I saw Alex yesterday at the mall and mentioned that Jackie was having a New Year's Eve party. I gave him the address. I really didn't expect him to show up."

"Are you still interested in him?" I queried, with a touch of disdain, fully expecting Amy to assure me that she was not. She did not assure me. Instead, she simply shrugged her shoulders.

About an hour passed, and midnight was quickly approaching. Alex casually strolled through the house, unencumbered, like he owned it. He grabbed Amy from behind, startling her. He put his arm around her waist, at the time when Dick Clark was performing his annual countdown ritual to the New Year. Ten, nine, eight . . . The ball dropped, bells and whistles sounded, and confetti showered Time Square.

After Avery and I rang in the New Year, 1983, I watched Alex kiss Amy wildly, while shy guy, Peter, watched the scene from the sofa. When they finally parted lips, Alex mumbled something, then split with his friends. Amy stood there static, dazed, and confused. That was the last time Amy had an encounter with Alex.

Chapter 46

THE SUNDAY AFTER NEW YEAR'S weekend, we welcomed a guest speaker to our high school Sunday school class. The topic entailed appropriate physical behavior between a boyfriend and girlfriend. Naturally, the speech emphasized abstinence, which was a no-brainer for a Sunday school class, but the speaker also accentuated the forbidden places to touch and reveal before marriage. The speaker supported his talk with many verses from the Bible, as well as Christian and secular works that have studied sexual attitudes and behavior.

"Nevertheless, to *avoid* fornication, let every man have his own wife, and let every woman have her own husband"— (1 Corinthians 7:2). This verse was used to clearly state that it is a sin to engage in sex outside the realm of marriage.

The speaker expounded, by saying that God desires singles to abstain from sex, by using the following verse that was written by the apostle Paul, "I say therefore to the unmarried and widows, it is good for them if they abide even as I. But if they cannot contain, let them marry: for it is better to marry than to burn" (1 Corinthians 7:8-9). *Whoa! Burn, as in burn with passion. I can relate to that! Ave and I better get the fire extinguisher out because there's no way we are getting married any time soon.*

There was major emphasis on the fact that the male in particular is instantly aroused visually, so any nudity was forbidden, as it could easily lead to other tempting sexual acts. Oral sex was out of the question. We were encouraged to not practice safe sex, but to abstain from sex altogether.

And above all, the speaker emphasized, "You should never ever proceed without mutual consent." He elaborated, "If one party says, no, then no means no, and that is the final word."

Upon hearing the word no in that context, I was catapulted back to the Martins' house, hearing my own voice screaming, no at Creepoid. *"NO! NOOO! NO! STOP, PLEASE STOP!"* Without fail, I relived that moment again, in the middle of the lesson, of all topics—sexual immorality. I could feel my body shaking within, and I caught my breath, which brought me back to the topic at hand.

The speaker continued to state that very conservative views defended the stand that the physical contact would cease at hand holding. Ultra conservative views contended that even holding hands was forbidden. In the end, it was up to the couple to decide what boundaries they would uphold in order to find favor in the Lord; to please God by doing what He desires.

I felt ashamed listening to all the boundaries Avery and I crossed. The looks from our classmates also caused some shame. Though Joey sat on the other side of Avery, he not once glanced in our direction, as he seemed to be intent on listening. I fidgeted in my seat and anxiously waited for the lecture to end. It would have been easier to get a root canal than hear that lecture.

After hearing the compelling verses to refrain from sexual immorality, the message rang true for both Avery and me as we discussed them together after church. We felt guilty for what we had already experienced. However, as it was explained, we were forgiven upon request and we could move forward without sin in that area of our lives.

Later that night, I reviewed scripture from the Sunday school lesson that was used to demonstrate it was sinful to have sex outside of marriage, "Marriage *is* honourable in all, and the bed undefiled; but whoremongers and adulterers God will judge" (Hebrews 13:4).

As I continued to read through the various scripture, it started to make sense that I felt guilty after Avery and I were too intimate. God was protecting the marriage bed and I somehow deep inside knew it was wrong to do those things. I learned that I was feeling convicted for engaging in sin. The Holy Spirit was letting me know that it was wrong. That was the reason for the uncomfortable feelings, the reason for the guilt and shame. It wasn't just about what happened that dreadful afternoon down the street from my house.

As a result, Avery and I both agreed we would only kiss on the mouth and would refrain from touching the reproductive organs, even with clothes on. Abstaining from our usual conduct proved challenging and frustrating at first—but, by the grace of God, we succeeded triumphantly. It was a matter of time before we fell into an acceptable pattern of physical behavior that we felt would be pleasing to God.

Chapter 47

A MONTH PASSED AND WE WERE celebrating Avery's fifteenth birthday on his actual birthday, February tenth, which fell on a Thursday. Like my mom did for me, Mrs. Evans prepared an exquisite meal for Avery—garlic-crusted roasted rack of lamb, with a side of asparagus, carrot soufflé, and roasted potatoes. It was truly scrumptious.

"Mrs. Evans, I hope that someday I can be half as good a cook as you." *She must have slaved over the hot stove all day to create this culinary masterpiece.*

She smiled sweetly, "Thank you, Christina. That's so sweet of you to say."

Mr. Evans also raved about the meal before us, "Yes, Maggie, you really outdid yourself this time. This is absolutely delicious!"

"Yeah, thanks for a fabulous dinner, Mom!" the birthday boy complimented the chef.

Behold, the pièce de résistance was a brownie trifle. And I thought the dinner was amazing! I had died and gone to heaven when I took one bite of the decadent dessert.

"Oh, my gosh! Mrs. Evans, this is awesome! Best dessert I ever had!" I blurted enthusiastically, covering my half-full mouth with my left hand, as I was getting ready to shovel down more of the tasty trifle.

"Christina, that has to be the most heartfelt compliment that I ever heard. Thank you!"

"Um," I said, swallowing some trifle. "You're welcome! Thank you for inviting me!"

"You know you're like part of the family, Christina! We love having you here!" *Aw, she's so sweet!*

"I love being here!"

And I did. It was my home away from home. Ever since the sex talk at Sunday school, Avery and I didn't spend as much time alone. Instead, we played board games, like Trivial Pursuit, with his parents and it was a lot of fun.

So, when it was time for Avery to open his birthday gifts, we did it all together. His mom handed him a medium square box, wrapped in colorful birthday balloon wrapping paper. Avery wasted no time tearing it open. When he saw that it was an autographed baseball from Mike Schmidt, the 1980 Philadelphia Phillies World Series MVP, he jumped up and screamed, "This is amazing! How did you get this?" His excitement was palpable. "Thanks, Mom. Thanks, Dad. I can't thank you enough. It's great! I love it!"

Like I'm supposed to follow that? I handed Avery my gift. He tore open the box to discover a black guitar strap crafted out of fine leather. "Wow, this is great! How did you know I needed a strap?"

"I asked your mom one day and she told me. I had no idea because I never watched you play."

"Avery, why don't you get your guitar and put the strap on?" Mrs. Evans suggested. The lightbulb went off in her head, "Maybe you can play for us. What do you think?"

"I'm not sure, Mom," Avery replied with hesitation.

"I would love to hear you play, Ave. I think it's a great idea," I encouraged.

"Well, all right. I'll be right back."

Avery came back, with not only his electric guitar, but the amplifier as well. He hooked on the brand new strap with ease, plugged in his amp, and began playing "Rock This Town" by Stray Cats. His fingers were nimble and his stage presence was phenomenal. It was as if he was meant to play the guitar. The birthday boy was quite impressive.

As soon as he finished playing, I said with enthusiasm, "That was incredible! Why don't you play more often?"

"I do, but not in front of people."

"That's what I mean. Why not? You're really good!" I remarked.

Avery seemed to ponder the question, "Thanks, but I guess I play for me."

Mrs. Evans piggy backed on my comment, "You're right, Christina, he should play more often for an audience. I love hearing him play!"

"That's not what you said three years ago when I started playing. You couldn't stand the noise."

Mrs. Evans replied, with a flick of her wrist, "Oh, Avery, that was different. You were just learning how to play and you turned up the amp so loud it was hard to think straight. It's different now because you honed in on your craft. You play remarkably well."

His dad chimed in, "I'm proud of you, Avery. You really do sound great! Those lessons are definitely paying off."

"Hey, thanks everybody. Maybe I will play for you from now on."

At that, Mrs. Evans clapped her hands in sheer delight. "This has been such a treat! I can't wait to hear more!" *She is too cute!*

Avery turned to me and said, "The strap is comfortable and believe me that makes a big difference when playing."

"Oh good, Ave. I'm glad you like it." I replied.

"Hey, would you like to learn how to play?"

"Uh." I couldn't get the words out. *I can't carry a tune in a bucket.*

"I will show you. It's really a lot of fun!"

"I can barely play the radio," I willingly admitted.

"Oh, come on. It'll be fun!" an enthusiastic Avery persisted.

"Now, you can't disappoint the birthday boy," Mrs. Evans stated.

Avery shot his mom a look that said, don't embarrass me. "Really, Mom . . . Birthday boy, come on . . ."

Mrs. Evans shrugged sheepishly. *Aw.*

"Why don't you two play down in the basement? You can crank up the amp that way," Mr. Evans suggested.

"Great idea, Dad. Thanks! Come on, Christina, I'll teach you how to play the guitar."

What? Uh, I don't think so. Really. I am not musically inclined. A monkey could play better than me.

Despite my reluctance to learn how to play the guitar, I got caught up in Avery's love for all things guitar related. *Maybe it won't be so bad.*

Once we were situated on the couch, Avery explained the parts of the guitar. He began as he pointed to the various components, "This is the bridge, this is the neck, these are the chords along the neck that cross over the sound hole, which is where you strum to create sound. These rectangular spaces between the brackets are called frets. This is the first fret, this is the second fret . . ."

I nodded, like there would be a test later.

"Here, why don't you hold the guitar now?" He placed the guitar on me and immediately the strap fell. The guitar felt awkward, foreign to me. *This is not going to work, but for you and only you, I am willing to give this a try.* He adjusted the strap and asked, "Here, how does that feel?"

"Uh, okay, I guess." *Now what do I do?*

"Okay. Hold this chord down with your finger."

"Like this?"

"No, tighter, or you won't get the right sound."

"This isn't very comfortable."

"Yeah, guitar players inevitably end up with calluses," he informed me. *Oh, great. That's all I need.*

He grabbed his acoustic guitar. "Okay, now try this arrangement . . ." He showed me an order of chords to play. *What? You have to be kidding. I can't remember all that and do it that fast.* I started to play and I fumbled big time.

"No, like this. Put the tip of your index finger on the chord and the tip of your middle finger and place them together like 'scouts honor' like this." I moved my fingers accordingly. "Great. Now strum." I strummed. "You can't have your hand block the other chords or you will block the sound. The chords have to remain open until you intentionally close them with your fingers. Got it?" I nodded, trying to pay close attention. "Okay, now do two down strums." I strummed twice. "Great, now strum up to add rhythm."

When I strummed up, it created an entirely new sensation. "Hey, I like the strumming up and down part."

"Good! I think you got it!"

Since it was a school night, we had to cut the lesson short. It was much more fun than I anticipated, so Avery promised me another lesson.

We had a great time celebrating his fifteenth birthday and it felt special that I was able to get to know Avery on a whole other level. I felt like we gained favor in the Lord in our relationship, as we were no longer putting ourselves in tempting situations.

This purity stuff isn't so bad after all. We got this!

And to think, a month ago we struggled with not crossing over any unacceptable lines in the eyes of God.

"Fear thou not; for I *am* with thee: be not dismayed; for I am thy

God: I will strengthen thee; yea, I will help thee; yea, I will uphold thee with the right hand of my righteousness" (Isaiah 41:10).

God is good!

Chapter 48

*A*S SPRINGTIME BROUGHT AN AWAKENING and rebirth in nature, with colorful flowers in bloom, and wild animals taking care of their younglings, it also brought an awakening in my relationship with Avery. We fell into a rhythmical pattern that suited both of us and our families.

Avery joined the baseball team and I followed suit, by joining the softball team. His outstanding performance landed him a spot on the junior varsity squad, while I stayed with the freshman team.

The bad news was that Avery didn't get as much playing time on JV, but they were allowed to use him on the freshman team. I, on the other hand, started every game at first base just as Avery predicted I would.

We didn't get to see each as often, due to our sports, but we made the most of our time together. Our relationship was easy, fun, relaxing. Since the sex talk at Sunday school, we stopped engaging in inappropriate sexual behavior, reducing our intimate time together to kissing. Neither of us seemed to mind.

At the very least, I didn't worry about anyone catching us in an embarrassing situation. No more guilty pleasures led to no more hysterical tears of shame. Thus, the end to the dopamine roller coaster ride regarding our physical time together.

Instead, some of our time was spent discussing just about everything under the sun, but never did I reveal anything about that terrorizing afternoon that occurred at my neighbor's house.

We still saw each other at homeroom, at gym, during lunch, and after school during our free period. No more walking home together, and I no longer volunteered at The Manor because it was too late to go after practice. I informed Miss Brenda that I wouldn't be coming around due to my new softball schedule.

Her response was typical, "Honey, you do what you gotta do. I know all about those crazy sport schedules. My Jerome was all about sports. You name it, he did it at one point or another: football, basketball, track . . ." She let out a chuckle, "He was always running!"

Avery and I did, however, continue to see each other on the weekends. Saturdays were for fun, and Sundays were for church and more fun. We continued to play our favorite video games— Pac-Man, Asteroids, Space Invaders. We also played board games with his parents on occasion.

Best of all, we practiced playing the guitar together. Even though I didn't have a guitar to practice on at home, I managed to learn part of a song, "Teach Your Children Well" by Crosby, Stills, Nash & Young. Avery praised in disbelief, "I can't believe how much you learned, considering you can only practice here."

"It's because you're such a great teacher, Ave." I winked. *I'm no Jimi Hendrix. Now, if I could sing and play at the same time, that would be something.*

Some days, depending on the weather, we would toss the softball. On a few occasions, we even inspired softball games with the guys at Joey's house—they were kind, always letting me play on Avery's team. I honestly enjoyed being one of the guys.

However, my social interaction did not end with Avery and his friends. Morgan, the social director, had slumber parties at her house where her dad served his amazing milkshakes. I attended a few of the overnight parties, but my mom put a halt to them for reasons she failed to explain.

Nonetheless, I was still Morgan's mix and match friend. I got together with the girls on Friday and—or—Saturday nights, when I wasn't babysitting or hanging out with my special guy. We went roller skating, rented movies, dined out, shopped at the mall . . .

Our friends got together too, which was always interesting, to say the least. After New Year's Eve, Jackie decided to have parties at her house on a regular basis. Fortunately, we had the house to ourselves like we did before, except the alcohol was no longer flowing freely. I could tell that some people were a little bummed about the lack of alcohol at her parties, namely Larry, John, Tom, Doug, Cheryl, Macey, Val, and Amy.

Tom complained, "Yo, Avery, remember when we partied all the time with alcohol?"

"Yeah, man, what's up with that?" John added.

"Yo, guys, there's the door if you don't like it," Avery shot back. Ave and I were more than happy to avoid Mount St. Mindy and her popular piglets at the keggers.

Then again, there was Macey. "It was more fun when we drank," she droned.

I rolled my eyes, especially since Macey managed to conjure up enough antics when she rallied the troops at Avery's alcohol-free party back in the fall. That was enough awkward to last a lifetime for me, but everyone else had a super time.

Per usual, Val agreed with her, "Yeah, I wish Jackie's mom was still cool about having beer." *One drinking party and they think they're part of a college frat house.*

Chapter 49

WITH THE BLINK OF AN eye, our freshman year concluded and summer arrived in all its glory. It was a terrific one too. We engaged in new activities, which brought on new responsibilities, like barbecuing. I took my dad's portable charcoal grill and set it up at the pool or in the park. The guys always grilled, like it was a rite of passage. *Men grill—boys don't.*

"There's nothing sexier than a guy flipping burgers," I couldn't resist saying, one sun-shining summer day.

After many times of paying admittance for Avery to be a guest at my pool, we were granted permission for him to be on my family's plan. Thank God, because I couldn't get enough babysitting jobs to afford to have him as a guest all summer.

Plus, his pool quickly became a very unappealing option. Mindy was a member and without fail, she tried to grace us with her royal irritating presence. She proved socially awkward and relentlessly vile. Her Delusional Majesty did not seem embarrassed by her pathetic attempts to steal Avery away from me.

For example, once, when Avery and I were goofing around in the pool, cooling off from a scorching hot day, Mount St. Mindy jumped in, intentionally landing directly in front of my boyfriend, splashing us both. "You were supposed to catch me," she whined to an annoyed Avery.

With a look of sheer disapproval, and a tone displaying utter exasperation, he gruffly told her, "Mindy, I'm here with Christina. Do you mind?"

"Yes, actually, I do. I am much more fun than Christina," she snippily declared. *Someone please take her off our hands. Maybe I could use my babysitting money to buy her a boyfriend. Hmm, who could I punish?*

Avery and I climbed out of the pool, yet unbeknownst to us, she followed. After we were comfortably situated on our towels, she stealthily kneeled behind Avery and began to give him a massage. My mouth agape, I incredulously watched the audacious display. He wasted no time swatting her arms away, as if she were a pesky fly, and we departed to his house to rid ourselves of Miss Intrusiveness.

Avoiding Mount Saint Mindy and the Miss Blue Lagoon Pageant were two of my most treasured victories. The freak show came and went that year and I was immovable in my resolve to avoid every last fleck of it. I had absolutely nothing to do with the silly carnival. I didn't even listen to stories regarding it. I was able to sidestep it like one sidesteps annoying potholes. It was as though it never even happened. I sent up more prayers of thanks and praise for the minimal reminders!

Chapter 50

SUMMER SLID INTO AUTUMN AND we were no longer freshman. Faith moved just before our sophomore year. She gave me the impression that she wanted to leave her life at Pennsford behind, so I didn't make much of an effort to keep in touch, thus ending a six-year, scholastic, and minimally social friendship.

It saddened me in a way, but I had countless distractions and tried not to take Faith's attitude personally. It felt that way, but I reminded myself often that her parents' divorce affected her greatly. It's true I considered the possibility that she never forgave me for eating lunch with Avery. Regardless, I wished her well and prayed for her to have an easy transition at her new school.

For a while it seemed like I was in a perpetual state of bliss. I had an unbelievable boyfriend, a knack for schoolwork, and my friends were consistently there for me, especially Morgan and Katie.

Katie eventually broke up with Sam the Man—a bummer because he, seemingly upbeat most of the time, was in fact, depressed. According to Katie, his mood swings were too much and too often as of late. "He's just so moody. One minute he is joking and laughing, and the next minute, he's down in the dumps."

Her words took my mind back to the Martins' where we first met after the dreaded pageant. He was chilling, not loud or cracking jokes, and he was not acting like a party animal. When I thought about it a little more, he appeared somewhat somber at times. However, it was just as well, because Sad Sam was away at college. I must admit that I missed my giant, jovial friend.

As for Morgan, she continued her role as Julie from *The Love Boat*. We were never at a lack of something to do, so long as *Julie* was at the helm. Whether it was scheduling a bowling party, a girl's night in with manicures and pedicures, or teen dancing at a local club, we all had an active social life, thanks to our very own personal social director. *Thanks, Julie! Wink.*

———◆———

Sophomore year proved much more challenging, academically, than freshman year. There was more homework, more group projects, and the tests were considerably harder. Plus, it was time to begin preparing for college. Logically, that meant more hours in the books and pouring over the dreaded SAT study guides. *Ha! Like that ever happened!*

I never returned to The Manor, even though I thought about it quite often. Alas, that was an end of an era, yet, I continually prayed for Miss Brenda. Never will I forget how helpful she was during such trying times. I didn't want to feel like a burden to her and felt like it was time for me to move on.

At some point, my guy joined the local youth group that several churches in the area sponsored together. Since I was afraid to ask my parents, I never once attended. I didn't want to push my luck with being able to spend time with Ave.

He thrived in that youth group. I could tell because he was elated as he spoke of the gatherings. At first, he didn't talk about it, because he feared it would upset me, but I assured him that I wanted to hear all the details. Apparently, they played a lot of games and kept the focus on Jesus through prayer, Bible studies, and memorizing verses. In a nutshell, it was good, clean fun.

The group even took turns going to different churches in the area and headed to campgrounds, with challenging outdoor obstacle courses, for retreats. In the winter, they traveled to ski resorts with all kinds of winter sports, like snowboarding, snow tubing, and, of course, skiing.

I was inspired by Avery's interest of pursuing God through fellowship, so I decided to pursue my Savior in my own way. I read daily Christian devotionals from the *Our Daily Bread* booklet that I picked up from church. Prayer was also a constant in my Christian walk.

The following verse prompted me to ramp up my study of the Bible, "This book of the law shall not depart out of thy mouth; but thou shalt meditate therein day and night, that thou mayest observe to do according to all that is written therein: for then thou shalt make thy way prosperous, and then thou shalt have good success" (Joshua 1:8). *Bring on the prosperity and success!*

I meditated on Bible verses like, "I can do all things through Christ which strengtheneth me" (Philippians 4:13). This verse became my mantra to keep the demons at bay that followed me from the Martins' house.

———•—•———

In the spring, we both reenrolled in our favorite sports. I was the starting first baseman again, but this year there was a lot more competition for my position. I managed to end the season with the most RBIs and stolen bases. Avery played first base too, and he ended up with the second most hits of the season. His record was especially impressive for a sophomore, as baseball was a seriously competitive sport at our school, unlike softball.

Overall, my sophomore year went off without a hitch—no terrorizing, no drama, no oinking, and plenty of thick, chocolate milkshakes. Sophomore year was a gift tied up into a beautiful bow—nothing like freshman year, which I spent anxious, worried, and sleep deprived.

I was walking closer to God by attending church and Sunday school, reading my Bible on a regular basis, and I tried to "pray without ceasing" (1 Thessalonians 5:17).

Those things turned my life around. I was becoming new. I was feeling strong.

Chapter 51

I ANXIOUSLY AWAITED SUMMER TO ARRIVE so Avery and I could spend all day together at my pool, hoping we would be granted the same privilege again of letting Avery be considered as part of our family.

The summer did not happen as I had planned. New management prevented us from spending time together at my pool because we couldn't afford to pay for Avery to be a guest. I tried to make the most of it by alternating my days with Ave and going to the pool to hang out with Katie and Amy.

However, I seemed to be spending less and less time with Avery as the summer progressed. When I asked him if something was wrong, he assured me that he still loved me but had other obligations. Often, he told me he was working on a project with our Sunday school teacher, who was also one of the youth group leaders. When I pressed him for more details, he avoided the topic. I assumed he didn't want me to feel bad, because I wasn't part of the youth group, so I let it drop.

Toward the end of July, Ave joined the youth group on a retreat down the Jersey Shore at Harvey Cedars on Long Beach Island. They spent a few days there and were all abuzz when they came home. It sounded like a blast. They sang worship songs, engaged in Bible lessons, as expected, but they also caught sun rays on the beach, played beach volleyball, surfed, parasailed, and wind surfed. Everyone who attended seemed to be rejuvenated and had even more of a fire for "walking the talk"—living out their faith—upon their return.

On occasion, throughout the summer my sweet boyfriend showered me with gifts like flowers—mostly roses in keeping with the theme of my name, a variety of fine chocolates, and gold jewelry. By summer's end, he had given me two more gold charms, a lock and a key. Of them, he said, in his typical Avery charming manner, "Christina, you unlocked the key to my heart." Nothing like melting a girl's heart.

Chapter 52

THE FIRST DAY OF JUNIOR year set the pace for impending despair over the upcoming weeks. I arrived at my locker as usual, with the anticipation of seeing Avery, but he wasn't there. No Ave in homeroom either. Suddenly, a dreadful sensation fell over me. I felt dizzy and nauseous. My heart was imitating a terrified scene from a horror movie as my body shook. Instinctively, I knew something was wrong.

On my way to second period, I overheard someone say that Avery was attending the local Christian school, Pennsford Christian Academy. I could hardly believe my ears. People constantly asked me to confirm the gossip. I ignored them, pretending that I didn't hear the barrage of questions.

Finally, I went to our usual lunch table to see if I could find Avery—I didn't want to believe the gossip—or one of his friends. Much to my relief, I spotted Joey. I ran over to Joey, crashing into people along the way.

My boyfriend's best friend was surrounded by people talking about Avery. When I arrived on the scene, Joey nodded in the coolest Fonzie-like manner and said, "Yo, I'll catch you all later, okay." Everyone dispersed.

I heard someone ask the wind if I was available. I wondered myself and panicked. The room was spinning. *What in the world is happening? Why don't I know anything? I should be among the first to know, not the last.*

I nearly hyperventilated. "Joey, what's going on? Where is Avery? Is he okay?" I cried in a desperate panic.

Joey answered my questions, but not in order. Avery was fine and he was attending the Christian school. Avery just couldn't tell me himself. Joey didn't know why. He simply continued, "Avery changed over the summer. Didn't you notice?"

Well, we didn't spend as much time together as we normally did. Come to think of it, Avery didn't have that same fervor to spend time with me. He was more interested in his youth group projects. When I asked Joey about those projects, he seemed pissed off about them. I mean, really pissed off—he was furious.

The start of my junior year shattered before my eyes. If the eyes were truly the windows to the soul, as the saying goes, then a black curtain fell over mine, shutting everything and everyone out.

Later that day, Avery and I broke up over the phone and I didn't even understand why. My once awesome boyfriend said he couldn't give me any reason in particular, only that he wanted to sever the life he had and start anew. *What the hell?!*

I wasn't at fault he claimed. He was following a calling. I didn't get what that calling was, or why I couldn't be a part of it, but he seemed determined to keep me out of his life. My perfect boyfriend vanished faster than you can swing a bat. Gone. Just like that.

After that devastating phone conversation, I tried to stop all communication with Avery. However, I couldn't stay away. Two days passed until I visited him after school unannounced.

His mom answered the door. She looked worried, yet graciously greeted me, "Hi, Christina. It's nice to see you." She hesitated. "I'm so sorry, but Avery's not home." Mrs. Evans must have read my disappointment correctly because she invited me in. "Why don't you come in for a few minutes, Christina?" We sat down in the living room.

She began, "Avery left explicit instructions for me to tell his friends that he is moving on and not to contact him. I know this is hard for you to understand, but Avery is protecting you. It's in your best interest to move on, at least for now. Perhaps by the grace of God you two will be together someday, but that day is not today." Her eyes welled up in the corners.

After a brief moment, the beautiful woman in front of me continued, "Avery is ending relations with all of his friends, not just you." Again, she was quiet. Her pain was palpable. She raised her hand and put it on mine and said through tears, "Christina, you've been like a daughter to me. I wish things would be different between you and Avery, but I have to respect his wishes.

You understand that, don't you?"

All I could manage was shaking my head in disbelief. *No, none of this makes any sense.* I pleaded with my eyes. At that point, I heard a door slam. "Hey, mom, I'm home!"

My heart leapt. This was my chance to convince Avery that we belong together. I turned around to meet Avery's eyes. He looked like he saw a ghost. A sprinter was running inside my heart wanting to break free. Mrs. Evans stood up, pressed her skirt and darted a look between us, "I'll leave you two alone."

It was my turn to stand up. Avery shot up a hand. His face was expressionless, cold. *What's going on? What happened to the guy who loved me . . . and so deeply?* "I told you that I was moving on. I need to. I'm sorry, but you need to leave." He nodded toward the exit.

"But . . ." He gestured with his hand up again. I sensed his misery and could no longer stand in it. Tears poured down my face without my consent.

Uncontrollably.

I left, reluctantly, without saying good-bye to Mrs. Evans, as her son was very abrupt and determined to get rid of me. I failed miserably in my mission to win my man back. He was adamant about not having any further contact.

When I got home, I replayed his final words to me as I stood in front of him, desperately seeking a suitable explanation, "Christina, I'm really sorry about all of this. Believe me, if I could change it, I would. I still love you. If you love me, you will honor my wishes. Good-bye, Christina."

I searched deep within my soul, and after much prayer, decided not to pursue him. Unbeknownst to me, an inexplicable peace surrounded that specific decision to not make any contact.

It was official, Avery broke my heart—more accurately, he shattered it. I cried continuously in the privacy of my home. I was an emotional wreck. People left me to wallow in self-pity early on.

I started to have dreams of falling off a cliff, usually while riding a bike. I awoke with a start, often finding myself falling off my bed.

I was tempted to cut again because the emotional pain was almost unbearable, but I resisted. Instead, I repeated my mantra, "I can do all things through Christ which strengtheneth me" (Philippians 4:13). Motionless, eyes closed, I repeated the verse over and over. It helped to center me. It gave me strength and courage. I prayed for the day to be free of those unnerving nightmares.

All along, my friends were supportive, especially Morgan. She made sure I didn't become a social recluse. Interacting with friends greatly improved my emotional state. Most of my friends didn't notice much of a difference in my demeanor, but Morgan and Katie were very aware of the devastation I experienced due to my recent break up.

Thankfully, my parents left me alone to find my way back. They knew that Avery and I were close, yet they didn't know how to pull me up and out of my misery.

I tried my best not to look like the pathetic end of a heartbreak. It wasn't easy, but through meditation, prayer, and the help of close friends, I was lifted out of a deep despair and was on the mend.

He still loves me.

Chapter 53

*A*VERY.

After Avery and I broke up, my nightmares came back with a persistent force. I couldn't completely shake the evening terrors, despite my efforts. I found myself praying in the middle of the night to get me through just one more sleepless night. As a result, I was frequently tired.

The last time I felt peaceful, I was with Ave. We were downstairs in his basement on a rainy summer day, watching MTV. Avery and I weren't as physical as often during those last months, at least not in a sexual way. We barely even kissed. We snuggled quite a bit, but that was the extent of it for the most part.

He said he wanted to stay true to his vow from Sunday school and uphold our commitment to each other to find favor in the Lord. In the end, I was so proud of our turnaround. Perhaps it was premature to think that we conquered our physical desires. Perhaps he was too tempted to abstain. Maybe that's why he went off to Pennsford Christian. Maybe our relationship proved too challenging for him after all. I never got any straight answers.

However, to be on the safe side, I let Avery go, because I didn't want to be a hindrance to him.

"Let us therefore follow after the things which make for peace, and things wherewith one may edify another. For meat destroy not the work of God. All things indeed *are* pure; but *it is* evil for that man who eateth with offence. *It is* good neither to eat flesh, nor to drink wine, nor *any thing* whereby thy brother stumbleth, or is offended, or is made weak" (Romans 14:19-21). Even though this passage mainly focuses on food, I learned that it applies to anything that may cause a believer to sin. Although it was the hardest thing for me to let Avery go, I felt like it was in his best

interest to do so. I refused to be the reason to cause him to stumble.
Brenda.

I was reminded of Miss Brenda often as I leaned into scripture.
She gave me, ". . . for he hath said, I will never leave thee, nor
forsake thee" (Hebrews 13:5).

The reminder of her thoughtfulness and strength prompted me
to write her a letter.

Dear Miss Brenda,

*I wanted to thank you for being there for me during such a trying time
in my life. I watched you go through an unimaginable tragic event, yet you
remained strong and courageous in your faith.*

*Someday I hope to be as bold and confident as you in the Lord. I also
hope that I will be able to help someone in their spiritual journey as you
have helped me.*

*I still refer to all the Bible verses you gave me throughout our time
together. They have helped me tremendously as I navigate through trials
and tribulations. I feel God's presence in my life, and I have you, especially,
to thank for sharing your faith and showering such kindness and love my
way.*

*You will always hold a special place in my heart. Thank you again from
the bottom of my heart!*

God bless and take care!

In His grip,

Christina De Rosa

Joey.

Joey was my constant, even though we never discussed Avery.
We continued to eat lunch every day, as we had our freshman year,
except this year there was an obvious void. Avery severed ties with
Joey and my lunch companion clearly didn't want to discuss it.

I could also tell that he, too, was sad, but in a different way, of
course. He lost his oldest and most loyal best friend.

I often wondered if Avery's decision had something to do with
Creepoid. I dismissed that idea because, according to Joey, Avery
cut ties with all his friends from our high school. Erin said he
didn't even talk to her at church or in Sunday school. This was in
keeping with what Mrs. Evans stated the day I tried to win Avery
back.

Like me, Joey stopped going to Avery's church. I suppose Joey and I found solace in each other. Day after day, week after week, month after month we ate lunch together. Just the two of us. Occasionally, we bumped into each other at parties, although I doubted that the bumping was entirely unintentional on Joey's part.

I wondered if being around me was like being around Sad Sam. *Poor Joey. His brother and I were both depressed.*

Sam.

The big difference was that Sam the Man had been up and down for years. However, I was determined to return to a healthy emotional state, as there were more and more glimmers of hope the more frequently I prayed, meditated, and memorized God's promises.

In addition, my newfound interest in classical music allowed me to be swept away by the dichotomy of soothing and riveting measures that lulled the pain and heartache and restored my heart back to being strong and vigorous. I enjoyed the brilliant classics of Mozart, Chopin, Beethoven, Vivaldi, Bach, Tchaikovsky, Handel, and Strauss, just to name a bunch. I wondered if Sad Sam had an arsenal at his disposal like I did to keep the melancholy at bay. Perhaps he did, since the jolly giant went away to the University of Pennsylvania to become a doctor of all things. Apparently, Sam the Man was brilliant. *Who would have thunk?*

God.

The holidays were approaching, and I was getting stronger and stronger. I heard God's voice, "But they that wait upon the Lord shall renew *their* strength; they shall mount up with wings as eagles; they shall run, and not be weary; *and* they shall walk, and not faint" (Isaiah 40:31).

In the beginning of my turmoil, I decided not to play softball, as I didn't have the energy, focus, or the drive. But, the voice in my head was persistent, so I changed my mind. "I can do all things through Christ which strengtheneth me" (Philippians 4:13).

My special verse gave me the will to start training on my own. I began to jog on a regular basis. Running helped me sort through my thoughts and helped me sleep a smidge better, yet I still struggled to get a full night's rest.

Chapter 54

ONE DAY IN NOVEMBER, DURING lunch, Joey finally mustered up the courage to ask me out. At first, I didn't know how to respond. People assumed we were already dating. "You sure?" I started to say. "I mean, I can hardly stand to be around myself." I still felt like I was unworthy, even though I had more moments of hope each day.

"Don't say that, Christina. Let's give it a try."

Reluctantly, I agreed. Not because I didn't like Joey, but because I loved Joey. I loved Joey like a brother. He was so sweet and dear to me, like I'd expect a protective older brother to be—but like a brother, I wasn't attracted to him. It wasn't that he wasn't good-looking—he was. He was, in fact, very attractive. It was, put simply, my heart—it just wasn't free.

So, there I was getting ready in my bedroom for my big official date with Joey—reminiscent of how I used to get ready for Avery. My parents told me they were relieved that I was going on a date, finally moving on from Avery.

Joey came to my house and greeted my dad. My dad had met Joey a few times and liked him well enough. We headed to the movies and saw *Purple Rain,* which was peculiar, depressing, and disturbing all at the same time. It resembled my life, yet in a completely different way. I was getting much better, but Prince was on a downward spiral.

I sensed that Joey wanted to hold my hand during the movie, but he never made the attempt. Undeniably, there was a discomfiture between us. We managed a few cordial words throughout the evening, but the tension was almost unbearable.

Our once easy conversation was now strained. It made the night flat and quiet. Neither of us dared to order milkshakes at the diner after the movies. *Whew.*

I couldn't help but remember going out with Avery. Even though it had been a while since we dated, I couldn't shake the fond memories that turned out to be a living nightmare to live without my Prince Charming—my knight in shining armor, who rescued me and protected me from the evil villain.

When Joey drove me home, he walked me to my door. He held his head low, while I fretted over how to handle the situation before me and grappled with my options. *Should I kiss him? If so, on the lips? On the cheek?* After much wringing of my hands and biting of my lip, I thanked Joey for a good night and settled for a kiss on the cheek. I didn't want Joey thinking that I desired to pursue a romantic relationship with him by kissing him on the lips. And I certainly didn't want to be the cause of any pain for him, so I did what I could—I prayed. Fervently. With haste. Right there. *God, please don't let this hurt him. Help him understand what I cannot say. I want this friendship. I treasure our friendship. Please let us have it.*

Later that night, I dwelled on the passage, "And be not conformed to this world: but be ye transformed by the renewing of your mind, that ye may prove what *is* that good, and acceptable, and perfect, will of God" (Romans 12:2).

I also found the following verse comforting, "Trust in the Lord with all thine heart; and lean not unto thine own understanding. In all thy ways acknowledge him, and he shall direct thy paths" (Proverbs 3:5-6).

I was so relieved when Joey called me the next day. "So, we're still friends, right?" he fished.

"Yeah, of course," I replied, incredibly grateful for his forthrightness, and God's answer of YES!

"Are we just friends?" He asked more boldly. I hesitated. An uncomfortable silence stood between us.

"Joey, I don't want to ruin another friendship. I like you as a friend and need you too much." *Please, God, let him accept this.*

"Hey, I get it. I'll see you at lunch at school then," he said, with the twin emotions of a glimmer of hope and subtle resignation in his voice.

"Yeah, I'll see you then."

My heart ached for Joey. He sounded disappointed, but I wasn't ready to be his girlfriend. I wasn't ready to be anyone's girlfriend. My heart still ached for Avery. I guess I haven't completely let go of my first true love. I replayed his words. *I still love you. How can he still love me and leave me with no explanation?*

I sobbed.

Chapter 55

OEY AND I CONTINUED TO eat lunch together and we
went to the movies as friends. My lunch buddy was a movie
buff. He loved going to the theatre. We didn't go to movies at night
because it seemed too much like a date. For some strange reason,
watching flicks during the day relieved the pressure of being a
couple who dated, instead of just hanging out, so we could relax
and spend time as friends.

One Saturday in January, we saw the movie *Footloose*. I absolutely
fell in love with the upbeat soundtrack. The movie put me in a
fabulous mood, one that was foreign to me since the first day of
school, the day Avery ceased to be a part of my life. I found the
music to be so riveting and the plot so compelling, that I didn't
mind when Joey held my hand. I was joyful. *Oh my gosh, I feel
happy. I almost forgot what it felt like.*

The brightness of the unseasonably warm winter day blinded us
when we walked outside from the darkness of the movie theatre.
We drove to a nearby park and walked to a remote gazebo near a
wooded area. Apart from hearing shouts of children in the distance,
we were alone. We made ourselves comfortable on the wooden
seat, when Joey took hold of my hand again.

I laid my head on his shoulder and closed my eyes. I felt so
relaxed and at ease with him. The cool breeze refreshed my body,
as the fresh air filled my lungs. Joey moved slightly and apologized,
not wanting to disturb our blissful moment. I opened my eyes to
find him smiling at me. I craned my neck and he leaned in and
kissed me. It was soft like a whisper, barely touching my lips. I
remained motionless. Joey leaned in again. I closed my eyes and
felt his curious lips on mine. We kissed for a moment. It was nice.
No fireworks, but pleasant.

He enveloped me with his arm and drew me closer to kiss me again. This time the kiss was moist and sweet, filled with longing. "You have no idea how long I've waited to do that," he said.

I had an idea but didn't dare say. Every time he looked at me, since our freshman year, his feelings for me were obvious. I released a smile. "I hope it was worth the wait," I teased.

My playfulness returned that warm spring-like day. Joey didn't say anything. Instead, he showered me with kisses. Each kiss grew more passionate, deeper, lengthier. Inwardly, I smiled. I felt lighter.

Joey and I talked about all kinds of subjects, especially the Bible, what it was like to be a Christian, the challenges we faced as teenagers. I even shared that I listened to classical music. "You will probably think this is strange, but I listen to Chopin, among others."

Joey encouraged, twining his fingers in mine, "Music is such a personal choice. You shouldn't hide your preferences. Hey, I might even give it a listen!"

I never told him about my cutting days. No one knew about the self-mutilation. No one knew about that unspeakable act at the Martins' either.

Chapter 56

IT WAS EARLY MAY AND Joey and I were headed to the Junior Prom together. We didn't make any arrangements with anyone else. It was just the two of us—no double dating, no group dating.

My gorgeous tuxedoed date picked me up himself. *Sixteen has its perks.*

As always, I waited until my dad told me that my chariot awaited, thus taking advantage of this special princess moment— the moment of a grand entrance down the staircase that landed in the foyer.

Taking hold of the railing, I glided downward adorning a long, flowing, baby pink, spaghetti strap gown. I couldn't resist blushing when I looked upon Joey's face. When he gazed in my direction, he appeared his usual cartoon character self, with his heart beating out of his chest while hearts flowed upward and popped away. Except this time, it was ten times more intense. "Christina, you look beautiful," he ogled in awe.

"You do look beautiful, Pooch," my dad complimented, then he called out to my mom. "Bea, are you going to see the kids off and take some photos?" Once again, my mom wasn't there, when I presented myself. *Sigh.*

My strikingly handsome escort was sporting a traditional black and white tuxedo—and wow, he looked fantastic. I bit my lip once I got the chance to properly assess my beau. His layered chocolate brown hair flipped to the side looked breathtaking against the dark formal attire that he filled out like a GQ model. *Yowza! Chocolate and Joey, my two favorite things! Talk about eye candy! I could just . . .! Down, Christina!*

"I have something for you," he stated, while presenting me with a matching pink wrist corsage. I held out my hand, so Joey could slip it on, which he did with care. He treated me like a princess, or a porcelain doll, as if I were breakable. I took that all in stride, as it was basically what I expected from my dashing prince.

After snapping a few photos, some of which included my parents, which Joey took, we headed to dinner at an elegant Italian restaurant, then to the opulent hotel in Delaware where the prom was held.

Upon arrival, we were expected to get our photos taken as a couple, and we naturally complied. Periodically, our teachers complimented us. Not only was Joey very handsome, especially in formal attire, but he was coming into his own academically. He was excelling in all his subjects as he hit his stride junior year. I couldn't blame Joey's teachers for liking him, practically flirting with him, but it was a little unsettling. *Jealous much?*

The challenging part was finding a place to sit, as seats were not assigned. Thank goodness we found Morgan and her new boyfriend, Steve, at a table with empty seats. The two were a super match—both were intelligent, athletic, and serious about school.

Soon, Erin and her date, and Katie and Glen—her new man— joined us. Katie respectfully kept her distance from Joey because of her breakup with his brother, Sam. I leaned in and whispered to Joey, "Are you okay with this?" Joey knew what I meant and nodded.

After greeting one another and settling into the evening, the music cranked up signaling it was time to get this party started.

Upon hearing "Material Girl," I grabbed Joey and raced onto the dance floor. Nothing got my blood pumping to dance like Madonna did. What a great way to kick off prom!

The festive mood exploded with "Relax" by Frankie Goes to Hollywood. The flashing colored lights, in tandem with the beat of the music, prompted us to perform abrupt and quirky dance moves. The special lighting effects rivaled that of any Hollywood studio.

The electrifying tempo segued to "Walking on Sunshine." Katrina and the Waves created the illusion of celebrating summer on a sandy beach while waves crashed on the shore.

Keeping the excitement alive, the DJ played "All She Wants To Do Is Dance," followed by Cyndi Lauper's "Girls Just Want to Have Fun." We were all having fun dancing—not just the girls.

When the song "Just a Gigolo" filled the room, Joey surprised us with his fabulous rendition of a dancing gigolo, showcasing swiveled hips and hip bumps. Cheers and screams of approval from both male and female voices reverberated throughout the room. Joey's debut as a talented performer was a smash hit.

After picking my jaw up off the floor, Joey and I settled into the slower paced sounds of "Crazy for You." My boyfriend mouthed the lyrics as we swayed to the music causing my stomach to flutter. Tossing my head backwards, I replied, "You are crazy." His endearing smile stirred up the butterflies from within. My toothless grin fell short of my feelings for Joey. *I'm crazy for you too.*

Another slow song, "Saving All My Love" allowed us to savor the tender moment we shared. No words were exchanged between us as we floated to the powerful and beautiful stylings of Whitney Houston.

The DJ spoiled us with more Madonna. My friends got into the groove with "Dress You Up," and we celebrated our special holiday with "Like a Virgin."

Glen demonstrated his impressive dance skills as he jammed to my favorite recording artist. Apparently, Glen was a true-blue Madonna fan too. Fortunately for us, Katie picked the fun-loving guys to be her boyfriend. Steve was on the borderline as he contemplated his dance moves. Morgan, Katie, and I cherished the efforts of our guys even more for expressing themselves. Everybody cut the rug with those lively tunes, except for Erin and her boyfriend as they walked off the dance floor because we were causing a commotion.

When we slow danced to "Can't Fight This Feeling" by REO Speedwagon, Joey gave me his endearing cartoon look, with his heart pounding outside his chest. I couldn't help but smile and felt a warm glow well up inside me. Peace and joy overcame me as Joey and I swayed on the danced floor.

The tempo changed to a faster pace when the DJ cued "Footloose." We let loose as soon as we heard it! The song was a pleasant reminder of the first time we kissed at the gazebo in the park after watching the movie, *Footloose.*

As the magical night was winding down, "You're the Inspiration" invited couples to glide to its words of declaration. Appreciative that Joey danced with me the entire evening, I cast a demure smile in his direction. Relaxed in his arms, I closed my eyes as I nuzzled into him.

"Careless Whisper" eased us into the final moments of Prom. Content, yet tired, couples danced their last steps. For some, the evening was just beginning . . .

Chapter 57

*A*FTER THE DANCE WE ATTENDED an after-prom party at Jackie's house. We stayed for only a brief time and left for a drive in the tranquil star-dusted night. Joey parked at a nearby hotel. He told me that someone booked a hotel room, but he and his girlfriend broke up, so it was vacant. I was at a loss for words because it was so unexpected. "I thought we could enjoy some time alone. We don't have to *do* anything.

It's all paid for. My friend doesn't want any money."

Up until then, Joey and I had only kissed—we were taking things slowly, perhaps because we discussed our faith quite a bit. The passion, the heat wasn't quite there with Joey. I liked kissing him, but usually had little desire to go to the next level and he never pressured me. My best friend seemed to be content with our physical status, but then I began to question his current motives. "We can leave if you want to,"

he said, casually. "Again, no pressure."

"Uh, I don't know. Is this even legal?" I asked, feeling like a doofus after the words spilled out.

"Yeah, it happens all the time." How did he know that? I didn't ask. *It would be a shame to waste a perfectly good and generous offer. Why not?*

I agreed to go to the hotel room. It was beautiful. The bedspread was a rich purple and gold sheen that matched the drapes. Another *Purple Rain* Prince craze I assumed. There was also a small wooden table and chairs in the room. Above the dresser was a mirror, framed in ornate gold. "This is nice," I said trying to cut the tension. Joey nodded nervously, as he surveyed the room.

The boy in front of me felt like a stranger. He wasn't the Joey I knew and adored. He was acting uneasy, fidgeting, while he looked about the room, which in turn made me feel uncomfortable.

At some point during the course of the evening, my dapper date had already taken off his bow tie and jacket and unbuttoned his shirt. I felt way over dressed in my pink gown and heels. "My feet are killing me," I stated.

"Here sit down," Joey said, indicating to the love seat across the room. "Why don't you take off your shoes?" I readily complied. Silence. He remained seated at the edge of the bed while I was still sitting on the love seat. Although there were only a few feet between us, it seemed like a million miles.

"Christina."

"Joey." We said each other's names at the same time.

"You go first," he insisted, always the gentleman.

I was at a loss for what to say. Joey seemed totally committed to the oath he made to remain chaste in Sunday school, even more so than Avery. I was completely confused and needed clarification, so I went for it. "What exactly did you have in mind?"

He padded the area beside him. "Come here," he said, nonchalantly. I walked over and sat next to my date. He looked debonair, even after losing the tie. We stared at each other. I tried to figure out what was going on in that brain of his. He held my hand like he did many times before.

"Christina, you don't have to do anything you don't want to. I didn't bring you up here to have sex with you." *You didn't?* "I still want to wait until I'm married. You know that, right?"

I nodded, while he cupped my chin. "I thought we could enjoy a little privacy," he said repeating his earlier statement. "Christina, I love you," he declared for the first time. I knew for a while that's how Joey felt about me but was relieved that he never said those magic words because I wasn't ready to hear them.

"I love you too!" rolled off my tongue so easily that I surprised myself. And I did. I really loved Joey. He was incredibly sweet, tender, protective, and considerate, and he put me on a pedestal.

He leaned forward and kissed me. "I *really* love you, Christina!" He kissed me with more intensity. My stomach began to quiver like a feather tickling my insides.

Gently he laid me on the bed. Our bodies were pressed against each other when he caressed my cheek.

I thought about how I liked to be on the bottom and hated

myself for thinking of Avery. Visions of Avery would crop up periodically. It was like the start of kernels of corn popping in a hot oiled pan. I couldn't help it, and I never told Joey, of course. *I still love you* echoed in my brain.

We never discussed Avery. Ever. Avery was long out of the picture. He made it abundantly clear that he didn't want me to pursue him, so I respected his wishes, as painful as it was. *Stop it, popcorn Avery! Get out of my head! Why are you tormenting me like this?*

I was with Joey now and I owed my devoted boyfriend my full attention. By then, Joey was on top of me kissing my neck, nibbling my ear, as he descended along my neckline. He was caressing my body while we both groaned in sheer pleasure.

Shortly after, Joey asked, "Are you comfortable?" Truthfully, I wasn't. My gown bunched up. I leaned forward and tried to reach the zipper along my back—Joey aided me quite willingly. I stood up and let the gown fall to my feet. I gracefully stepped out of it, and with a sigh of relief, turned to my boyfriend, who was leaning on the bed, with the wide-eyed look of anticipation.

He stood up and took in the sight before him, while I was still wearing a lacy bra with matching underpants. Joey stood before me, taking me in like a refreshing drink. I thought Joey was going to have a heart attack by the look on his face when he saw me that exposed for the first time, as I always wore a one-piece swimsuit.

With focus and dexterity, I unbuttoned his tuxedo shirt, draped it off his shoulders, and let it flutter to the floor. Then he began taking off his socks. After he threw his undershirt on the floor, he kissed my neck, my ear, while one hand was on the hook of my bra. I shook my head knowing that nudity could lead down a forbidden path.

He put his hand on my shoulder, ever so tenderly, and began kissing me in such a way that I was never kissed. His lips were moist and warm, full of passion. It was heavenly. And it was clear to me that Joey adored me. Even idolized me. Maybe he talked so much about his faith to keep him from doing what we were doing. Only this time our teenage bodies took over.

Slowly our completely entwined bodies landed on the bed. His passion ran through me. I felt electrified, mesmerized. He moved me in such a way that I rolled on top of my brawny boyfriend. He looked at me with wonderment in his eyes, as I draped over him. "I have loved you since our freshman year," he confessed. But I already knew that. Avery knew that. Even during our freshman year, it only took an instant to recognize that Joey was in love with me, although no one ever articulated the obvious in my presence. I secretly relished how he adored me, but I also hated myself for it.

I didn't love Joey as I loved in the past. Maybe I would never experience that type of love. Maybe it was rare, almost unheard of. *Am I settling for second best?* I didn't feel like I had a choice. Avery and I didn't exist anymore. Maybe this was a good as it gets. *And this is awesome—and this guy is awesome.*

I smiled at Joey and leaned forward to kiss him. I mean really kiss him. The kiss was deep and sensual. A groan escaped him. I let the electricity run through me. My body pulsated with his. "This is even better than I ever imagined," Joey shared.

"Shhhh," I said, as I gently placed my left index finger on his lips. I continued to kiss him feverishly. I ran my fingers on his bare chest. I moved to his sculpted abdomen. Joey and his rock-hard abs. The mini Hercules had been working out on a regular basis, yet it wasn't until recently that he developed a super buff body. *Oh, baby! My heart be still.* I bit my lip.

He wrapped his arms around my body, as his hands wandered all over my back, my rear, my thighs. Our breathing was harsh and ragged. We were getting too intimate, too close.

At that moment I realized, with sudden clarity, that *I* can choose my destiny. I couldn't let my tainted past dictate who I was or what to do anymore. That awful day down the street was not my fault. I was free from guilt and shame and I was no longer going to be a victim—to be held prisoner, as if I were at fault, when I was violently violated. *I'm the creator of my destiny. No one has the power to take that from me.*

"What are you doing?" I asked.

"What?"

"Stop. You need to stop," I said, abruptly. I rolled off of Joey and he rolled over towards me. "What's wrong?"

"I can't do this. We can't continue like this."

"Like what?"

"We're on the verge of . . . of . . ." I shook my head, not able to spit out the words.

"Christina, I told you. I'm waiting." My confused mind swirled, as

I tried to wrap my head around Joey's mixed messages. "Christina, I'm so sorry. You thought I wanted to . . ."

I collapsed on the bed utterly embarrassed. I figured he talked a good talk, but at the last minute changed his mind. It seemed like his intentions changed and I couldn't be a willing participant, not after we pledged to each other to abstain.

He leaned over to me and gripped my chin, "I want to make love to you, but I have to wait. I just have to," his soft chestnut eyes pleaded with me.

"Then why did you let us get this far?" I asked, in my defense, recalling his presence during the Sunday school talk about inappropriate premarital physical behavior.

Joey shook his head. "I'm really sorry. Please don't be mad at me."

I wept. My emotions ran amok. I got caught up in the heat of the moment and let myself go, finally letting Avery go free and now this. I was mortified. I buried my face in my hands and turned away from the person I thought I could trust.

"Christina, please understand. I would never deceive you like that. *I love you!*" he said emphasizing each word. "I thought you knew that." Joey pleaded insistently.

"I need . . . a tissue," I managed in between sobs. Joey stood up and walked into the bathroom, returned with a tissue and handed it to me. He sat at the edge of the bed next to me, stroking my hair, while I wiped my face. So many emotions flooded me at once. I felt guilty for giving up on Avery, even at his insistence, even after all this time.

I thought Joey wanted me, despite what he said about waiting before marriage. We ignited a passion that clouded my judgement. I should have never let it get that far. I knew better than to expose myself like that—it's risky behavior. I fanned the fire and I felt like a complete idiot, acting like a mistress in a Harlequin romance novel. *Why did I let it get that far? Dear God, I'm so sorry for my sexual immorality. Please forgive me!*

I lay there, suddenly ashamed of my bareness, so I slipped on Joey's undershirt. I flung my arms around his body and buried my head in his chest. We cuddled. Surprisingly, we decided to stay and snuggled under the covers. I lay on his chest, as he soothingly stroked my hair. *It was all a misunderstanding.*

"I love you," he whispered over and over. My eyes were closed, while my ears listened to the rhythm of his heartbeat. I felt relaxed and comforted in his herculean arms. "I love you too," I said softly, and eventually drifted asleep.

Chapter 58

AYS PASSED. MAY WAS IN full swing and the school year was winding down. Joey and I were inseparable, and my trust in him was regained from prom night. I reminded myself not to engage in tempting situations and that I was, in fact, captain of my destiny.

Most importantly, I finally rid myself of the guilt and shame I felt from that awful afternoon at the Martins'. What Creepoid did to me was wrong and I was done blaming myself for playing a part in that horrific act. HE WAS AT FAULT, NOT ME! I don't know why it took years to come to that conclusion, but I finally did, and it was absolutely liberating!

I was gaining more understanding in knowing what I could control and what I could not, to take responsibility for the actions that were under my control, and to not feel guilt or shame when I was wronged. It was a lot to process over the month, and I figured that I was just peeling the layers.

In the meantime, I wanted to embrace life the best I could, and to put my faith in God to keep me on the straight and narrow path. I appreciated God's blessings, and thanked him, especially, for giving me good health, a good family, good friends, and a good boyfriend.

I was able to watch a couple of Joey's baseball games because softball season ended earlier. He was an amazing athlete and led the varsity team to states, but they lost three to two, in the ninth inning. My ballplayer was one of the two runs scored! *Way to go, Joey!*

He finished his junior year with a record number of hits, but no home runs. There seemed to be an underlying joke with his teammates about that, but he ignored it, for which I was thankful. *I'm not that girl, after all.* I breathed a sigh of reassurance.

Although, each day I was feeling more confident in who I was, I still hated being the center of attention, and Joey was somewhat sensitive to that. It was obvious to everyone that he adored me. Even when he stood at bat, he looked over at me, with a huge grin on his face, and nodded towards the outfield as if to say, "This one's for you."

Chapter 59

SCHOOL LET OUT IN MID-JUNE. My summer plans were uncertain because my parents decided not to join the swim club.

Ever since Joey became serious about fitness, he was in constant training and included me in his activities. It worked for me because I liked staying fit, and the results of his efforts caused me to drool. The more he worked out, the more he bulked up. *Hubba, hubba!* Even college girls checked him out. *You can look, but you can't touch. He's mine!*

We hung out at the park, held hands, kissed, rode bikes, and jogged together. I also jogged on my own—it helped to reduce life's stressors. I noticed how much better I felt after a run. It was therapeutic. *Free therapy. Works for me.*

Frequently, we threw the ball around to hone our ball skills. Sometimes we even went to the batting cages to practice hitting the ball. That was a lot of fun, but it used up our spending money.

Sam the Man was home from college and tagged along with us on occasion. He was doing much better with his manic-depression since he started taking prescription medicine. It seemed to work wonders for him.

One day, when the three of us were hanging out at the Glosser's house, Sam whispered in my ear, "I'm glad he has you and I'm glad you have him too." He gave me an approving wink, and I knew Sam the Man was going to be okay.

We went to the mall or to the movies on rainy days. There was a local movie theatre that showed older movies for free on Tuesdays, so we went faithfully. We saw films like *Airplane, The Empire Strikes Back, Ghostbusters, Raiders of the Lost Ark, Sixteen Candles, The Karate Kid,* and *Gremlins.*

Morgan hosted a Bible study that Katie, Amy, and a few other people attended. We ate pizza and Mr. Ricci always made us his famous milkshakes afterward. I cherished that time to fellowship with friends to learn more about God.

My faith wasn't "in your face" but I know people, including my parents, noticed that I wasn't so anxious or depressed anymore. One summer day, my dad surprised me with precious words, while enjoying the Italian Festival at Penn's Landing, along the Delaware River in Philadelphia. He said in an earnest tone, that exuded love, "Christina, you know I'm incredibly proud of you. The way you handle yourself in the face of challenges is remarkable." He paused to gather his thoughts, "I know you had a rough go of it the beginning of the school year, but you pulled yourself out of it. I know that couldn't have been easy."

I returned my appreciation for having such a supportive dad by smiling and simply replied, "Thanks, Dad." I looked upward, knowing that, by the grace of God, I was able to pull through a devastating breakup, as well as the unimaginable, and silently repeated my mantra, *"I can do all things through Christ which strengtheneth me"* (Philippians 4:13).

Chapter 60

Y SENIOR YEAR, MY MOM hounded me to get a job after school and on weekends. I don't know what came over her, but it was like she was demon-possessed. Every word out of her mouth was about me getting a job. The poltergeist said I had to get a job because I wasn't playing a sport. She also constantly reminded me that I needed money for college. "We're not footing the bill for college, so you have to get a job if you want to go to college!"

"Okay, okay! I'll get a job!" I screamed one day, after the possessed one badgered me for the millionth time—and I did get a job. I really showed her!

The job wasn't too exciting, but I made the most of folding, stocking, and selling clothes at a clothing store in the mall. I received a thirty percent discount off the clothes and was able to get special employee deals. I bought myself a few over-sized striped shirts, a royal blue, pleated miniskirt, and a hot pink, flared, tank dress, all for five dollars each with my stupendous discount. *Go me!*

Unlike my peers, I didn't have the urgency to get my driver's license, so my mom or Joey dropped me off and picked me up at work. I could get used to being chauffeured. *Oh right, I am already used to it. I don't know any different.*

Joey had a few baseball scholarship offers that he had to sift through: Temple, Bloomsburg, West Chester University, Shippensburg University, University of Delaware and University of Virginia. *My man is set!* I was banking on my solid GPA to help me find a school.

Joey and I didn't have any classes together our senior year—not even lunch. Thankfully, I didn't have any classes with Creepoid either. I noticed that I saw less and less of the jackalope as time marched on. I thanked God for his grace, by sparing me the constant reminder of what happened that unspeakable day, as my prayers were answered. "Be careful for nothing; but in every thing by prayer and supplication with thanksgiving let your requests be made known unto God" (Philippians 4:6).

On graduation day, Joey and I had our pictures taken alongside our families before and after the formal ceremony. My brother was present, along with Sam the Man. "Look at you two," the older brother said, finding a moment to tease us. "Who would've thought that you'd be together after all these years. Must be the power of milkshakes." *What?!* Sam went from being Sam the Man to Sam the Super Soaker to Sad Sam to Nonsense Sam. I guess all that medical studying made him even wackier. Do not study medicine. It makes you crazy. One career eliminated, only one billion to go! In all seriousness, I didn't worry about Sam. He was able to be comical without diving into the dark recesses of despair.

Joey and I headed out to Jackie's party and, like prom night, weren't expected back until the next day. Neither Joey nor I gave our parents any reason not to trust us. *I'm still not that girl.*

At the party, we signed year books and reminisced about old times. Sometimes Avery's name popped up and it made my heart ache. Joey and I never talked about our once-close mutual friend, but he was ever present, even after a year and a half of dating. *Ah, Avery.*

Chapter 61

M Y FRIENDS ASKED ME TO join them for senior week in an efficiency apartment in Ocean City, New Jersey, where everyone else from our graduating class was staying. Joey and I drove down together. He was staying in a house several blocks away with his friends. We made plans to meet up later after he dropped me off. He said he would come by and pick us up to take us to the boardwalk.

When I entered, Morgan informed me that her mom made a pan of baked ziti. Katie and Amy brought some food too. It never occurred to me to bring any food as we never discussed it.

I felt stupid not bringing anything. "Drinks are on me then," I declared, and everyone seemed to appreciate my gesture, but by drinks, I didn't mean alcoholic, as Ocean City was dry, and I was only seventeen—too young to purchase alcohol.

We walked around to check out the rest of our current digs. As it turns out, Val, Jackie, Cheryl, and Macey were staying across the hall from us. *Ugh, Macey—major eye roll! Why does she make my skin crawl?*

Morgan's boyfriend, Steve, was pacing back and forth with his head down, near a detached cottage that stood in the middle of the complex. I assumed he wanted to see her.

The next thing I knew Steve and Morgan were vehemently arguing about something. Her hands were flailing. She was irate. *She is fiery when angry! What is going on?*

Morgan darted into the apartment building. Amy, Katie, and I followed. We found a hysterical Morgan sobbing profusely in our small apartment.

She informed us that she and Steve just broke up because she found out that he cheated on her—with Macey of all people!

We were horrified to discover that Macey would betray her friend in such a despicable way. I knew Morgan was waiting for her wedding day to have sex, but apparently Steve had other ideas.

The following scripture came to mind, "Flee fornication. Every sin that a man doeth is without the body; but he that committeth fornication sinneth against his own body" (1 Corinthians 6:18).

An impatient Steve cheated on Morgan. His likability ratings just took a major nosedive. *Poor Morgan!* I

felt horrible that my closest friend was going through such a devastating and public breakup, during what was supposed to be our first taste of freedom after high school.

Katie and Glen broke up two weeks prior, and she was still reeling from it. I felt for both Morgan and Katie. Sometimes it felt like yesterday when Avery and I ended our relationship. Other times it felt as if an eternity passed.

Amy never had a boyfriend all through high school. Peter never mustered up the courage to ask her out.

Her mom told her that the special girls waited until college to have a boyfriend. Didn't that make the rest of us feel special?

We didn't mind though, because we kind of felt sorry for Amy. She turned out to be a neat person, fun-loving, smart with a broad sense of humor, not to mention she lost some weight and was looking better than ever.

As promised, Joey picked us up. He brought his friends Peter, Adam, and Doug.

Utterly devastated, Morgan looked a mess as she had been constantly crying. Mascara ran down her face. My dear friend looked like a raccoon.

I couldn't help but wonder if Katie still had the hots for Doug and if Peter still liked Amy.

We walked all over the place. First, we headed to the boardwalk only a few blocks away.

Joey bought me chocolate frozen custard on a waffle cone. Oh, how I loved frozen custard! My relationship with anything chocolate, especially cold, ran deep. It was almost like I was cheating on Joey. *Delicious!*

Several other schools planned their senior week the same week, so the parties were endless. When we ran into Val, Cheryl, Jackie and, unfortunately, Macey, on the boardwalk, Macey couldn't even face Morgan. Morgan and I kept our distance from Macey, which was perfectly fine by me. The groups exchanged party locale information and parted ways. *See ya, Macey! Or not!*

We went to one house and, oddly enough, they asked us to sign in with our name and address. We all wrote fictional names and addresses.

For example, Joey wrote that he was Fred Flintstone from Bedrock. Amy inscribed she was Ginger from Gilligan's Island, while others outside of our group took the guest book seriously. *Creativity at its finest!*

It wasn't long before we realized that this party was not for us. They were smoking pot and snorting cocaine. We were all straight-laced, no drugs.

It was weird, because we thought they were going to be serious and geeky, with them having the sign in sheet, but we thought we could shake things up. We should have known better than to judge a book by its cover.

The next party was more our style. Val, Cheryl and Jackie greeted us, enthusiastically. Those girls got their wish to drink. Macey was cowering from Morgan and looked like she could use a drink.

Joey was careful not to drink, since he typically refrained from drinking. He was strict about what he consumed because he treated his body like a temple.

The following verse popped in my head, "What? Know ye not that your body is the temple of the Holy Ghost *which is* in you, which ye have of God, and ye are not your own? For ye are bought with a price: therefore glorify God in your body, and in your spirit, which are God's" (1 Corinthians 6:19-20).

I wished I had such discipline, as I overindulged with the chocolate. What a shocker, I know!

The party was a blast. Everyone had a great time, even though not all of us drank, especially Morgan and me. We danced, we sang, we cheered!

A bit later, I noticed Katie downed a few beers, not that it mattered to me. She needed to chill a little bit and it wasn't like she was in danger of drinking and driving.

Late into the evening, after grabbing a beer, an intoxicated Katie wobbled with Morgan by her side, as they passed by Macey flirting with some random guy she met at the party. Macey turned her head and looked over her shoulder as the girls passed her and laughed flirtatiously. Katie, with a look of determination like that of a world heavy weight boxer before the bell rang for the start of the fight, spun around without warning and hurled her drink on Macey, drenching her. "That's for Morgan! You disgust me!" Katie yelled. Obviously, Sam the Super Soaker left a lasting impression on Katie.

As Macey screamed and wiped her hands on her soaked clothes, a horrified Morgan pulled Katie to the side of the room. Macey went charging after them with fury in her eyes. I bolted toward Macey, jumped in her way, put my hand up in front of her, and stated sternly, "Macey, you've done enough harm. Let it go."

By then, Val came to Macey's side and begged her to stand down. With clenched fists, Macey turned toward Katie and Morgan's direction, then back to Val and me with the crazed look of embarrassment and vengeance in her eyes of betrayal.

A brave Val firmly placed her hands upon Macey's shoulders and looked her dead in the eyes when she said, "Don't do it, Macey. Just drop it. Please." Time stood still while we waited for Macey's next move. She growled as she violently released her closed fists and stomped away. That may have been the first time Val stood up to Macey and it was for someone else's benefit. *Way to go, Val!*

Relieved with the outcome, I walked over to the latest super soaker and Morgan. Morgan began, "Thanks, guys, I appreciate your loyalty, but I would rather God, in his great justice, to handle this. Macey will get what is coming to her. Trust me. In the meantime, we should probably take you back to the room, Katie."

It was time to go. The guys walked us home and I noticed that Doug and Katie were hitting it off.

After Joey and I kissed good-bye, I watched Katie stagger inside, waving good-bye to Doug. I prayed she wouldn't puke all over the inside of our apartment. Not to be insensitive, but that smell makes me gag and is terrible to get rid of.

———◆———

We slept in since there was no hurry to do anything right away. It was a beautiful, sunny day, about eighty-two degrees, and breezy. Joey stopped by. We all decided to go to the beach.

While sitting on the beach, Morgan shared with Katie, Amy and me that although she was upset with Steve and Macey's betrayal, she was leaving it up to God. "I'm not going to lie, this is one of the hardest things I've ever had to deal with, but I have to give this to God. I can't seek revenge."

Morgan panned the azure sky as she let the sand slip through her fingers and said, "I memorized this verse, 'Dearly beloved, avenge not yourselves, but *rather* give place unto wrath: for it is written, Vengeance *is* mine; I will repay, saith the Lord.' That's Romans 12:19."

She placed her hand on Katie's leg and continued, her green eyes shining brightly in the midday sun, "I know you were trying to help, Katie, and I appreciate that, but it's in God's hands. He's judge and jury. I trust that he will provide the perfect justice."

I felt bad for what Morgan was going through, although triumphant in her dealing with it. I couldn't even imagine the type of heartbreak she was experiencing. She was always good to Macey—generous, kind, inclusive—and for Macey to stab her in the back like that was unforgivable, as I put it.

In turn, Morgan replied, "There's another verse that I committed to memory. It's Ephesians 4:32. 'And be ye kind one to another, tenderhearted, forgiving one another, even as God for Christ's sake hath forgiven you.' That's been my life verse. It's what I live by. I've been fortunate to learn this at an early age, so I had a lot of practice living like this."

Inwardly, I shook my head in awe of Morgan's maturity and godliness. I always knew she was a wonderful friend, but, more so, she was an amazing person. The more I got to know her, the more I could see God in her.

In contrast, I never liked Macey to begin with, and the more I was around her the more I disliked her. Needless to say, Macey kept her distance from us. That was a huge blessing in and of itself! *Wahoo! No Macey! God is good!*

I was appreciative to have such extraordinary friends and knew that all I could offer Morgan at that time was prayer and to honor her wishes not to retaliate on her behalf, or even hold a grudge. She reminded us, "This is our time to enjoy. Let's make the most of it."

How could we not appreciate God's manifestation as we were surrounded by sand, surf, and sun? Ah, a day at the beach with good friends. We took Morgan's sage advice and relished in our newfound freedom. It was so relaxing to bask in the sun and invigorating to ride the waves in the ocean.

That summed up how it was for the next few days. The evenings were filled with walking the boardwalk, followed by parties. All with a handsome hunk by my side!

Chapter 62

O NE NIGHT, JOEY SAID HE wanted to hang back at his rented shore house so we could spend some alone time together. I enthusiastically agreed. Joey and I hadn't spent any time alone, as we were constantly surrounded by our friends. Later that evening, while we were making out on his bed, Joey blurted, "I want us to get married." I stopped and looked at him. I was speechless. "What? Not like right now. I mean someday," he clarified. *Oh, whew!*

Funny how we never discussed our future like that, especially with our futures looming over us—college in the very near future, only a couple months away. As much as I loved him, I didn't see us married. Joey read my reaction accurately. "Oh, I see," he said with such great consternation. He sat up, leaned forward, and covered his face with his hands.

I put my hand on his back to comfort him, not knowing what to say, except, "I'm sorry."

"What have we been doing all this time? Was this a game to you?" He hesitated, then continued, "What, I'm not good enough for you?" He raked his hair with his fingers.

"I never said that," I cried in my defense.

"I can't live up to Avery. That's it, isn't it?" He said it. He finally addressed the elephant in the room after a year and a half of dating, and almost two years since Avery broke it off with me.

"I never said that," I repeated in tears. I didn't have to and we both knew it.

I still loved Avery and we both knew that too. I tried to shake Avery from my being. I thought I did once and for all. I only fooled myself and in doing so, deceived Joey. I felt horrible. Sick to my stomach.

Joey shrugged me off. Then stood up. "You better go," he said, devastated, without looking at me.

I knew I deeply hurt him. He was always so protective of me, even when I was dating Avery. He must have been truly upset to have me leave alone at night, in the dark, several blocks away from my apartment, with all of the crazies on the street during senior week.

I tried to smooth things over, so I pleaded, "Joey, I love you, doesn't that account for anything?!"

"I thought I could do this, but I can't. I will always be in Avery's shadow," he said, without any hope of changing his mind. "I'll walk you home to make sure you get there safely."

Maybe there was hope after all.

I got up off the bed and placed my hands on Joey's arms. "Joey, please, we can work this out. I love you! Just give me more time," I protested.

I kissed him as passionately as I could to prove to him that I did in fact love him. The kiss was wet, wild and urgent. He kissed me back with the same intensity. We fell onto the bed in a heated fervor.

Suddenly, Joey stopped, dead in his tracks, and exclaimed with frustration, "I can't do this. As God as my witness, I love you, but I can't do this, not when your heart belongs to someone else. It hurts too much." He shook his head, got up, and sat hunched over on the edge of the bed.

I reached out and touched his sculpted abs. I looked up at him and cried. I hurt too.

I was infatuated with Joey, I even loved Joey, but I was still deeply and hopelessly in love with Avery. He was right. My heart belonged to Avery.

Was I forever doomed to never be free of someone who wanted nothing to do with me? Was Joey forever going to have to take a back seat to his former best friend—first with Mindy and then with me?

Strangely, we comforted each other by embracing one another. It wasn't sexual, but heartrending. We held hands as Joey escorted me back to the apartment. I prayed he would give me a second chance.

He walked me to the front of my apartment and tenderly kissed me on the cheek. "I loved you for almost five years, Christina, and I have a feeling I will love you for five more. Good-bye, Christina."

I reached for Joey, but he stopped me. I pleaded with my eyes. Tears streamed down my face. He shook his head and said, "I won't be coming by. I hope you can get a ride home. Take care, Christina."

As I watched Joey walk away, I caught a glimpse of two figures kissing along the pathway leading to the efficiencies. The streetlight revealed that it was Steve and Macey.

Seconds later, I watched another couple holding hands, heading towards the cottage. From what I could see, it looked like Glen and Mindy. *No way!* A feeling of disgust enveloped my body.

Suddenly, the urge to cut washed over me. Since I was in a room filled with girls, I didn't cut that night. I couldn't take the chance, although I seriously entertained the notion.

The last time I cut was the time when Avery and I started dating the second time around. Over the past few years, I had grown stronger in my faith, as a result of studying scripture. In addition, I used other coping mechanisms, like jogging and meditation, so cutting seemed like a distant memory, and I prayed fervently that it would stay that way.

I also thanked God for putting Joey in my life for that time. Even though it didn't work out between the two of us, I felt like our relationship was nonetheless an enormous blessing. Joey got me through a tough time and for that I was eternally grateful.

Epilogue

THROUGHOUT THE SUMMER, I SEARCHED my soul and I thanked God for putting two great guys in my life, yet I realized I could no longer depend on guys to make me feel happy, whole, and secure. Rather, I had to trust in the Lord, and put my faith in the God Almighty, and not rely on others for inner strength.

I learned so much more from Morgan's Bible study, church, and Sunday school. I was learning how to be single, how to do life without a boyfriend. Friends and verses provided some of the tools I needed to successfully navigate life. But it didn't end there.

Jogging continued to be a fabulous outlet for me. Without it, I would have been devoid of energy and clarity. Instead, I felt surprisingly fantastic. I pushed myself to run longer, faster. I made a game out of it, which helped keep my mind off of my most recent breakup.

One day, during one of my more intense workouts in my neighborhood, my nosey next-door neighbor asked, "Are you training for a race?" When I told her I wasn't, she replied, "You look so intense. Maybe you should consider signing up for one." *No, thanks. I run for me, not to compete. Besides, this is free therapy. Paying to run defeats my purpose of saving money. I have college tuition to pay for after all.*

In any event, I came across the following verse that struck a chord with me, because of the running analogy, "Know ye not that they which run in a race run all, but one receiveth the prize? So run, that ye may obtain. And every man that striveth for the mastery is temperate in all things. Now they *do it* to obtain a corruptible crown; but we an incorruptible" (1 Corinthians 9:24-25).

I decided to go for the gold in life, to search deeply within, to live the way God wanted me to. Jogging helped my thoughts come to the surface. It helped to make sense out of the zaniness. It released the built-up tension from past mistakes, allowing me to move forward and to step into a place where God wanted me to be. I knew that I had done wrong in relationships, and I asked for forgiveness knowing that I needed to move on.

After a run, I deliberately sought Joey out in person to apologize to him for leading him on, although unintentionally. We met up at the gazebo, where we had our first kiss, hoping to set the stage of more fond memories.

I looked into his puppy dog eyes and listened to his response. "Christina, it's not just your fault. I bear the responsibility too. I'm sorry things didn't work out between the two of us." He paused, thoughtfully, "What we had was special, but there was someone else in the way that stopped it from being extraordinary." He shook his head and his lips formed a line. "I wish it could be different, but . . . I can't take a backseat to anyone in a relationship. It's not fair to me."

In an attempt to explain myself, I returned with more authenticity than intended, "Joey, I thought I let go! You have to believe me! I would have never gone out with you otherwise. Please forgive me!"

With that Joey replied, "Christina, I know you didn't mean to hurt me, and for that I forgive you, but it doesn't hurt any less. Like I said, I have loved you forever, and you will always have a special place in my heart." I watched as his chestnut brown eyes clouded over a bit while I was choking back the tears.

I managed the words, "Joey, I honestly loved you. In fact, I still do. You believe me, don't you?

"Christina, I believe you loved me as much as you were capable. In the end, it just wasn't enough."

"What can I do, Joey? How can I change? I tried. Believe me, I tried."

Joey shook his head. With sorrowful eyes, he responded, "I'm not sure there is anything you can do. I don't really fault you. It's what I find so endearing about you . . . how you love and care for others so deeply when you allow them to get close. I don't regret our time together and I hope you don't either. It's just the way it is. It's time to move on."

Swallowing back the tears, I replied, "Joey, I don't regret our time together. It was beautiful and amazing and I thank God every day that He brought you into my life. I just don't want it to end between us. What we had was fabulous. I still love you!"

Joey put his hand on mine, "I can't do this anymore. You still love Avery. You can't deny it even though I know you fight it." He closed his eyes for a second. "Please, just let me go."

Hearing the name Avery brought me to tears. No, I couldn't deny it. All I could say was, "I'm so sorry, Joey!" I slowly shook my head. "I'm so sorry. I wish . . . I wish I could stop . . ." I was sobbing at that point. "But, but I can't."

Joey stood up. "I wish you all the best." He walked away, leaving me to wallow in my tears of a forbidden destiny.

There was nothing left to say.

Even though it didn't work out with either Avery or Joey, I felt strongly that God put them in my life to help me through agonizing times. Without either of them, I couldn't even imagine what might have happened. At different seasons for different reasons, each of them had become a godsend. And for that I was truly thankful for the experience to be a part of their lives.

The End

A note from Maria

Dear Reader,

Thank you for reading my little contribution to the universe. I truly hope you enjoyed reading *NOT AGAIN* and would be grateful if you would write a review on Amazon and Goodreads. One sentence is all it takes.

I would be honored if you tagged me on social media, especially as a newbie to the publishing world. As an extrovert, I thrive on the social interaction, so don't be shy. Feel free to give me a shoutout.

FOLLOW ME, MARIA T. HENRIKSEN,
ON SOCIAL MEDIA:
FACEBOOK, TWITTER AND INSTAGRAM.

www.facebook.com/PurpleNchocolate/
www.facebook.com/groups/292254218386413
www.Twitter.com/MariatHenriksen
www.instagram.com/maria_t_henriksen

Visit my website for the most current information on my writings and subscribe to my blog for the most up-to-date announcements and events. New subscribers will receive a relaxation audio download created by yours truly.
www.mariathenriksen.com

Contact me directly via email:
authormariathenriksen@gmail.com

Acknowledgements

First of all, I would like to thank my family for supporting me throughout this entire endeavor. I spent summer days alone down the shore in a quiet house revising my novel, while everyone else was on the beach basking in the sun, surf, and sand.

Countless hours were spent around the clock to make this novel come alive as prompted by my editor, S.E. Swann, who had the confidence in me to make this more than just a worthwhile read. I'm not complaining, as I loved every minute of the writing process.

During this time, I grew as an individual, along with my main character. I incorporated the scripture and lessons I learned into the novel, and in turn I learned from the characters in my book. Specifically, I was inspired to forgive, despite what my stubborn nature ill-advised, and experienced a breakthrough in a friendship.

I would like to thank my friends Katie Treisch, Debbi Hicks, Skye Harris, Kristin Tovey, Kaitlin Bowen, Claire Smith, Helen Forgrave, and Maureen and Collin Foley who read my novel and provided valuable feedback. A heartfelt thanks to my bestie, Loreen Dietz, who took the time to dig deeper—for that I am truly grateful!

The scrumptious Pink Moose Ice Cream Café and Catering in Royersford, Pennsylvania deserves a shout-out for hosting the photo shoot for the book cover and trailer. Their milkshakes are amazing!

Last, but not least, I extend a special thanks to Willard Carpenter for introducing me to the world of publishing, and to Lori Chasko for offering unlimited support in the final days of the compilation of my novel.

My biggest desire is that this novel will have a positive and powerful impact on the lives of many! Most of all, I hope that my readers will enjoy the novel as much as I enjoyed writing it!

Much love,

Maria

Author Bio

Maria T. Henriksen is a lover of reading and writing, but her interest in reading didn't become realized until her thirties. Publishing a novel was a childhood dream of hers, but she knew she needed to immerse herself in reading first before pursuing her dream of becoming a published author.

Helping others in any capacity is what drives Maria. This novel was created with the intent of arming teens with the necessary tools to navigate life with peace, passion and clarity. She hopes that all readers, not just teenagers, will be able to employ those methods to overcome the stress that plagues us all.

Maria has a passion for health and fitness, and exercises on a regular basis. She can be seen running on a track, trail or along the road several times during the week, especially in the summer. Her favorite place to run is down the shore, along the bay.

This born-and-raised Philadelphia suburbanite resides with her husband, Dave, of over two decades, along with their teenage twins, Brandon and Kathryn. As a family, they bond over their love for sports, and each member makes every effort to cheer each other on at their competitions. Maria feels extremely blessed to have such a close family and continues to find each of them as a source of daily inspiration.

Resources for Help & Support

NATIONAL SEXUAL ASSAULT HOTLINE/RAINN

1-800-656-HOPE (4673) Free. Confidential & 24/7
RAINN website: https://www.rain.org or online.rainn.org
https://hotline.rainn.org
For support, information, advice, or a referral, trained support specialists are ready to help.

CRISIS TEXT LINE

Self-Harm Text Hotline | Crisis Text Line
Text CONNECT to 741741 for 24/7 support
Crisis Text Line website: https://www.crisistextline.org/selfharm
Hurting? Get free help for self-harm and self-injury.

THERAVIVE

Theravive is a network of licensed and professional clinical counselors, therapists, and psychologists who uphold clear, compassionate values in therapy for effective and lasting change.
https://www.theravive.com/

SiOS: Self-injury Outreach & Support

SiOS is a non-profit outreach initiative providing information and resources about self-injury to those who self-injure, those who have recovered, and those who want to help.
http://sioutreach.org/learn-self-injury/

NHA: Mental Health America

800-273-TALK
NHA is the country's leading nonprofit dedicated to helping ALL people to live mentally healthier lives.
http://www.mentalhealthamerica.net/

NAMI: National Alliance on Mental Illness

NAMI is the nation's largest grassroots mental health organization dedicated to improving the lives of persons living with serious mental illness, and their families.

http://www.nami.org/

S.A.F.E ALTERNATIVES
https://selfinjury.com/referrals/sites/
Provides a list of sites – Safe Alternatives

Made in the USA
Monee, IL
12 August 2020